Orchard of Hope

A NOVEL

ANN H. GABHART

Published by Fleming H. Revell
a division of Baker Publishing Group
P.O. Box 6287, Grand Rapids, MI 49516-6287

Printed in the United States of America

Library of Congress Cataloging-in-Publication Data

Gabhart, Ann.
Orchard of hope : a novel / Ann H. Gabhart.
p. cm.
ISBN 10: 0-8007-3169-7 (pbk.)
ISBN 978-0-8007-3169-4 (pbk.)
1. Teenage girls—Fiction. 2. Motherless families—Fiction. 3. Kentucky—Fiction. 4. African American families—Fiction. 5. Race relations—Fiction. I. Title.
PS3607.A23073 2007
813'.6—dc22 2006035314

Scripture is taken from the King James Version of the Bible.

To my children with love—
Johnny and Leah
Tarasa and Gary
Daniel and Carrie

1

The Hollyhill noon siren jolted David Brooke awake. He couldn't believe he'd dozed off at his desk, at least not until he read over the editorial about Monday night's town council meeting he'd been working on for the next issue of the *Banner*. Three paragraphs of nothing but snooze news.

David glanced through his scribbled notes and then clicked on his little tape recorder to review what went on at the meeting. Mayor Palmor's voice boomed out on the tape as he pushed the council to authorize funds for new Christmas decorations for the lampposts on Main Street. Councilman Jim Jamison interrupted to say the old decorations looked fine to him. The mayor came back at him with "I'll bet you don't even know what the old decorations look like, Jim."

The tape kept rolling with nothing but a scratchy playback sound. That was while Jim had stalled and wiped the sweat off his forehead with his handkerchief before he said, "It's way too hot to think about Christmas decorations. It's August, for gosh sakes. What we really need to be talking about is painting crosswalks before school starts. Now that the schools are fixing to desegregate, crosswalks might be especially important."

"Why's that, Jim? You think our Negro boys and girls don't know where to cross the street?" It was easy to hear the irritation in the mayor's voice.

David clicked the recorder off and read the note he'd written and blocked off with dark lines in the middle of his scribbles about the meeting. *Write editorial on new beginnings.* Peaceful *new beginnings.* The *Banner* had carried a front-page story a few weeks back when the Hollyhill School Board had voted to desegregate the schools. Congress had passed the Civil Rights Act in July, so it was high time Hollyhill stepped into the modern era. As true as that was, David thought the closing of the elementary school up in the West End where virtually every black family in Holly County lived actually had more to do with the old school needing a roof than with the Civil Rights Act. Desegregation was going to happen. It was just a matter of when.

Nobody in Hollyhill was expecting problems. The superintendent, Aaron Boyd, had told David the only reason the schools hadn't been desegregated already was that the black community hadn't wanted to give up West End Elementary and Mrs. Rowlett, who taught fifth through eighth there. Some said she was the best teacher in the county. This fall she'd be teaching Latin at Hollyhill High. David grabbed the pad he kept by his phone for story ideas and wrote *interview Francine Rowlett.* Then with a sigh, he clicked the recorder back on to hear more of the arguing.

Jim was answering the mayor, not quite in a shout, but almost. "I just think the safety of our kids should be a priority. All our kids, and crosswalks might help."

Harry Williams was talking now. "We'd have to check into the state regulations on where to put the crosswalks and how wide they should be." Harry's son was an attorney over in Grundy, so he considered it his duty to bring up any possible legal issue.

Mayor Palmor's voice got a little louder as he said they were talking about city streets so it didn't matter what the state said. David clicked the recorder off again. Nobody had said much worth hearing after that anyway, with nothing getting done about anything until finally Ramona Sims, the clerk who kept the minutes, had yawned into her hand, looked at her watch, and announced she had to go pick up her son at baseball practice. She'd clicked her ballpoint pen, folded up her notebook, and ended the meeting.

So David was trying to write an editorial about how the council members and the mayor should work together for the good of the town, but after looking over what he'd written so far, he decided it might be more interesting watching the paint dry on those crosswalks if the council ever agreed on where to put them. Maybe he should write his editorial on the proper placement of crosswalks. He wanted to hold off on the "peaceful new beginnings" one until the Wednesday school started.

He would have to pick his words carefully for that one. He didn't want to be the kind of hometown newspaper editor who used his pen to stir up trouble just to come up with fresh headlines. Hollyhill had never had any racial problems. Mayor Palmor had told David just last week that Hollyhill was lucky to have such "good Negroes who weren't out doing sit-ins and marches just to cause problems."

David hadn't pursued the subject. He'd let it slide into whether or not the heat wave was going to ease up any time soon. He felt cowardly when he thought about it now. He should have reminded the mayor that the Lord saw all men the same. And women. Centuries ago Paul had written to the Galatians, *There is neither Jew nor Greek, there is neither bond nor free, there is neither male nor female: for ye are all one in Christ Jesus.*

David should be writing the same sort of thing to the people in Hollyhill. How all people were guaranteed certain inalienable rights in their country. But instead, he was just filling space with words that wouldn't do anything except put his readers to sleep. David crumpled up the paper and threw it toward his wastebasket. He missed.

He stared down at the new blank sheet on his notepad and felt his eyes getting heavy again. At least it wasn't his sermon for Sunday he kept falling to sleep on, although he'd been in the doldrums trying to come up with an idea for that too. He felt as stagnant as the Redbone River had looked when they passed it last night on the way to prayer meeting, and Aunt Love had declared the dog days of summer officially here.

It wasn't easy coming up with fresh ideas week after week for editorials or sermons. Of course, he trusted the Lord to supply the sermon ideas, but David had to do his part by praying and searching the Scripture. He couldn't expect to just stand behind Mt. Pleasant's pulpit come Sunday and open his mouth and have a fine sermon spill out.

It took time to come up with the right message, the Lord's message. It took time to come up with editorials that were more than just fillers. It took time to lay out the *Hollyhill Banner*, even if it was only published once a week. And time was what had been in short supply in David's life ever since the tornado had swept away Clay's Creek Baptist Church in July and dropped an oak tree limb on Wes, practically crushing his right leg.

David depended on Wes to keep the press in working order. Thank goodness nothing major had broken since Wes had been in the hospital recovering from the surgery to piece his leg back together. He knew Wes took the papers out to the post office for the mail delivery and to the grocery stores, the drugstores, and the Grill to be sold. He knew Wes blocked out most of the ads. What David hadn't known was how many hours that took until he started doing it all himself.

Everybody had the same number of hours in the day, David reminded himself. The Lord had given him this day, August 13, 1964, and hadn't held back a single hour. But lately twenty-four hours hadn't been enough. Sometimes David felt as if his own life had been hit by a tornado, with all that had happened since June.

It wasn't only the *Banner*. He'd just taken on the full pastorate at Mt. Pleasant after the people there decided they could be served by a pastor with an ex-wife out in California and an unmarried daughter expecting a baby the end of September. The thought of Tabitha's baby, his grandbaby, made him smile.

In the past couple of weeks after the word about the baby got around, some folks had stopped him on the street to tell him how sorry they were about Tabitha's "trouble" while they tried to come up with a polite way to ask if she planned to give the baby up for adoption. A baby did need a loving mother and father. It was God's plan.

But that didn't mean the Lord wouldn't help with a new plan if the first plan went awry. The Lord had helped him find a way nearly fourteen years ago when Adrienne had handed Jocie over to David to raise.

He remembered holding Jocie after Adrienne had gone back into the bedroom and firmly shut the door. Jocie had been so tiny—fragile almost, as she'd weighed in at just over five pounds—that for a moment he was terrified. But then she pushed open her eyes and seemed to look directly at him while her lips had turned up in a smile. It didn't matter that the experts said newborn babies couldn't focus on anything and only smiled because they had gas and hadn't gotten it straight which way was smiling and which way was frowning. He felt her very being reaching out to him. At that moment she captured his heart and became his forever.

Thank goodness she hadn't been hurt in the tornado. David looked at his watch. Where was Jocie? She was supposed to be there to go with him to pick Wes up at the hospital. They had to get him checked out before three, and it was a long drive even if they didn't get caught behind a rock truck on Highway 27. At least all the trips to see Wes at the hospital had given David plenty of one-on-one time with Jocie. The Lord could make good come out of anything.

David shoved his notes in a folder and plopped it on top of the pile of papers in his to-do basket. Jocie might be waiting for him back in the pressroom. She'd been helping set up the ads, working practically full time except when she had to help Aunt Love at the house. That's where she'd been this morning, helping Aunt Love get a bed set up in their living room for Wes. The man couldn't very well stay by himself in his rooms over the newspaper offices. He'd never get up the back stairs to begin with.

Wes could barely walk across his hospital room using his crutches, and no wonder with the way the rods holding his bones together stuck out of his cast. He was beginning to really look like the alien from Jupiter he sometimes claimed to be.

The doctors had suggested Wes go to the Hollyhill Nursing Home until his leg healed enough to get a smaller cast, but David couldn't imagine Wes in a wheelchair in that place where old people went to die. Wes wasn't that old or that feeble. His leg was going to get better. It had to. David needed him back helping put out the *Banner*. And telling Jupiter stories to Jocie. David needed things to get back to normal, but maybe normal wasn't possible after a tornado hit your life.

2

Jocie panted a little as she pedaled her bike up Locust Hill. The hill wasn't really all that steep, but it was long and had two curves. Jocie stood up and worked the pedals. For a minute she thought she was going to make it to the top, but then the chain slipped on the old bike and the left pedal spun loose away from her foot.

"Piece of junk," Jocie muttered as she hopped off the bike and began pushing it. She could practically see Aunt Love frowning and quoting some Scripture at her. Maybe something like, *In all things, give thanks*. That had to be one of Aunt Love's favorites.

And she was right. Jocie was grateful Matt McDermott, the head deacon at Mt. Pleasant Church, had dug around in his barn and found the old bike for her. It was rusty, but she could paint it. She'd been able to knock the biggest dents out of the fenders. And it wasn't all that much trouble to pump up the tires whenever she needed to ride it. She and her dad had already patched the inner tubes a couple of times, but the tubes were old and kept springing new leaks.

At least the chain hadn't come off its cogs again. She definitely didn't have time to be prizing it back in place. She was already late. Even before the twelve o'clock siren went off a couple of miles away in Hollyhill, she knew it was high noon. Her shadow was crawling along right beneath her. She should have called her father at the newspaper office before she left the house.

The sun beat down on the road until the blacktop practically burned her feet through her tennis shoes, but she didn't let the heat slow her down. She pushed the bike faster.

Still, thankful or not, she missed her old bike. She could pedal to the top of the hill on it. Not that it had been new or anything. But that bike was gone with the wind. Her father had found one of the wheels, crumpled and bent with the spokes sticking out every which way, but the tornado must have blown away the rest of it to Jupiter along with Clay's Creek Church.

People were still showing up at the newspaper office to get their pictures in the *Banner*, holding the back of a hymnbook, the splintered plank off a pew, a Sunday school chair, or whatever bit of the church building they'd found in their fields. Zella, who manned the reception desk at the paper, had printed out a sign last Monday saying "No more church fragment pictures needed," but Jocie's dad made her take it off the door. He said community relations were worth a little film and newspaper ink. Besides, folks still seemed interested in where the pieces of the church had ended up. Somebody came in nearly every day to ask if anybody had found the collection plates. As if they'd be full of money or something.

It was funny how some things had survived the storm and some hadn't. Wes's motorcycle ended up on its handlebars, but with hardly a dent. Not that Wes could ride it. Zella said she didn't see how he'd ever ride it again, but Jocie knew he would. His leg would heal. Jocie prayed about it every day, and the Lord answered prayer. She knew that without a doubt after this summer, with Tabitha coming home from

California and Zeb waiting with his funny dog grin every time she went out of the house and Wes living through the tree falling on him. And her father being her father.

As Aunt Love was always saying, *O give thanks unto the Lord, for he is good.* Psalm somewhere, Jocie was sure. Aunt Love would know exactly where. She had hundreds of verses on file in her head. Lately she'd even done better remembering other things. The beans hadn't been too salty or the biscuits burned past eating for weeks. Of course Tabitha and Jocie tried to be Aunt Love's backup memory, taking things out of the oven or off the stove before the smoke started rolling.

That was about all Tabitha helped with. Not that Jocie had expected her to help rearrange the living room that morning so they could put up the cot for Wes. Tabitha couldn't very well push furniture here or there now that she was so obviously expecting a baby. She spent most of her time sitting right in front of the electric fan, chewing on ice.

Jocie was beginning to understand why her own mother had hated being in the family way. Nobody in their right mind would volunteer for that nine-month tour of duty. Tossing your breakfast every day for months, looking like you'd been wrung out like an old dishrag, propping up ankles as puffy as old Mrs. Johnson's at church, groaning every time you stood up, keeping hold of your belly all the time for fear something might fall out . . . But the really weird part of it all was that, in spite of every miserable thing, Tabitha was practically glowing she was so happy.

Maybe once Wes was home, he could help Jocie make sense of some of it. She and Wes hadn't gotten to talk, not really talk, for days. Another reason Jocie was having to practically run up the hill, pushing her bike. She had to get to town in time to go with her father to pick up Wes at the hospital. She had to be the one to tell him they had everything ready for him at the house and how much they wanted him to stay there until he got well enough to hop back up the steps to his own rooms over the newspaper office.

She'd already told him as much a dozen times, but it would be different when the nurse was rolling him out of the hospital. He might decide Aunt Love was too old, Tabitha too expectant, Jocie's dad too busy, and Jocie too young to take care of him. He might decide he was a bother and look for a way to go back to Jupiter, the planet—or Jupiter, the town in Indiana or Ohio or wherever he'd come from before he'd shown up at the newspaper office back when Jocie was just a little kid. She couldn't let that happen even if she had to stay home every other day from school. She had to take care of Wes. She was the reason he had been in that churchyard with the church and trees flying over their heads. It was her fault that he needed somebody to take care of him.

A couple of cars eased past her, and Jocie thought about ditching her bike and flagging down one of the drivers to hitch a ride. But she was nearly to the top of the hill, and it was mostly downhill the rest of the way to Hollyhill.

Her dad would wait for her or come looking for her if she didn't show up soon. He'd been paying more attention to where she was, ever since the tornado. Of course, that could be because she was always underfoot, going with him to see Wes or at the newspaper office helping get out the *Banner*. About the only times she wasn't close enough for him to yell at her if he needed something was when he was taking Tabitha to the doctor over in Grundy or when he was down at the courthouse talking to Leigh Jacobson.

Aunt Love said Jocie's father and Leigh were sparking even if they hadn't really gone out anywhere except to church or to see Wes at the hospital. And Leigh did show up regular as clockwork to help fold the *Banner* on printing night every week now. That was okay with Jocie. Leigh always brought brownies.

Jocie wasn't saying a stepmother prayer the way she had the sister prayer ("please let Tabitha come home") and the dog prayer ("please let me have a dog"). She'd asked her dad if she should, and he'd said to leave that prayer up to him.

At the top of the hill, Jocie paused long enough to wipe the sweat off her forehead with her shirttail before she got up on the bike seat. She glanced back at the rear tire to be sure it still had enough air in it. She really did need some new inner tubes. Then she took off down the hill, happy to feel the breeze on her face, what with the way the sun was roasting the top of her head.

Up ahead of her, she spotted another bike. It wasn't one of the little kids from the houses along the road. This kid was big, bigger than Jocie. Maybe not a kid at all. No one Jocie recognized, at least from the back. It was pretty uncommon seeing somebody in Hollyhill she didn't recognize. It was even more uncommon to see a stranger riding a bike to town. She generally knew everything about any new family that moved into the neighborhood long before their bikes were unloaded.

She started pedaling faster, curiosity making her forget the heat and how thirsty she was. Worse, she forgot that the old bike didn't handle speed very well. The chain started clacking. Jocie braked, but it was too late. The chain had already slipped off the cogs and the pedals were useless. She was freewheeling down the hill.

She still might have been okay if the bike up ahead of her hadn't been passing by the Sawyers' house. Butch, the Sawyers' big German shepherd, lunged off the porch toward the road. Butch never let any bike pass his house unchallenged, and the thing to do was either pedal as fast as possible to get by with no bite marks, or walk by because as soon as your feet were on the ground instead of on pedals, Butch turned into a big pussycat.

The person on the bike in front of Jocie obviously didn't know that. He slowed his bike down to keep an eye on the dog.

"Watch out!" Jocie yelled, as she barreled down the hill toward him.

The boy looked over his shoulder and pushed hard on the pedals to get out of the way. The dog was barking and nipping at his front wheel. Jocie tried to swerve around them, but Butch jumped in front of her. Without thinking, she laid the bike down rather than hit the dog. The dog jumped sideways and banged into the other bike's rear wheel. They all ended up in a heap in the ditch. Butch quit barking, jumped on top of Jocie, and started licking her face. Her leg was hurting some, but the dog's front paws digging into her shoulder hurt worse, so surely nothing was broken.

Jocie pushed Butch back and peeked around the big dog to look at the boy on the other side of the spinning bike wheels. She'd been right about him being a stranger. He looked about fifteen or sixteen, with curly black hair cut close to his head and angry dark brown eyes staring at her out of his black face. Blood was trickling down from a nasty scrape on his forehead.

"Are you okay?" Jocie asked. She was glad the bikes were between them.

3

"Am I okay?!" he shouted. "Do I look okay?"

Jocie winced. "Well, no. Your forehead's bleeding a little."

He touched his forehead and then looked at the blood on his fingers.

"It doesn't look too bad," Jocie said. "I mean, from what I can see."

"No thanks to you and your dog," he said as he wiped his fingers on the grass.

The boy yanked his foot out from under his bicycle and sat up. The better to glare at Jocie. She put her arm around Butch for courage and said, "He's not my dog."

"He's not your dog?! Then why's he trying to lick your face off?"

"He just likes me. At least as long as I'm not on a bike. He doesn't like anybody on a bike."

"No kidding."

"And I didn't aim to run into you. The chain came off my bike and I couldn't stop. Didn't you hear me yelling at you? And it was just bad luck Butch jumped in front of me. I'm really sorry. I hope nothing's broken." Jocie looked at her bike. The wheels had finally stopped spinning.

"You mean on us or on the bikes?" The boy was still frowning.

"Both. I've already totaled one bike this summer."

"What's the other poor guy look like?" the boy asked.

"Not too good actually," Jocie said. "He's in the hospital."

The boy looked at her and suddenly burst out laughing. Butch started barking and jumping around them.

"It's not really all that funny." Jocie made a halfhearted attempt at a smile just to be agreeable, but what she really felt like doing was crying. She was still a mile from town. It'd take her forever to get the old bike straightened out and the chain back on. She could run, but when she stood up, her ankle hurt. She must have sprained it. She might walk on it, but running was definitely out.

The boy wiped the laughter tears off his cheeks with the back of his hand. "I'm sorry, but it really is."

"Look, I'd love to stay and keep you laughing, but I've got to get to town." Jocie picked up her bike and looked at it. It was hopeless. She let it drop back down in the ditch. She'd have to work on it later.

"What's your hurry?" the boy said. "You haven't even told me your name yet. If I'm going to charge you with reckless bike riding, I need to know your name."

"Jocie. Jocie Brooke. I live down the road about a mile. And charge me with whatever you want to. I told you I was sorry and that it was an accident." She gave Butch one more pat on the head before she started down the road.

"Hey, are you hurt?"

"I'm not bleeding. At least I don't think I am." Jocie stopped to feel her face and look at her hands and legs. Nothing but dirt and grass stains.

"You're limping."

"And you're bleeding."

"But you said it looked like I'd live," the boy said.

"Me too. I just won't be able to run for a while." Jocie

was walking again. Butch ran ahead a couple of steps and waited for her to catch up.

"You want to run?" the boy asked as he picked up his bike and set it on its wheels out on the road.

"I'm late to meet my dad," she said over her shoulder without stopping.

"Aren't you going to ask me my name? Or do you just ask white kids for their names?"

Jocie stopped walking and turned around to look at him. "What's that supposed to mean?"

"That you didn't ask me my name, I guess."

"Well, actually I've been told I shouldn't talk to strangers at all, much less ask them their names."

"We can't be strangers after we've been down in a ditch together." The boy wasn't smiling, but his eyes were still laughing at her.

Jocie took a deep breath and blew the air out of her lungs slowly. She wouldn't let herself get mad. After all, she had run him over on her bike, so if he wanted to laugh at her, that was better than yelling at her. She kept her voice calm. "Okay, good point. So what's your name?"

"Maybe I don't want to tell you. Maybe I want to stay a stranger."

"Then suit yourself." Jocie turned around and started walking again. She didn't have time for whatever game this boy was playing. She tried to keep from limping, but she couldn't. At the edge of the Sawyers' yard, she scratched the spot right in front of Butch's tail and pointed him back to his porch. To her surprise the dog went.

"Are you sure that bike-biting terror is not your dog?" the boy asked. He was pushing his bike along beside Jocie.

"He's not my dog." Jocie looked over at him. "I'm glad your bike wasn't banged up too bad."

"How about my bloody head?"

"I've already told you I was sorry about that."

They kept walking without saying anything. Finally the boy said, "Your ankle looks swollen."

"Yeah. I must've twisted it," Jocie said.

They went a few more steps before the boy said, "Look, I know you're a little white girl and I'm a big black boy and I just moved here and I'm not sure what the rules are around here about this kind of thing, but do you want a ride?"

"I'm not a little girl. I'll be fourteen next month. And it's my guess you aren't much older or you'd be driving a car instead of riding a bike."

"So I lack a little being sixteen. I'm still a big black boy in a white neighborhood, and I don't bow and scrape too good." The boy grimaced and touched his forehead. "Well, that might not have been the best word to use right now, what with this scrape on my head. But now that the dog's gone I'll give you a ride."

"You forgot about the stranger part," Jocie said.

"I bet you've never met a stranger."

"Somebody who doesn't want to say his name is pretty strange."

The boy laughed again. "Your point."

"Maybe my point, but your serve," Jocie said.

"You play tennis?"

"No. We don't have any tennis courts, but I've played badminton sometimes. All you need is a yard and a net for that."

"I told my mother this place was too backward to move to. We should have stayed in Chicago. Lots of tennis courts up there."

"You play tennis?"

"How come you sound so surprised? Because I'm black and black people don't play tennis?"

"Do you?"

"Well, no, but I might someday. So how about the ride? Yes or no?"

Jocie stopped walking and looked straight at him. "How about the name? Yes or no?"

He stopped rolling his bike and smiled at her. "Noah Hearndon at your service, Miss Brooke."

"Pleased to meet you, Mr. Hearndon, and I'd be more than happy to take you up on that offer of a ride if it's not too much trouble."

"Climb aboard." Noah straddled the bike and waited while Jocie tried to figure out the best way to sit on the back fender.

"I don't think this is going to work," she said finally.

"Not unless you grab hold of my waist," Noah said. When Jocie still hesitated, he laughed and added, "I promise the black won't rub off on you."

Jocie wasn't a bit worried about the black rubbing off, but she hadn't grabbed hold of a boy since she used to wrestle with Teddy Whitehead in second grade. Still, she'd told Noah she wanted a ride, and she couldn't ride without holding on. She took a deep breath and put one hand gingerly on each side of his waist. His muscles felt hard under his sweaty T-shirt.

Noah gave her a look over his shoulder and said, "Hold on and pray."

Jocie was already praying. She just wasn't sure exactly what she should be praying for the most. That she wouldn't fall off? Surely this couldn't be that much different than riding on the back of a motorcycle, and she'd done that plenty of times with Wes. But with Wes, she just wrapped her arms around his waist without a second's thought. She couldn't very well hug this boy like that.

Or maybe she should be praying that she wouldn't make Noah laugh at her again. She didn't know why she cared if he did or not. After all, she really didn't know him. She didn't know where he lived. She didn't know why he was in Hollyhill. She didn't know why he went from being mad to laughing his head off in a second's time. And she didn't know which she was going to make him do next or how.

One thing for sure, she wasn't going to find out any of the answers without asking. Now seemed to be as good a time as any.

"You move in somewhere around here?"

"You don't think I biked down from Chicago, do you?"

"I haven't heard about anybody moving into the neighborhood."

"And you'd have heard if I moved into your neighborhood. That's for sure."

"Okay, so you don't live in Chicago or my neighborhood. Where do you live? Or did you just fall out of a spaceship?" She knew he wouldn't know what she was talking about, but she didn't care. That was what Wes was always telling Jocie. That he fell out of a spaceship and landed in Hollyhill.

"My misguided parents moved down here to plant an orchard out on Hoopole Road. I bet you don't even know where that is. It's so far out in the sticks that nobody could know where that is."

"But I do. My father's the preacher at Mt. Pleasant Church just over the hill from Hoopole Road," Jocie said.

"A preacher's kid. You have my sympathy."

"I don't need it. I like being a preacher's kid," Jocie said.

"All the time?" He glanced back over his shoulder at her.

"Well, my father's the newspaper editor too, so I can be the editor's kid part of the time."

"I'll bet nobody ever forgets you're a preacher's kid, though."

"I don't want them to," Jocie said. Just a few weeks ago she'd been more worried about people not believing she was the preacher's kid. "Are you a preacher's kid too?"

"My father a preacher? No way." Noah was laughing again. The bike wobbled a little before he paid attention to keeping his wheels straight. "He doesn't have much use for preachers."

"Why not?"

"Beats me," Noah said. "Now my mother, that's a different matter altogether. She might have been a preacher if the job was open to women. Instead she just preaches at me and anybody else who will stand still five minutes."

"What's she preach about?"

"Anything and everything, according to her mood. But mostly freedom. She's what some might call an activist. Went to the March on Washington with the Reverend Martin Luther King Jr. last summer."

"Oh yeah. My dad had me read Rev. King's speech because he thought it was so good. He kept saying he wished he could hear him preach in person sometime."

"Yeah, that part about having a dream really grabbed people. My mother came home all charged up, but my daddy said that's all it is—a dream. A dream that won't ever come true, but my mama says it will if we make it happen." Noah looked over his shoulder at Jocie. "I don't know how you people here in the big town of Hollyhill feel about blacks in general, but one thing for sure, you're going to know it when my mama comes to town. Your little town will never be the same once Myra Cassidy Hearndon gets hold of it."

Jocie didn't say so out loud, but she thought the same might be said about Myra's son, Noah Hearndon.

4

Jocie pointed out the newspaper office when they got to Main Street.

"People are looking," Noah said as he stopped the bike in an open parking space in front of the office.

"Just because they don't know who you are. We expect to know everybody we see in Hollyhill." Jocie climbed off the bike and stepped down gingerly on her ankle. It still hurt.

"Yeah. I'm sure that's it and that it doesn't have a thing to do with me being a little dark around the edges and you being so lily white."

"We have black people in Hollyhill."

"You ever ridden on the backs of any of their bikes?"

"Not yet. They know me well enough to stay out of my way when they see me coming on my bike."

"Smart guys," Noah said, smiling again.

Jocie stood on the sidewalk and looked at Noah. "You never did tell me why you were coming to town."

"You're sort of nosey, aren't you?"

"Maybe." Jocie didn't let what he said bother her. "I guess it comes from helping my dad get stories for the paper."

"I know. And being a preacher's kid."

"That too." Jocie waited for him to say why he was in Hollyhill, but he just balanced himself with one foot on the road and one on his bike pedal and looked at her without saying a word.

She eyed him, then gave a shrug. "Okay, don't tell me. The *Banner* just came out yesterday anyway, and your story, whatever it is, would be such old news by next week's issue that nobody would care." She nodded toward the door. "But come on inside and meet my dad. And you can clean up the scrape on your head. If you were looking for a job or something, you wouldn't want to show up bleeding."

"What makes you think I need a job?" Noah asked, but he got off his bike, sat it up on the sidewalk, and kicked down the stand.

"You're almost sixteen and you want to drive a car instead of ride a bike," Jocie said.

"Deductive thinking. You must be a regular female Sherlock Holmes."

"That's me. Come on and I'll get you a Band-Aid and a copy of this week's *Banner*. I don't remember any help-wanted ads, but there might have been one or Dad might know somebody that needs help. Of course, there are always farmers working in hay and stuff."

"I've already got a line on something like that. The guy who sold us the farm said he might need some help with fencing and painting his barn roof in a week or two."

"Who was that?"

"Harvey McMurtry. You know him?"

"Sure. Mr. Harvey goes to my dad's church."

"Small world, isn't it?" Noah said and then looked up and down Main Street before making a face. "Real small."

Jocie stepped into the newspaper office and set the bell over the door to jingling. Zella looked up from her typewriter. "Where in the world have you been, Jocelyn? Your father's been calling everywhere to try to find you." Her eyes narrowed as she took a closer look at Jocie. "Good heavens, Jocelyn. Don't you own a comb or a washcloth? You look like you've been wrestling pigs or something."

"No pigs, just a bike wreck. I ran into a newcomer to Hollyhill. Literally," Jocie said and stepped aside so Zella could see Noah. "This is Noah Hearndon. Zella Curtsinger, Noah."

Zella's eyes popped open wide when she saw Noah. Zella had been working at the *Banner* ever since Jocie could remember, probably ever since her father could remember too. As long as Jocie had known her, she'd looked exactly the same—with the same dark-rimmed glasses, the same tightly curled black hair, the same red lipstick that she sometimes had to wipe off her teeth with the pink tissues she kept at hand on her desk, and the same twist to her mouth as if she'd been eating green persimmons whenever she looked at Jocie.

Jocie just had a way of getting under Zella's skin even when she didn't try, and most of the time she tried. Zella was always reciting the proper behavior rules for girls to Jocie, and she looked as if she was about to explode with several of them now as she stared between Jocie and Noah.

Finally she dabbed her upper lip with one of her pink tissues and managed to say, "Pleased to meet you, I'm sure."

"Same here, ma'am," Noah said. He looked as if he wanted to not only smile but burst out laughing the way he had at Jocie after the bike wreck.

"Noah's family bought a farm out on Hoopole Road," Jocie said. "He was coming to town when me and the Sawyers' dog managed to knock his bike out from under him. He needs a couple of Band-Aids."

"Certainly," Zella said as she pulled open a desk drawer

quickly. She held out the Band-Aids to Jocie and let her eyes skip across Noah's face. "Your father's a farmer?"

"Now he is," Noah said. "That's not against the law here in Holly County, is it? Having Negro farmers?"

"Well, no, certainly not, or at least I suppose not," Zella said as she fanned her face with her tissue. "I don't think we've ever had one before. Some of the boys who live up in the West End work on the farms now and again, of course, but nobody who actually lives on a farm."

"Oh, what do the Negroes here do?" Noah asked.

"Well, they have jobs like anybody else."

"Lawyers, bankers, sheriff's deputies, mailmen?" Noah said.

Zella's eyes narrowed on Noah. "I think you need to learn some manners, young man, when you're talking to your elders."

"Yes, ma'am, you're probably right," Noah said. "I sometimes forget my place."

Jocie could tell Noah was baiting Zella. She'd done the same plenty of times herself, but it seemed different somehow when somebody else was doing it. "Come on, Noah. I'll show you where the bathroom is so you can take care of your forehead."

Noah followed her away from Zella's desk. "Are they flesh-toned Band-Aids?"

"Not your flesh tone, I'm sure," Jocie said. "You have a problem with being black or something?"

"Not me. It's everybody else that seems to have the problem."

Jocie decided not to bite on that one and just pointed Noah toward the sink in the bathroom. "I'll get Dad."

"Is he going to have a problem with me being in his restroom?"

"Beats me," Jocie said. "You can ask him." She wasn't going to be baited like Zella. She could almost hear Zella steaming at her desk behind them before she started banging extra hard on the keys of her typewriter. Jocie went through the door into the pressroom. "Hey, Dad. You back here?"

"Jocie, it's about time. I thought maybe I was going to have to call the sheriff and send out a search party. Aunt Love said you left there almost an hour ago." Her dad stood up from the worktable and took a better look at her. "What have you been doing?"

"The chain slipped off my bike, and I had a wreck."

"Are you okay?" He moved closer to look at her better.

"Bummed up my ankle, but I'm okay. I sort of hit somebody else. He banged up his head."

"You ran your bike into somebody? How could you run into somebody on your bike? I mean, you had the whole outdoors out there to steer around him, didn't you?"

"You'd think, but I had help," Jocie said. "He was on a bike too, and Butch, you know the Sawyers' big German shepherd, was chasing him and I couldn't stop and he did. It's a long story."

Her father sighed. "Maybe I better get the short version for now. You can tell me the details on the way to get Wes. Who did you hit? And how bad is he banged up?"

"Noah Hearndon, and not too bad."

"Hearndon?"

"His family just moved here. He said they bought a farm from Mr. Harvey out on Hoopole Road."

"I heard he sold some land, but I hadn't heard to who. Some welcome to Hollyhill, huh?" her father said. "Do we need to pay for his doctor's bills?"

Noah came through the pressroom door. "I don't think

I'll need a doctor," he said. "A couple of Band-Aids and I'm good as new. Or almost."

"Dad, this is Noah," Jocie said. "He gave me a ride to town since my bike was pretty much out of commission and his was still rolling. And so I thought the least I could do was let him bandage up his head at our sink."

"I should think," Jocie's dad said as he stepped forward with a smile and held his hand out to Noah. "David Brooke. I'm sorry my daughter ran you down. Thank goodness she's not old enough to get her driver's license for two more years."

"She's a terror on wheels, for sure," Noah said, taking Jocie's father's hand. He was smiling. A real smile and not the laughing-at-the-world smile he'd been wearing most of the time since Jocie had bowled him over.

Jocie breathed a little easier. She wasn't going to have to run interference between her father and Noah the way she had with him and Zella.

"Jocie said you'd moved in out on Hoopole Road. That's a long way on a bike."

"And relatively uneventful until about a mile from town, if you can call this place a town."

"Noah's from Chicago," Jocie put in.

"Then I guess Hollyhill does look small to you. It'll take some getting used to," her dad said.

"I'm sure. On both sides," Noah said.

Jocie's dad looked puzzled by that remark but didn't ask what Noah meant.

"Noah may be looking for a job," Jocie said. "I told him he could have one of this week's *Banners*, but I don't remember anybody advertising for help."

"No, but then some people don't like to spend money on ads." Jocie's father looked over at the press and the pile of paper waiting for their next run. "What kind of job did you have in mind?"

"I worked for a grocery store back in Chicago, stocking shelves, that kind of thing."

"Our grocery is a family affair. Got a couple of nephews working for them," Jocie's dad said.

"Is everything around here a family affair? Jocie said she worked on the paper here."

"I just help out," Jocie said. She didn't want her father to think she'd inflated what she did for the paper.

"I couldn't make it without her," Jocie's dad said. "In fact, while Wes has been out, we haven't been making it too good anyway. I might could use a little extra help, say two or three afternoons a week."

"You mean sweeping the place out, that kind of thing?" Noah asked.

"I suppose the place could use a good sweeping, but I was thinking more along the lines of whatever needs doing from setting the type to blocking out ads to making deliveries or running errands."

"I don't know how to set type or . . ." For the first time, Noah looked a little unsure of himself. ". . . what did you call it? Blocking ads."

"You can learn. So what do you think? You want to give it a try for a couple of weeks? I can't pay much. I'll have to check with Zella on that. She keeps the books. And it'll only be until my regular hand, Wes, is back on his feet again."

"Is he sick?" Noah asked.

"Remember the other totaled bike I told you about?" Jocie grimaced. "And the guy who ended up in the hospital?"

"Now, Jocie. Wes doesn't hold any of that against you. It wasn't your fault a tornado blew a tree down on top of him. But he may hold it against us if we don't get up there and get him out of the hospital. He's had all the doctors and nurses he can stand for a while." Her father looked at his watch.

"I'll go wash my face and hands," Jocie said.

"Good idea. I'll show Noah how the press works while you're getting cleaned up."

Jocie washed the sweat and dog slobber off her face as fast as she could. Then she ran her fingers through her shoulder-length brown hair and limped back to the press-room. She didn't want to miss anything.

When she went back through the door, her father was saying, "So tell you what. You talk it over with your folks, and if they say it's okay, you can start next week."

"I don't need to talk it over with my parents. My father said I could take whatever I found." Noah held out his hand to Jocie's dad again. "It's a deal."

"Great." Jocie's dad shook Noah's hand. "We'll give it a trial run next week and see how it works for both of us."

"The lady out front might not be too happy about it," Noah said.

"Oh, Zella's okay once you get to know her," Jocie's dad said with a quick look at Jocie to be sure she didn't contradict him. "Right, Jocie?"

"Sure, Dad. She keeps things straight around here. We'd be broke without her. If you don't believe me, just ask her."

"She does keep us in the black. Now we better get on the road."

Noah walked out with them. As he passed Zella's desk, he said, "Thanks for the bandages, ma'am."

"You're perfectly welcome, I'm sure," Zella said without looking up from her typewriter. "Will I need to lock up when I leave today, David?"

"You'd better. We probably won't be back till late, and then we'll have to get Wes settled in at the house," Jocie's father said.

"Very well," Zella said, her eyes still on the paper in her typewriter. "I hope Wesley makes the trip all right."

"I think he'll do fine if we can get him in the car with that cast," Jocie's dad said.

Noah leaned over close to Jocie to whisper, "I guess I was lucky to only need a Band-Aid."

"I told you," Jocie said.

Out on the sidewalk, Noah got on his bike. "Thank you, Mr. Brooke, or should I call you Rev. Brooke? Jocie told me you're a preacher."

"I am, but David will do fine while we're working."

Noah hesitated a moment and then looked straight at Jocie's father. "Jocie said you preached at that church out close to where we live, so maybe I should warn you that my mother might show up for church Sunday morning. She asked Mr. McMurtry about his church when we moved in."

"Well, that will be fine. She'll certainly be welcome. Your whole family will be welcome."

Noah smiled a little. "Then in that case, she probably won't come. My mama don't necessarily like to go places where she's welcome. She likes to go places where she has to make herself welcome."

5

The nurse who wheeled Wes to the front door of the hospital took one look at their car and frowned. "Didn't anyone tell you Mr. Green would need an ambulance?"

"I don't think so. At least not that I can remember," David said. "But my backseat's pretty big."

The nurse mashed her mouth together in a thin line and made a sound somewhere between a snort and a sigh. It was just their luck that Nurse Army Boots was on duty. Wes had names for all of the nurses. Nurse Merry Sunshine was always smiling, Nurse Stinky had to be eating garlic three times a day to try to ward off germs, Nurse Maybe Someday never came when he rang the call button, and Nurse Sweetie-Pie talked baby talk to him.

But Nurse Army Boots was definitely the worst of the bunch. She was bigger than Wes and Jocie's dad put together and looked ready to knock aside anything and everything in her path in order to see that things got done her way. She'd already spent more than a half hour lecturing Jocie's father on the care Wes was going to need when he got home, without even a glance toward Wes as if he couldn't hear just because his leg was banged up. Then she shoved the mustard brown plastic washpan full of various other mysterious mustard brown plastic hospital stuff at Jocie and ordered her to make herself useful.

Now Jocie tried to do just that by tucking the washpan

under one arm and running around the wheelchair to swing open the car's back door.

"This is not going to work." The nurse's frown got deeper. "Surely you can see that Mr. Green cannot bend his leg to get in a car. I'm afraid he'll have to stay until you can provide proper transportation."

"I can try to get hold of Gordon Hazelton, but Albert Bowen's funeral was this afternoon. I don't know whether Gordon can spare anybody to bring the ambulance over today," Jocie's dad said. The only ambulance they had in Hollyhill was an old hearse the funeral director had fixed up for emergency runs. They rarely ever had an emergency in Hollyhill that conflicted with a funeral, so it usually worked out okay. And getting Wes home wasn't really an emergency.

"Then Mr. Green will just have to stay another night. Probably should anyway. His doctor surely believed Mr. Green was going to a nursing home when he signed the discharge papers," the nurse said and started to turn the wheelchair back toward the doors.

"Hold everything," Wes said as he flicked the wheelchair brakes down so the wheels skidded on the sidewalk and stopped. He picked his crutches up off his lap and sat the ends down on the ground. "You ain't taking me back inside that place."

"Don't be ridiculous," Nurse Army Boots said as she reached forward to release the brakes.

"Don't touch that brake." Something in his voice made the nurse stop. Or maybe it was the way his white hair seemed to raise up off his head as if he'd just grabbed a hot electric wire. He kept his eyes hard on her and began pushing himself up out of the chair as he said, "Now stand back out of the way."

"Really, Mr. Green, don't be difficult. I'm just here to help you, and I know your family wants to do what's best for you as well," the nurse said even as she took a step back away from the wheelchair.

"I'm not the least bit kin to either one of these people. They just came down to give me a lift home, and I aim to take it even if I have to ride with my foot sticking out the back window." Wes looked at Jocie. "Roll it down for me, Jo."

Jocie stowed the washpan of stuff in the front seat and rolled the back window down. Without a word, her father was helping Wes get his crutches fixed under his arms. Wes hopped over to the car and slowly turned on his crutches until his back was to the door. He handed the crutches to Jocie and then held on to David until he was sitting on the backseat. "Now hold up my leg a little while I scoot on in here. Just be sure the door on the other side is shut good, or I might scoot right out on the road." He groaned a little as he inched himself back along the seat.

Jocie crawled in the front seat and leaned over it to push down the lock on the back door. She looked at Wes. His face had gone white and beads of sweat rolled down his forehead. "You sure you're going to fit?" she said.

"One way or another," Wes said between pants. "I'll chop my foot off before I go back in that hospital."

Jocie looked over the seat at him. "Maybe you should let Dad call Mr. Hazelton."

"Nope. I've ridden in worse shape and I ain't so big that I can't sit sideways in a backseat even with this contraption on my leg." He smacked his hand against the cast.

Jocie peeked back out at the nurse standing on the sidewalk, her feet spread apart and her hands on her hips. Jocie lowered her voice. "Nurse Army Boots is going to report you to your doctor. They'll probably make you do a hundred leg lifts or something."

"I'm already doing that, and if I ever get away from here,

I'm never coming back. Doc Markum has a saw. And if he don't, I know where I can buy one."

Jocie forced herself to look at his cast. She didn't like to. It made her stomach squeeze up in a hard knot and drop like lead inside her. Of course, it wasn't as awful as his leg had looked the day the tornado had dropped the tree on it. Then she might have just fainted away at the sight of the blood and bones if she hadn't been so busy trying to help Wes and taking pictures of what the tornado did to the Clay's Creek Church building.

Her father said the tornado hadn't blown away the church, because the church wasn't the building. The church was the people who went there. And Jocie guessed he was right since the people were still meeting. Every Sunday morning they set up folding chairs on the church floor, which was about all the tornado had left behind. One of the members had taken some pictures of the preacher with nothing but blue sky behind him, and they'd run the picture on the front page of the *Banner* last week. Of course, it was black and white in the paper so you had to imagine the blue sky.

They'd used almost all the pictures Jocie had taken after the tornado in the *Banner* too. She hadn't wanted to take the pictures, but Wes had told her she had to. For proof that they actually went nose to nose with a tornado and lived to tell the tale. So it was almost as if she were two people that day—one girl who wanted to curl up in a ball and cry, and another girl who just kept doing what had to be done.

Wes struggled to scoot along the car seat with the cast that went all the way up to his hip and had metal rods sticking out here and there below his knee. Now, as she watched, she felt more like the girl who wanted to curl up in a ball and cry. Wes wasn't very big, not much taller than she was since she'd grown a couple of inches over the summer. He was always saying he was scrawny, but tough. But when Jocie looked at the cast, she was afraid he wouldn't be tough enough. She was afraid Wes might never be able to walk again without crutches. She'd heard the doctors tell her father that. And she was the reason Wes had the cast.

Wes had told her it wasn't her fault. Everybody told her it wasn't her fault, but it was. She was the reason Wes was in the tornado's path. If only she could go back and live that day over. But she couldn't. As Aunt Love said, each day brought its own trouble. Aunt Love had a Bible verse she quoted about it, but Jocie could never remember exactly how it went. Something about sufficient unto the day the evil it was going to have.

Jocie thought that verse too depressing to memorize, but her father had told her it was just telling her not to worry about everything and anything. Said there was no need worrying yourself to distraction about things when what you were supposed to do was trust in the Lord. Besides, once something happened, it was done. Jocie couldn't change the fact that Wes had hurt his leg because of her. She just had to figure out how to help him get better. Right now she had to help Wes get in the car before Nurse Army Boots decided to pick him up and carry him back in the hospital.

"Another inch and I think we can close the door," she said. "Or maybe we could get a rope and tie it to the other door to keep it mostly closed."

"I don't know about that, Jo," Wes said as he scooted closer to the door until the armrest had to be digging into his back. "The way your dad drives, he'd go around a corner, the rope would come loose, and I'd slide right out of here and maybe break my other leg instead of my head, and you guys would want me to come back to this hospital, and I already told you and anybody else who wants to know, I ain't never going back in there again."

Jocie looked over her shoulder at the nurse who was giving her father an earful. "I know that's what you said, but I don't know how much longer Dad can hold off Nurse Army Boots, and she's bigger than all of us put together."

Wes grabbed hold of the back of the seat and pushed himself back a little more. "Okay, stick that wash pan you carried out under my heel."

Jocie helped Wes lift his leg and pushed the wash pan under the cast. The plastic bent but didn't break. "Now what?" she asked.

"Now shut the door and grab your dad before old Army Boots calls for reinforcements."

The door pushed up against the bottom of the cast, but it clicked shut. Jocie went over to where the nurse was still talking to her father. "Excuse me, Dad, but Wes is ready to go. He said he'd like to get home before his pain pill wears off."

The nurse glowered at her. "He wouldn't take a pain pill."

"Oh," Jocie said. "Well, maybe he said so we could get home before the drugstore closed and he could get his prescription filled. Maybe it's the one for the pain pills." Jocie knew she'd heard something about pain pills in the lecture the nurse had given her father up in the room. "And he wanted me to tell you how much he appreciated all you nurses who took care of him these last few weeks." She smiled at Nurse Army Boots and avoided her father's eyes. It wasn't much of a lie. Wes might have said it if he hadn't been so worried about the nurse trying to roll him back inside. And Jocie wanted to say something to make the nurse forget about calling for reinforcements.

"Well, did he really? I didn't expect that," the nurse said, a smile actually breaking out on her face. "I'll be sure to tell the others." She went over to the car window and leaned down to look in at Wes. "If you have any problems, Mr. Green, you just give us a call."

They were on the interstate headed home before Wes said, "Fat chance."

Jocie looked over her shoulder at him in the backseat. "What's a fat chance?"

"That I ever call that woman."

"She might be single," Jocie said with a grin.

"I would've bet on it, but Nurse Merry Sunshine told me she was married," Wes said. "Poor man is all I've got to say."

Jocie's father laughed. "She's probably sweet as pie at home, and she was just doing her job watching out for you. She really liked you telling Jocie to thank her for the way she'd taken care of you."

"I think that must have been more Jo talking than me," Wes said.

"It got us out of there, didn't it?" Jocie said. "And I'm sure you would have said the same thing if you'd thought of it."

"That and some other things," Wes growled.

"Then maybe it's just as well that you let Jocie deliver the message." Jocie's father glanced up in the rearview mirror at Wes in the backseat. His smile turned to a worried frown. "You don't look very comfortable. Is the way you're squeezed in there hurting your leg?"

"Not enough to bellyache about," Wes said.

"We should've brought some pillows," Jocie said.

"No, we should've brought the ambulance."

"Or a pickup truck with a chair in the back," Wes said. "How long did they say I was supposed to keep this thing on?"

"At least a month," Jocie's dad said. "Then they'll do more x-rays and decide what to do next."

"Doctors," Wes said. "What do they know?"

"A lot, we hope."

Jocie searched for something to say to lift the mood in the car. She hated it when Wes got all cranky and discouraged sounding. Before he hurt his leg, he'd sometimes dipped into a bad mood but he'd never carried it around with him. Her father said when people were hurting you couldn't expect them to be smiling all the time and happy. He told her it was really hard on Wes not being able to move around the way he wanted and that she should be more worried about how Wes was feeling than how she was feeling.

Still, sometimes if she could pull out the right thing to say, she could make Wes smile and then they both felt better. So now she said, "Didn't you have doctors up on Jupiter before you came down here and fell out of the spaceship?"

For a minute she didn't think he was going to pick up on it, that he was just going to keep his eyes closed. But then he said, "We didn't have need of doctors, as best I recall."

"You didn't get sick or hurt?"

"Not sick. No germs on Jupiter. Injured sometimes, but say like somebody hurt their leg, they just went to the warehouse and found a new leg the right size, unscrewed the one they had, and screwed in the new one. Some Jupiterians paid attention to color and others didn't, so sometimes you'd have a body walking around with one blue leg and one red leg."

"That was sort of weird, wasn't it?" Jocie said.

"No, just colorful. Very colorful."

Relief bubbled up in Jocie, and she laughed. She looked straight at Wes. "And what was that about you telling Nurse Army Boots you weren't kin to me? You're my granddaddy, remember, and there's no way you can get out of that."

"All right, if you're sure you want a Jupiterian grandpappy." Wes wasn't smiling much, but he was smiling. "But you can just forget about taking me to school for show-and-tell."

6

What Wes hated the most was feeling old. Old and helpless. He could put up with the pain. Even when it thumped through his whole body the way it was doing now as he lay his head back against the window and felt the wheels rolling under him, taking him back to Hollyhill. He wrapped his mind around the pain, absorbing it and letting it carry him as he rode out the worst of the pain like a rodeo rider staying on the back of a raging bull until the horn sounded.

Wes had followed the rodeo trail for a while before he ended up in Hollyhill. He'd never ridden the bulls. He was one of the even crazier clowns who waved flags in front of the bulls' noses to keep the fallen riders from getting stomped. He got pretty good at scaling fences or jumping into the barrels when the bulls charged him. So he knew about pain. He could handle pain.

But he'd never felt old before. Helpless, but not old. And the last time he'd felt helpless he just ran away from the feeling. Ran away and became a new person. A person who might have fallen out of a spaceship the way he was always telling Jo. She didn't believe him anymore the way she had when he first showed up in Hollyhill and started working for her dad. She was just a little squirt then. Now it was more of a game they played.

He wished he could catch a ride on a spaceship and go somewhere that he could unscrew this old leg and screw in a new one. Then maybe he could stop feeling so old and helpless. And useless. A man who couldn't work wasn't worth much, and Wes couldn't even walk, much less work.

David was always talking about when Wes came back to work at the *Banner*, but Wes wasn't all that sure that even David believed it. Jo did. Jo couldn't believe anything else. She wanted everything to be the way it was, when she should know, after all the things she'd been through, that nothing could ever be the way it was. Things happened. And there wasn't any going back.

Wes kept his eyes half closed as he watched Jo and David talking in the front seat. Every once in a while he caught a word when Jo glanced back at him as if she thought he was part of the conversation, but he couldn't really hear what they were saying. Too much wind whipping in the windows and bringing in road noise.

He should have taken the pill old Nurse Army Boots had tried to shove on him. He might have, in spite of the way the things made his head spin, if he'd known how he was going to have to wedge himself into the backseat. Who'd have thought his leg would be that long? Of course, his legs had always been long for the rest of him. His mother used to tell him his legs started under his armpits. Now, with the crutches, they did. He almost grinned at the thought.

In the front Jo let out a laugh. That did make Wes smile. He was glad she'd survived the storm intact with no more than a few scrapes and bruises. And she seemed to have weathered the emotional storm as well. She and her father were as tight as ever, maybe tighter. And she wouldn't let go of this granddaddy idea. He'd told her maybe uncle would be better, but she said uncle wasn't close enough. It had to be granddaddy. He pointed out that even the name sounded old, but she just laughed. In her young eyes, he probably looked ancient even before the tree fell on him and knocked a few years off his life.

When he thought about it, he probably was old enough to be her granddaddy. Actually, no probably about it. He was past sixty. He didn't think about exact years. He'd always told himself years didn't matter, but now he felt every one of them plus. Fact of the matter was, he could be a real granddaddy to somebody somewhere. He didn't know it if he was, but he could be. No, more than could be. Probably was. He'd had a son back in that life before he fell out of the spaceship and landed in Hollyhill.

Just because he cut the boy loose some twenty years ago and hadn't made the first attempt to even check to see if he was still living, that didn't mean he wasn't. He was married when Wes took off. Wes frowned, trying to remember the boy's wife's name. Michelle or Madeline. Something with an M for sure. As best he could remember, she'd looked like the type who would want children. Most every woman did. And a good thing. It's what kept the old world spinning.

He wished it wasn't spinning quite so much right at this particular moment. He guessed the pain was making him light-headed. And the heat. Air was flowing through the car, but it had to be close to a hundred outside. The sun coming through the window was cooking his shoulders. He tried to shift in the seat a little, but he couldn't move his leg.

"You all right back there, Wes?" David called over his shoulder at him.

"Fine as frogs' hair," Wes lied.

"You want to stop and take a break? Move around a little or get something to drink?"

"Better go on in, David. I ain't sure we could prize me

back in this car if I got out." He met David's eyes in the rearview mirror.

"I'll speed up a little."

That was the trouble with David. He always knew when Wes was lying. He never tried to pry out the truth, but he always knew. And he cared. He was full of the fruits of the Spirit. Wes might not go to church, but he recognized the genuine article when he saw it, and David was it. Goodness oozed out of his pores.

Just like now, taking him home with him when he didn't have to. Not only didn't have to, but probably shouldn't. The man had a house full of problems already. He didn't need to add a crippled-up old man. A crippled-up old man who couldn't shake the dark cloud hovering over his head.

The doctor back at the hospital had told Wes there wasn't a thing unusual about a man feeling low after he'd gotten his leg about mashed off. He offered him some pills for that too. For the low feelings. But Wes hadn't ever been much for taking pills even when he was in the kind of crowds where pills were handed out like candy.

Wes let his mind freewheel to try to keep away from the dark thoughts of never walking again. Of being old and helpless. And useless. He looked at Jo in the front seat and tried to hear what she was saying, but he couldn't. She'd grown taller even in the short time he'd been in the hospital. Or maybe it was only because he felt shorter on the crutches.

She was growing up. He hadn't aimed to ever get close to anybody again after the wreck that took his wife and daughter from him back in the old life. And he hadn't, until he stopped in Hollyhill to get an odd job to put a little more gasoline in his motorcycle before he went on down the road. But then Jo came to work with her daddy. She couldn't have been more than three, and as soon as she laid eyes on Wes, she walked right over to him and held her arms up to him. Before a week went by, he'd have died on the spot for her.

He never had the opportunity to prove it until the tornado came barreling at them back in July. He'd have fought winds twice as strong and trees twice as big and passed out of life gladly as long as she was safe. Maybe she was right about him being her granddaddy.

At last they drove through Hollyhill. Wes looked over at the newspaper office and wondered if he'd ever see the inside of it again. He liked keeping the contrary old press in running order. He liked ink under his fingernails. Wes looked down at his hands in his lap. Not the first sign of ink, and even the mashed thumbnail had about grown out.

"Maybe you should let me try the steps up to my place, David. I could just hibernate there for a while till my leg gets better. Jo here could bring me wieners and coffee."

"In a few weeks maybe," David said. "You wouldn't want to cheat us out of the blessing of taking care of you for a while first."

"It may not be such a blessing. Old Nurse Army Boots could've warned you about that," Wes said. "I'm not sure Lovella is up to it."

"I'll be there to help," Jo said. "And Dad too."

Then they were out of the town, and Jo was pointing at an old bike by the side of the road. She looked around at Wes. "There's the bike I told you about. The one Mr. McDermott found for me."

"What's it doing there? Did it run out of gas?" Wes asked.

"I had a wreck. I'll have to tell you all about it after you get settled in at the house. It's too crazy a story to tell in the car."

"Did you get hurt?" Wes asked.

"My ankle's a little sore," Jo admitted.

"So that's why you were limping. And I thought it was just sympathy pains."

And then they were pulling up in the yard beside the end of the porch where it was only a little step off the ground. Lovella and Tabitha were waiting on the porch in the rocking chairs. Tabitha stood up. No doubt about it, the girl was blooming, but happily, it appeared from her face and all David had told him. She might be a dead ringer for her mother, but perhaps thc resemblance was only skin deep. If she wanted to be a mother, that would have to be true. For sure, Adrienne had never wanted to be a mother. Had never actually been one. To Jo at any rate.

It was a bigger ordeal getting out of the backseat of the car than it had been getting in. For one thing, he didn't have old Army Boots to inspire him. He just had Jo watching him and looking as if she was going to burst out in tears any second. The poor kid had a load of blame slung in a sack over her shoulder. When Wes felt better, when the dark cloud quit drifting over his head, he'd have to try to get her to throw that sack away. He'd never been able to do it about Rosa and Lydia. But that was different. There weren't any tornadoes that night. Just the road and the car and him behind the wheel.

He turned his mind away from the memory of the wreck. He couldn't think about that now. Not unless he wanted to get lost in the black cloud that kept trying to settle over his head. And right now he had to get out of the car.

Jo had hold of his cast, and David had his hands and was trying to tug him out of the car. Trouble was, Wes could barely move. His backside and other leg had gone numb during the ride home. It would have been funny if they hadn't all been looking at him as if he were going to turn purple and blow up any second.

Then Jo's ugly dog, Zeb, came racing from somewhere and started dipping in and out under his leg and barking. Lovella shouted at the dog and then started reciting something. What with the blood thumping in his ears and the dog's barks echoing off the side of the house, Wes couldn't make out the words, but he could tell it was Scripture. David was saying something too. His mouth was moving as the sweat dripped off the end of his nose while he pulled on Wes.

Maybe he was praying over Wes. It wouldn't be the first time. He knew David prayed for him even if the man never said so in so many words. After all, the man was a preacher, a man called of God. He had to pray for everybody. It was part of his job.

Wes couldn't remember the last time he'd prayed. Maybe when he was a kid tagging along with his mother to Sunday school. Maybe never. Not a real prayer. He might have said words. *Our Father up in heaven, hallowed be thy name*. For years, he'd thought it was "Howard be thy name." Wes had a brother named Howard and had once asked his mother if she'd named Howard after God. She laughed as if he'd told a good joke when she finally figured out what he was talking about. That was the best thing about his mother. The way she could laugh. She died when he was fifteen, so many years ago that he could barely remember her face, but he remembered her laugh.

Now the dog, maybe dizzy from all his running back and forth, banged into Jo's knees and knocked her backward. She let out a little squeal as her hands slipped off his cast.

Wes stiffened and braced himself for the pain of his leg jarring against the ground, but Zeb, as if he really knew what was happening, scooted under the cast and stopped, letting the weight of it land on his back. He stopped barking and looked over at Wes almost apologetically. Then the dog started panting with his tongue near to dragging on the ground as the poor creature's legs almost buckled under the weight of the cast. He turned his head to direct a little hurry-up woof at Jo, who was scrambling to her feet.

"That's the craziest thing I've ever seen," Tabitha said. "Do you think he aimed to do that or he just got under there at the wrong time?"

"Well, of course he aimed to," Jo said as she grabbed hold of the cast again so the dog could move out from under it. Zeb wobbled over to the shady side of the car and collapsed. "He didn't want to hurt Wes. He was just excited."

"Come on, Jocie," Tabitha said. "He's just a dog."

"Try telling him that," Jo said.

"Why? You think he might bite me or something if I say he's a dog? He is a dog." Suddenly Tabitha didn't look all that sure. "Isn't he?"

David smiled at Wes as he tugged him a little closer to the edge of the car seat. "He looks like a dog, he sounds like a dog, and heaven only knows, he smells like a dog. So I think we can be pretty sure he's a dog."

"But smarter than any other dog you'll ever meet on this planet," Jocie said. "Right, Wes?"

"Oh, no, not the out-of-Jupiter stories again." Tabitha smacked the palm of her hand against her forehead as if her head had started hurting. "You guys are weirder than anybody I ever met from here to California and back."

Wes laughed. He was out of the car at last and on his feet, or foot might be more accurate. The good leg was tingling awake. He needed to stomp it, but it was hard to stomp when only one foot was in working order. He shoved the crutches up under his arms and didn't pay the first bit of attention to the complaints his arms and shoulders started shouting at him. He just kept laughing. That somehow seemed a better thing to do than cry, especially with Jo watching him.

"'A merry heart doeth good like a medicine.'" Lovella smiled at him.

"'But a broken spirit drieth the bones,'" Wes said.

"Proverbs 17:22. I didn't know you knew the Scriptures, Wesley," Lovella said.

"There was a Bible in the table drawer at the hospital. And a lot of time for reading if I could get the nurses to let me alone."

He let them help him up on the porch and into the house. They'd shoved all the living room furniture to the side of the room and put up a cot for him with a table beside it. The bed looked awfully low to the floor, but maybe if they set a straight chair beside it he could pull himself up out of it. Jo must have gone to his rooms and brought him a stack of his books. An easy chair with a footstool sat right by the table with a floor lamp over the chair. He could feel Jo watching him to see what he thought of how they'd fixed it up for him. He let the smile hanging around from the merry heart stay on his face and tried not to think about broken spirits drying up bones as he looked at her. "You guys have got me fixed up so good, you may never get rid of me."

For a minute he thought Jo was going to start bawling. He was glad she fought it off, because he wasn't sure he might not have joined in. And then the merry heart medicine would have been down the tubes.

7

Things were always a little wild on Sunday mornings at the Brooke house as they all scrambled to get ready for church. Before Tabitha came home from California, Aunt Love had kept David and Jocie on schedule. If either of them stayed too long in the bathroom, she rapped sharply on the door and got them moving. But it was hard to move somebody out of the bathroom who had morning sickness. And it was beginning to look as if the only thing that was going to ease Tabitha's morning sickness was having her baby. Her doctor had told Tabitha some women were just unlucky that way.

David still had a hard time thinking of Tabitha as a woman. He'd lost so many of her girl years after she'd left with Adrienne that he wasn't ready for her to be a woman, even if she was only a few weeks from being a mother. She had settled in better back in Hollyhill than he ever imagined she would after they came home from church a couple of months ago to find her on the porch. She'd ridden a bus all that way. By herself. Holding the secret of her baby close within her for weeks after she was home. Aunt Love had finally insisted Tabitha tell him what he'd been too blind to see. So many surprises already this summer.

Sometimes David was almost afraid to stick his head out from under the covers in the morning for fear of what the Lord might send his way next. But then when the sun started pushing light in through his window, David would say his morning prayer. "Oh, Lord, be with me today." And the Lord's answer would echo back. *Lo, I am with you always, even unto the end of the world*. The Lord's promise was good to the disciples who faced much more perilous times in those New Testament days than David could even imagine facing, and that same promise was good to the Lord's followers now. David just had to lean on the Lord and in all things be thankful.

And he was. He was thankful Tabitha was home. He was thankful for the child on the way. He was thankful for a church that trusted David to lead them. He was thankful Jocie had weathered the storms of the summer. He was thankful Wes had survived the tornado. He was thankful that it was so easy to smile when Leigh was around. He still didn't know exactly what he should do about Leigh. If only she wasn't so young, but maybe it was her being young that kept him smiling.

But none of that made it one bit easier to get out the door on time to leave for church. Or easier to decide what to do about Wes. David wasn't having second thoughts about bringing Wes home with him, but he was having second thoughts about their ability to take care of him, especially Aunt Love's and Tabitha's and Jocie's when David wasn't there to help.

On Saturday, they had all three volunteered to stay home with Wes on Sunday. And now Tabitha had found David going over his sermon notes in his bedroom and was trying to convince him she should be the one to stay home. "Let me stay with Wes. Nobody will miss me at church."

"Everybody will miss you," David told her. "Whenever you're not there, they all ask about you."

"Probably to see if I'm properly ashamed of myself yet." Tabitha made a little face as she touched her rounded stomach.

David stood up from his desk and went over to hug her. "You know that's not true. The people out there have been nothing but kind to you. Haven't they?" He peered down at her face. Maybe there was something he didn't know. Maybe the Martin boy was at it again. It had been Ronnie Martin's ugly words in Jocie's ears that had sent her reeling earlier in the summer.

David and the boy's father, Ogden Martin, one of the deacons at Mt. Pleasant, had talked it out, then prayed together on their knees in the men's Sunday school room until the Lord helped them find a way to both continue on in the same church. Ogden made his son apologize to Jocie, something she stood still and endured even though she didn't want to. The words were said, but David didn't sense a genuine feeling of sorrow in the boy over what he'd done any more than he felt any hint of forgiveness in Jocie. He wouldn't be surprised if Ronnie was already making more trouble.

But Tabitha was shaking her head. "No, they don't say anything outright. It's just the way they look at me with those 'oh poor pitiful thing' eyes like I had leprosy or something instead of just expecting a baby. And then if I tell them I'm doing fine, they look at me like I shouldn't be doing fine, like I should be sitting over in the corner staring at my hands and crying big crocodile tears or something."

David tightened his arm around her shoulder and smiled a little. "We don't always act the way other people think we should."

Tabitha looked up at him. "Well, I mean, I know I did wrong, that I should have waited till I was married, but if I had, this baby would've never been. And Aunt Love helped me pray and tell the Lord I'm sorry. She said the Lord would forgive me if I did that."

"And the Lord did. In the Bible it says if we ask for forgiveness the Lord will separate us from our sins as far as the east is from the west."

"How far is that?" Tabitha asked.

"If you were to start walking east and never turned around, you would never go west. You would just keep walking east forever around and around the world."

"Really? I'd never thought about that." Tabitha looked as if a light had come on inside her head. But then she was frowning again. "But the women at church want me to be miserable instead of happy. They think I'm sinning if I smile when I feel little Stephanie Grace kicking."

"Oh, I don't think they're that bad." David had given up sticking in a word here and there to prepare Tabitha in case her baby didn't turn out to be the girl she was so sure she was carrying. She said she was having a girl. She was naming her Stephanie Grace, and that was that.

"But why can't they just be glad for me? I'm glad. Why can't they be?"

"Tell them that. Tell them you're glad about the baby and hope they will be too."

"I couldn't do that." Tabitha looked half scared at the thought. "They'd really think I was awful then."

"No, they wouldn't. They'd think you were a mother who loved her baby just the way they loved their own babies before they were born." David brushed Tabitha's forehead with his lips.

"I'm not sure about that. They already think I'm half heathen because I've got this rose on my cheek." Tabitha touched the small tattoo on her left cheek. "And I'm probably causing you enough problems at church without saying all the wrong things the way DeeDee used to when she went."

"Your mother never liked being at church."

"I remember," Tabitha said.

"I suppose you do." David hadn't realized until Tabitha came home how much the girl had known about the problems between David and Adrienne. He thought he'd kept it all hidden so well. "But you're not causing me any problems, and when your baby comes, the people at Mt. Pleasant will be won over by his or her first smile."

"If you say so, but somebody has to stay home with Wes. It can't be you. You have to preach. And Aunt Love likes to go to church too much to miss. I guess Jocie and me can take turns, but let my turn be first. Please."

"Okay, if you promise to call Mr. Crutcher next door if you need help. If Wes were to fall or something, you couldn't try to help him up."

"Mr. Crutcher goes to church too, doesn't he? Doesn't everybody in Holly County go to church except Wes?"

"Well, I'm not sure the whole county is that faithful, but just in case, I'll tell Wes not to try to walk to the bathroom till after church time," David said.

"Maybe you'd better ask him instead of telling him. Nicely," Tabitha said. "Wes doesn't take orders too well. He was even cranky with Jocie last night when she was trying to get him to eat."

"We may be expecting too much out of him. He's lived by himself for years now, and we plop him down in the middle of what he calls Brooke Central Station. He told me that it wasn't even quiet around here at midnight with the way Grandfather Brooke's clock bongs out the hours."

"I'll go out and sit on the porch today and let him have all the silence he wants."

"He'll probably appreciate that," David said.

Jocie didn't protest when he told her Tabitha was going to take the first turn staying with Wes. She just said, "Okay. I forgot to get somebody to help Miss Vangie in my place with the Beginners' Class today anyway. I'll ask Paulette if she can do it next Sunday."

Letting Jocie help with the Beginners was how David had found a way to keep her out of Sunday school with Ronnie Martin. David believed in avoiding confrontation in church if possible. The Lord instructed his followers to love one another, and David believed that with the Lord's help it was possible to love all people. Liking them enough to sit in Sunday school class with them for an hour was a whole different matter.

"I'm sure Miss Vangie would appreciate that," David said, but he could tell Jocie was thinking of more than Miss Vangie. After all, Miss Vangie had managed the Beginners' room alone for nearly twenty years before Jocie started helping her.

Jocie saw his look. "I know Miss Vangie would be okay without me there, and I don't mind staying instead of Tabitha, but I just thought that if Noah and his family did decide to show up for church this morning, I maybe should be there. You know, since I've met Noah already."

"If they come, I'm sure Noah will be glad to see a familiar face."

"Do you think they will?"

"I don't know, Jocie. I haven't visited them yet or talked to his parents."

"He said that his father didn't go to church, but that his mother was half preacher. She went on that march in Washington with Reverend Martin Luther King."

"She sounds like an interesting woman."

Jocie hesitated a second before she asked, "Do you think people will get upset if they do come?"

He didn't have a sure answer for Jocie then, nor did he have a sure answer for Harvey McMurtry when Mr. Harvey pulled him aside before the Sunday school assembly.

"You knew I sold my farm on Hoopole Road, didn't you?" Mr. Harvey said as he ran his fingers down the inside of his black suspenders. He'd been a member of Mt. Pleasant all his life. He and his sister, Sally McMurtry, still lived in the house where they'd both been born sixty-plus years ago. Neither of them had ever married. Mr. Harvey said he was always too busy on the farm to go courting, and Miss Sally said nobody ever asked her.

"So I heard," David said.

"Good people. A nice family. Name of Hearndon. Moved down here from Chicago. Got four kids." Mr. Harvey hemmed and hawed a bit. "I asked them to church."

"I should hope so since they're in our church community. You think I should go visit them this afternoon and extend a pastor's invitation to them as well?"

"Well, uh, that might be good, Pastor." Mr. Harvey rocked forward on his toes and then back on his heels before he stopped flat-footed and leaned a bit closer to David. "But just so's you know, they're colored folk."

"Right," David said. "I met their boy Thursday. He's going to be helping me out at the paper until Wes gets back on his feet."

Mr. Harvey looked relieved David already knew his news. "Well, that's fine then. The boy helped me put up fence Saturday. Polite, good worker. Better than some I've had working for me." Mr. Harvey frowned a little.

"He won't be working for me every day, so he can still help you out when you need him."

"I'm not worried about that, Pastor."

"You seem worried about something, Mr. Harvey. You want to tell me about it?"

"All right. I'll just be out with it and quit beating around the bush. Do you think the folks here will get upset if the Hearndons do take me up on my invitation?"

"I don't know. What do you think? You've been part of this church a lot longer than I have."

Mr. Harvey sighed and looked a little sad. "I guess it will be like anything else. Some will and some won't. The same as with your girl. Some understand and some don't."

David was a little surprised by Mr. Harvey's honesty with him. He knew there were people in the church who hadn't fully accepted that Tabitha was going to keep her baby even though she wasn't married, but nobody had spoken the words directly to him. David put his hand on Mr. Harvey's shoulder and said, "We just have to pray for the ones who don't. And for ourselves too, that we'll say and do the right things."

"It's not like we've never had colored folks in the church before. When it was founded back in the 1820s, a third of the members were black."

"Is that right?" David asked, surprised.

"Slaves of the founding members."

"Oh," David said. "That might be something you wouldn't want to bring up to Mrs. Hearndon if she does decide to attend church here. At least not right away."

"You sound like you've met her," Mr. Harvey said.

"No, I was just going from what Noah said about her."

"Well, you got the right idea." Mr. Harvey smiled and shook his head a little. "She'd grab that in a minute and be gone with it. She's something. Just wait till you do meet her. Fact is, I might ought to worry more about our members than her if she comes. She'll probably set us all on our ears."

"Maybe we need to be set on our ears every once in a while."

"You could be right, Pastor. You could be right."

8

They had six beginners in the class that morning, all under the age of six—counting little Murray McDermott who wouldn't be a year old until October, but he was happy as long as Jocie was carrying him around. Miss Vangie somehow managed to get them to sit around the little table and listen when she told them stories about Jesus. Of course, she kept the lessons short. Stuff like Jesus loves you and God made the world and how to say, "Thank you, Lord."

Miss Vangie said singing had never been her best talent, so she turned that part of the class over to Jocie. Jocie loved the way the little boys and girls kept their eyes tight on her while they were singing. She liked the way they shouted out the "Yes, Jesus loves me" part, and she couldn't keep from laughing when they got the deep and wide mixed up when they sang about God's love. She was having more fun in Sunday school than she'd had since she was a beginner herself in some other church years ago.

This Sunday she sang "Jesus Loves the Little Children" with them because of the line in the song that said "red and yellow, black and white." All through Sunday school she kept peeking out the window at the parking area in front of the church, but so far there weren't any cars she couldn't match up with regular members.

With the singing part of the class over, Jocie set Murray down on his feet in front of the open window to give her arm a rest. He wasn't walking yet, but he liked to stand up holding on to the windowsill and look outside. Behind her, Miss Vangie was handing out crayons and coloring books along with vanilla wafers. It was the time of Sunday school when Jocie began to count the minutes until the bell rang because the kids were beginning to get tired of being confined in one little room. And today it was an extra hot room.

A four-year-old named Sandy came over to show Jocie her picture of a church she'd colored blue and red and to share one of her cookies with Murray. "What a pretty picture and how sweet of you to share your cookies, Sandy," Jocie said, emphasizing the word "share" to be sure the little girl knew that was a good thing to do. Jocie moved over a little. "You want to look out the window with me and Murray?"

"What are you looking for?" Sandy asked.

"I was just watching all the people coming to church this morning."

"Why didn't they come for Sunday school?" Sandy asked. "My mommy says everybody should come to Sunday school to learn about Jesus."

"Maybe they'll all come to Sunday school next week," Jocie said.

"Miss Vangie will have to bring more cookies," Sandy said.

"She might." Jocie laughed.

"Look." Sandy put her finger against the window screen to point out toward the parking lot. "There's your daddy's girlfriend."

"Oh, really. Who's that?" Jocie said, even as she watched Leigh climb out of her tan and white '59 Chevy with the fins in the back that looked like wings.

"Her." Sandy shoved her finger a little harder against the screen. "Mommy told me."

"Oh, you mean Leigh. You know, your mommy might be right," Jocie said as she watched Leigh pick up her Bible and purse and then try to shut her car door with her free hand. The door didn't budge. Leigh said the hinges must be broken or need oil or something. Sometimes when Jocie was with her, they both had to push on it to get it to shut. Now Leigh gave up trying to close it with her free hand and stepped around behind the door to push it shut with her backside. Jocie could hear the hinges creak all the way across the churchyard.

Leigh was wearing the new dress with the white top and yellow-and-white-striped skirt that she bought when she took Jocie shopping for school clothes last Monday after they'd visited Wes at the hospital. She'd lost almost ten pounds, and she said that kind of effort deserved a new dress.

She looked nice, Jocie decided, as she watched Leigh brush off the back of her skirt and head across the yard toward the church door. She was still what some of the church ladies might call pleasingly plump and far from skinny like Jocie was. Jocie was too skinny. If she stuffed her hair under a baseball cap and wore jeans, nobody would even guess she was a girl just by looking.

Leigh had laughed when Jocie had told her that as they were driving home from their shopping trip. "Better to be too skinny than too heavy. At least you can eat all the cakes and doughnuts you want without feeling guilty."

"But don't you think I should be starting to develop?" Jocie had asked.

"Develop what? Hives?" Leigh looked over at her with a smile.

Jocie didn't smile back. "That sounds like something Wes would say."

"It does, doesn't it? His Jupiterian wit must be rubbing off on me." Leigh laughed. Leigh laughed a lot.

"It's not funny. You know what I mean. Something to fill out those new bras you helped me buy." They'd bought the smallest cup size the store had, and they were still too big. "After all, I am almost fourteen."

"I know. September twelfth. Chocolate cake with white and dark blue icing so our teeth can turn blue when we eat it."

Leigh was a great cook, and the chocolate cake she had helped Jocie bake for Tabitha's birthday in July was the best Jocie had ever eaten. Still, Jocie hadn't been worried about chocolate cake right then. She just stared down at her hands without saying anything.

Leigh reached over to touch Jocie's shoulder lightly. "I'm sorry, Jocie. But you really are beautiful just the way you are." Leigh took her hand away and smacked the steering wheel. "Ooh, I can't believe I said that. That's what my mother used to tell me when I worried about being so chubby. It never made me feel the least bit better, and I'll bet it didn't you either."

"Not really," Jocie said.

Leigh let out a long sigh. "I guess it's just a girl thing not being happy with the way we look."

"I never thought about it much before, but I'm going to start high school. I don't want to still look like a sixth grader."

"You won't. You're way too tall. I'll bet you've grown an inch this summer."

"Two inches, but all up and none out in the right places."

"You will. I promise. Any day now. Some girls just take a little longer to develop than others."

"I only have two weeks till school starts."

"Well, it might not happen by then," Leigh admitted.

"I know. I thought about praying about it. Dad says the

Lord wants us to pray about everything, but I wasn't sure about a give-me-boobs prayer." Jocie looked over at Leigh. "I probably shouldn't even say 'boobs.' That's not a very nice word, but 'Lord, please give me breasts' sounds like I want the first pick off a plate of fried chicken."

Leigh laughed again. "Jocie, you're one of a kind. But you know what? The Bible says the Lord knows what we need. And I know he's going to develop you into the most beautiful girl in Hollyhill."

Leigh had said it as if she really believed it, but Jocie had a mirror. She could see what she looked like. Big eyes, wide mouth, an okay nose, brown hair that just sort of hung there on her head. Most of the time she didn't give a thought to how she looked. She was too busy to worry about makeup and curling her hair. Maybe before she started high school she needed to buy some lipstick and one of those glass bottles of makeup that Paulette, her friend here at church, dabbed all over her face and then smoothed out with her fingers.

Jocie's dad must have been watching out his Sunday school window too, because he met Leigh halfway across the yard. He wasn't running away from the idea of Leigh liking him anymore. Far from it, from the smile Jocie could see on his face as he welcomed Leigh to Mt. Pleasant as if this was her very first Sunday there, when in fact she'd been coming every Sunday for two months. Jocie wouldn't have been surprised to see him lean down and kiss Leigh. Maybe not on the lips right there in the middle of the churchyard, but on the cheek. But he didn't. He just took her hand and smiled.

Of course, with the way Zella said Jocie's dad was backward in the romantic department, he might not have kissed Leigh on the lips even if they'd been standing all alone in the dark on the tiny landing outside Leigh's apartment. Jocie had told Zella her father wasn't backward, just out of practice. After all, it had been eight years since Jocie's mother had packed her bags in the middle of the night and left. As far as Jocie knew, her father hadn't kissed any females since then except her and maybe Aunt Love and Tabitha now that she was home, and that wasn't exactly the kind of kiss Zella was talking about. Zella was talking about the kind of kiss she read about in the romance novels she kept hidden in her desk drawer at the paper.

Wes said that reading about it was the only way Zella could know anything about kissing, since if any man had ever kissed her it had been so long ago that she wouldn't be able to remember a thing about it. But whether she had experience or not, Zella had set herself up as matchmaker and romantic expert on the premises at the newspaper office and as the final authority on how things should be between Jocie's dad and Leigh.

But now, as David and Leigh stood out in the middle of the yard together, the sun seemed brighter where it shone on them. It might have just been her yellow dress and his white shirt, but the air sort of radiated around them, and they looked as if they might have stepped out of a romance novel.

Beside her at the window, Murray had run out of cookie and let out a squeal for more. Jocie's dad looked around and saw them in the window. He waved and so did Leigh. The shaft of sunlight that had spotlighted them melted away, and they drifted over to where some other people were talking before going in for church.

The warning bell that Sunday school was almost over sounded. Jocie picked up Murray and turned away from the window to help Miss Vangie put away the crayons and coloring books while the boys and girls lined up at the door to wait for the second bell.

After the bell rang and the kids rushed out into the hall to find their parents, Jocie went back into the Beginners' room to get a tissue to clean the cookie mess off Murray before she turned him over to his mother. She took one last peek out the window and finally saw a car she didn't recognize pulling into the parking area. Jocie watched as Noah climbed out of the passenger side of the front seat and reached back in to pick up a little boy who looked about two. Jocie hadn't thought to ask Noah about brothers and sisters. Another girl of maybe nine or ten climbed out of the backseat and then picked up a little girl who looked the same age as the little boy Noah was carrying.

"They must be twins," Jocie told Murray as if the baby knew what she was talking about. "I wish Tabitha was here to see this. She's half scared of you, Murray baby. She'd faint if she had to think about having two."

"Two what?" Murray's mother said behind her. When Jocie looked around at her, she went on. "I waited out in church, but thought you might be having trouble with Murray."

"No trouble. He's never any trouble. I was just cleaning off his hands and face. Vanilla wafers and drool make cookie mud."

"Here, I've got a wet cloth in my bag somewhere." She dug down in her purse until she came up with a wet washrag in a plastic bread sack. "But two what?" she asked again.

"Two babies."

"Oh, my heavens. One at a time is enough. Has the doctor told Tabitha she's having twins?"

"No. I was just looking at the two little kids out there and guessing they might be twins." Jocie moved to the side so that Mrs. McDermott could look out the window too.

Together they watched Noah's mother climb out of the car. She was tall and slender and moved with total confidence. Her skin was a beautiful bronze and her black hair was swept back in a neat roll on the back of her head. At least Jocie was guessing the woman might be Noah's mother. She really didn't look like anybody's mother. She looked way too regal for that.

"She's beautiful," Jocie said.

"She is, isn't she?" Mrs. McDermott agreed. "They must be the family that bought Harvey McMurtry's farm. I'd heard they'd moved in."

"Did you think they would come to church here?" Jocie asked.

"Well, I didn't know, but I'm glad they decided to give our church a chance. Let's go meet them before church starts."

"I met Noah—that's the boy Thursday."

"Oh, good. So he'll know somebody." Mrs. McDermott took Murray and led the way down the hall to the sanctuary.

As Jocie followed her, she knew again why she liked Mrs. McDermott so much, why most everybody liked Mrs. McDermott. She didn't just talk about loving her neighbor. She did it. She always wanted to believe the best about anybody and didn't want to listen if somebody else tried to point out the parts that weren't best. And she always knew the right thing to say.

Jocie hoped Mrs. McDermott would do most of the talking now, because Jocie was feeling strangely tongue-tied. Maybe she'd just say hi and play with the toddlers. She was good with little kids. Kids liked her. Kids and dogs.

9

Each Sunday David was amazed at how much he could tell about the kind of week the people in his congregation had had just by looking at them in the pews as he welcomed them to the morning service. "Good morning," David said as he made mental notes of the ones he needed to seek out after church for an extra word. "Is everybody warm enough?"

That brought a laugh since it had to be almost ninety outside, and the cardboard fans donated by the Hazelton Funeral Home were getting a workout all over the church. "Well, I just wanted to be sure everybody got a warm welcome today," David went on with a smile before he called on Ogden Martin for the opening prayer and then returned to his chair on the podium behind the pulpit while Jim Sanderson led the first hymn.

Jim wasn't the greatest singer in the world, but he was willing and loud and looked as if he enjoyed singing so much that everybody in the church felt compelled to join in. If he went off key, his wife, Jessica, just played the piano a little louder until they got back on the right notes. Singing in church was all about making a joyful noise unto the Lord anyway, and most mornings they sounded joyful if not always on pitch.

This morning everybody was sounding a bit tentative as they started out on the first verse of "Bringing in the

Sheaves." And then a strong soprano voice rose up out of the third pew from the back, and even Jim almost forgot to keep singing for a moment. Myra Hearndon's voice was as beautiful as she was, and she didn't seem to give the first bit of notice to the fact that half the church had seemed to lose their voices as they looked over at her when she started singing. Or maybe she did notice and sang a bit stronger and truer because of it.

She and her family had come in and nearly filled up one of the pews. The McDermotts had settled in the pew in front of them although they usually sat closer to the front. Jocie sat beside Noah and already had one of the twins, Elise, in her lap. The little boy, Eli, was in Noah's lap. The girl, Cassidy, was sitting very close to her mother, helping her hold the hymnbook and singing along. Aunt Love was in her customary spot three rows back, and Leigh had joined her there instead of crowding the Hearndons by sitting with Jocie.

Three families had moved across the aisle to settle in different pews than usual, but at least no one left when the Hearndons came in and sat down. That was something to give thanks for, David thought as he watched his congregation. Some had even welcomed Myra Hearndon and her children. The McDermotts. Mr. Harvey and Miss Sally. A few more.

Several others smiled over at the woman and her children but seemed hesitant to speak to her for fear they wouldn't say the right thing. Myra Hearndon had kept a friendly smile on her face the whole time. Yet David thought he caught the hint of a challenge under her smile, as if she was waiting for someone to say the wrong thing, perhaps even ask her to leave so that she could refuse.

Before the service started, David had introduced himself

to her as he shook her hand. "We're so glad you are here this morning."

"Are you?" she said with that challenge in her eyes.

"Of course. Noah said you might come when we talked last week."

"Oh, yes. He told me you had offered him a job at your newspaper." She bent her head just a bit like a queen granting favor to a subject. "Thank you, but he'll have to clear the hours with his father. My husband is working very hard to get the ground ready to put in some apple trees this fall."

"Noah can let me know what hours might suit him best. Tuesday is the day I need the most help because that's the day we run the paper, but we can talk about that later. Now I hope you enjoy our services."

"Is that what you think the Lord wants? For us to enjoy church?"

The question had surprised David. "Yes, I do. Don't you? The Bible does say to come before him with gladness."

"So it does," she had conceded with a smile that showed perfect white teeth. "And perhaps I will enjoy worshiping with you and your congregation."

"It's our prayer that you do so."

Now with the last verse of the song winding down, David was praying. He had his eyes open as he sang along, but he was praying at the same time. *Dear Lord, let these people you have allowed me to shepherd have open minds and hearts. Let us all be here in your church to receive your message and your love and to share that love generously and without prejudice with one another.*

David was preaching on Paul's conversion on the road to Damascus. His focal verse was the one where Paul asked, "Lord, what wilt thou have me to do?" That was a question every Christian needed to ask themselves. It was a question David had asked many times since the first time he'd felt the Lord in his heart. It was a question he'd asked even more times after the Lord had laid his hand on him and called him to preach.

Could a man ever be absolutely certain that he was following the will of the Lord instead of his own will? Every Sunday when David stood up behind the pulpit he prayed his sermon would be what the Lord wanted him to say and what the people needed to hear. Sometimes he felt the message move through him and become more powerful as it left his mouth, and other times he felt he failed completely.

Now as he watched Ogden Martin and Harvey McMurtry bring the offering plates with the tails of bills and checks sticking up out of them back to sit on the table in front of the pulpit, he said the prayer he said every Sunday before he preached. *Not my words, Lord, but thine.*

The heat was building in the church. Already David's shirt was sticking to his back, but he didn't loosen his tie. He took hold of the pulpit on both sides so that no one could see how his hands were shaking. He'd been preaching for almost twenty years, but he still got nervous, still had to swallow his fear of speaking in front of people. He reminded himself he wasn't speaking. He was preaching, and the Lord would give him the power to do that if he only reached toward him in faith.

He began reading Acts 9. He read the sixth verse twice. "'And he trembling and astonished said, Lord, what wilt thou have me to do? And the Lord said unto him, Arise, and go into the city, and it shall be told thee what thou must do.'"

And then the sermon was there spilling out of his mouth, some of the same words as he'd prepared the night before and some new words put into his mouth by the Lord. The people listened. They waved their fans back and forth in front of their faces but they listened. For a while, they even seemed to forget that something unusual was happening at Mt. Pleasant on this Sunday morning. Something that probably hadn't happened for almost a hundred years in Holly County. Blacks and whites sharing the same church pew.

After the invitation hymn had been sung and the final prayer said, David stood at the door and shook the hands of his people. The Hearndons were one of the first families out the door. When Myra Hearndon took his hand, her hand felt cool as if she could even will her body not to feel the heat that had gathered in the church building during the service.

"Thank you for coming," he said.

"I appreciated your sermon," Myra Hearndon said. "It's a question I ask myself every morning when I get up. What would you have me do this day, Lord, to make the world a better place?"

"And do you get an answer, Mrs. Hearndon?"

"Some days, and some days I find my own answers."

"May the Lord guide you to the right answers."

"And the same for you."

"That is my prayer," David said.

She studied his face a moment before she nodded. "I believe it is. Thank you for your welcome, Rev. Brooke, and for the welcome of your people."

"God's people. We're all God's people."

"Yes."

"May I come out to meet your husband? Alex, didn't you say?"

"He's working. He might not stop for a visit from the preacher."

"Perhaps I can help him in whatever he's doing."

"On the Lord's Day, Preacher? The day of rest?" She raised her eyebrows at him.

"A preacher does little resting on Sunday," David said.

"No, I suppose not. Come if you want." She started to step out the door, but then smiled at David over her shoulder and added, "I'll hide the shotgun."

The girl, Cassidy, slipped past David without letting him shake her hand and hurried after her mother.

Noah, still carrying Eli, shook David's hand. "Mama shouldn't have said that. Preachers might not be Dad's favorite people, but he's not that bad. He won't shoot at you."

"That's good to know," David said.

"Mama just likes to test everybody to see if they're as brave as she is."

"I doubt I could measure up to her standards."

"Yeah, well, join the club," Noah said. "Look, I'll come to work tomorrow about noon if that's all right."

"Sounds great," David said.

Noah looked down at the little boy he was carrying. "Tell the preacher good-bye, Eli."

The little boy obediently waved his hand and said, "Bye bye."

Jocie, who was right behind Noah still carrying the other twin, Elise, flashed David a quick smile and said, "Aren't they cute?" She went on out of the church where she gave the little girl to Noah. He easily balanced the twins, one in each arm, and carried them to the car where his mother was waiting.

David kept smiling and shaking hands as the Mt. Pleasant members spilled out of the church and spread out in the shade of the oak tree out front. A few of them stopped talking to watch as Myra Hearndon backed her car out of the parking area and drove off. Harvey McMurtry waited till everybody else went out the door, except for Miss Sally who was gathering the money out of the offering plates, and Nora Hayes, the housekeeper, who was back in the Sunday school rooms making sure the windows were closed and all the lights were off.

Mr. Harvey's forehead wrinkled in a frown. "Did anybody say anything to you?"

David smiled as he shook the man's hand. "No, and I don't think they will."

"Well, they will to me. They're liable to run me out of church."

"I don't think that would be possible, Mr. Harvey. Mt. Pleasant wouldn't know how to open its door without you and Miss Sally being here."

"I don't know. I got some looks this morning, but I'm glad they came."

"I am too," David said.

"She can ever more sing, can't she?"

"I have a feeling Mrs. Hearndon can do many things well."

"I have a feeling you're right," Mr. Harvey said. "Sally says you're to come to our house for dinner today."

"I know. I hope Miss Sally didn't go to too much trouble cooking for us."

"Oh, you know women. They have to cook everything in sight when the preacher's coming. We'll have leftovers for a week. So tell your girlfriend to come on over and eat with us too." Mr. Harvey put his thumbs behind his suspenders and grinned.

David's cheeks warmed. He hadn't even allowed himself to call Leigh his girlfriend yet. But as the word echoed in his ears, it didn't have a bad sound.

Sally McMurtry had come up behind her brother in time to hear his words. She put her hand on David's arm. "Now don't you let Harvey give you no bother. He sometimes opens his mouth and lets fly before he thinks. But we do have plenty and we would love for Leigh to come eat with us if she can. She's such a sweet girl."

"I'm sure she'd like to do that if she doesn't have other plans for the afternoon."

"You know, I have a pretty good idea that she'll have the afternoon free," Miss Sally said with a smile and a knowing look in her eyes.

David followed Miss Sally out of the church and down the steps. She made her way purposely toward Leigh and Aunt Love, who were passing the time of day with Dorothy McDermott and Pam Jackson. Jocie and Pam's daughter, Paulette, were taking turns swinging little Murray McDermott back and forth in their arms.

Bob Jessup stopped David before he reached his family. "Brother David, can I have a word with you?"

"Of course, Bob." David tried to keep the reluctance out of his voice as he stopped beside Bob. Bob and his wife, Charlene, drove out from Hollyhill every Sunday. Charlene said Bob kept talking about joining one of the big town churches, but she liked going to Mt. Pleasant where she'd grown up. Bob owned a furniture store in Hollyhill and didn't mind letting people know how successful he was. He made sure everybody saw the two twenties he put in the offering plate on Sunday mornings. David was glad enough to see the twenties—churches couldn't operate without money—but he didn't like the way Bob thought the twenties bought him more right to decide what happened in the church than the people who put in ones or fives.

Now David only half listened to Bob complimenting

him on his sermon. Instead, he was watching Leigh smile and nod a little as Miss Sally talked to her. She raised her eyes up to look over Miss Sally's head toward David as if to be sure going to dinner with them would be okay with him. Her cheeks were bright red, but that just made her look prettier. David's heart started beating a little faster as he smiled over at her.

Maybe *girlfriend* was the right word. Maybe it was time to ask her out on a real date instead of just expecting her to show up at Mt. Pleasant on Sunday mornings or to help fold papers on Tuesday nights at the newspaper office. What was it Zella had told him he should ask Leigh to do last week? A candlelight dinner. When he'd told Zella he didn't think the Hollyhill Grill had candles on their tables, she'd just rolled her eyes at him as if he was hopeless. He didn't have much argument with her on that when it came to dating. Of course, Miss Sally might put candles on the table if he asked her to.

David's smile disappeared as Bob moved away from David's sermon to what he'd really wanted to talk about. "Don't you think somebody ought to tell that Mrs. Hearndon about the colored church up town? She and her children would surely be happier going to church there, you know, with her own kind, and it isn't all that far. Charlene and me drive the same distance out here every Sunday morning."

"I think we should let Mrs. Hearndon decide on her own which church she and her family want to attend." David looked straight at Bob. "And as long as I'm pastor here, our doors will be open to anybody who wants to worship."

"I wasn't suggesting they wouldn't be, Pastor," Bob said. "But I'm not sure this woman is a bit interested in worshiping with us out here. I think she just wants to stir up trouble. She was in the store one day last week, and she's not your run-of-the-mill colored woman. I hear she's been all over the South doing sit-ins and marching in the streets down there. I tell you, she just wants to upset the natural order of things. That's the only reason they bought Harvey's old farm."

David took a deep breath and kept his temper under control. "Mr. Harvey says they're getting ready to plant apple trees, start an orchard."

"That just goes to prove what I'm saying. You can't grow apples on that old farm. Take my word for it. All they're wanting to start is trouble."

"I guess that remains to be seen, Bob." David pushed a smile across his face and prayed for patience. "But the Lord only holds us accountable for our own actions and thoughts, so as I said this morning in my sermon, we need to ask what the Lord would want us to do before we borrow any trouble. Don't you agree?"

"You don't want to divide the church over this, Brother Brooke," Bob said.

"No, Bob, I don't. Do you?" David kept his voice low, but he could tell the people around them were listening. David could almost feel the people shifting to this side or that in the yard.

Bob didn't answer his question. Instead he said, "I pass two other churches on the way out here. I can stop at either one of them."

David kept his voice calm and as loving as he possibly could, with the way he was having to clamp down on the anger rising inside him. "You and Charlene are part of our family here, Bob. We'd hate to lose you."

Bob's voice rose a little. "Your words don't mean much if you're choosing that colored family over mine."

"I'm not choosing any family over any other family, nor does the Lord. We're all part of the family of God if we have made the decision to follow the Lord."

"Are you trying to say that I'm not right with the Lord?" Bob's face had gone beet red.

"No, Bob, I would never say that. You know in your heart where you stand with the Lord," David said.

But Bob had stopped listening. He took hold of Charlene's arm and jerked his head at their daughter as he headed for their car. Everybody in the churchyard stopped talking and watched them get in the car and drive away.

Ogden Martin moved up beside David. "That's the last we'll see of him. And his money. Guess we'd better be tightening our belts around here."

"I'll talk to him," David said.

"No offense, Brother Brooke, but I think you might have already talked to him too much."

Again David had to clamp down on his irritation and the feeling that Ogden Martin was taking pleasure in David's discomfort. "You could be right, Brother Ogden. Perhaps you should be the one to talk to him instead."

"And what should I tell him, Brother Brooke?" Ogden Martin said.

"Whatever the Lord puts in your heart to tell him." David looked straight into Ogden's eyes. "I know your prayer is always to do what's best for the Lord and our church body."

Ogden slid his eyes away from David's. "Sometimes the devil has a way of sneaking right inside a church and tearing it apart no matter what most of the people are wanting."

"Then we need to stand together as pastor and deacons and church members, hand to hand, heart to heart. We need to stand strong in the gap to keep our people away from that kind of destruction."

Ogden looked over David's head at the church building behind them. "I've always stood in the gap for *my* church."

David kept his eyes on Ogden's face, willing him to look back at him. He and Ogden Martin had their differences, probably always would. But it was important that they try to find a spiritual common ground for the good of the church at Mt. Pleasant. David chose his words carefully, overlaying each with a prayer. "And I thank the Lord you're there, Ogden. I thank him that we can stand together on the most important matters in the church."

Ogden looked back at David and met his eyes. "I've never done things for the preacher, Brother Brooke. I do things for the Lord."

"That's all the Lord asks of any of us."

Ogden looked down at the ground and then at some place over David's left shoulder as he said, "The wife is planning to have you all to dinner some Sunday whenever Miss Sally says there's an opening on the list."

"Well, that's great, Ogden. We'll look forward to it." David smiled. It wasn't much of a lie. And it was a good first step to healing the problems between them, putting their feet under the same table to eat. He'd just have to make sure Jocie stayed home with Wes that Sunday.

10

Jocie liked going to the McMurtrys' house for Sunday dinner better than any of the other Mt. Pleasant members' houses. Miss Sally made the best yeast rolls in the county, and she didn't act the slightest bit upset if Jocie passed up the green beans to save room for an extra roll or two. She'd just wink at Jocie and pass her the butter while telling Aunt Love, "She'll eat an extra portion of your beans and corn next week, Love."

Aunt Love was about ten years older than Miss Sally, but Jocie couldn't tell much difference in them except, of course, Miss Sally hadn't started losing her memory the way Aunt Love had. At least she never burned the rolls. Still, they both liked to sit in the living room and talk about the church and how much things had changed since they were girls. Sometimes they'd run out of things to say and the only sound would be the ticking of the old clock that had been sitting in the same spot on the mantel ever since Miss Sally could remember. That didn't seem to bother them either, even if one or the other of them dozed off for a few minutes.

Best of all, Miss Sally didn't expect Jocie to just sit there with them listening to the clock tick. She let her explore. The last time they'd been there, Jocie had played the old records on the windup Victrola in what Miss Sally said used to be the parlor. She told Jocie the parlor was where she was supposed to have received her gentlemen callers, but that she guessed they must have forgotten to call. After Miss Sally's father died and her mother got too feeble to climb the stairs to one of the upstairs bedrooms, they set up a bed in the parlor for her.

Her mother had passed on years ago, but Miss Sally never bothered turning the room back into a parlor. "I was way too old for gentlemen callers by then anyway, and the parlor had always been Mama's room even before we put the bed in there."

So Miss Sally's mother's hats were still on the hat stands on the chest. Her glass perfume holder on the dresser still smelled faintly of lily of the valley. A quilt stitched by her sisters and cousins for a wedding gift lay folded at the bottom of the bed. As Miss Sally helped Jocie read the names embroidered in the quilt squares, Jocie ran her fingers over the threads and half expected ghosts to come out of the walls to tell her their stories.

Everybody had stories. Sometimes it didn't seem like it when they were trying to find enough Hollyhill news to fill up the pages of the *Banner*, but news stories and people stories weren't always the same. It was funny, but ever since Zeb had found the baby's bones in the cave in the woods and Jocie had heard Aunt Love's story, she hadn't been able to look at old people the same way. Before, she might have looked at Miss Sally and just thought she was a nice old lady who was always good for a piece of chewing gum at church. But now Jocie wondered about her. Why hadn't she married? Had she wanted to? Had she been happy never leaving the house she was born in?

And then Jocie wondered what her own story would be. She couldn't imagine leaving Hollyhill now. But if she didn't, would she be old someday and wish she had? Wasn't she supposed to want to leave home and see the world?

Jocie sometimes almost exploded with all the questions she had. She wanted to know everything all at once, but her father told her it took a lifetime to get even some of the answers. He said the search for the answers was sometimes more important than the answers, especially when she was finding out answers about the people around her. A week later he'd given her a wire-bound notebook and a new ink pen. "So you can write down the stories you find out," he said. "And your own story a day or week at a time."

So she'd started a journal. She liked that better than a diary. She'd tried diaries before, but it was always too boring writing down what she did every day. *Got up, ate breakfast, rode my bike, got ink on my new shirt, got fussed at by Aunt Love, and went to bed.* But in a journal she could put down what she was thinking instead of just what she was doing. She could write about Wes being from Jupiter, or Tabitha changing into a mother in front of her eyes, or Miss Sally saying she didn't have any kind of story that would interest anybody. That she'd been happy and content even if she hadn't married or had children.

Miss Sally had smiled and touched Jocie's cheek as she talked. "I've borrowed the children at Mt. Pleasant over the years. Made them mine in many ways, but it might have been nice to have been called Granny by some child born to the job. A granddaughter perhaps. But I have no regrets with the life the Lord has seen fit to bless me with."

Jocie wrote down what Miss Sally had told her almost word for word, and in her journal she wondered if she should call her Granny. But then she remembered Miss Sally saying the child had to be born to the job, and Jocie hadn't been. She would only be a substitute. Jocie knew about that. About how sometimes people tried to substitute for what they thought you were missing.

There'd been a few women at the churches she and her father had attended who tried to be a substitute mother for her, but she didn't really need one. She had her father. And Wes. And for a few years her grandmother, Mama Mae. Aunt Love, who'd moved in after Mama Mae died, never tried to be a mother to Jocie. She cooked for them and did her best to keep Jocie on the straight and narrow path a preacher's daughter should travel by dipping into her vast resource of memorized Scripture to whip Jocie into line. There'd been few smiles and no hugs over the years before Tabitha came home.

Jocie hardly recognized Aunt Love now sometimes when she saw her sitting out on the porch knitting blankets and sweaters for Tabitha's baby. Her face would be all gentle and smiling, and she would be humming and not just hymns Jocie knew, but other songs. Livelier songs. Songs that made Jocie think of banjos and dancing. So maybe they could teach Tabitha's baby to call Aunt Love "Granny."

Of course, Tabitha's baby would have a grandmother. DeeDee out in California. Jocie liked calling her mother DeeDee in her thoughts and writing that for her name in her journal. That was what DeeDee had made Tabitha call her after they left Hollyhill. She'd never wanted to be a mother to Jocie, and it looked as if she didn't care the first thing about being a grandmother to Tabitha's baby either. Tabitha had told Jocie a few days ago that she hadn't heard a word from DeeDee. "And I doubt if I will," Tabitha said. "She didn't want me to have the baby."

"What did she want you to do? I mean, you couldn't do much about it once the baby was on the way, could you?" Jocie said.

Tabitha didn't meet her eyes. "DeeDee doesn't think the same way about things as people back here in Hollyhill do."

Jocie didn't worry about her mother that much anymore. Once she'd come to the conclusion that her mother had deserted her long before she left Hollyhill, Jocie shoved all her memories of her into a box in her mind and pushed it back out of the way where she could forget all about it. Maybe someday she'd want to pull the box out and open it up again, but not now. Now she had other things to worry about, such as starting high school and helping Wes get better and figuring out how she felt about her dad getting all googly-eyed over Leigh.

Jocie buttered her third roll and watched her father talking to Mr. Harvey, but his eyes kept slipping back to Leigh's face. It was easy to see he was glad Miss Sally had insisted Leigh join them for Sunday dinner.

Mr. Harvey scraped a bite of roast beef up on his fork and chewed it slowly before he said, "Do you think we should go visit the Hearndons this afternoon, Brother David?"

"This might be a good time if you want to ride over there with me," her father said.

"I want to go too," Jocie said quickly.

Her father looked at her. "You'll get to see Noah at the paper tomorrow."

"I wasn't thinking about Noah. I wanted to see the twins again. They're so cute. Do you think there's any chance Tabitha will have twins?"

"I hope not," her father said.

"She's not having twins," Aunt Love said. "She's not big enough for that."

"She might be bigger if she wasn't throwing up all the time," Jocie said.

"Jocelyn, we're at the table," Aunt Love frowned across the table at her.

"Oh, sorry," Jocie said, glancing at Miss Sally and then

Leigh. Leigh had her mouth twisted a bit to hide her smile. Neither of them looked as if talking about throwing up had upset their stomachs.

Miss Sally got up to cut one of the butterscotch pies she'd made for dessert. As she distributed huge slices all around, she said, "I got a little carried away baking pies, more than me and Harvey will ever eat up. I was planning to let you carry one home and then take another one over to the Hearndons. Why don't we all just ride along so I can deliver my pie?"

"That sounds good, but first, let me call Tabitha and make sure everything's going okay with her and Wes." Jocie's father got up and went into the living room where the phone was. When he came back, he reported all was well, that Tabitha had stopped the pendulum on Grandfather Brooke's clock so they could sleep all afternoon without anything bonging them awake.

"My heavens. I never even hear that clock," Aunt Love said as she stood up to help Miss Sally with the dishes.

So after they cleared the table, they all piled into Mr. Harvey's old Buick. Even Leigh.

She'd made noises about going on home, but Miss Sally looked at Jocie's father and said, "Brother David, you tell her to stay so she can come back to church with us tonight. They can do without her at First Baptist better than we can do without her down here. Now isn't that true?"

Leigh was still easing toward the door until Jocie's dad said, "It is." He'd put his hand on Leigh's arm. "Why don't you stay? I'll follow you home, and Jocie can ride back to town in your car."

Jocie had thought for a minute that Leigh was going to sparkle she was so happy, and she had to be even happier now wedged in between Mr. Harvey and Jocie's dad in the front seat. Jocie wasn't sure how happy Noah's mother was going to be when she saw them all coming up to her door. But most people were polite when the preacher came calling, even if they weren't especially glad to see him. Of course, the preacher didn't usually drag along five extra people. Maybe there would be safety in numbers. Then Jocie wondered why she'd thought about safety.

She told herself the Hearndons were just people like anybody else in the church community, but it wasn't true. Jocie had never gone to church with a black family. She'd never even been inside a black person's house. She knew a few black people. Willanna, who cooked at the Grill and her little girl, Shamece, who was a couple of years younger than Jocie. She liked talking to Linc who worked with the vet. He knew more about animals than anybody she knew. He'd even given her some worm pills for Zeb a few weeks ago. Just in case, he said, seeing as how the dog was a stray and all.

Plus, she supposed she could say she knew Noah. They'd ended up in the same ditch. They'd ridden together on the same bike. Perhaps not a conventional way of getting acquainted, but they had definitely met. Noah wasn't much like any other kid Jocie knew, but she didn't think that had much to do with his skin color. Kids from big towns were always different from kids who'd grown up in Hollyhill. They thought they were smarter, better somehow just because more people lived in the towns where they were born.

But Jocie was pretty sure she'd never known anyone a bit like Myra Hearndon. So she didn't have the first idea what Mrs. Hearndon might do when they all showed up on her front porch. Even her father looked a little unsure as he led the way across the yard and up the steps to the

Hearndons' front door. No dog came out from under the porch to bark at them. It was so quiet that her father's rap on the wooden screen door sounded extra loud.

Then Myra Hearndon was at the front door, throwing it open wide and smiling just as widely at all of them. A real smile. A glad smile that welcomed them on her porch. Somehow that was the last thing Jocie had been expecting.

"Rev. Brooke," she said. "What a pleasure to see you and your family. And Miss Sally and Mr. Harvey."

Miss Sally stepped forward to give Mrs. Hearndon the pie. "I had extra so thought maybe you would like to try my butterscotch pie."

Myra Hearndon's face softened as she leaned over to touch her cheek to Miss Sally's in a quick embrace. "Would we ever! It looks delicious." She took the pie and moved back to let them come into the living room. "Please come in. Alex and Noah are out in the field. Alex says the more rocks he picks up, the more rocks come to the top of the ground. You didn't seed the fields with rock, now did you, Mr. Harvey?"

"Somebody must have before I bought the place. I've picked several tons of them up off the fields myself." Mr. Harvey smiled at her. "Are they down in the long acre field where he's intending to put in the first trees?"

"They are. He's hoping to do the first wave of planting in a couple of weeks. It's sort of scary thinking how long it will be before the trees start bearing. We're looking to other things before then, but of course it's too late this season to grow anything. Or so Alex says. I'm afraid I'm a novice when it comes to farming."

"You could try hogs," Mr. Harvey said. "They pay off pretty quick if the market stays steady."

"Hogs," Mrs. Hearndon said. The word didn't seem to

fit naturally in her mouth. "My friends in Chicago would never believe it."

"What did you do in Chicago?" Jocie's dad asked as he sat down on one of the chairs Mrs. Hearndon carried in from the kitchen. Mr. Harvey took the rocking chair while Miss Sally, Leigh, and Aunt Love settled on the couch. Jocie leaned up against the wall and looked around for some sign of the twins or Cassidy.

"I taught English in one of the high schools there," she said. "Alex worked for the city, repairing streets mostly, but he grew up in the country and has always wanted to own his own place. And I think he was hoping getting me this far out in the country would slow me down a bit, maybe keep me home and out of jail."

The word *jail* seemed even more foreign than *hogs* coming out of Myra Hearndon's mouth. Jocie stared at the beautiful woman who was smiling a little as if she knew she was shocking them and the idea pleased her.

11

David prayed the Lord would put the right words in his mouth as he followed Mr. Harvey out of the yard and across the barn lot down toward the field where Alex Hearndon and Noah were working. They'd left the women and Jocie back at the house where they'd gotten a surprisingly warm welcome from Myra Hearndon, but David had no idea what her husband would think or say when he saw them coming across the field. On another day wearing other clothes besides his Sunday preaching garb, David might have been able to impress the man with his willingness to get his hands dirty by helping clear the field. David knew about hauling rocks. That had been one of those never-ending chores when he was a boy growing up on the farm.

"I've been wondering about something," David asked as he and Mr. Harvey walked past the barn. "How did the Hearndons find out about you having your farm for sale? Do they have family in Hollyhill?"

"No, it's the other way around. I have family up in Chicago. My aunt Clara's boy, Ben. He worked with Alex up there. Ben told Alex about me having the place for sale, and then Ben called me up and said he knew a good family that was looking for a farm to grow some apple trees." Mr. Harvey looked over at David. "He didn't bother to tell me they were colored folk. I guess that was something he thought might be better for me to find out after the money had changed hands."

"Would it have mattered?"

Mr. Harvey looked over at David. "I could pretend it wouldn't have, Brother David, but that would be just pretending. It's not that I have anything against colored folk, but I'd have worried about upsetting the neighbors."

"Are they upset?"

"Some of them." Mr. Harvey reached down and broke off a long stem of grass and put the end in his mouth.

"And were you upset? With your cousin, Ben?"

"Not that much. I'm not saying we weren't a little surprised when me and Sally first saw them, but Ben's a good judge of character. And even if I had been put out with Ben, I wouldn't have been able to hold on to any of the ill feelings because of the way Sally and Myra hit it off from the first time they laid eyes on one another. Sally says she can't explain it, but that she has to believe the Lord is behind it. Like maybe the Lord knew she needed some young ones to love like family." Mr. Harvey twisted the blade of grass around his fingers and then threw it away. "Me, I never really missed having a family, but Sally, she did. She don't talk about it, but I know Sally. I've been watching out for her ever since she was born when I was four. Hoping for a brother, but blessed by a sister."

"The two of you have certainly been a blessing to me at Mt. Pleasant," David said.

"Well, that's kind of you to say, Brother David. I guess we all need blessings. Take Myra back there." Mr. Harvey jerked his head back toward the house. "She tries to act all sure of herself like she knows everything, but the truth is, she needs something too. Some rock-solid base maybe. Somebody that never has the first doubt that the Lord is in control. Somebody like Sally."

They went through another gate and David spotted a red tractor at the far end of the field. "What about Alex Hearndon?" David asked. "Anything I should know before we walk over there and start talking?"

Mr. Harvey stopped walking, took off his hat, and fanned his face for a moment. "He's a man. Shoulders like you might imagine Samson having in the Bible. Keeps his nose to the grindstone. I might have seen him smile once. But nobody ever said you had to smile to be a good man."

"But some say the eyes are the window to one's soul."

"His eyes are fine."

"He's not going to be happy to see us, is he?" David looked across the field at the man picking up rocks and piling them on the wagon behind the tractor.

"I don't know, Brother David." Mr. Harvey gave David a considering look before he went on. "Me maybe, but probably not you. Says he don't have much truck with religion the way it's practiced this day and age."

David smiled. "It's okay, Mr. Harvey. I've been plenty of places I wasn't very welcome, and Mrs. Hearndon promised to hide the shotgun."

A worried look chased across Mr. Harvey's face. "I hope they don't have a shotgun or any kind of gun to hide."

"Why not?" David was surprised. "It seems to me a shotgun is about as much a tool on the farms around here as a grubbing hoe and a shovel. You know, for varmints and such."

"Some varmints just get madder when you shoot at them, and it's better to just let them do their growling and leave."

"You're not talking about normal varmints."

"No, I'm not." Mr. Harvey looked straight at David. His face was uneasy. "I maybe shouldn't talk about it. All I'm hearing are rumors and idle talk, but somebody told me the Klan was making noises."

"The Klan? The Ku Klux Klan?" Just saying the words seemed to bring a shadow over Mr. Harvey and David as they walked on across the long open field.

"Nothing but tale carrying as far as I know," Mr. Harvey said quickly. "Trying to put a scare into us. They're mostly just a bunch of cowards hiding under sheets anyhow. They probably wouldn't really do anything, but I'd just as soon not see guns get involved if they did."

"No, I suppose not," David said. "But I haven't heard anything about the Klan around here since before I went into the service."

"Sometimes we don't want to know things about the people around us," Mr. Harvey said. "And there hasn't been any reason for the Klan to be showing up in Holly County since we've pretty much been keeping the races separate. But now here the schools are desegregating this year, and then I up and sell a colored man a farm out here where no colored man has ever owned property before. And not only that, as much as I admire Myra Hearndon, she is an agitator. Alex himself says she chases after this what they call the freedom train. Fact is, she's already seen the inside of a jail cell three or four times for taking part in those sit-ins or boycott marches down south. She's even had the kids marching a time or two. I'm thinking it put a kind of strain on their marriage."

"He doesn't do the freedom marches with her?"

"I think he's done give more than he wanted to give to that cause. Myra told Sally that Alex had a younger brother killed down in Mississippi or maybe it was Louisiana a couple years back. The boy was down there on one of those marches. Said the family never really found out exactly what happened, but the boy ended up dead. Anyhow, now all Alex wants is for folks to leave him alone and let him grow his apple trees. And his kids to be safe." Mr. Harvey looked across the field to where Alex Hearndon had straightened up and stood waiting for them with his hands on his hips. "It seems a reasonable enough hope. I've been praying that it's one he can see realized."

"I'll add my prayers to yours," David said.

Mr. Harvey looked over at David and lowered his voice as they got closer to where Alex and Noah were waiting. "But we'll just let them be unspoken for the time being, Brother David. I'm not sure Alex is open to the idea of prayer for him or about him right now."

"Everybody needs prayer."

"You won't get no argument about that from me, Brother David, but let's just take it slow with Alex and let him come around to our way of thinking on his own. With the good Lord's help, that is." Mr. Harvey turned his eyes back toward Alex Hearndon, let a big smile move across his face, and stepped faster across the last few feet that separated them.

Alex Hearndon didn't smile when Mr. Harvey introduced David to him, but he did take off his leather glove, brush his hand off on his blue jeans, and reach out to shake David's hand. He had a working man's hands, calloused and rough. His handshake was firm, but at the same time controlled as if he was aware of his strength. "Pleased to meet you, Reverend," Alex said. "My boy told me you'd given him a job. He'll work hard for you."

Still no smile as he glanced behind him at Noah, but there was a lightening in the man's dark brown, nearly black eyes. It was easy enough to see the father's pride for a son who might not yet be able to step up and fill his father's shoes, but was growing into the job. It was also easy to see why Mr. Harvey had compared Alex Hearndon to Samson, even if the man's hair was clipped off so close to his head you could see his scalp. He was tall and so muscular that he looked as if he might be able to pick up the jawbone of an ass and dispense with an army of Philistines. Now he pulled a blue bandanna out of his back pocket and wiped the sweat off his forehead as he waited for David to say whatever he had come all the way across the fields to say to him. Not a thread of his blue cotton shirt was dry.

David met his eye squarely and didn't let the man's lack of a smile keep his own away. "I just wanted to come by and welcome you and your family to the community. We were pleased to have Mrs. Hearndon and the children in church this morning."

"They said they had a kind welcome from you and some others," Alex said. "We expected as much if the other members there at your church are anything like Mr. Harvey and Miss Sally." And finally there was something approaching a smile on the man's face. Just a bare lifting of the sides of his mouth, but there when he looked over at Mr. Harvey.

"Not all of our folks are as fine of a Christian example as Mr. Harvey and Miss Sally, but we're working on it."

"Now, Brother David, Sally will bake you another pie without you buttering us up like that," Mr. Harvey said with a laugh.

Nobody suggested moving off to the side of the field into the shade, so they stood there with the sun beating down on them and talked about the rocks in the field and how long the dry spell was going to last. "The ground's cracking open and getting hard as these rocks we're hauling off the field," Alex said. "We're hoping for some good rain before time to plant the trees."

"The rain will come. We're praying for it at the church," Mr. Harvey said.

"Mr. Harvey's the kind of man who brings his umbrella when we have a prayer meeting for rain," David smiled at Mr. Harvey, then looked around. "So you're planning to turn this field into an orchard."

The man turned to stare out over the field, his field. His shoulders relaxed a bit and the lines of strain on his face disappeared. He pointed. "Up there at the top of the field is where the first trees are going in. The ground's better there. Not so many rocks. I'm hoping to put in somewhere around fifty trees this year and then build on that number as the years go by. Down here we might try pumpkins or maybe some sweet corn. We might even try Christmas trees. I've heard there's a market for them in the cities."

David looked where Alex pointed and had no problem sharing Alex's vision of a field of trees with limbs drooping low to the ground from the weight of their fruit. "'I made me gardens and orchards, and I planted trees in them of all kind of fruits,'" David said.

Alex looked at him. "Is that Scripture?"

"It is. From Ecclesiastes. The writer's not exactly writing about hope, but sometimes a verse can reach out and touch you one on one as the Lord puts his own special meaning for it into your heart. And now imagining what this field can be under your stewardship, the verse sounds full of promise."

"A preacher should know the Scripture," Alex said.

"That he should. Along with all who want to do the will of the Lord."

"I'm not much on preaching, Reverend. I've done my time in church buildings. Now I meet up with the Lord out in the open."

"As did Elisha. He was plowing with oxen when the Lord called him to follow Elijah."

Alex's eyes narrowed a bit on David. "I'm not aiming on having that kind of meeting, Reverend. I'm just aiming to put me in an orchard."

"I'll pray the Lord will bless those plans, Mr. Hearndon," David said. "And when you do get the field ready to put those trees in, have Noah let me know. I'd like to come down and help you do some planting."

"I'll remember that." Alex looked at him a moment before he asked, "Where did you say that verse was?"

"Ecclesiastes. I'm not sure exactly which verse, but I think it's the second chapter."

"I'll look it up tonight if I get the chance."

They talked a little more before David and Mr. Harvey went back across the fields to the house where Myra Hearndon had iced tea waiting for them. By the time they all piled back in the car to go back to the McMurtrys' for the supper of leftovers Miss Sally would insist they eat, David thought it had been a successful visit. Yet the shadow of Mr. Harvey's words on the way down through the fields stayed in David's mind.

Things had felt so good out there in the field, even with the unrelenting heat of the sun beating down on them, as they talked about a time for planting, a time for hope. David didn't want to think about a time for hate that might come to this family. That was the trouble with Ecclesiastes. Within the beauty of its words were hard truths. In every life there was a time to plant and a time to pluck up what was planted. A time to weep, and a time to laugh. A time to love, and a time to hate. A time of war, and a time of peace. That's what David would pray for fervently for this family. A time of peace.

12

Jocie was up early the next morning. She got up early every morning to make sure Zeb was out of the house before Aunt Love noticed him sleeping beside Jocie's cot out on the glassed-in porch. Jocie had been sleeping on the porch ever since Tabitha came home from California. Being pregnant and all, her sister needed a room worse than she did.

Jocie didn't miss her room all that much. She liked it out on the porch. She liked counting stars until she fell asleep. She liked the way the windows swung up to attach to the ceiling to let in every bit of night air, especially the last few weeks when the heat of the day had gathered and lingered in the house through the night. She liked being able to smuggle her dog in at night to sleep beside her bed. Of course, she'd told her dad Zeb was coming in, but the subject hadn't come up with Aunt Love. Jocie was doing her best to make sure it never did.

Come winter, Jocie supposed she'd have to move in off the porch to a warmer spot, but she didn't know where. By then Tabitha would have had her baby and would need her own room more than ever. There was the couch in the living room, but they'd turned that into a room for Wes. The way it was looking, he might not be gone by the time the snow started flying.

He'd want to be. Being an invalid was wearing on him. Everything was a struggle with that heavy cast weighing him down. It was all he could do to pull himself to his feet by holding onto the straight-back chair beside the bed they'd set up for him in the living room. Every time Jocie saw him struggling to stand up, she felt a little guiltier. And a little more worried. She was afraid Wes wasn't ever going to be his old self again. Sometimes it looked as if it took all his energy just to smile.

She'd come in from church the night before and told him all about going to Miss Sally's house for dinner and her father making eyes at Leigh. At least that brought a half smile to his face.

"I guess it's about time," he said. "Your daddy's lucky the girl didn't give up on him and move on to the next guy before he started paying attention."

"She says there aren't any next guys. That everybody in Hollyhill is already married and got five kids or something like that," Jocie said. "Except maybe you, and she's too scared of riding on your motorcycle to go after you."

Wes looked over Jocie's head toward the open window. "It would be a good night for riding. A little wind in my face might cool me off."

"You'll be riding again soon. If you can get your handlebars straightened up a little."

"That ain't all I need to get straightened up."

"Looks like to me, your problem is that your leg is too straight." Jocie tapped his cast softly.

"You got that right, Jo. They need to make a hinge on this thing."

And at last she'd gotten a real smile out of Wes. She thanked the Lord for that when she said her prayers before she fell asleep.

Now with the early morning sun coming in the kitchen window, she was slicing some of the tomatoes the church people had loaded them down with, while Aunt Love scrambled the eggs from the Rileys, who had a yardful of chickens. Her dad had gone out on his prayer walk before breakfast, and Tabitha was sleeping in the same as always.

"Will you need me here today?" Jocie asked Aunt Love. "To help can tomatoes or anything?"

"Not today. The tomatoes need to get a little riper before we make juice."

"Everybody out there at church must have a garden."

"For which we should give thanks."

Jocie nodded. She didn't have any problem giving thanks for tomatoes. Cabbage was a different matter. "The Hearndons didn't have a garden. I guess they moved in too late for that." Jocie looked up at Aunt Love. "Maybe we could share some of the stuff people give us with them. Do you think they'd like some cabbage?"

"I'm sure they would," Aunt Love said. "But I don't know that we should give away what the church people have given your father. A congregation's gifts to a pastor are a special way they show him love, whether it's vegetables or money."

"Doesn't the Bible say we should share the love?"

"The love, but maybe not the cabbages," Aunt Love said. "'Every man is a friend to him that giveth gifts.'"

Jocie wasn't sure exactly how that verse was supposed to help her see why they couldn't share their bounty of vegetables with the Hearndons, but she didn't ask Aunt Love to explain. Sometimes Jocie thought Aunt Love just reached in her head and pulled out whatever verse was handy. "Sounds like Proverbs," she said as she resigned herself to more boiled cabbage.

"So it is," Aunt Love said.

"You should teach Sunday school class, Aunt Love. You know so many verses by heart, you wouldn't even have to use a Bible."

"Oh, no. The teachers all have to study out of those newfangled books from the Sunday school board. I couldn't do that." Aunt Love rubbed her hands off on her apron and started setting plates on the breakfast table, but she sounded pleased.

"The Bible's the important book to know," Jocie said.

"True enough. 'All scripture is given by inspiration of God, and is profitable for doctrine, for reproof, for correction, for instruction in righteousness.' Second Timothy 3:16," she said as she handed Jocie a plate. "You'd best fix Wesley a tray. He's not up to coming to the table yet."

"So you think I need to stay here and help take care of Wes?" Jocie asked as she put a couple of slices of tomatoes and a biscuit on the plate.

"No, go on with your father today. Wesley just needs time to heal, and you can't speed that up no matter how much you want to, child. It's going to take weeks."

Jocie held in a sigh. "I know." She put some eggs and bacon on the plate, poured a cup of coffee, and carried the tray into the living room. Wes was in the chair with his cast propped up on the stool. Jocie smiled and said, "Good morning. Coffee's here. Of course, it's not that real stuff you make at the paper, but we do the best we can."

Jocie set the tray on the floor and handed Wes the coffee cup. She carefully placed the card table over his legs and put the tray on it. "You are going to eat this morning, aren't you?"

"I guess a man has to eat," Wes said as he picked up the fork without much enthusiasm. "Did you cook this?"

"Some of it. Just be glad I got up in time to keep the biscuits from burning."

"Lovella does make a fine biscuit." He broke off a piece of biscuit, put it in his mouth, and chewed dutifully.

"You've got whiskers." Jocie reached over to touch his cheek before she sat down on the cot to keep him company while he ate.

"No Nurse Army Boots around to make me shave," Wes said. "Thought I might just see how much I can start looking like old Santy Claus."

"You're way too skinny for that. You'd have to eat double breakfasts and dinners and all the time between."

"I could get some pillows," Wes said.

"And the ho, ho, ho?" Jocie asked.

"I've got plenty of time to practice on that. Months and months."

Jocie smiled. "Then do it. Every church I've ever gone to, they have a hard time finding a Santa to hand out candy canes at the Christmas programs. You can fill the need."

"That's what every man wants. A need to fill." Wes pushed his eggs around a little more with his fork.

"You need some salt for those?" Jocie asked. "Ketchup maybe?"

"No, they're fine." Wes put down his fork. "I just haven't got much appetite. All this laying around, I guess."

"You have to eat, Wes," Jocie said.

"Don't you worry none about me, Jo. You just leave the plate there. I'll eat it in a little while. I just need to swallow down some more coffee first to wake up my stomach." Wes picked up his coffee cup and took a sip.

Jocie tried to think of the right thing to say to make him want to eat, to make him feel better, but she couldn't think of anything. Wes had always been the one who made her feel better when something was wrong. She wanted to do the same thing for him, but she didn't know how. Everybody—her father, Aunt Love, the doctors—said Wes just needed time to get better, and that she needed to give him that time. But Jocie worried everybody was wrong. She worried Wes needed something more than time, something she needed to make sure he got, if she only knew what that something was.

Jocie pulled her bare feet up on the cot, wrapped her arms around her legs, and leaned her chin on her knees. "Can I get you anything before I go with Dad this morning? Or maybe go up to your place and get you some more books or something?"

"I haven't read the ones you brought me already." Wes nodded toward the pile of books on the table beside his chair. "Funny thing about reading. When you're busy working all the time, you think it'd be good to just sit down and read all day, but then when you can just sit and read all day, your eyes get tired or the books all get boring after a while."

"Even Nero Wolfe?"

"Well, maybe not old Nero, but I finished the latest one about him back in July. It'll be awhile before he makes another appearance on the pages of a book."

"Maybe you'll get something in your book club mail." Jocie dropped her feet to the floor and sat up straight. "Or even better, you can start writing that *Hollyhill Book of the Strange* we're always talking about."

"Now that's an idea. I'll think on it today," Wes said, but he didn't sound as if he really would. He took another sip of his coffee. "Your daddy says that boy he got to help at the paper is supposed to start today."

"Yeah. I don't know how much help he'll be. He doesn't know anything about setting up ads or anything." Jocie broke off a piece of one of the biscuits on Wes's plate before she scooted back on the cot and got comfortable again.

"You can teach him. And it don't take a lot of know-how to do most of the stuff I was doing."

"That's not true." Jocie frowned over at Wes. "Me and Dad have been having a prayer meeting at the press every morning to keep it working until you can get back. Dad says we'll be up a creek without a paddle if it breaks down on us."

"He could fix it."

"Yeah, right." Jocie took a bite of biscuit and chewed a minute before she said, "What's more likely is that we'd have to load you up and make you come tell us which piece to change or screw to tighten or whatever. So you'd better hurry and get well before the press starts missing you too much. It's already making funny noises."

"You are oiling it regular, aren't you?" Wes said, showing the first real interest in anything Jocie had said.

"I guess," Jocie said with a shrug as she finished off the biscuit.

"You guess? You'd better know. It'll break for sure if you don't keep it greased up."

"I'll remind Dad today when we get there, but I don't think it needs oil. I think it just needs you." Jocie poked his arm with her finger. "And I know we need you. Noah won't be able to do half what you did."

"He'll learn." Wes set his cup down. "What's old Zell think about the boy coming to work?"

"She's not too excited about it. I'll have to bring Noah by sometime to let you meet him and you'll understand."

"You already told me he was black."

"It's more than that. I don't know how to explain it, but you know, I told you how he was when I bowled him over on my bike. Sort of ready for a fight or something. It's like he has his radar on full to catch even the hint of a slight, and of course, his radar was going full blast with Zella. You know how she is."

"Yep. There's only one Zell in the world."

"And he baited her a little."

"Oh, like you do sometimes when you're not wearing your halo?" Wes raised his eyebrows at her.

"As if you don't," Jocie shot back.

"Well, most of the time she asks for it," Wes said, a real smile creeping across his face.

"Maybe so, but we don't usually make her ask twice. But at the same time, she is sort of like family at the paper. I mean, Dad needs her to keep things running, and I kept feeling like I needed to jump in between her and Noah so neither of them would get too upset."

Wes rubbed the whiskers on his chin. "So you're worried you're going to get caught in the middle?"

"Maybe not the middle, but somewhere in a spot I don't know what to say or do."

"That is a dilemma. You don't want old Zell to go completely bonkers. Sort of bonkers is bad enough. And at the same time you want to get along with this new boy, and you're worried you won't say the right things because he's black."

Jocie looked down at her hands. Wes could always figure out what she was thinking even when sometimes she didn't know herself. "I don't want to do the wrong thing. Like when we were out at his house yesterday. I didn't see Noah. He was out in the field helping his father."

"So what happened?" Wes picked up his coffee and took another drink.

"Nothing really." Jocie looked up at Wes. "His mother was nice as can be. Way friendlier than she'd been at church.

Even with all of us showing up on her porch. Leigh, Aunt Love, me, Dad, Mr. Harvey, and Miss Sally."

"Quite a crowd."

"But she was okay with it," Jocie said.

"Then what's the problem?"

"I don't know. Maybe there isn't one, but I went out in the yard to talk to Noah's little sister, Cassidy. She was out there with the twins I told you about. Eli and Elise. They are so cute. Anyway, Cassidy, she's maybe ten. She acted afraid of me." Jocie shifted uneasily on the cot as if a spring had suddenly come up through the mattress to poke her.

"Maybe she's just shy."

"I guess, but you know, I thought for a minute she was going to run and hide behind a tree or something. It made me feel funny to think somebody might be afraid of me." Jocie pointed to her chest.

"Why don't you ask Noah about it?"

"Oh, I don't think I can do that," Jocie said. "He's already told me I'm too nosy."

"Newspaper people are supposed to be nosy."

"That's what I told him, but I can't just start asking him questions about Cassidy."

"Why not?"

"I don't know. I guess because I don't know him well enough."

"You will soon enough if he's working with you and your dad. And don't worry about him being black. After a week you won't even notice what color he is."

"You think so?"

"I know so." Wes looked at her over his coffee cup.

"Have you known a lot of black people?"

"We had all colors up in that spaceship I fell out of."

"Right," Jocie said, but she didn't follow up on the Jupiter bit. Instead she spit out another worry. "You know I'm going to start high school next week."

"So I've heard," Wes said with a nod. "I thought you were looking forward to it."

"I am. Mostly." Jocie hooked her hair back behind her ears and sat up a little straighter. "I guess I'm a little nervous about finding my classes and that kind of stuff."

"They'll point you in the right directions the first few days, and after that you'll be able to do the pointing."

"Yeah, maybe," Jocie said. "But things are going to be a lot different. What with the schools desegregating and everything."

Wes looked at her. "That's not bothering you, is it?"

"No, it just got me to thinking. I don't think I know a single black kid my age by name. Don't you think that's kind of strange?"

"For sure," Wes said. "Maybe that should go into that *Book of the Strange* you've been after me to write."

"I guess." Jocie pushed a smile out on her face even though she didn't feel much like smiling.

Wes leaned over to touch her on the shoulder. "It's not going to be a problem for you, Jo. You'll find out their names, and then you can be friends or not. And Noah will just be Noah. You can't take care of the whole world."

"How about just Hollyhill?"

"Not even all of Hollyhill."

"How about you?"

"That you can do," Wes said as he held out his cup toward her. "You can start by moving this table off my legs and getting me more coffee."

13

Jocie glanced at the clock on the pressroom wall. Almost lunchtime. She went in the front office to remind Zella that Noah was supposed to show up for work around noon.

"Dad wanted to be sure you hadn't forgotten."

"How could I forget that? We can only hope he remembers his manners this time." Zella yanked the paper out of her typewriter and glanced up at the clock over her desk. "But if your father wants him to have a welcoming committee, he'll have to do it himself. I'm leaving early to meet Leigh at the Grill for lunch."

"It's only eleven thirty."

"The special today is fried chicken. You know how crazy that place gets when Willanna fries chicken. There's no way you can get a decent table if you wait till twelve." Zella dropped the black plastic cover over her typewriter. "I'd ask your father to come along, since heaven only knows, he's too backward to ask Leigh to lunch himself, but it wouldn't be proper you being here alone with that colored boy."

"What's proper got to do with it? Noah's just going to be working for Dad."

"Proper has everything to do with it," Zella said as she patted her hair to be sure all her perfectly round curls were still in order. Then she pulled a mirror out of her desk drawer and applied a fresh coat of lipstick. She popped her lips together before she went on. "It was bad enough with

Wesley back there. That man has to be running from the law or something. Who knows what he might have done before he showed up here in Hollyhill? But something for sure, or he wouldn't be so secretive about his past."

"He's not secretive. He tells me stories about where he came from all the time," Jocie said just to egg her on a little. She'd heard all Zella's theories about Wes dozens of times. He was on the run from the law. He had an ex-wife or even wives after him. He owed the IRS money. Lots of money. Or if not the IRS, he owed the kind of people it was dangerous to owe money to.

"Don't start with those silly Jupiter stories. Wesley Green is no more from Jupiter than a pig, and you know it, Jocelyn. It's high time you started paying attention to what is true and what is only stories. After all, you're almost fourteen."

"But stories are fun," Jocie said.

"There's more to life than having fun."

"Don't you ever try to have fun?" Jocie asked. The question made two spots of color appear on Zella's cheeks, but Jocie hadn't asked it to be mean. She really wanted to know. A few days ago she had tried to write something about Zella in her journal and realized she didn't really know all that much about her. She knew Zella had never married but sighed over romance novels. She wore bright red lipstick. She could type sixty words a minute without making even one mistake. She could fold a whole pile of newspapers without getting the first spot of ink on her clothes. She was as much a part of the newspaper office as the press in the back. Still, what she did when she wasn't at the newspaper office was a total mystery to Jocie.

"Well, of course. I have fun all the time." Zella peered in her mirror and grabbed a tissue to wipe a bit of lipstick off her tooth.

"How?"

"Well, there's my bridge club. And I'm always doing things with my Sunday school class. You're the one who doesn't know a thing about anything." She dropped the mirror back into the drawer and slammed the drawer shut. "You're way too young to understand how a person can be satisfied with life the way it is. You're just all filled up with fantasies and dreams."

"Didn't you like to dream about things when you were my age?"

"I didn't have time for that kind of nonsense. I had to help my parents on the farm."

"I can't imagine you feeding chickens or pigs," Jocie said.

"Well, I did, but I never planned to make a career of it. So after my father died, Mother and I moved to town and I got a job here at the paper. That was while Mr. Henry still owned the paper. He was such a nice man."

"Dad's nice too."

"Well, of course he is. I never implied he wasn't. Your father's problem is that he's too nice for his own good sometimes."

"How can you be too nice?" Jocie asked.

"The same way you can ask too many questions." Zella snatched up her purse and stalked out the door and up the street.

As Jocie watched her go, she wanted to call out a couple more questions. How could she be a dreamer and ask too many questions at the same time? Didn't dreamers come up with their own answers without having to ask anybody anything? Not that she would have expected an answer to either of those questions from Zella.

Her father was always telling her she couldn't expect

to get an answer to every question. Or every prayer. But with prayers, a person just had to trust God to send the best answers at the right times. And the Lord did. She'd been praying Tabitha would come home for years, and now she had. Maybe the same was true with questions. She just needed to give the answers some time to come clear.

She couldn't know whether Noah would show up for work and be willing to let her teach him how to do things. She couldn't know how long it would be before Wes would be back helping them. She couldn't know what was going to happen next week when she started high school. Would she get lost and not be able to find the right classrooms? Would the older kids laugh at her just because she was a freshman? Would she start worrying, the way Paulette did, about whether boys thought she was cute?

Of course, Paulette was cute. She had a figure and long blonde hair that curled up at the ends, and her mother let her wear lipstick. Jocie was straight as a stick, had brown hair that she hooked out of her face behind her ears, and she didn't even own a lipstick. Some questions weren't even worth wondering about, Jocie decided as she headed back to the pressroom to help her father get the paper ready to print.

Noah showed up just as the noon siren sounded. Then the clock on top of the courthouse started its twelve slow bongs. On its heels, the Christian Church bells rang and then played "Rock of Ages" the way it did every Monday at noon. There was a different hymn for each day sort of like day-of-the-week underwear. One thing for sure, nobody in Hollyhill was going to forget that it was time to eat lunch. That was what Jocie and her father were doing when Noah tapped on the pressroom door before he pushed it open.

"Nobody was at the desk out front," he said. "So I just came on back." He had on jeans and a plain white T-shirt.

"Come on over and grab a chair," Jocie's dad said. "We're just finishing up lunch."

Jocie pulled a sandwich out of the paper sack. "I made extra if you want one. Bologna and cheese. And we have tomatoes. Boy, do we ever have tomatoes."

"I ate before I came. I don't expect you to feed me," Noah said.

"Suit yourself," Jocie said as she laid the sandwich on the table. "But there it is if you want it. Me and Dad won't want it and Zella wouldn't eat it even if she was here. She says nobody would eat bologna if they gave the first thought to what they put in it. She's probably right, so I don't think about it." Jocie took a big bite.

Noah looked back over his shoulder toward the door. "Where is Miss Curtsinger?"

"Zella?" Jocie said. "Oh, she usually gets lunch up at the Grill or goes home. She's not much for eating at her desk."

It sounded funny hearing Zella called Miss Curtsinger, but maybe it would be better if Noah stayed extra polite to her for a while until Zella got over what she called his impertinence last week.

Noah pulled over a chair and eyed the sandwich a minute before picking it up and saying, "There's no need letting it go to waste."

"No need at all," Jocie's father said. "We're trying to come up with which story we've got that might sell a few extra papers this week."

"Nothing much happened in Hollyhill this week," Jocie explained. "At least not newspaper-type stuff. First Baptist is having a revival, and we have a piece about the evangelist they've brought in from Louisville, but that's for the church page. And we've got some pictures of the schools being cleaned up for school to start."

Noah looked over at Jocie's dad. "But aren't the schools being desegregated? That should be a big news story in a little town like this. Actually, it's a pretty unbelievable story that the schools aren't already integrated. I've never gone to a school that wasn't integrated."

"You're farther south now," Jocie's father said as if that explained everything. "Besides, school doesn't start till Thursday next week and the *Banner* goes out on Wednesdays. So we'll print those stories next week." He gave Noah a look. "Do you like to write? If you do, you could write something about how different starting school here is from what you were used to in Chicago or something like that."

"You might not like what I wrote," Noah said.

"Then I wouldn't print it." Jocie's dad fastened his eyes on Noah. "We might as well get one thing clear right at the beginning, Noah. The *Banner* is just a small-town paper. We put out one issue per week. We're here to serve the community by reporting on what happens in Hollyhill and Holly County. We don't do national news like what Congress is up to or what's happening in Vietnam unless it has a local handle, such as one of our Hollyhill boys flying the bombers over North Vietnam or one of our senators coming through town. Neither of them ever has, but if they did, it would be front-page news for the *Banner*. We leave the national and state news to the daily papers out of Lexington and Louisville."

"So how do you sell papers if you don't have anything much to write about?" Noah asked.

"We manage," Jocie's father said. "Folks here want to read about what happens in town and at the schools. They like seeing their pictures or their kids' pictures in the paper."

"Sounds pretty dull," Noah said. "I thought newspapers tried to come up with controversial stories to keep people interested."

"I don't print stories to stir up trouble just for the sake of stirring up trouble."

"But sometimes trouble needs to be stirred up in order to get wrongs righted," Noah said.

"Then that would be a different matter, but I always want to walk the peaceful route first," Jocie's dad said.

"That's fine by me." Noah took another bite of his sandwich and chewed a minute before he went on. "The peace road is a fine one to walk if people will let you walk it. But the fact is, they've put my mama in jail three times for walking that road or trying to walk that road down in Mississippi and Louisiana. The Reverend Martin Luther King Jr., he doesn't do anything but talk the peace road, and they've put him in jail a few times too. According to Mama, he and a few thousand more walked on your state capital here in March. Did you print anything about that then?"

"They didn't march through here. People got that news in the daily papers."

Jocie had stopped eating her sandwich as she watched them talk. They weren't exactly arguing, but Jocie could hear an edge of irritation to her father's voice. He was trying to hide it, but it was there. Having Noah in the pressroom wasn't going to be a thing like having Wes there to back up her father in whatever he wanted to do. Noah had questions and he didn't seem to want to wait for the answers.

"Do you really think your Hollyhill is going to be that much different when the black people here decide they want to go in the front door at the courthouse or sit at the counter to eat at the restaurant uptown?" Noah said.

"I hope so," Jocie's dad said. "And I pray so."

Jocie spoke up. "What do you mean, go in the back door at the courthouse? Can't anybody go in any door they want to?"

Jocie's dad looked uncomfortable as he answered. "I'm sure they can now."

"What do you mean 'now'?" Jocie asked.

"Well, there used to be a sign. I don't think it's there anymore, but it could be I just haven't been paying attention. Is there a sign there, Noah?"

"I didn't see one, but it wouldn't surprise me if there was," Noah said. "There are signs like that all over the South that white people don't pay much attention to until black people quit paying attention to them too."

"What signs?" Jocie asked.

"Saying colored people should use the back door or 'whites only' signs that say they shouldn't come in at all." Noah took another bite of sandwich as if he was just talking about the weather or something.

Jocie stared at Noah. "There's no sign like that here."

"So maybe there isn't," Noah said with a shrug. "But whether the sign is still there or not, it's still in people's heads. A few of them told my mother as much when she went in the courthouse when we first came down here. Of course she went right on through the front door and out it again when she'd finished her business there."

"As she should have." Jocie's father crumpled up the wax paper that had been around his sandwich and threw it in the trash can. "I know we're far from perfect here in Hollyhill, Noah, but I think if you and your family will give the people a chance, they'll come around. Desegregating the schools is going to change things."

"Things need to change," Noah said.

"You're right. There's no place for the kind of things you're talking about in our town."

"Do you think there'll be trouble next week when school starts?"

"No, I don't. Not in Hollyhill."

Jocie's father sounded sure of his answer, but Noah didn't seem ready to believe him. "There's been plenty of trouble in other places in the South."

"We're not that far south."

"Then how come the schools aren't already desegregated?"

"The black people here didn't want to give up their community school."

"All the black people live in one community?"

"They did till your family moved in," Jocie's father said.

Noah sort of smiled as he said, "I guess my mama will have her chance to stir things up even when she's not trying. She promised my daddy she'd stay off the Freedom Road for a while." Noah's smile disappeared. "Things are just getting too bad. People, even women like Mama, have been getting dragged off to jail and beat up by the police. Others just come up missing down there on the Freedom Road and then show up later, dead."

"Nothing like that will happen in Hollyhill," Jocie's father said.

"But if it did, would you report it in your newspaper the way it really happened instead of trying to say it was the colored people's fault because they were out there trying to breathe the same air the white folks were breathing?" Noah looked at Jocie's father as if his answer was especially important to him.

"I would report the truth."

"Even if it meant half your subscribers would cancel their papers?"

"Even if it meant all my subscribers canceled their subscriptions." Jocie's father's mouth was set in a hard line. "I look to the Lord to lead me to do and say the right things both at church on Sundays and here at work the rest of the week. But like I said, I don't make trouble just to make trouble, and if you want to work here, Noah, I'll expect the same out of you."

"Wait a minute." Noah held up his hands as if to protect himself from Jocie's father's words. "You've got me all wrong, Brother David. I don't want trouble. I hate trouble."

"Good. Then let's get to work on this week's issue."

Jocie tore the crusts off what was left of her sandwich and tried to think of something to say to get some of the tension out of the air. Wes would have been able to if he'd been there. He'd have said something about Jupiter or how they didn't have anything but snooze news for this week's paper. But before she could think of anything, Noah spoke up. "I think the top story should be about the drought. Or is it always this hot and dry here?"

"No, it's extra hot," Jocie said. "Hey, Dad, didn't you take a picture of a dried-up pond somewhere last week?"

"That might work," Jocie's father said. "I'll work on that while you show Noah how to start setting up some of the ads."

Jocie pitched the rest of her sandwich in the trash and moved over to the table to start work. She was relieved when Noah followed her and paid attention to what she told him to do. Maybe they'd be able to work together. Still, it might be that she should start praying harder for Wes to be able to come back to work soon. Real soon.

14

As David went out of the pressroom, leaving Noah and Jocie with their heads together over one of the ads, he couldn't keep the thought away that maybe he had made a mistake offering Noah a job. It seemed like the right thing to do at the time, but as Zella was quick to point out to him earlier that day, he hadn't even given himself time to pray about it.

He'd talked to Zella as soon as he'd gotten to the office that morning about what he could pay Noah. Zella kept the books, made sure the bills got paid on time, wrote out their payroll checks, and kept them straight on taxes. She'd been doing it for years, even before David started working at the *Banner* when he came home from the service after the war. She kept them out of the red. And David was grateful, but sometimes Zella acted as if the money was hers. Especially when he proposed a new expense like hiring Noah.

They had the means. David kept his eye on what came in and what went out, so he knew the paper had been bringing in more money this summer. The tornado issues had sold out, and they could count on a boost in church ads with end-of-summer revivals and homecomings in the fall. Plus Zella had already sold a whole page of ads for the big sidewalk sale the downtown merchants were having over Labor Day weekend.

So he didn't think it was beyond reason that the paper could hire an extra hand for two or three afternoons a week, even if they did keep paying Wes his salary. And the truth was, if they didn't get extra help before Jocie went back to school, then the paper might not get printed on time. Late papers brought complaints, and no paper meant no revenue.

That's what he'd told Zella, but she hadn't bought it. She'd just looked up at him standing beside her desk and said, "It's not like you to do this kind of thing without taking time to think and pray about it."

"What kind of thing? You mean hiring some help? We need to get the paper out."

She just kept looking at him. "You're borrowing trouble. That's what you're doing, David. Borrowing trouble."

"What makes you think that? Because Noah's black?"

"It's not just that he's colored. He has a chip on his shoulder. Worse than a chip. A whole block. The boy will make problems. And besides that, you won't be able to let him and Jocelyn work back there alone the way you did Wesley and her. While Wesley certainly can't be the best influence on a young girl like Jocelyn, even so, you could rest easy knowing he'd take care of her."

"He's the same as family," David agreed.

"Well, this boy very definitely isn't family." Zella pointed her ink pen at David. "And you can't expect me to supervise them every minute while you're out gathering stories or covering meetings or whatever. I have to do my work up here."

"Jocie knows how to behave," David said.

"Jocelyn has been doing whatever she's wanted to do for years. Why, half the time you don't even know where she is or what she's doing." Zella waved her pen around.

"That's not true." David frowned at Zella. There were limits and she had just about reached his. "Jocie is a good girl."

Zella seemed to realize she'd gone a step too far. "I didn't mean to imply she wasn't, but she has had a different upbringing than most girls in Hollyhill. Working here since she was a child. As far as that goes, she's still a child. She's only thirteen. But even if she does want to do the right things, how do you know that boy will?"

"I'll make sure that he does," David said.

Zella mashed her lips together as if to keep from saying whatever else she wanted to say, but decided not to because of the look on David's face. After a couple of seconds, she simply shook her head a little and said, "If you wanted to get some extra help, you should have hired one of the local boys. People aren't too happy already about the Hearndons buying that place out there. Things might turn ugly, and if their boy's working here, it's liable to rub off on us. People might cancel their subscriptions."

"I offered him a job, Zella," David said flatly. "I plan to stand behind that and give him a chance. I'll have him keep his hours, and we'll pay him a dollar an hour."

"You're the boss," Zella said as she started typing again. "But like I said, if you ask me you're borrowing trouble. As if you didn't have enough already. Sometimes it looks like you go out hunting it."

Now David was sitting at his desk, staring at the picture of the dried-up farm pond and trying to come up with a headline, but he couldn't keep from wondering if Zella was right. Maybe he was borrowing trouble. He didn't really know anything about Noah. Still, he'd always prided himself on being a good judge of character. Except of course with Adrienne.

Adrienne had been the biggest mistake he'd ever made, and he'd done that on impulse. He let her talk him into running off to get married twenty-four hours after he'd come home on leave for his father's funeral, but then there was a war going on. Everybody was making fast, sometimes rash, decisions. A man didn't know whether he was going to live long enough to make a slow decision. And she hadn't had to talk all that much to convince him. He was carried away by the sight of her. Whatever else anybody said about Adrienne, nobody was ever able to deny she had looks.

The decision to hire Noah wasn't anything like that. Impulsive maybe, but David hadn't been carried away by emotion. The boy was okay. A person could tell. Noah wasn't going to cause any problems, David told himself even as he sat extra still in his desk chair and listened to see if he could hear what was going on back in the pressroom. All he could hear was Zella, back from lunch, pounding on her typewriter just outside his office, and he had to make himself not get up to go back to the pressroom to make sure everything was all right.

He told himself again that Noah wasn't going to cause problems. At least not that kind of problems. The boy was going to shake things up. Shake David up. He had already done that.

David had never thought he was prejudiced. He had studied Paul's sermon to the Athenians in Acts where Paul said God gave breath to all life and made all the nations of men of one blood. David never doubted that the Lord loved all people regardless of color or station in life. The Lord looked on the heart of man, not the outward appearance.

But what was the Lord seeing in David's own heart? Love for all neighbors or only love for those David chose to be his neighbors? Was he only willing to love his neighbor if it was easy? If it made him feel good? Perhaps the Lord had sent Noah his way to jolt David out of his comfortable thinking and make him see in a new way.

David bowed his head and prayed silently. *Dear Lord, open my mind and heart and help me step forward with faith on the path you are putting before me. Now give me the words I need to get this week's* Banner *ready. May your love and mercy ever surround me. And mine. Amen.*

He opened his eyes and stared down at the picture of the pond with its cracked mud bottom. He wrote "HEAT PARCHES COUNTY" in big letters over his article about the drought before he carried it back to the pressroom where Jocie and Noah had several ads blocked out and ready to run.

Jocie looked up at David with a big smile. "Noah's catching right on. Together me and him are almost as fast as Wes." Jocie's smile disappeared. "I'll bet Wes wishes he was here."

"I'm sure he does," David said. "Maybe in a couple of weeks when he gets a smaller cast he can come back and boss us around."

"We're going to have put in a super long day tomorrow, aren't we, Dad? Maybe we should pack our lunch and our supper. Or maybe we can beg Leigh to bring some sandwiches along with her brownies tomorrow night. She is coming, isn't she?"

"I don't know," David said. "I haven't had time to talk to her today."

"She'll be here," Jocie said with a smile. "She told me she thinks folding papers is fun. And of course, she likes the company."

"Is that the lady that was with you at church?" Noah asked.

"Yep. Leigh makes great brownies. Wait till you taste them," Jocie said.

"There's more to like about Leigh than just her brownies," David said. "You shouldn't make it sound as if we're just wanting her to show up for the food."

"I know, Dad." Jocie's smile got even wider as she turned to Noah and whispered loudly, "Leigh's my daddy's girlfriend."

"A friend, at any rate," David said.

"She is a girl," Jocie said. "So if she's a girl and a friend, doesn't that work out to girlfriend?"

"Just get to work and save your girlfriend/boyfriend nonsense for next week when you start school." David went over to the press and pretended to give it the once-over.

There was that word again. *Girlfriend.* Could a man his age have a girlfriend? Maybe a better question was, should a man his age have a girlfriend? Especially a man about to be a grandfather. But at the same time, he wished he could slip out the back door and walk down the street to the courthouse where Leigh worked.

Ever since Sunday he'd been thinking about how he might ask her out on a date. A real date. He'd almost asked her the day before, but he didn't know what people did on a real date nowadays. When he was in high school, he'd taken girls to the drive-in movies over in Grundy. And with Adrienne their first and only date had been running off to get married.

Jocie probably had more ideas about what to do on a date these days than he did, but he couldn't very well ask her for dating advice. He supposed he could ask Zella. As far as David knew, she'd not been on a date in all the time he'd been working with her, but she read all those romantic stories.

The only love stories David read were in the Bible, and some of those weren't exactly something a person would want to copy in his own life. Other matches were literally arranged by the Lord. Some took the intervention of angels. David thought it might take the intervention of an angel to help him get off square one in the dating game.

The very word *date* made him uneasy. But at the same time, *girlfriend* wasn't sounding nearly so strange to him these days. While he had no idea why a young woman like Leigh would ever want to be his girlfriend, he sort of liked the sound of it. Maybe he'd take time to slip down to the courthouse later before Leigh left work to see how her day had been going. Maybe he'd see if she was planning to walk the next day. He could pick one of the red roses out behind the house and go walk with her. He'd walked with her one morning several weeks ago, and they'd been comfortable walking and talking together.

Of course, it would be hard to get away from the house that early now that he had to help Wes get cleaned up and dressed in the mornings. And he needed to make time to go by and see Ben Atkinson who'd had a tumor removed last week. Wednesday he had to take Tabitha to the doctor over in Grundy, and then there was his interview with Mrs. Rowlett that he had scheduled for Thursday. He wanted to have his story about her going from teaching at the West End School to the high school for next week's issue.

Time. The hours were all too full and went too fast. But sometimes if a person didn't grab hold of an hour and keep it for himself, life just passed him by. Somehow he'd manage to pick that rose in the morning and be there at the park when Leigh got there for her morning exercise walk. She said she was trying to lose weight.

Maybe tomorrow morning he'd tell her she didn't have to lose weight to look nice. Maybe he'd find the right words to ask her on a real date—if he could figure out what that was and carve out another hour or two. He wanted to. It surprised him how much he wanted to. And right on top of that surprise was another. Without summons, the memory of her hugging him on the day Jocie had run away and the tornado swept Clay's Creek Church off its foundation came to mind. Her arms around him had felt right. Maybe it was time for him to return the hug.

15

Tuesday morning, Leigh's alarm jerked her away from a dream. A good dream. The kind of dream she wanted to hold on to and enjoy to the end, but as soon as she opened her eyes to grab the clock on her bedside table to stop its buzzing, the dream slipped away. All she had left was the vague feeling that if only she'd had five more minutes to sleep, something really wonderful would have happened.

She lay back on her pillow and shut her eyes to see if she could recapture the dream, but it was only feathery mists in her memory. She kept her eyes shut anyway to block out the morning light. The sun wasn't up. She'd set her alarm early to have time to walk before work, but maybe she'd just sleep in. The air the fan was pulling in through the open window across from her bed already felt hot. It was going to be another scorcher. Her boss, Ralph Mitchell, had a noisy window air conditioner that kept his office bearable, but only teasing hints of cool air leaked out to the counter in the large office next to the hallway where Leigh and Ralph's wife, Judy, waited on the people wanting to get married, go fishing, vote in the next election, or license their cars. If Leigh went out walking this morning and got hot, she'd be sweating all day.

Still, she had lost ten and a half pounds when she weighed in on the courthouse scales last Thursday. She only let herself weigh once a week since she'd started trying to lose weight back in the spring. It was too depressing when the needle on the big scale crept up instead of down. That hadn't happened for a few weeks. She'd been faithful to her walking and no-potato-chips plan. But she did eat two pieces of that butterscotch pie at Miss Sally's house on Sunday. Not that she had much choice about that. She had to eat when she went to people's houses on Sunday with David.

With David. She savored those words a moment and whispered them out loud. "With David."

She hadn't exactly gone to church with him. She drove out there herself. He didn't exactly ask her to go to the McMurtrys' with him. Miss Sally did. But he did ask her to stay for the evening service. The lost dream inched back closer to her consciousness. It had surely been about David. Surely. A smile slipped across Leigh's face and she sighed.

Then she remembered the two slices of pie and the problem at hand. She put her hands on her stomach. It didn't stick out too much when she was lying down, and it wasn't as soft and flabby as it had been. Still, it wasn't flat. She shouldn't have eaten the pie, but the Mt. Pleasant women expected her to eat twice as much as she could hold or they got insulted. Leigh didn't know how David and Jocie stayed so slim. Sometimes it seemed as if everybody in the whole world was slim but her.

Leigh's mother said carrying a little extra weight ran in the family. Leigh wasn't worried about a little extra weight. She was just tired of carrying a lot of extra weight. She figured she needed to lose fifteen more pounds before she got down to that little-extra-weight size. That wasn't going to happen if she didn't put her feet on the floor and get out of bed to go walk. She opened her left eye and then her right eye and let the mists of the dream completely vanish as she sat up.

In the bathroom, she splashed cold water on her face before staring critically at her reflection in the mirror as she jerked a comb through her almost-blonde hair. She wondered if the people at David's church would think she was a hussy if she put highlights in her hair. More to the point, would David?

Maybe she should just concentrate on her eyes. Everybody always said her eyes were her best feature. Cornflower blue. And eyes didn't get fat like the rest of a person's body. But this morning her eyes looked bloodshot and tired. She shouldn't have sat up so late watching that stupid tearjerker movie, but it had been too hot to sleep. She dug the shorts and T-shirt she'd worn to walk on Monday morning out of the dirty clothes. It didn't matter how she looked. She hadn't seen anybody in the park for weeks. Everybody else was sitting in front of their fans drinking iced tea for breakfast.

Leigh made herself down a whole glass of water before she went out the door and tiptoed down the outside stairs to the ground in her socks before she put on her tennis shoes. She didn't want to wake up Mrs. Simpson who lived below her and rented her the upstairs apartment. There weren't that many good apartments for rent in Hollyhill, and Leigh had been lucky to get this one over Mrs. Simpson. But the woman had to keep her ears tuned on high level all the time. She complained if Leigh so much as dropped a big spoon on the kitchen floor. Heaven only knew what would happen if she dropped a pan.

Her landlady did regularly fuss about Leigh's music, but there were some things a girl just had to do. And one of those was play an Elvis record now and again.

Sometimes Leigh wondered if her mother wasn't behind Mrs. Simpson's complaints. She knew her mother called Mrs. Simpson at least once a week. Her mother wasn't happy with Leigh living in Hollyhill. She wanted Leigh to come back home to Grundy. She wanted her back in her old room with the frilly little girl curtains and princess bedspread. Leigh had hated that bedspread since the day she'd gotten it on her eleventh birthday. She'd never been anybody's princess. Not even her mother and father's. Not that she hadn't tried.

She'd worked hard to be the perfect daughter. She ate everything on her plate. She put away her toys without being told. She didn't complain when her mother made her wear her hair in ringlets even though none of the other girls at school did. She hid her tears when some of the kids called her a big fat baby. She didn't once doubt the fault was hers when her father never seemed to have time for her. She spent hours studying to get the top grades in her classes. She stayed home and got a job right out of high school because her mother cried when she'd talked about going off to college.

Her mother had cried again when Leigh moved to Hollyhill years later, but Leigh shut her ears. She loved her mother, but she wanted to have a life on her own and not be a child forever in her parents' house. Now five years later, her mother hadn't given up on finding a way to bring Leigh back home.

She'd called just the night before. She usually only called on Thursday, so Leigh had not expected to hear her voice when she picked up the phone. Her mother didn't bother with the usual greetings. Instead she went straight into guilt trip number three thousand and six. "Your father's sick."

Leigh took a deep breath and sat down at the kitchen table. She twisted the curly telephone cord around her hand and wished for the hundredth time that she could remember to get a longer cord for the receiver so she could move around while she talked. Leigh couldn't even reach the refrigerator to get something to drink. She was stuck at the table until her mother was ready to say good-bye.

Leigh picked up an envelope off the table where she'd thrown the mail when she'd come in from work and fanned herself. "Oh gee, that's too bad. What's wrong with him? Nothing serious, I hope." She wasn't too worried. Her mother was always talking about somebody being sick or going to be sick. Of course it was usually herself and not Leigh's father.

"Who knows? It could be, but you know how your father is. He won't go to the doctor, but something's wrong with him. He's been complaining for over a week now about a pain in his back."

"Maybe he just strained it somehow," Leigh said.

"But he hasn't done any lifting or anything." Her mother's voice took on a little whine. "I thought you'd be home to see us this weekend, and I was going to tell you about it then, but you didn't come."

"I was busy, Mother. I told you I wouldn't be there this weekend when I talked to you last week."

"How could you be too busy to come see your parents?"

Leigh fanned a little faster and mentally counted to ten before she said, "I'm planning to come home to see you Saturday afternoon."

"But I thought you were coming on Sunday. You know that's a better day for visiting. Your father is always out playing golf on Saturday."

"He's always out playing golf on Sunday too," Leigh said. "Besides, I thought you said he was sick."

"Well, you know your father. He'd have to be on his deathbed to not play golf. Especially on Saturday afternoon."

"If he's not there, we can go shopping," Leigh suggested.

"Shopping? How can you even talk about me shopping? You know my legs are in too bad a shape to do any shopping. Besides, your aunt Wilma was going on about how you hadn't been coming home very much lately, and I told her that you'd be here for sure on Sunday. Jenny and Aaron always take their kids and go for dinner at her house on Sunday. And me, I'm just stuck here all alone."

Leigh took another deep breath. Her cousins had done everything on schedule. Married, moved three streets over, produced grandchildren for Aunt Wilma. "I'm sorry, Mother. Why don't you go over to Aunt Wilma's on Sunday afternoon and see the kids? I'll bet Jenny's little Teri Jean is growing like a weed. What is she now? Three?" Leigh tried to get the conversation to a better level, but it didn't work.

"Almost four and it's a madhouse over there on Sunday with all Wilma's grandkids running around screeching like a bunch of wild hyenas. Wilma spoils them rotten."

"Oh." Sometimes no matter what Leigh said, it was the wrong thing. But she held back her sigh and gave it one more try. "Well, then I'm sure there are some other ladies at the church who might like to go out for dessert or maybe to a movie. The theater would be air-conditioned."

"They all have family coming home. Sons and daughters who don't just forget all about them when they move off away from home. Sons and daughters who remember what their parents have sacrificed for them. Sons and daughters who remember their parents want to see them."

Leigh let the sigh come out. "Now, Mother. You know I haven't forgotten all about you, but I think I'm going to be busy Sunday." At least she hoped to be. David had been coming by the county clerk's office nearly every day to lean on the counter and talk to her and Judy and sometimes Ralph, if he ventured out of his air-conditioned office. The last couple of Fridays, David had looked straight at Leigh and said he hoped he'd see her at church. While that might be a little vague to count as a real date of any kind, it was an invitation that Leigh wasn't about to ignore. Not even if her mother started crying on her. Leigh braced herself for what was sure to come next.

"You're still chasing after that preacher, aren't you?" her mother said. She didn't wait for an answer. "I can't see why you couldn't have found a boy more your age to chase if you were going to run after somebody. I hear that preacher has a daughter almost as old as you are."

"Tabitha's a lot younger than I am. Twelve and a half years younger."

"And obviously without the first hint of morals. Why, Mrs. Simpson tells me she's going to have a baby but that she doesn't act one bit ashamed that she's not married. And a preacher's daughter to boot. What kind of preacher lets that kind of thing happen in his own family?"

"That kind of thing happens in a lot of families," Leigh said patiently. "And you always used to say we shouldn't judge others unless we've walked in their shoes."

"I'm not judging anything. I'm just looking at the facts. Facts that you'd better pay more attention to if you're foolish enough to want to throw away your chances on that man."

"He's a nice man, Mother. You'd like him. Maybe sometime when David takes Tabitha to the doctor in Grundy, I could ride along and we could drop by to see you and Dad."

Leigh wished the words back even before her mother let out a shriek as if Leigh had stabbed her with her words. "You're talking about bringing him home to meet us!? With his daughter about to have a baby out of wedlock!? Your father would take to his bed."

"I doubt it. He'd probably like David. You would too. Nearly everybody does."

"If he's such a saint, how come he's divorced? Mark my

words, Leigh Catherine, there must be something wrong with the man."

"For heaven's sakes, Mother! He's a preacher. There's nothing wrong with him. There was something wrong with his ex-wife." Leigh had tried to keep her voice calm, but the irritation had bled through.

Now Leigh shook away the memory of her mother's phone call as she picked up her pace along the street toward the park. Her mother should be happy for her. Her mother should be glad Leigh wanted to try her wings. She should be wishing Leigh's wings would be strong and carry her far. She should be happy that such a man as David had noticed that Leigh was alive. She should be praying along with Leigh that he would go past noticing and fall in love with her.

Leigh's cheeks got red at the thought of praying for love, but what could be more important to pray about than the man she wanted to spend the rest of her life with?

So he had family. So he was going to be a grandfather. He was going to be a young grandfather. And she loved babies. She wouldn't mind the thought of a baby or two of her own, although she didn't let that idea come to the surface of her mind often. After all, she was already thirty-two. She didn't have a lot of years to think about having babies, and David might not want to think about having babies at all.

Her cheeks started burning as if they'd caught fire. She must still be dreaming to even think about the possibility of her and David having babies. Leigh opened her mouth and blew out air. Jocie had taught her that trick. And it seemed to work.

She needed something that worked. She colored up easy as pie so everybody always knew when she was embarrassed. Of course if they noticed her red cheeks now, they might just think it was the exercise. If anybody had been out to notice. The only people she'd seen were a couple of women in their housecoats coming out to pick the Lexington daily paper up off their porch steps.

The *Banner* wouldn't be out until tomorrow. Leigh had baked brownies last night even though the heat from the oven had made the small apartment nearly unbearable till after midnight. But she had to have brownies to take to the newspaper office tonight when she went to help fold the papers. Another time when she'd just sort of made her own invitation into David's routine. Tuesday night folding papers. Sunday morning church. And last Sunday she'd stayed for the night service. That was surely progress.

Sunday morning he'd come out to meet her in the churchyard. He seemed glad to see her. He kept his eyes on hers when they talked. But he didn't kiss her. Not that she expected him to kiss her in the middle of the churchyard, but he followed her home after the evening service. He got out of his car to say good night, even walked her up the stairs to her door. Then they both just stood there in the dark for an awkward moment before David lightly touched her arm and said good night.

A missed opportunity, Leigh thought now. She should have reached out and hugged him the way she had the day Jocie had run off, but that had been a crisis situation. He might have let anybody hug him that day the same way you let people you barely know hug you when they come to the funeral home to pay their last respects to somebody in your family. Thank goodness they hadn't had to pay any last respects that day, and Jocie and Wes had survived the tornado. Still, the hug was nice. Another hug would have been even nicer, and a kiss would really mean progress.

Yesterday at lunch, Zella had said, "Of course, he hasn't kissed you. I'll bet you haven't been alone with him more than five minutes. He has family hanging off his arms all the time. Or church people. The man is hopeless."

"Maybe I'm the one who's hopeless," Leigh had stabbed at the lettuce in her salad and hit a tomato, squirting juice on her white blouse. "See. I'm a klutz."

"You're not a klutz. A little clumsy sometimes, but not a klutz and certainly far from hopeless," Zella had said matter-of-factly as she fished a piece of ice out of her tea. "Here, rub this on the tomato juice. Then blot it with your napkin. It'll come right off."

And Zella had been right about that. Leigh hoped she was as right about some of the other things she'd said. Like Leigh was perfect for David. Like sooner or later David would see that. Like they were making progress even if there hadn't been a kiss. Like it wasn't really hopeless.

Leigh picked up her pace a little as she went through the entrance into the park, past the empty picnic tables and swings on the playground, past the inviting turquoise blue of the water in the community pool that was locked away until noon, down the gravel road that led to the back baseball field where some team was either practicing or playing every evening. At this time of the morning, she nearly always had the field to herself.

But not this morning. A man was leaning against the concrete block dugout on the third-base side of the field as if he was waiting for someone. As if he was waiting for her.

Leigh's heart started beating faster as she wondered if she should turn and go a different direction. The man pushed away from the dugout and took a couple of steps toward her before he stopped and waited again. Leigh's heart pounded even faster. It was David.

Maybe she was still dreaming. Maybe she hadn't really put her feet on the floor and gotten out of bed, but instead had drifted back into her dream. Leigh pinched the inside of her upper arm. No, she was definitely awake. She had a sudden mental image of how she looked. Maybe she should just pretend she hadn't seen him and turn around and walk the other way. Of all mornings to go out without fixing her hair and wearing the rattiest T-shirt she owned. Maybe she shouldn't just turn around. Maybe she should run before he got a good look at her and decided he never wanted to see her again.

But she kept walking toward him as part of a Bible verse popped into her mind. *Be strong and of good courage.* It was part of the Scripture when David preached about the Israelites entering the Promised Land a few weeks ago.

This was Leigh's promised land. She had prayed for this moment when David would step up to meet her. She certainly didn't want to run away from the Lord's answer to her prayer. Besides, she was close enough to see that David was holding something in his hand in front of him. Something red. A rose.

She could see his face now. He was smiling, and she started smiling too. Clothes didn't matter. Sweaty faces didn't matter. Messy hair didn't matter. What mattered was what was in the heart. And in her heart she didn't want to run away from David. In her heart, she'd been running after him for weeks. She wouldn't stop now just when he had turned to face her.

And nobody had ever, ever brought her a rose. She hoped she didn't cry when he gave it to her.

16

Be strong and of good courage. David wondered where the bit of Scripture came from. Of course, he knew where the Scripture was in the Bible. It was sprinkled throughout the story about the Israelites going into the Promised Land. He'd preached on that passage just a few weeks ago. What David didn't know was why the verse had popped up in his mind at this particular moment.

He'd been in plenty of situations where he'd needed courage. Courage while serving in the war encased in a submarine stalking the enemy through the black ocean waters. Courage to believe the Lord had called him to preach. Courage to step behind a pulpit the first time to deliver the Lord's message. And even now he still needed courage every time he stepped forward to preach.

This, standing here at the edge of a deserted ball field, waiting for a young woman to walk close enough so he could hand her a rose, shouldn't take any courage at all. But it did.

It took courage to step out of the shadows where he'd been hiding out ever since Adrienne had left him. He had stayed faithful to his marriage vows even though she had not. She'd divorced him two years after she left. He signed the papers that came in the mail. It seemed futile not to, but he had still felt married. If not to Adrienne, then to the past.

Now he was turning the past loose. He was standing there holding a rose and ready to step into the future. And even though he had no idea where that first step would lead him, he wasn't sorry he had come. He'd prayed about it that morning even before he'd gotten out of bed. Then he'd looked for signs that the Lord was in favor of his early morning mission. The day had dawned clear—which wasn't much of a sign since every morning had dawned clear and hot for weeks. He'd dressed and slipped quietly down the stairs in the fuzzy gray light of dawn to see Wes sitting up on his cot, waiting for David. That seemed more of a sign.

"Are you okay, Wes?" David asked.

"Now, that's a pretty dumb question, David. If I was okay, I wouldn't be camped out here in the middle of your living room, would I?"

"No, I guess not. But I was meaning, are you in extra pain? Do you need some kind of painkiller?" David looked at Wes. The man had lost pounds he didn't have to lose. His cheeks were sunken in, and he had a mashed look to his mouth.

"No, them pills the doctor give me just make my head swimmy and don't help all that much. The pain ain't nothing I can't handle." Wes shifted his leg that he had propped on a pillow in a chair. "I just couldn't sleep, so I been sitting here thinking."

"What about? Anything interesting?"

"Nope," Wes said.

A little more light crept into the room. David peered at Wes's face before he sat down across from him. "You need to talk about something?"

"Nope."

"You aren't going to shut out an old friend, are you?"

"Nope."

David waited a minute for Wes to add something to prove he meant it, but Wes was silent. "You are going to get better, Wes," David said finally.

"If I don't die first." Wes kept his eyes straight ahead on the wall in front of him. "It might've been better if I'd just bled out that day at the church. Just gone on."

"The Lord wasn't ready for that to happen." David leaned forward in his chair, but Wes wouldn't look at him. "And neither was Jocie or me. We need you here a little longer, Wes."

"It would've been hard on Jo," Wes admitted. "But this ain't easy on me. I ain't sure how much longer I can take being anchored to the ground with this thing." He hit his hand on his cast.

"A few more weeks. That's not so long in the whole of a man's life."

"It's this sitting still. It gives a man too much time to think about the whole of his life."

"What do you mean?"

"All men have demons that bite at them more when they can't stay busy and outrun them." Wes was still staring at the wall.

"Do you want to pray about it, Wes?" David leaned closer and touched Wes's arm.

"Nope," Wes said, moving his arm away from David's hand.

David leaned back in his chair and was silent for a few seconds. It was easy to see the man was struggling with something, but David didn't want to say the wrong thing. He chose his next words carefully. "The Lord can help."

"I ain't doubting it, David, but I think I'm too old to change my stripes now."

"Nobody is ever too old. And it's not a matter of changing your stripes. It's just a matter of trusting the Lord with the stripes you have."

Wes looked down at his hands. "You could be right, David. But then again I think I may be like some of the old reprobates I've known. Past saving."

"You're not a reprobate, Wes. The Lord's camping right outside your heart, but he won't come in unless you ask him to."

Wes kept his eyes away from David's face. After a couple of minutes, he said, "I sure could use some coffee to tide me over till breakfast. And how come you're up and about so early anyhow? You got a date or something?"

"Or something." David let Wes change the subject. But somehow he knew the door hadn't been completely closed. Still he could only pray that Wes would decide to push that door back open himself. David couldn't push it open for him, as much as he wanted to. So David had prayed as he made the coffee and helped Wes dress. Silently to himself, even as he admitted to his early morning mission with the rose.

Wes had smiled at him as he left the house. "The girl will like the rose. And old Zell will swoon when she hears about it."

"It's not Zella I'm trying to make swoon."

"Leigh's way too sensible a girl to swoon, but her eyes will light up and her cheeks will go rosy. She don't know it, but she's a right pretty girl when her cheeks go all rosy."

Now as David stepped forward to meet Leigh, he could see Wes had called it right. Leigh's eyes were shining. Her cheeks were red, and she was pretty. He held the rose out toward her. "A pretty rose for a pretty girl."

Her cheeks went redder, but she looked happy. "How sweet," she said as she took the rose and held it up to her nose to breathe in its fragrance. "It smells heavenly."

"I hope you don't mind me coming out to walk with you this morning," David said.

"Of course not. Not if you don't mind me looking a mess. I thought I'd walk and then clean up for work." Leigh pushed her hair back from her face.

"You look fine. Better than fine," David said as he kept his eyes on hers.

"Now come on, preachers aren't supposed to tell fibs," Leigh said with a little laugh. "My hair's a mess. I'm sweating like a pig, and I probably stink."

David laughed along with her. "Who cares about hair? And the good Lord intended for us to sweat when we get hot, and I can't smell anything but roses." He took her elbow and turned her toward the baseball field. "How many rounds are you going to make this morning?"

"I was thinking two, maybe three," Leigh said as she carefully placed the rose in the shade by the dugout before they went out on the field. "But we can walk all morning if you want. Of course, Ralph might send the sheriff out to hunt me."

"And the *Banner* wouldn't get printed," David said.

"Then I guess we'd better just do three. I might could hide out from the sheriff, but the people in Hollyhill expect their paper on Wednesdays."

"Whether there's any news to print or not," David said.

"A slow news week?"

"If Wes was here, he'd say every week was a slow news week in Hollyhill, or at least almost every week. Next week there should be plenty to print."

"You mean because of school starting and desegregation?"

Leigh asked as they passed by first base and headed toward the outfield fence. "You think there will be problems?"

"I hope not, but I don't know. Did I tell you I hired Noah Hearndon to help at the paper until Wes is back on his feet?"

"I heard you talking about it Sunday," Leigh said. "Zella said he was supposed to start yesterday afternoon. She didn't sound too happy about it."

"Zella thinks I made a mistake hiring him. She thinks I'm asking for trouble."

"In what way?" Leigh looked up at him as they walked.

"With our subscribers. With Jocie. With Noah. I don't know."

"Are you sorry you offered the job to Noah?"

"No. I think he'll be a quick learner and a good worker, and we needed the help."

"Then there you are," Leigh said as if that settled everything. "Your subscribers will just be glad to get their papers on time, and you can keep your eye on Jocie. But I think she was more entranced by Noah's little twin sister and brother than she was by Noah on Sunday."

"She does love babies," David said.

"I guess that's good with Tabitha's baby just weeks away. Tabitha told me she was due around the last of September. The twenty-sixth, wasn't it?"

"Right. Sometimes I wonder if I'm ready for that," David said. "It's been a long time since I've had a baby in the house."

"I've never had a baby in the house. I always wished for a little brother or sister, but it never happened. Mother said one was enough."

"Were you that hard to handle as a kid?" David smiled over at her.

"No, not at all. I was always too good. Sometimes I think I'm still too good." Leigh frowned a little. "I guess that's a weird thing to say. I mean, you can't be too good, can you?"

She stopped walking and waited for his answer. Her face was so open and innocent. She really was young, more in experience than years. He probably wasn't doing her any favors bringing her that rose and encouraging her to pin her hopes on a man of his age. But he didn't feel all that old standing there beside her, looking down into her beautiful blue eyes.

A bead of sweat was rolling down her forehead, and he reached over and gently wiped it off. A charge ran through him when his finger touched her skin. She must have felt it too as her eyes popped open wider. He had the sudden urge to kiss her, but he fought the feeling. It was too soon.

Still, even as he told himself that, he dropped his hand down to trace her lips with his thumb. They were incredibly soft. Her lips parted a bit, and he could feel the warmth of her breath on his fingers. He clamped down on the feelings rising inside him and pulled his hand away. He turned and started walking again.

ꕤ

Leigh stayed rooted to her spot as she watched David take one step and then two steps away from her. She felt as if she were on a roller coaster. One second she was at the heights, the next second crashing to the bottom. And suddenly anger pushed through her, sweeping away all thoughts of propriety and good sense. She put her hands on her hips and said, "Stop right there, David Brooke."

David looked back at her, his face surprised. She didn't care. She was going to surprise him some more. He hadn't answered her question about whether a person could be too good, so maybe she was answering it herself. That she wasn't all that good after all. She looked him straight in the eye and said, "Do you or do you not want to kiss me, David Brooke?"

"The thought had crossed my mind," David said, his surprised look slowly being replaced by an amused smile.

That just made Leigh angrier. "What? That you did or didn't?"

"Your lips are very enticing," David said.

"Then kiss them." Leigh took a step toward him and stopped. The anger drained out of her. She felt near tears, scared and vulnerable, as she whispered, "Kiss me."

David took the other step back to her and put his hands on her shoulders. "Are you sure?" he asked.

"I've never been more sure of anything in my life," she said. At the same time, she felt awkward. She was forcing him to kiss her. She shouldn't have done that. A lady should wait until the man was ready to kiss her, not demand a kiss. Especially out in the middle of a dusty baseball field with the early morning sun warming their shoulders. How romantic was that?! And what was she supposed to do with her hands? Just let them hang down by her sides? Should she shut her eyes? She should have thought this through before she started demanding a kiss. What if she did it all wrong?

"Relax," he said as he gently put his finger under her chin and tipped her face up toward his. "It won't hurt."

He was smiling but he looked a little nervous himself, and she remembered Jocie saying her father was probably out of practice kissing, the same as Leigh was. Of course, Leigh had never been in practice. She met his eyes and said, "Do you promise?"

"I promise," he said and dropped his mouth down to gently cover hers.

Leigh shot back up to the top of the roller coaster and fireworks started exploding overhead. Without even thinking about what she was doing she stepped into David's embrace and wrapped her arms around him. It was as natural as breathing.

After the most amazing moment of time Leigh had ever lived, David lifted his head away from hers, but he kept his arms around her for another few seconds. Then she was stepping away from him. "I'm sorry, David," she said. She wasn't sorry he'd kissed her. She was ecstatic. But on the other hand she shouldn't have forced him to kiss her. "I shouldn't have made you do that if you didn't want to."

"Did it feel like I didn't want to?" he asked.

"No, it felt wonderful. At least on my side of the lips."

He put his hand on her cheek and turned her face toward him. He touched his lips to hers again softly, but he didn't let them linger. "You won't have to ask me the next time."

Leigh practically floated the rest of the way around the ball field as they continued their walk. She had no idea what they talked about or if they even talked. It didn't matter. David was there beside her. He'd kissed her. She'd kissed him. That was progress. That was more than progress. That was right off the chart.

17

The night before school started, Jocie jerked awake a dozen times before it was time to get up. She didn't know if it was because she was afraid she'd oversleep or because she'd rolled her hair up on some old bristle rollers Tabitha had found when she was cleaning out her closet to make room for baby things. Jocie had never slept on rollers, and no matter how she lay, the rollers were digging into her head somewhere. But she wanted to look good on the first day of school, and Paulette said all the girls at high school curled their hair.

Finally when Jocie turned on the lamp at four a.m. so she could check the time yet again, even Zeb ran out of patience with her. The dog stood up and gave her a long look as if enough was enough before he trotted to the back door to be let out. Jocie climbed out of bed and tiptoed over to open the door for him as quietly as possible. Then she stood by the open window and looked out at the stars still bright in the sky.

She couldn't see even a wisp of a cloud. No sign of rain. It had been so dry that most mornings only a bare trace of dew kissed the ground. The smell of the brown orchard grass in Mr. Crutcher's hayfield drifted across the fence to her there at the window. Everything was drying up. Even the Mt. Pleasant Church folks' gardens were suffering. They'd only gotten a small bucket of tomatoes last Sunday and no corn at all. Of course, they still got cabbage and zucchini.

Rain was on every church's prayer list in the county. Springs were drying up, and people were hauling water from town for their cisterns. The farmers her father had interviewed for the drought story in last week's *Banner* had said it was the worst dry spell they could remember since the thirties. Back then, it had gotten so bad that some farmers had cut down trees so their cows could eat the leaves. Her father searched back through the *Banner*'s files and found an old picture of a herd of cows grazing on a downed tree. They put that on the top fold instead of the picture of the dried-up pond and sold all their extra papers.

This week's issue had a picture of the high school on the top fold. Just thinking about school made Jocie feel as if ants were running races inside her veins. One minute she couldn't wait for the sun to come up so she could get ready to walk into school as a freshman, and the next minute she was scared to death. Her father had told her whenever something scared her to take a deep breath, say a little prayer, and then look whatever she was afraid of right in the face and see if there was really that much to fear.

She could do the first two. She took a deep breath of the almost-cool night air coming through the window and whispered a prayer. "Dear Lord, thank you for this day. For the stars up above. Please send rain for the farmers' crops. And help me not be scared today at school."

But the last thing she couldn't do. She had no idea what she was going to face at school. Seniors and juniors making fun of her because she was a green freshman? Being lost in the halls with no idea where her classes were? Looking stupid?

Noah had told her on Tuesday as they ran the paper that she didn't have to worry about that last one. He said it was a sure thing and she might as well accept it. All freshmen looked stupid. He claimed he wasn't a bit nervous about starting school, but she didn't believe him. He had to be nervous starting a new school.

Jocie took another deep breath and wished she could talk about it to somebody who understood. Tabitha hadn't. She'd just told Jocie that starting high school wasn't going to kill her, that she would surely hardly notice since she'd be going to school with the same kids she'd always gone to school with, except for the black kids, and black kids were just like any other kids. Tabitha said she'd gone to school with black kids, Chinese kids, Indian kids, Mexican kids, every kind of kid you could think of. Then Tabitha said she'd been the new kid at so many schools while she was with DeeDee that she couldn't even remember them all. And look at her. She had survived.

Jocie wasn't worried about surviving. She was pretty sure she'd survive. She just wanted to know what to expect so she could be prepared. She'd tried to talk to her father the night before, but he hadn't been much help. He'd been acting funny all week. Not hearing half of what she said. Being gone extra early nearly every morning. She reminded him three times the day before that he had to drive her to school this morning. Aunt Love said he was off "courting that girl." Aunt Love still couldn't remember Leigh's name even though Jocie had written it down for her a half a dozen times.

Something was different between Leigh and her father, but Jocie wasn't able to quite put her finger on what. On Tuesday night, Jocie had noticed her father smiling a little extra at Leigh as they folded papers, and Leigh had either started wearing rouge or had a permanent blush.

Zella must have noticed something different going on too. She'd caught Jocie off to the side while they were folding papers and grilled her about what she knew about it all.

"Nothing, Zella. Dad hasn't told me anything," Jocie had admitted. "Hasn't Leigh been keeping you up-to-date?"

"She just says things are progressing, but she won't tell me how." Zella looked over her shoulder at Leigh. "After all I've done to get her this far, you'd think the least she could do is tell me what's happening."

"Maybe it's too private."

Zella looked back at Jocie. "What could be too private?"

"I don't know. I'm not the romantic expert. That's you."

Zella's eyes narrowed a little. "She'd have surely told me if he had finally gotten up the nerve to ask her out on some kind of real date."

"Maybe he kissed her," Jocie suggested, just to have something to say.

"She would have definitely told me that."

"Maybe not. Maybe she thinks that's something just between her and Dad."

"Well, we'll see about that." Zella gave a little snort before she headed back to her spot at the table to start folding papers again.

Jocie had stayed where she was and watched her father smiling at Leigh. An uneasy idea had wiggled awake inside her. Maybe if her father had fallen in love with Leigh, really in love, he wouldn't have time for Jocie anymore.

A noise from the kitchen jerked Jocie back to the present. Surely Aunt Love wasn't up already. It was only four thirty, a long time before even her father got up. Then Jocie heard the clunk of Wes's crutches hitting the floor. Maybe he was thirsty. Jocie went to the kitchen door and peeked in. In the light spilling out of the open refrigerator door, Wes was leaning on his crutches and trying to maneuver a broom to sweep something either under the cabinet or out from under the cabinet.

"Can I help?" she said.

He jerked around, and for a minute she thought he was going to fall. She rushed toward him, but she didn't know how to help. So she just jumped around him while Wes dropped the broom, wobbled on his crutches, and finally caught his balance by leaning back against the cabinet behind him. "Criminy Pete, Jo, don't sneak up on a feller like that."

"Sorry," Jocie said. "I just wanted to help. Are you okay?"

"You mean other than Mr. Jupiter having to restart my heart." Wes put his hand flat against his chest. "Let me get my breath here."

"Can he do that from up on Jupiter?" Jocie asked. "That seems awfully far away."

"Mr. Jupiter has his ways, but don't expect me to explain them right now. I ain't got over the scare yet."

"I didn't think you scared that easy."

"Well, maybe scared ain't the exact right word. Startled might be better." Wes peered at her in the dim light. "Except you are looking pretty scary with those wire contraptions sticking out of your head. They some kind of weird antenna to contact somebody in outer space?"

"No, silly, they're just curlers. I want to look good for school today."

"I hate to be the one to tell you, Jo, but they don't improve your looks all that much."

"I'm not going to leave them in. They're just supposed to make my hair curly."

"What's wrong with straight hair?" Wes asked.

"I don't know. It's just too plain. I don't want to be plain today."

"There ain't a thing plain about you, Jo. Never has been and never will be."

Jocie touched her curlers. A couple of them were about to fall out, but she just left them alone. It didn't seem worth it to reroll them now. "I want to make sure today. And Paulette says none of the girls at high school have straight hair."

"None of them?"

"That's what she said. None of them."

"So she's an expert?"

"I guess. More of an expert than me anyway," Jocie said. "She has a cousin who's a senior this year."

"Ah, so maybe she does know," Wes said. "But back to the matter at hand. You think me dropping the broom has woke up the whole house?"

"I don't know." Jocie stood still and held her breath to listen. "I don't hear anybody, so I guess not." She leaned over and picked up the broom. "What were you doing?"

"I was throwing something in the trash can and missed. I was cleaning it up."

"By sweeping it under the cabinet?"

"Why not? There's probably plenty of other stuff under the cabinet for it to make friends with, and I couldn't exactly lean down and maneuver a dustpan, now could I?"

"But you could have waited till morning and let us clean it up for you."

"I could have. And since you're here, go to it."

Jocie swept a little pile of white dust and chunks of plaster into the dustpan. "What is this?"

"Would you believe Jupiter dust?" Wes asked.

"I don't think so," Jocie said as she let the plaster slide into the trash can.

"Then make me some coffee and I might tell you."

"Coffee now in the middle of the night?"

"It ain't the middle of the night. It's nigh on morning and we're both wide awake. I might as well have some coffee so I'll have an excuse for not sleeping." Wes looked at her in the light still spilling out of the refrigerator. "What's your excuse? Besides curly hair wires."

"Would you believe it's too hot to sleep?"

"I don't think so. You've got the only air-conditioned room in the house out there on the porch with all those open windows."

"I pay for it in mosquito bites."

"Make the coffee and then we'll sit in the dark and talk about it." Wes slowly pivoted around on his crutches and headed back toward the living room. With his uncombed white hair and long white nightshirt, he looked almost like a ghost in the dim light.

She told him that when she went in to sit with him after the coffee started percolating. He'd settled in the chair, his back to the box fan propped in the front window. Outside the night was giving way to dawn, and the air the fan was pulling in off the porch looked so grainy and gray that Jocie thought she should be able to feel it between her fingers. If a real ghost had materialized out of that, she wouldn't have been all that surprised.

"Sometimes I feel like a ghost," Wes said. "A ghost of my old self."

Jocie didn't know what to say to that, so she just said, "Where did that stuff come from? It looked like plaster."

"Good guess." Wes used both hands to lift his broken leg up on the stool in front of the chair.

"Your cast?"

"You always were sharp."

"Is your cast falling apart or something?"

"Or something." Wes picked up his pocketknife off the

table beside him and rubbed the bone-handle casing. "To be truthful, I've been doing a bit of whittling at night when I can't sleep."

"On your cast?" Jocie looked at the cast sticking out from under his nightshirt. "Do you think that's a good idea?"

"I do. Them hospital people got carried away with their plaster, put the thing clear up to my hip, and it was just too blame heavy. I've been taking off an inch or so at night when I can't sleep. It gives me something to do, and a man needs something to do."

"I could go get you a tree branch to whittle."

"I might try that once I get this thing whittled down to size," Wes said.

"But the doctors must have thought you needed it that big for your leg to heal right or they wouldn't have put it on."

"Doctors don't know everything. And besides, I left it alone till a few nights ago. I figure my bones have had time to knit together enough that they won't be breaking apart now just because I take a few inches off the top."

Jocie reached up and, without thinking about it, pulled a couple of the curlers out of her hair. Her head seemed to breathe a sigh of relief. Maybe that was how Wes's leg was feeling. "What's Dad say about it?"

"I don't know that he's noticed."

"He has to have noticed. He's been helping you get dressed and stuff, hasn't he?"

"He's had other things on his mind this week."

"Tell me about it," Jocie said. "I think Leigh has finally caught his eye big time."

"That would be my guess. He's acting pretty twitterpated."

"What's that? Some kind of Jupiter word? Twitterpated?"

"No, straight earth term. It means his pate—" Wes slapped his hand against his head—"that's his head. That his pate is all a-twitter over this female he's noticed. I think the rose he took her last week must have done the trick."

"He took her a rose?"

"He did."

"How do you know?"

"He told me."

"She didn't tell Zella."

"You don't say." Wes stroked his chin and nodded a little. "Then things must be getting serious."

"You think he's kissed her?"

"Could be," Wes said. "It's been known to happen before when a man and a woman form a mutual admiration society. You got a problem with that? Is that what's given you the wide-eye here before dawn?"

"Maybe. I don't know." Jocie frowned as she thought about it. "I like Leigh. I can't see Dad kissing her, but I don't think that's what's keeping me awake. I think it's more school starting today. I guess I'm a little nervous about that."

"Oh yeah, afraid your hair won't curl so you'll look like every other girl at the high school."

"It probably won't." Jocie reached up and pulled out another couple of curlers. She couldn't feel much curl there.

"Tell you what. It sounds like the coffee's quit perking, so run get me a cup and then we'll talk about how you're going to take the school by storm, curls or no curls."

18

In the gray light of early dawn, Tabitha eased down the steps to the bathroom. She never made it through the night now without at least one trip to the bathroom. She moved as quietly as possible to keep from waking up the rest of the house and especially Wes since she had to pass right through the living room where he was sleeping to get to the bathroom. But the bottom two steps squeaked no matter how lightly she tried to step on them.

The truth was she couldn't do anything very lightly these days. In spite of still flipping her cookies nearly every day, she looked like a pregnant walrus with her round full belly pushing her normally cute little inny belly button out until it looked like it might explode. And she still had over a month to go unless the baby came early. She was hoping for early, but at the same time she was terrified at the thought of actually giving birth.

Women were always sharing horror stories about giving birth. How bad it was. How much it hurt. How they'd suffered, bled, even almost died. But at the same time some of the ones who told the worst stories were sitting beside Tabitha in the doctor's waiting room because they had another baby on the way. Surely if it was as bad as they claimed, they would have never decided to go through it again. When Tabitha had told one of the women that, the woman smiled as she touched her extended belly and said that whatever it took, a baby was worth it.

And each time Stephanie Grace did a little somersault inside her womb, Tabitha knew it was true. She could hardly wait until she could hold the baby in her arms. Her father kept reminding her that she couldn't be sure she was having a girl and not a boy, but Tabitha knew. She was sure. She wanted a girl. She had to have a girl.

A boy might look like Jerome, and Jerome didn't deserve any part of this baby. Before he had split without saying so much as boo to Tabitha, he'd given DeeDee money to "take care of the problem" and make the baby disappear.

Tabitha supposed that had worked. Maybe not the way Jerome had planned and the way DeeDee had advised, but it had made the baby disappear from California. Tabitha had used Jerome's money to buy a bus ticket home to Hollyhill. Now there were other reasons to hope her baby had no part of Jerome. In California it hadn't mattered all that much that Jerome had black skin and she had white, but Hollyhill wasn't California.

A long way from it. People here held tight to the same old-fashioned ideas they'd always had. Still, the church people out at Mt. Pleasant hadn't fired her father as preacher when they found out Tabitha was expecting a baby without benefit of matrimony. That had been a surprise. And a relief. So maybe a few things had changed.

But probably not the black and white race stuff. Of course, who knew if she would even stay in Hollyhill after Stephanie Grace was born? Tabitha couldn't see herself living there cocooned in her father's house forever, but for now it felt good to be where she was safe and loved.

That's what she wanted for little Stephanie Grace after she was born. Love and security. If Tabitha didn't think her baby could have that in Hollyhill, then she'd take her where she could be loved and accepted no matter what color her skin turned out to be. Even if that was all the way back across the country to California.

Not that she could look to DeeDee for any help. Tabitha had written to her mother, but she hadn't heard the first word back from her. DeeDee didn't want to hear about being a grandmother. She hadn't even wanted to be a mother.

Tabitha had never thought that much about whether she wanted to be a mother or not. She certainly hadn't planned on being a mother this soon. She'd just been carried away by the moment with no thought about the future. But once she'd realized the baby was growing inside her, all her thoughts changed. She not only wanted to be a mother, she was a mother from the first moment of awareness of the baby inside her.

And as a mother, she'd do whatever she had to in order to give Stephanie Grace the best chance of a happy life. Her own happiness didn't matter, even though she did sometimes dream of meeting someone who would love not only her but her baby as well. She didn't let herself think about that very often. She wasn't sure she deserved to find love. But she couldn't deny that her heart yearned for it.

At the bottom of the stairs, Tabitha took a peek over toward where Wes slept. She was surprised to see him sitting up in his chair drinking coffee. And he wasn't alone. Jocie was sitting on his cot, her lap full of curlers and her hair sticking out in odd angles. Tabitha stopped moving. "Oh, I guess I can quit tiptoeing now."

"Never no need in tiptoeing," Wes said. "I told you it don't bother me none for you to come down to the toilet."

"Morning, Tabitha," Jocie said. "I didn't know you ever got up this early."

"This isn't early. It's the middle of the night," Tabitha said.

"It's daylight," Jocie said.

"What's daylight got to do with it? And I'm not up. I've just got some urgent business to take care of."

Wes held up his coffee cup toward her. "After you take care of that business, come join us for some middle-of-the-night coffee."

"The doctor says I shouldn't drink coffee," Tabitha said with a look at Jocie. "And you shouldn't either, Jocie. You're not old enough for coffee."

Jocie held up her cup. "Iced tea."

"In a cup?"

"Why not?" Jocie took a sip.

"Okay. Whatever," Tabitha said as she hurried on to the bathroom. "Bring me some saltines to go with it so maybe I can keep from flipping it."

When Tabitha came back from the bathroom, a cup of iced tea and a package of crackers were waiting for her. Tabitha lowered herself on the cot beside Jocie.

"Thanks," she said as she pulled one of the big square crackers out, then passed the package to Wes and Jocie who both took one too. "You guys have these middle-of-the-night tea parties often?"

Wes broke his cracker up into four smaller squares. "Not often. Just on the nights Jo here starts high school."

Tabitha looked over at Jocie, who shrugged and said, "Too excited to sleep, I guess."

Tabitha took a sip of her tea and then a nibble off her cracker. Usually crackers stayed down even in the mornings. "What have you done to your hair?"

Jocie touched her hair gingerly. "I rolled it up."

"She has to have curls," Wes said. "All high school girls have to have curls. It's an established fact."

"Not in California." Tabitha pulled a strand of her long honey brown hair over her shoulder. "There everybody wanted long, straight hair. I knew this one girl who even ironed her hair every morning. But not me. I didn't mind a few waves."

"I may have to iron mine to get it to lay down." Jocie made a face as she combed through her hair with her fingers. "I don't think it curled."

"It looks like it might have rebelled a little instead," Tabitha agreed.

Jocie looked down at her cracker. "Maybe I'll just be sick and not go to school."

"It doesn't look that bad," Tabitha said. "Go get a brush and we'll work on it. And if we can't comb it out, you've still got plenty of time. You can just wet it and start fresh. Trust me, everybody won't have curly hair."

"For sure, if I don't." Jocie didn't look happy, but she got up and went to get a brush.

When she came back, she sat on the floor in front of Tabitha and let her brush her hair. "You didn't bring a mirror," Tabitha said.

"I'll just look at Wes and tell by the look on his face how bad it is."

"It looks better now that you've got them wire contraptions out of it, but I can't really say I'm much of a judge on hairstyles. I just sort of let mine go where it wants, Jupiter style."

"What is Jupiter style?" Tabitha asked. She'd gotten used to hearing Wes and Jocie's Jupiter stories since Wes had been at the house. It was sort of fun to go along with them. Maybe that's what she'd tell people about Stephanie Grace's daddy. That he was from Saturn or somewhere. She hadn't come up with a very good story yet. Her father said she didn't owe anybody an explanation, and that was okay for most people. But someday she'd have to tell Stephanie Grace something.

"The kind of style where you just let your hair grow whichever way it wants without bothering it with combs and such," Wes said.

"Well, Jocie might rather have an Earth style." Tabitha combed Jocie's hair back and to the side. There were a few humps where the curlers had been, but no real curls. "A little more brushing and you'll be good as new."

"You mean just like always." Jocie sighed as she leaned back against Tabitha's stomach.

"Better than Jupiter style," Tabitha said with a laugh. The baby jumped inside her and pushed with her feet against the front of Tabitha's belly.

"Hey, she kicked me," Jocie said, leaning forward. She turned around and put her hand on Tabitha's stomach. "She's getting really strong."

"Swimming around in there like crazy," Tabitha said. "She must like tea parties in the middle of the night. That doesn't bode well for the future."

"You want to feel her, Wes? She's really kicking." Jocie looked at Wes and then Tabitha. "You don't mind, do you? I mean, if Wes is my granddaddy, that makes him Stephanie's great-granddaddy."

"Now hold on there," Wes said. "I ain't going with this great-granddaddy stuff. I may be old, but I ain't that old."

Tabitha laughed. "You can be the favorite uncle. So go ahead and tell her hello, Uncle Wes."

Wes hesitated, then reached out his hand and laid it flat on the front of Tabitha's stomach. Stephanie Grace performed right on cue and bounced her feet off his hand. "I think she's dancing," he said. He took his hand away and leaned back. "Thank you, Tabby. There ain't nothing like a new baby."

Tabitha looked at him. "You sound like you're speaking from experience."

"I wasn't in a spaceship all my life." An odd look passed over his face.

Jocie was staring at Wes. "You've never told me anything about babies, Wes."

"Nobody ever knows anybody else's whole story, Jo," Wes said as he held up his hand to stop her before she could say anything else. "And you ain't going to find it out today, so don't start in with your questions. You got plenty enough to worry about with having to be the no-curl trendsetter this morning."

"There aren't any curls then?" Jocie said, looking first at Wes and then at Tabitha. "I slept on those rollers for no good reason?"

"Sorry, kid. No curls." Tabitha patted Jocie's shoulder.

"But look on the bright side," Wes said. "We got to have a middle-of-the-night tea party. Now I think I hear your daddy stirring upstairs, so you'd better go put on another pot of coffee."

Tabitha stood up and yawned. "Stephanie Grace is worn out from all that dancing. Me and her are going to get the rest of our beauty sleep." She handed Jocie the brush. "Your hair looks fine the way it is, Jocie. Besides, it's the eyes that really matter, and you have the best eyes I've ever seen."

"I do?"

"You do."

"But boys like curves," Jocie said. "I don't have any of those."

"Who cares what boys like? That just gets girls like us in trouble. Look at me. I'm a prime example. The important thing is being true to yourself."

"And to the Lord," Tabitha's father said as he came down the stairs to join them. "Did somebody forget to tell me we were having breakfast an hour earlier this morning?"

"Talk to these two." Tabitha pointed at Wes and Jocie. "It must be some kind of Jupiter ritual on the first day of school."

19

Walking into the high school wasn't as scary as Jocie had imagined. Her heart was beating extra hard when she told her father good-bye and climbed out of the car in front of the school and the nervous ants were dancing around inside her skin, but she never once thought about not walking up the steps into the school. Instead, she practically ran up them to the door.

Right inside the door, a big sign directed all freshmen to the gym. A few teachers were standing around to point the way down the hall to the double doors that led out to the gym if freshman stupidity kept any of them from moving in the right direction.

As Jocie walked toward the gym, the nervous ants worn out from all that dancing fell asleep, and she forgot about being scared. It didn't even bother her when she saw Ronnie Martin and some of his buddies leaning against the wall, giving the freshman girls the eye. She had acted as if Ronnie Martin was invisible for weeks at church. It wasn't a bit hard to carry that over to school. So if he was invisible, the boys with him could be invisible too.

When she passed by them she thought she heard somebody say, "Hey, look, there's the preacher's kid. She looks more like a fourth grader than a freshman. Hey, little girl, you sure you're not lost?"

She looked around, but since Ronnie and the others were invisible, she just stared straight through them at the wall.

"Where's your darkie shadow, huh?"

For a second she almost saw Ronnie, but then his shape just sort of melted away in front of her eyes. She didn't care what Ronnie Martin had to say. Her father and Ronnie's father had forced them to face one another at Mt. Pleasant one Sunday after church while Ronnie pretended to apologize for the awful things he'd said to Jocie and she pretended to accept the apology, but they both knew they were pretending. Not a thing had changed in his heart. Or in hers. Some things were just too mean to forgive.

She didn't really want to think about what her father was always preaching the Bible said about forgiveness. About how a person had to forgive to be forgiven. That was in the red-letter part of her Bible, which meant it was Jesus talking, but surely the Lord understood that some forgiving took longer than other forgiving. Sometimes Jocie thought about talking it out with her father, but there just hadn't been the right time. And besides, her father thought she'd already forgiven Ronnie when she'd put on that big pretending act at church.

She pushed all that to the back of her mind. She didn't have time to worry about that now. She had to think about being a freshman on her first day of high school as she moved along with the other kids toward the gym. She knew nearly all of them, so she supposed Tabitha had been right about starting high school with all the kids she'd always gone to school with not being all that hard. And Tabitha had been right about the curly hair too. Some other girls had hair just as straight as Jocie's, and some looked sort of like Jocie had looked before Tabitha had brushed the weird kinks out of her hair that morning. At least Jocie had bra straps under her new blouse. She might not need them, but she had them.

What Jocie really needed was a camera. All around her she saw pictures that would be great on the front page of the *Banner*. One of Mr. Madison, the principal, handing out schedules to three or four black kids might have made the top fold. Jocie took a closer look to see if one of the boys was Noah, but it wasn't. She idly wondered if he was there yet before she let her mind go back into picture mode. The back of the freshman kids in front of her moving toward the gym like so many lemmings to the sea would be another great shot. She could have gotten a good portrait study of Mr. Hardin, the basketball coach, checking out how much the boys had grown over the summer. His eyes really narrowed in on the new black boys. The black high school over in Grundy had a great team nearly every year.

But her father hadn't let her bring her camera. He said she needed to think about her first day of high school and not about pictures for the *Banner*. He promised to take a few shots out front before he went over to the elementary school. Cute little first graders sold more papers than high schoolers.

Practically the whole front page of this week's *Banner* had been about school starting and desegregation. It was the news of the week in Hollyhill, and would be next week too when they ran all the pictures her father was taking today. He'd probably even want her to write some kind of article about what went on at the high school. Jocie had gotten her first byline for the paper when she was twelve. Her father said she had a natural talent for writing the news, maybe because she'd practically grown up in the pressroom. Breathing all the newspaper ink had probably done something weird to her brain.

She made herself quit snapping imaginary pictures and really look around. Paulette had promised to keep an eye out for Jocie after her bus got to school, but the school buses were unloading at a different door so Paulette was probably already in the gym. Jocie spotted three black kids in the group going up the stairs to the gym. One girl and two boys. When one of the boys looked her way, Jocie smiled and waved a little hello. The boy glanced over his shoulder to see who she might be looking at.

Jocie's cheeks went red, but she kept her smile bright as she tried to inch over toward the black girl. She wanted to know her name. It didn't seem right not to know the name of a girl her own age who lived in Hollyhill. The town was so small that not only did everybody know everybody, they knew everybody else's business. Who their parents were and where they worked. When they were sick or in trouble. When somebody in their family was born or died. Where they went to revival meetings and what they planted in their garden.

In every issue, the *Banner* published ten community news columns sent in by somebody, usually a sweet little gray-haired lady, who kept up with what was going on in their neighborhoods. Her father didn't pay them. The columnists' sole reward was seeing their bylines in the paper and having an excuse to be nosy.

The West End news was reported by a Mrs. Washington who brought in her column every Monday. So-and-so had visited so-and-so. So-and-so's daughter had a new baby in Grundy. So-and-so had a nephew in the army. So-and-so was being baptized by this or that church. Jocie had to proof the names as they got the column ready to print, but she'd never been all that curious about the faces behind the names. Now she was. Especially the names of the kids her age.

Before she could work her way over close enough to talk to the girl, they passed through the doors into the gym and Paulette ran up to Jocie. "There you are. I was about to decide you'd chickened out and stayed home," she said.

"I'm not that chicken." Jocie gave Paulette the once-over. Her blonde hair hung down to her shoulders in the kind of soft, curly waves Jocie had imagined her own hair would have when she'd wrapped the strands around the curlers the night before. She had on lipstick and a touch of color on her cheeks that might have been makeup. Her blue blouse showed off her curves and matched her eyes. Jocie wasn't a bit surprised that every boy who passed them gave Paulette an extra look. "You look great," Jocie said.

"Thanks. So do you, except I thought we decided you should curl your hair."

"I tried. It didn't cooperate."

"What do you mean it didn't cooperate? You sound like your hair has a mind of its own." Paulette frowned at her a little.

"I guess it does. You should have seen it this morning. It looked like I had stuck my finger in a light socket or something. Believe me, straight is better."

Paulette laughed. "You're so funny."

"And I've been told I have great eyes, so maybe that'll make up for the straight hair."

"You do have nice eyes," Paulette said even as she kept her own eyes busy sweeping across the kids around them. "Did you see Derrick this morning? He's looking extra good today."

Derrick was the latest boy Paulette had decided to have a crush on. He was a senior and so far hadn't given the first indication that he even knew Paulette was alive.

"I didn't see him," Jocie said. "But some of the guys in here seem pretty interested in how you look."

"Freshman boys are such babies."

"We're freshman girls," Jocie reminded her.

"But girls mature earlier than boys," Paulette said. "At least on average."

"I never liked being average anyway," Jocie said.

"I didn't mean you, Jocie. Besides, you may not have the figure yet, but you're very mature. Mentally."

"Well, that's something." Jocie looked around. The gym was filling up. "Let's go find a place to sit. How about over there by her?" She pointed at the black girl she'd been trying to catch up with earlier. She was sitting on the third bleacher up, and everybody was leaving plenty of space around her.

"By who? That black girl?"

"Sure, why not?"

"Well, come on, Jocie," Paulette said as if Jocie should already know the answer to her question. "Look, let's go over there by Linda and Janice. They'll make room."

"We already know Linda and Janice. I want to find out this girl's name."

"Why?"

"Because I don't know her, and I should if she lives in Hollyhill, don't you think?"

"No. I mean, we have to be nice to them and everything, but we don't have to try to be buddies or anything."

"But she looks like she needs a buddy," Jocie said.

"For gosh sakes, Jocie, we're not in church. You don't have to try to be nice all the time just because you're the preacher's kid."

Jocie looked at Paulette. "You think I'm too nice?"

Paulette frowned. "No, sometimes you're not nice at all—like now, trying to mess up our first day at high school."

"What do you mean?"

"I mean if you want to go sit by her, go ahead, but I'm going to go sit with Linda and Janice." Paulette started toward the other end of the bleachers.

Jocie took a couple of steps after her then stopped. She didn't want Paulette to be mad at her, but Jocie didn't want to go sit with Linda and Janice. She wanted to go find out the black girl's name. She felt as if it was an assignment for a story she needed to write for the *Banner*. She had to do it. She reached out and touched Paulette's arm. "I'll catch up with you later. Maybe at lunch."

"Sure thing," Paulette said, but she wasn't smiling anymore.

"It's just something I need to do. You understand, don't you?"

"Not really. Why can't you just be normal and have fun? Why does everything have to be about saving the world or something?"

"I'm not trying to save the world," Jocie said. "But I promised myself I'd find out the names of the kids I didn't know. And I don't know hers."

"Then go ask her. She'll probably just think you're nosy."

"Probably," Jocie agreed. "And I bet Derrick notices how cute you are today."

At least that made Paulette smile at her before she rushed on across the floor to climb up beside Linda who scooted over to make room. The black girl didn't have to scoot over to make room for Jocie. There was plenty of room.

"Hi," Jocie said. "Is it okay if I sit here?"

"I don't think we've been assigned numbers. You can sit wherever you want." The girl looked at her without smiling. She didn't look as nervous now. More just resigned to her fate.

Jocie smiled as friendly as she knew how and said, "I'm Jocie Brooke."

"I know," the girl said.

"You do?"

"Of course. Your daddy owns the *Banner* and is a preacher." Her voice was soft and there was the beginning of a smile deep in her brown eyes. "But you have no idea who I am, do you?"

"Nope. That's why I came over here. I wanted to ask your name. Are you going to tell me?"

"Sure, why not? Charissa Boyer. Now guess what my daddy does?"

Jocie searched through her memory of the names in the West End community column. She remembered Boyer. She looked closer at Charissa. "He's the preacher at West End Baptist Church."

Charissa laughed and her eyes lit up. "Good guess."

"Maybe that's why I wanted to find out your name," Jocie said. "So we could compare notes about being PKs."

"It's not something to be wished on the fainthearted," Charissa said. Her smile disappeared. "But from the looks of it, you aren't a faintheart. Your girlfriend didn't look too happy with you."

"Oh well, she'll get over it. She ought to know me well enough by now to know when I get my head set on doing something I'm going to do it."

"Why did you get your head set on sitting by me?"

"Because I didn't know your name, and I thought I should. We both live in Hollyhill. We're both the same age."

"And both PKs."

"And I thought it was just my curiosity getting the best of me when it must have been the Lord's hand pushing me across the floor, saying go talk to her. She'll understand."

"Understand what?" Charissa asked.

"I don't know. Whatever needs understanding, I guess."

Charissa shook her head a little. "I think you must have heard him wrong. I'm not understanding anything too good this morning."

"Why? You don't like it here?"

"Not much so far. It would have been easier to go on to school over in Grundy, but Daddy said we had to do this. To come here." She looked as if she was talking about chopping up cabbage or some other yucky chore. "It's really worse for my big sister. Anna's a senior and her boyfriend is at Grundy. She's been begging Daddy for weeks to let her keep going to Grundy. She cried all the way to school this morning. Says she wants to die or quit school or something. Anna's very dramatic. Me, I don't have a boyfriend, and all the kids I was in eighth grade with are here somewhere." She peered around her. "We don't look like very many mixed in with all of you. Some of them must've not come."

"Why wouldn't they come?"

"Too scared, I guess."

"I was scared this morning," Jocie said.

Charissa looked at her. "Because of us?"

"No, because of me. I was afraid I wouldn't know what to do and that everybody would think I was stupid or something."

"So what if everybody thinks you're stupid as long as you know you aren't."

"But sometimes I guess I'm not all that sure," Jocie said.

"That makes two of us." Charissa's smile went all the way across her face.

"You're really pretty," Jocie said.

"Tell that to that boy who works for your daddy."

"Who? Noah?" When Charissa nodded, Jocie went on. "Do you know him?"

"He came with his momma to church one Sunday a couple weeks ago."

"Aren't his twin brother and sister the cutest?"

"I wasn't looking at them all that much. I was thinking Noah was the cutest. Don't you think so?"

The same look was on Charissa's face that Paulette had on hers when she talked about Derrick earlier. What was the matter with Jocie that she wasn't drooling over any boys like that? Maybe she had a case of arrested development. She decided that was pretty obvious, given her lack of curves. "He's okay, I guess," Jocie said.

"Just okay?" Charissa gave her a long look. "Girl, you haven't been looking, or maybe you don't think it's proper for a white girl to look at a black boy."

"I hadn't thought about it."

"Well, don't. I don't need any competition, especially competition that rubs elbows with him."

"I wouldn't be much competition."

"Don't sell yourself short, Jocie Brooke. You're one of those people that other folks notice. Like Noah's momma."

"I don't know what you're talking about. Mrs. Hearndon is drop-dead beautiful."

"She is that," Charissa said. "But as my daddy is always saying, true beauty comes from inside, and he says that lady has plenty inside. That she aims to make a difference wherever she goes. And that's you too. That's how come you're sitting here beside me instead of over there with your girlfriends."

"Flattery will get you anything," Jocie said with a little laugh. "So why don't you come on down to the news office any Monday or Tuesday to see me? That's when you-know-who will probably be there."

"It wasn't flattery. It's the truth. But since you offered, I might take you up on that visit next Monday."

A bell sounded somewhere deep in the school, and the kids on the bleachers straightened up and looked out toward Mr. Madison, who was walking to the middle of the floor in front of them. His footsteps were loud on the gym floor.

"Ready or not, here we go," Jocie whispered.

20

Friday morning, Zella got to the newspaper office more than an hour earlier than usual. She went in and dropped her purse in the bottom drawer of her desk the way she did every morning, but she didn't sit down and uncover her typewriter. Instead she went back and pushed open the door to the pressroom. She never went into the pressroom unless she had to. It was too dirty and too noisy. Of course, it was silent as death now. The press, which always made Zella a little uneasy with its clanging and clacking as it ate up the blank newsprint, somehow looked even more forbidding as it sat so still and dark in the middle of the room. It was almost as if the thing was watching her, as if it knew what she was up to.

Zella hesitated, then whispered under her breath, "Don't be an idiot, Zella Curtsinger! It's just an inanimate object. The thing doesn't have eyes."

She stepped through the door the way she might have stepped across the border into foreign territory. The front of the office was more home than her own house, but the pressroom was David and Wesley's domain. She wasn't sure she'd ever even been in the pressroom when nobody else was there. Usually David or Wesley was back there making some kind of unholy racket with the press, or Wesley and Jocelyn were carrying on with their foolishness and thinking up new ways to irritate her. Or they were all back there doing the dreadful folding job so the papers could go out on Wednesday morning. That hadn't been so odious lately with Leigh showing up every Tuesday night.

Zella sighed just thinking about Leigh and David and the way they'd been smiling at each other last Tuesday night, as if they knew a secret none of the rest of them knew. Zella might not know it yet, but she would. Leigh wouldn't be able to keep any secrets from Zella about what was happening between her and David. After all, if it hadn't been for Zella and all she'd done to shake David out of his self-induced coma when it came to women and romance, Leigh would have never had the first chance of getting the man to notice her.

Zella liked Leigh. The girl was young, but she would make a perfect preacher's wife, a perfect wife for David. She'd have a handful with that Jocelyn, but then who wouldn't? David had always been too lenient with that child. Letting her write up news stories when she should have still been playing with dolls. Letting her be disrespectful to her elders, to Zella, with only the pretense of taking her to task. And now this letting her work shoulder to shoulder, nose to nose with that colored boy. It was just begging for trouble.

Not that Zella could totally blame David for how Jocelyn acted. He'd done the best he could in a bad situation. The child had never had a mother. Not from day one. Nor David a proper wife. Zella hadn't been the first bit shocked or the least bit sorry when Adrienne took off for parts unknown. Good riddance was all she had to say.

But while Zella couldn't do a thing about Jocelyn, she could do something for David. David was like a little brother to her. She cared what happened to him. He deserved better than what life had handed him so far, so Zella had set out to bring him to the door of happiness. He needed romance and love the same as the men in the novels she read, but just like most of them, he was too blind to see it.

In those romance books, it took about two hundred pages for the hero to get to a spot where he began to see the heroine as the girl of his dreams and to realize he couldn't live without her. In the real world it hadn't been quite that easy or the ending so sure. The ending still wasn't sure. Endings in real life never were, but David was finally heading up the walk to the happiness door. And Zella was standing there poised and ready to give him another shove or two if he needed it. When something needed to be done, Zella found a way to get it done.

She'd told Leigh as much early on when Leigh had been discouraged by their lack of progress with David. That had made Leigh wonder aloud, "Then how come you never found the way to the right man for yourself?"

Zella remembered exactly where they were when Leigh asked her that question. It was last April and they were driving back from Grundy after watching Nadine Richardson's son marry some slip of a girl over there. There was nothing like a wedding to make a single girl feel depressed. Especially a single girl like Leigh who didn't want to be single. That wasn't Zella. She explained as much to Leigh. "I'm quite happy with my life the way it is, and I never met a proper candidate to make me think about changing things."

The fact of the matter was even if a Prince Charming had ridden up to Zella's gate and paced his steed back and forth begging entrance, she might not have unlatched the gate to let him in. Prince Charmings had a way of turning into froggy old husbands who expected their wives to spend all their free time cooking and cleaning and picking up their dirty socks off the floor while they sat on the couch and watched golf on television. Why in the world would anybody want to watch golf on television?

And then Leigh said the most ridiculous thing Zella had ever heard anybody say. "What about Wes? He's sort of cute in a weird kind of way."

It was a good thing that Leigh was driving instead of Zella. Zella would have probably run right off the road and turned the car upside down. That's what would have to happen to the world before Zella ever took the first look at Wesley Green as a candidate for anything personal. The world would have to turn upside down.

Of course, a lot of people were saying it already had, with how President Kennedy had gotten shot last fall, and now President Johnson was bombing some country halfway around the world in the name of freedom, and Congress was passing all these laws about civil rights and everything. As if people didn't know how to run their own lives without some senators up in Washington telling them what to do. The truth was, even if most people did manage to make a complete mess of how they lived, some things just couldn't be legislated.

But the very idea of Leigh even thinking Zella would give Wesley Green the first consideration in that way. Even if he had been handsome, which he was not; even if he had been gentlemanly, which he was not; even if he had any redeeming qualities at all, which he did not, Zella wouldn't have given him a second thought. The man was some kind of outlaw. Zella had known that from the very first time she'd laid eyes on him. He'd done nothing over the ensuing years to convince her otherwise—which brought her to the matter at hand. The key to the upstairs apartment.

In the other room, the phone started ringing. Zella

slapped both her hands against her chest as her heart started banging against her ribs. She took two deep breaths while her heart slowed its thumping.

"Now who in the world would be calling here at this time of the morning?" she muttered to herself. She had half a mind to go in there, pick up the phone, and tell whoever it was to look at a clock. The office wouldn't be open for business for at least an hour. David wouldn't be there for a half hour after that. Zella was counting on it. And she wouldn't have to worry about Jocelyn. She would be at school. That was why Zella had waited until now. She'd known she was going to do this ever since the tornado blew through and Wesley had ended up in the hospital practically at death's door. It was something that had to be done. She'd just been waiting for the right time to do it.

It was for his own good.

There was really no need for her nerves to feel all jangly. She stepped quickly across the floor, past the press, and lifted the key off the hook by the back door. She stared at it for a minute as if just looking at it would give her the answers she was determined to find. But of course it was only a key.

She looked around until she found the old broom that obviously, from the looks of the pressroom floor, wasn't used nearly enough. She stepped out the back door and around to the steps that led up to Wesley's apartment. His motorcycle was parked under the landing. Somehow it had survived the tornado in better shape than Wesley. Zella wished it had been blown to kingdom come so that Wesley would have been forced to buy some more sensible mode of transportation. From the looks of his leg, though, he might never be able to get back on the seat of his motorcycle. Or climb the steps to his apartment.

As Zella started up the stairs, she swept a leaf off a step here and there. That was her cover story if anybody happened by and caught her on the steps. She stopped and looked around as the bells on top of the Christian Church tolled out the hour of seven. She didn't see a soul. A car door slammed in the parking lot out behind the courthouse. Probably Hal going to open up the courthouse and sweep out the hallway. Hal always walked with his head down as if searching for pennies, so she didn't have to worry about him noticing her even if he didn't take the shortcut across the parking lot straight to the back door of the courthouse. A car went by on the street behind the newspaper office, but luckily, the person in the car was looking straight ahead at the road.

She blew out her breath and told herself to stop acting like a scared rabbit. It didn't matter if somebody did see her. She had her broom. She was sweeping the steps. They'd probably just think that was part of her job the way it was Hal's job to sweep at the courthouse. Not that she was the *Banner*'s janitor or anything.

By the time she got to the top of the stairs, her forehead was damp with sweat, but that didn't have the first thing to do with nerves. It was hot. The sun was coming up bright and strong already without even a whiff of a promise of rain. Every church in the county had been praying for rain, but so far the Lord hadn't seen fit to send them any. David said he would, that sometimes the Lord answered prayers in his own time.

Zella wished he'd hurry. Her rosebuds were drying up on the bushes without even opening up, and that was with her carrying out the water she rinsed her dishes in to pour on them. The mayor had issued a ban on watering lawns and flowers. They'd run the notice in the *Banner* the last two issues. Police Chief Simmons had even handed out a citation to Perry Phillips who'd been caught watering his grass in the middle of the night. Perry set great store by his grass, but he couldn't be any fonder of it than Zella was of her roses. Her mother had planted most of those rosebushes. Still, Zella wouldn't break the law to keep them blooming.

It wasn't the best time to be thinking about breaking the law, Zella thought, as she stuck the key in the lock. But she wasn't breaking and entering. She had the key. She wasn't breaking anything. She was just entering.

She pushed open the door, quickly stepped inside, and yanked the door shut behind her. It was twice as hot inside as it had been outside. And stuffy. And it smelled. Not just that closed-up stale odor but like printer's ink and press oil and coffee. Like Wesley. Dust stood in the air and a cobweb stretched from the ceiling light to the door facing above her head.

No windows or doors had been opened up there for weeks except when Jocelyn had come in to hunt for a book, some clothes, or whatever for Wesley. The place needed a good airing out. Maybe she'd tell Jocelyn as much. Maybe she'd even offer to help. That would give her another opportunity to hunt for clues to Wesley's past if she couldn't find them fast enough this morning.

Zella waved her hand in front of her face to push a little extra air toward her nose. She had never been in Wesley's apartment. She'd never been invited, and even if she had been, she wouldn't have come.

The place wasn't exactly dirty, just dusty and cluttered. Books were piled everywhere. Zella picked up a couple of them. Nothing she'd ever think about reading. Still, a bit of admiration stole into her mind for a man who read that many books.

It was a small apartment with a kitchenette tacked on to the living room. He didn't even have a stove, just a hot plate on a tiny table. Beside it was a half-size refrigerator that she wasn't about to open. No telling what might be growing in there. Wesley surely wouldn't hide anything in there anyway. A glass and cup sat on a towel next to a small sink.

Zella slowly swept her eyes around the room. She wasn't sure exactly what she was looking for, but she was sure she'd know it when she saw it. Somewhere there would be a letter or a paper or a picture that would lead her to the truth of Wesley Green's past. He would have kept something. Everybody did.

Wesley didn't have a telephone, so there wouldn't be a telephone book where he might have scribbled down a number. She pulled open a drawer in the table by the old couch, but there was nothing in there but pencils and pens. She found a quarter and three pennies under the couch cushions. She picked them up and dropped them in the drawer with the pencils.

She took a peek at her watch. A quarter after seven already. She needed to hurry. She intended to be sitting behind her desk by seven thirty.

She straightened up and looked around. He might have stuck something in a book, but unless she was just lucky enough to pick the right book, she'd never find it in the time she had left. A Bible. People didn't throw away Bibles. She kept her mother's and her grandmother's Bibles in a special place at home. She'd heard dozens of stories about soldiers carrying their pocket New Testaments through this or that war. Maybe Wesley had carried a Bible away from his past with him.

She went across the room into the small nook where

Wesley slept. The cover was thrown back on the bed as if he had just gotten up and gone down to the newspaper office. There was even still an indention in the pillow. It was almost enough to make Zella give up her quest and run for the door.

"You're here. Wesley isn't here. Look for the Bible," she told herself firmly.

She didn't find a Bible, but she did find a road atlas under the bed. She blew the dust off the cover and opened it up. In the front was a map of the whole United States. Wesley had traced so many black routes on the roads between the states that it looked like a spiderweb. Zella couldn't even begin to comprehend how many miles the lines represented. There were lines to California and Oregon, to Florida and Maine.

Moving closer to the small window above the bed, she pulled the curtain back to let in more light. Then she narrowed her eyes and studied the map until she located the end of a line somewhere close to where a dot for Hollyhill, Kentucky, would have been if the town had been big enough to be on the map. Painstakingly, ever conscious of the minutes ticking by, she looked for another end of a line. Finally she found it.

She had closed the curtain and was putting the road atlas back under the bed when a picture slipped out of the atlas and fluttered to the floor. Zella picked it up and stared down at a much younger Wesley with his arm around a beautiful woman. A boy and a girl stood in front of them in one of those frozen-moment-in-time vacation shots where the sun was shining and a stranger must have offered to take a picture of everybody smiling and having a great time.

Zella very carefully placed the photo back between the pages of the maps and shoved the book under Wesley's bed. Then she practically ran to the door. She told herself she didn't need to feel guilty. She hadn't done anything wrong. She had never planned to turn Wesley in to the authorities or anything even if she did find something that proved he was running from the law. She was doing this for his own good.

The man could die. He almost had died, and if that happened, they needed to know who to contact. He wasn't from Jupiter. That of course went without saying. But he was from somewhere. He would have relatives. That picture proved it.

Zella remembered to lock the door before she hurried down the steps. She remembered to put the key back on the hook in the pressroom. She totally forgot about the broom.

21

Wes had been awake for hours before anybody stirred at the Brooke house on Saturday morning. He'd kept his eyes shut and even let loose a fake snore when Tabby had come down to the john around three a.m. The girl was beginning to waddle. It wouldn't be long now until there'd be a baby crying in the middle of the night to keep Wes entertained through the long dark midnight hours.

Of course he didn't plan to be camped out in the Brookes' living room all that much longer, so unless she had the baby soon, he might miss out on that. He'd got the cast trimmed down to just about six inches above his knee. He could put on his clothes without help, although it took him awhile to get his split britches leg up over the cast. He'd been practicing on the steps some when nobody was in the house. And he'd been feeling extra itchy for days. And not just under his cast where he couldn't get to.

This was a different kind of itch. The kind he had before he landed in Hollyhill, where he'd stuff his extra shirt and pants and his road atlas in his knapsack, get on his motorcycle, and move on down the road. But he wasn't sure he was itching to leave Hollyhill. He was just itching to be out of the middle of Grand Central Station in Brookeville. A man needed some time to be alone. A man needed some time to think.

Then again it could be all the time he'd had to think in

the middle of the night that was causing the itch. That and the Bible reading. He'd been doing a lot of Bible reading since the tornado had blown through his life. Sometimes he felt like a tornado was blowing through his soul when he picked up the Bible and started reading wherever the pages fell open. At first he'd read the Bible at the hospital because that was the only book there. Some Gideon had put it there, according to the front cover.

It wasn't that he hadn't ever read the Bible before. He'd been faithful in Sunday school as a little tyke, and Rosa had set great store by church while they'd been married. At one time Rosa thought their boy might even end up a preacher. For all Wes knew, the boy could have done it. He might be leading revivals all over.

Fate or the Lord or Mr. Jupiter, whoever it was who pushed the buttons that made things happen, had a funny sense of humor anyway. Here Wes was sleeping in the living room of a preacher whose daughter was wanting to call him Granddaddy. Jo was the reason that no matter how strong the itch got he wouldn't leave Hollyhill. If he left Jo behind, he might as well just ride his motorcycle off a cliff somewhere and face whatever eternal reward was waiting for him.

He hadn't spent a lot of time thinking about eternal rewards until the last few weeks. A man could sort of ignore the inevitable even when he knew how fast the inevitable could happen, the way it had with Rosa and Lydia. One afternoon they'd been on the beach in the full of the sunshine of life, and the next day, gone. Wes had done a lot of going since then, running away from even the memory of love until he'd gotten to Hollyhill and Jo had needed him. Or maybe it was him who had needed her.

Wes lay still and held his breath to see if he could hear

any movement out on the porch where Jo was sleeping. Another reason he needed to move on out of here. It would be too cold for her to sleep out there once winter came. She'd need his spot in the living room. The Brooke house was running over at the top with people. And who knew? What with the way the man had been humming when he got up in the mornings lately, David might be thinking about moving in another female. Wes was pretty sure David's song of choice hadn't been out of a hymnal the morning before. It had sounded suspiciously like an Elvis number, "Love Me Tender."

Wes didn't hear a thing from out on the porch. Jo didn't have the excitement of school to pull her out of bed early. She'd done all right at high school just the way he'd known she would even without the curly hair. She'd been typical Jo and jumped right in the middle of everything. The first day of school she had come home and sat on the porch with Wes, talking nonstop until Lovella made her help put supper on the table.

Jo was going to be okay. She was almost fourteen and she knew how to find answers to her questions. She'd be okay even if he wasn't. Some days he thought he might hobble on through the valley he was in and come out okay on the other side. Other days the black of the valley closed in around him until he lost even the glimmer of hope of finding his way out.

He wished the sun would hurry up and get close enough to the eastern horizon to put some light in the day. He wanted to find that chapter in Philippians that he'd read the day before. He couldn't remember all of it, but one verse stuck in his head. *I can do all things through Christ which strengtheneth me*. But that was Paul writing. And Paul was a man who knew what the Lord wanted from him. And why wouldn't he? The Lord had literally knocked him down and told him what that was. Wes wasn't hardly ready to put himself anywhere close to being in the same category as Paul. Even if there was another spot in the Bible someplace where Paul had said he was the chief of sinners. If old Paul was the chief, Wes wasn't sure where that might leave him.

Still it had seemed like a sign when the Bible had fallen open to that "strengthening" verse twice in a row. Especially since Wes had been giving a lot of consideration to whether he had the strength to make it up the stairs back to his apartment. He was hoping he wouldn't feel quite so old and helpless if he was living on his own again.

And there was another reason. He wanted to see if this drawing he was feeling toward the Bible was just rubbing off on him from David and Lovella and Jo. Maybe he'd forget all about Bible reading and go back to reading his science fiction or mysteries again. Maybe back in his old apartment he'd be able to lean on his own strength again.

He was sort of hoping he could, because he didn't know what he was going to do if he kept feeling the Lord hanging out around his heart. He hadn't been in a church building since Rosa and Lydia died. Swore he'd never go in one again after their funeral. He'd held them dying in the wreck against the Lord, as if the Lord had been driving instead of Wes. But living here, with David being so good to him and Lovella talking Bible verses with him and Tabitha letting him share in the wonder of her baby and Jo loving him so pure and simple, Wes could feel his heart softening. Twice already he'd thought about asking David to say that special prayer he sometimes talked about praying with people. The one where a man asked the Lord to save him. The one that David said the Lord always answered. The one that would change a man's life forevermore.

But could Wes change? And if he did, what would people, what would the Lord, expect him to do next? Would he have to walk down a church aisle and look a bunch of church people in the eye and confess to his need for the Lord?

Maybe it would be better to just hole up in his apartment and never admit he felt a thing. Sometimes it was as if there was a war going on inside his heart. One he had no control over. One he had no idea who was going to win.

22

When David came down the stairs as the sun was beginning to push fingers of light over the horizon, Wes was in his chair, already dressed and sipping coffee with a couple of books in his lap, but he wasn't reading. "Don't you ever sleep?" David asked. "And where did the coffee come from? Is Jocie up already?"

"Ain't heard a peep out of her. Don't think she's even put the dog out yet. As for the coffee"—Wes lifted up his cup toward David—"I ain't totally helpless. There's a whole pot if you want to get a cup and join me. That is, if you ain't on the way to walk with the girl."

David looked toward the door. He hadn't walked with Leigh for days. He'd wanted to, but he had to take Jocie to school. It was part of their father-daughter routine. He always dropped her off at school before he went to the newspaper office. He couldn't just suddenly tell her she'd have to start riding the school bus. She might think he was deserting her. She might think it had something to do with what had happened in July. She was already carrying around enough worry about that with feeling so to blame for Wes getting hurt. David didn't want to add any more worry and certainly not even the shadow of doubt about how much he loved her.

But today was Saturday. David could go. It was still early. The sun was just peeking over the horizon. Maybe he could even work up the nerve to ask Leigh out to dinner. She'd told him the day before when he went by the courthouse that she was going to visit her parents that afternoon, so maybe he could meet her somewhere in Grundy. Someplace where they had candles on the tables. Then he tried to remember how much money he had in his pocket. Probably not enough for a restaurant that keeps candles on the tables.

David looked back at Wes. The shadows under the man's eyes were getting darker. The skin was just hanging off his bones. The man was fading away in front of David's eyes. His friend was hurting and not just because of his broken leg. This went deeper. Some kind of soul sickness. The doctor in Lexington called it depression when David had called to see if there was anything he could do for Wes. Dr. Curtis had offered medication but said Wes had turned the pills down while he was still in the hospital.

"I'll see if he's changed his mind," David had told the doctor. "But I doubt it. We can't even get him to take an aspirin when the pain starts thumping in his leg."

"He did seem set against taking any kind of pills," the doctor agreed. "Failing medication, you can try to get him to talk it out. Is he eating all right? Sleeping okay?"

"Not eating much or sleeping well."

"Classic symptoms," Dr. Curtis said. "He isn't suicidal, is he?"

"Suicidal?" David hadn't even thought about that, although he knew what depression could do. He'd preached funerals of people who had put a gun to their head rather than face another day. But Wes wouldn't do something like that. Not as long as Jocie was around. "No, I don't think so."

"Then patience might be your best avenue. Most people

weather these storms, and when Mr. Green is once again able to do some of the things he could do before he was hurt, he'll most likely move away from his depression. Still, it might be best if you kept a close eye on him. Not every person who thinks about suicide talks about it."

So now David smiled at Wes and said, "Sure, coffee sounds great."

"It's extra strong," Wes said.

"Of course it is, if you made it. You need a refill?"

Wes held out his cup. "I could use it. I couldn't carry it but half full."

David looked at the cup, then at the crutches lying by the chair. "How did you carry it at all?"

Wes clamped his teeth on the handle of the cup and held his head sideways as he demonstrated. He took the cup out of his mouth and said, "I had to move pretty slow to keep from sloshing it out."

"Did you ever consider you might be too addicted to coffee?" David said with a laugh as he took the cup and went out to the kitchen.

When he came back and handed Wes his filled cup, Wes said, "Better coffee addictions than some others."

"That's for sure. But speaking of that, I talked to Dr. Curtis the other day."

Wes took a sip of his coffee before he asked, "How come?"

"I could say it was to do with you going back to get the rods out of your cast, but that wouldn't be entirely true." David looked straight at Wes. "We need to do that next week, but that wasn't why I called."

"I told you I wasn't going back over to that hospital. Dr. Markum can take the cast off here."

"If you haven't already trimmed it off yourself, right?"

David looked down at the floor and was relieved when he didn't see any plaster dust there.

"I haven't been whittling on it since I told you I'd wait a spell."

"Dr. Markum can't do the rods. You'll have to go back to Lexington for that, Wes. After that, he said he could handle it from here. It'll just be one more time to the hospital."

"One more time until the next time. Them city doctors like to bleed a man dry." Wes took another drink of coffee. "So why did you call him, David?"

"I was worried about you, Wes." He kept his eyes on Wes's face. "I am worried about you."

Wes just looked at him for a moment before he said, "I appreciate all you've done for me, David. I really do, but I ain't a child. I'm a grown man, and you don't have to take me on as a new responsibility. You've got enough of those as it is."

"You're not a responsibility. You're my friend, and I can't just sit here and watch you sinking so low without trying to help."

"No, I guess not. So what did the good doctor say? Slip pills in my coffee?"

"I wouldn't do that," David said. "Although he did say he could prescribe some pills if you wanted them."

"Nerve pills. He said something about them before, but he couldn't give me no guarantee that they wouldn't just make me crazier."

"You're not crazy. You're just feeling down because of being hurt."

"I do feel down," Wes admitted. "Sometimes down for the count."

"And you're not eating or sleeping."

"I eat some and sleep some."

"But not much. Not enough." David searched for the right words to say. Words that would help Wes walk out of the dark valley he was in. He wasn't sure the words that came to his mind were the right ones, but he said them anyway. "I've been praying for you."

"I know you have, David. You and Jo and Lovella. I feel hedged in with prayers here," Wes said, but he didn't look upset.

"The Lord sometimes hedges us in with blessings."

Wes stared down at his coffee cup. "He took the blessing hedge away from Job."

"He did," David admitted.

"If he'd do that to a good man like Job, what might he do to a man like me?" Wes looked up at David. "So maybe it's better to stay outside the hedge in the first place."

"I don't think so," David said. "I always want to be inside the hedge of the Lord's love and mercy, and I'll try to be like Job and trust him in the face of whatever happens."

"But I ain't sure I've got that much trust, David."

"Maybe you need to start with just enough trust to trust what you're feeling and stop fighting against it."

"You could be right, but I want to be sure it's me doing the trusting and not just me leaning on the trust that echoes in this house. Doesn't it have to be my own doing and not just what somebody else wants?"

"It does. I can pray for you, but somewhere, sometime, you'll have to take that prayer over and make it yours."

"That's what I thought." Wes looked back down at his coffee again.

David waited a minute hoping Wes would say more, but when he didn't, David asked, "Do you want to take the prayer over?"

Wes mashed his mouth together and then after a moment, sighed. "Not yet, David. I think I need to get out of here, out of the hedge of your caring for me, so that I can make sure it's me doing the praying for me and not me only pretending to pray to please you and Jo. You see what I'm saying?"

"I think so, Wes, but there's one thing you have to realize. You can never get out of the hedge of our love for you. Whatever you do, whatever happens, you're part of our family now. You always will be. If you decide to join the family of God, we'd celebrate your decision with you."

"I don't think I could walk down a church aisle."

"Once you say the prayer and mean it, the Lord will give you strength to do whatever needs to be done."

"'For I can do all things through Christ which strengtheneth me.'"

"Paul in his letter to the Philippians," David said with a nod.

"I've been thinking maybe I've been getting strengthened up enough to make it up the steps to my apartment. I think it's time." Wes smiled a little at David. "Now that I can make my own coffee."

"You need more than coffee," David said.

"Wieners aren't hard to cook. I can get me a hook and hang a bucket on my crutches to carry things in. And Jo can run errands for me. She needs to work off some of her guilt anyhow."

David looked at Wes and didn't know what to say. He was afraid to let Wes go back to the apartment, afraid he'd sink too low to remember the hedge of their love back here at the house. "How about you wait until we get the rods out of your cast? Or even better, until after Jocie's birthday. She's been looking forward to you being here to watch her blow out her candles. That's not but a couple of weeks away."

"You can bring me back for that."

David thought fast. "Tell you what. Let's make a couple of trial runs. I've been thinking about seeing if you'd go to the office with me sometime to look at the press. It was doing some mighty creaking last Tuesday."

Wes sat up a little straighter and said, "Did you oil it like I told you to?"

"I did, but it's still creaking. I think it's a one-man press. It needs you to look at it."

Wes smiled. "Well, I guess I could ride along if you think I can get in the car."

"You'll fit with no problem. Everything about you has shrunk since you came home."

"Then I guess we could try it this morning. If you're sure I won't be getting in Cupid's way and keeping you away from walking with your girl."

"I'm not sure we can call her *my* girl yet."

"If you don't mind, she won't mind," Wes said. "You can lay money on that."

"I think you probably need to have at least one date before you can claim couple status." David stared down at the coffee in his cup and tried to think of a way to change the subject.

"Some people just get blown right through the dating stage to something else."

"That might be a good way to describe me and Leigh. Something else." David looked up at Wes and laughed.

Wes smiled back as he said, "Why don't you ask her out tonight?"

"When would I study my sermon?"

"Leigh would probably let you practice on her. And I'm betting you already have it all blocked out anyway. What are you preaching on? Love for your neighbor? No matter what color they happen to be?"

"I've been thinking on it, but how'd you guess?"

"Your editorial in this week's *Banner*. You was preaching some in it."

"You think so? I was trying not to, but sometimes it's hard not to preach a little when you see things going bad." David took a sip of his coffee. It was cold.

"Are things going bad in Hollyhill?"

"I don't know, Wes. Things seem peaceful enough. Mrs. Hearndon's been back to church once with her children and a few more people didn't bother moving to the other side of the church. Jocie said there weren't any fights at the high school, and the little kids don't seem to even notice anything's different at the elementary school. And we've only gotten a couple of letters complaining about me putting the article about Mrs. Rowlett being the best teacher in the county on the front page. At least one of the best."

"So what's bothering you, David?"

"I don't know. Maybe I'm just worried it's the calm before the storm."

"There don't have to be a storm. Maybe it's just time for Hollyhill to give up its old ways and move into the twentieth century since we're done past halfway to the next one. Skin color shouldn't make a difference in where a person goes to school. Or buys a farm."

"It's the farm that has me a little worried. I think the schools being desegregated isn't going to be a problem. But the Hearndons, that's a different matter."

"Why's that?" Wes asked.

"Harvey McMurtry, you know he's the one who sold them the place. Anyway, he says he's been hearing rumors about the Klan getting active around here."

"That ain't good news." Wes frowned and shook his head a little as he looked at David. "I got invited to a Klan meeting, conclave, whatever they call it, once."

"Really?" David was surprised.

"I was down in Mississippi and I guess the fellow I was working for thought I looked like a good old boy. I was curious so I went."

"What happened?"

"I didn't stay long enough to find out. Five minutes was all it took for me to know I was in the wrong place. I waited till nobody was paying me any attention. Then I slipped away, got on my motorcycle, and didn't stop till I was a couple of hundred miles away."

"What did they do?"

"I don't know that it was what they did, but more what they became when they all got together and put on their pointy hats. It was like they sort of joined together and became some kind of monster with a hundred heads." Wes shivered a little at the thought. "One thing sure, they had a mighty attraction to fire. Had this huge bonfire that looked like it might have burned down the whole state if the wind had got up."

"I can't see that kind of thing happening in Holly County," David said, but even as he said it he thought it was more hope speaking than sureness. "Our people wouldn't do that kind of thing."

"People can surprise you. Those people down there surprised me. Of course it wasn't all local folks. The guy I worked for said men came in from all over the state when they had those meetings or whatever they were."

"But did they do anything besides talk?" David asked.

"Beats me. I didn't stay around long enough to hear the talk. I might have done some foolish things in my life, but

I ain't no fool. I took one look around and got a real bad feeling that maybe my invitation didn't have a thing to do with me joining the club and a lot more to do with me being a beatnik on a motorcycle and somebody they might be wanting to practice their hate on."

David looked down at his coffee as if he might see the future in its dark liquid. "That's a kind of hate we don't need in Holly County. I'm praying what Mr. Harvey heard was just rumors and nothing more."

"Well, that's a prayer I can join in with you without a problem," Wes said. "Not that the good Lord above has any reason to listen to me the way he does you."

"He listens," David said. "He hears every prayer."

"Then maybe your sermons both in the *Banner* and the pulpit will do the trick."

"We can only hope so. And pray so."

23

It wasn't so hard getting Wes in the car this time. Not only had the cast shrunk thanks to the whittling he'd been doing on it, but Wes had shrunk himself. The foot of his cast was still jammed against the car door, but Wes didn't appear to be in as much discomfort as he had been on the ride home from the hospital. Once the car door was shut and the engine started, it was only a five-minute ride to the newspaper office. Wes assured David a man could stand anything that long.

Jocie had begged to go with them, but Aunt Love wouldn't let her. Said it was too good an opportunity to do some cleaning without having to worry about disturbing Wes.

"It's too hot to clean," Jocie had protested.

"It's not one bit hotter here than it will be at the newspaper office," Aunt Love said. "And houses need cleaning whether it's hot or cold."

"I can clean tomorrow while Wes sits out on the porch."

"Tomorrow's Sunday," Aunt Love reminded her.

Jocie looked ready to cry. "Please, can't I do it next week?"

"Never put off till tomorrow what can be done today," Aunt Love insisted.

"That's not in the Bible, is it?" Jocie said, looking at David.

David had wanted to let her come with them, but he

couldn't go against Aunt Love. "Maybe not in those exact words," he said. "But Aunt Love is right that we shouldn't put off our chores. After you do what Aunt Love wants, you can ride your bike to town."

"But it takes forever to clean. I'll probably have to dust and everything, and then who knows if I can even get my bike tires to stay pumped up long enough to get to town."

David had helped Jocie bend her bike wheel back out after her wreck with Noah and patch the tubes again, but the old bike was still in bad shape. "Well, give it a try. It'll probably make it to town one more time, and then we'll see about those new tubes soon."

"You've been saying that for a month," Jocie said.

"I know. I'm sorry." David kept putting off buying the tubes because there was a brand-new bike hidden in the back of Sanders Hardware Store just waiting for Jocie's birthday to get here. Leigh had come up with the idea after she'd taken Jocie shopping for school clothes over in Grundy and had caught her admiring the new bikes in the Sears Roebuck store. So Leigh had gotten some people to pool their money to buy Jocie a bike. Zella had even pitched in a couple of dollars, and Miss Sally at church had slipped David five dollars to give toward the surprise birthday gift.

David was almost to the cemetery on the edge of town when Wes said, "Why don't we take a little tour of the town?"

"You want to ride around Hollyhill?"

"Why not? My leg's not hurting over much, and it might be good to see what's been going on besides everybody's grass turning brown."

"It is dry."

"Even out at the park? Maybe that's where we should start the tour."

"The park? What in the world are you up to, Wes?" David looked at Wes in his rearview mirror.

"Well, the truth is, David, I'm feeling some guilty keeping you from maybe getting to walk with the girl this morning. It's not so late now, and she might not have gone so early seeing as how it's Saturday. We could just buzz through there and see if maybe she's hanging around waiting for you to show."

"She won't be there this late. It's already almost nine and getting too hot to walk."

"You could be right, but it won't take but a couple of minutes to drive out that way to see."

"Are you joining in on this matchmaking stuff?"

"Not me," Wes said. "I just hate for the girl to be disappointed if she's out there walking slow, waiting for you to show up. I feel like I owe her something for the times she came to see me in the hospital. She brought cookies a couple of times, you know."

"I know, and I also know I'm too old for her," David said even as he turned onto Broadway to go out to the park instead of heading down Main.

"Age is all in your head. Me, I'm too old for her. You, you just feel old 'cause you're about to be a granddaddy, but forty whatever you are ain't all that old. You could start in and have a whole new family."

"Are you trying to make me have a heart attack? I've got more family than I can handle now."

"Didn't you say the Lord would give you strength for whatever he wanted you to do?"

"Now you've got the Lord matchmaking?" David glanced up at Wes in the rearview mirror again.

Wes was smiling. "There's folks that say some matches are made in heaven."

"You must have been reading some of Zella's books."

"Most all books have a little romance in them. Even the Bible."

"Okay. Just remember I'm only doing this to humor you," David said as he turned in to the park. "Besides, some softball team will probably be out there practicing this morning to beat the heat."

"Naw. They'll be playing this afternoon. They don't care if it's hot, but if you're needing an excuse for cruising the park, you can set your camera up on the dashboard and act like you're out here to take some pictures."

"Or I can just say I had to humor a crazy old man in my backseat."

"Wouldn't bother me none," Wes said. "You can print it in the paper if you want. Won't be no kind of news flash or anything. The folks around here have thought I was crazy ever since I showed up in Hollyhill."

David drove past the swimming pool where Missy Hawkins, the lifeguard, was dipping bugs out of the water to get ready for the onslaught of swimmers at noon. On around the gravel road, the baseball field was deserted. No ballplayers. Nobody walking around its edges for exercise.

"Nobody here," David said.

"You sure?" Wes raised up and peered over the seat out the windshield. "Well, looky there. I think I see somebody over there on the bleachers. Looks to me like maybe whoever it is might be just sitting there waiting for somebody to show up and offer her a ride home."

ꟹ ꟹ

Leigh could hardly believe it when she saw the car raising dust on the road back to the ball field. She'd told herself she was just resting a little while in the shade before she walked on back to her apartment and started getting ready to go visit her parents. She'd told herself she needed a few minutes of quiet out where the birds were singing to put her in a better mood before she had to go listen to her mother telling her how she was doing everything wrong. Especially how foolish she was to be making eyes at a preacher. But what she'd really been doing was sitting there wishing that preacher had come to walk with her. She'd been almost positive David would show up here at the park this morning.

He had hinted he might the day before when he'd stopped by the courthouse. He hadn't said he would. She hadn't asked him if he would, but there was some kind of unspoken promise between them. And then he hadn't.

She'd walked three extra turns around the field until the sun had gotten higher in the sky and hotter. The heat was merciless now. The night before she'd put a bowl of ice on a tray in front of the fan to try to cool off her apartment enough that she could sleep. And this morning the grass out in the outfield was extra crisp under her feet. Every time she passed home plate she said a little prayer. "Please, Lord, send us some rain, and bless David wherever he is."

She'd wanted to pray, *Let David come to the park today*, but she hadn't. That didn't seem to be a proper prayer. *Bless David. Be with David. Thank you for David.* Those sounded okay and she'd been praying them for months. But she felt uncomfortable asking for David to love her. Maybe her mother was right and she shouldn't be chasing after a preacher. Maybe it was unseemly. It had surely been unseemly the way she had demanded David kiss her that morning last week. He'd come out to the park to walk with her a few times since then before he had to start taking Jocie to school every day, but there had never been the first sign that he might be thinking about kissing her again.

At least he did still seem to want to talk to her. He came by the courthouse every day. Sometimes twice a day. She hadn't gone by the newspaper office to see him. Mostly because Zella was about to drive Leigh crazy wanting to know every detail of what was happening between David and her. And some things a person didn't necessarily want to tell. Some things a girl just had to hold close to her heart and savor. And she had all week long, and then this morning when she'd been so sure David would come walk with her, he hadn't. The doubts began to seep in.

Maybe David thought she was unseemly. Ungainly. Too fat. Ugly. Pushy. Maybe he'd noticed how she sometimes snorted when she laughed. Leigh had always hated doing that, but sometimes a snort just came out right in the middle of a laugh. The only way she knew to stop it was to not laugh, and that seemed a little severe. She liked to laugh. But sitting there on the old wooden stands with splinters poking into her legs, she felt more like crying than laughing. Until she saw the dust following the car up the road to the ball field.

She stood up and then sat back down. Should she climb down and go meet David as if he'd come calling at her house? Or should she stay where she was and wait for him to come up to her? Why did she have to worry about every move she made? Why couldn't she just do what felt right?

She knew the answer to that. If she did what she wanted to, she'd climb off the bleachers, run to meet David, and throw her arms around him. But she remembered the worry about being unseemly and held herself back. David had told her straight out that she wouldn't have to ask for a kiss the next time, so she just had to force herself to wait.

David pulled the car up right beside the bleachers, opened the door, and got out. The dust cloud the car had raised drifted up and over the field and the bleachers. Through it, Leigh could see Wes in the backseat of the car. Leigh forgot about being coy and climbed down off the bleachers as fast as she could. When she got to the ground, David was there waiting.

"Is something wrong with Wes?" she asked, looking past David toward the car. Wes stuck his hand out the open window to wave at her.

"You mean besides the usual mashed leg and Jupiter stubbornness?" David smiled and didn't wait for her to answer. "No. We're just on the way to the office. I wanted him to check over the press."

"Oh, good. I was scared something was wrong. I mean, I don't know why you'd be coming out here to the park if something was wrong." Leigh looked at David. "I guess I might not know why you'd be coming out here to the park anyway. It's not exactly on the way to the newspaper office."

"Wes insisted."

"Oh," Leigh said. "And why did he do that?"

"He thought you might still be here walking."

"Was he planning to walk with me or something?"

"More like 'or something.' He's playing Cupid."

Leigh could feel her cheeks going red, but it was so hot, David might think she was flushed from the heat. "So, you're only here because Wes wanted you to come?"

David reached over and laid his hand on Leigh's cheek. He dropped his voice to where only she could hear. "No, that's not right at all. I wasn't here earlier because Wes needed me to have coffee with him. I'm worried about him. You'll understand when you see him. But Wes, he must read minds or something, and he knew he'd kept me away from seeing you so he insisted we come. He said you might be waiting for me."

Leigh put her hand over David's on her cheek. She could feel her heart beating. His touch was almost as good as a kiss. "I guess he can read minds long distance too."

"I'm glad you were still here," David said. "I was thinking. Maybe we could go out and get something to eat tonight."

Leigh's heart did a somersault. "That would be great."

"I could drive over to Grundy and meet you somewhere or come by your parents' house if that would be better."

"No, no. I'll be back in Hollyhill by then," Leigh said quickly. She still needed time to convince her mother that David was the perfect man for her. She didn't want her mother's disapproval to put a damper on this first date. A real "he asked me out" date and not something she'd just pushed him into doing.

"There aren't many restaurants in Hollyhill," David said.

Leigh heard reservation in his voice. "Are you worried about people seeing us together here in town?"

David smiled. "No. I just wanted to take you somewhere nice. Zella says I need candles on the table."

"Zella reads too many books. Anywhere would be fine with me. The Grill. Hillside Drive-in. Peanut butter sandwiches at the *Banner*." Leigh stopped talking and made a face. "Gee, I probably sound too eager."

David laughed. "You sound just perfect. Makes an old man like me feel good, but we can probably do better than peanut butter at the office. Let me think on it today and surprise you."

"I like surprises," Leigh said. "Good surprises anyway."

Then David surprised both of them by pulling her close to him in a hug and kissing her quickly on the lips. It was a good thing he offered her a ride home after that. Her legs were way too weak to do much walking.

24

Jocie dusted and swept as fast as she could, but it was still nearly noon before she pumped up her bike tires and headed for the *Banner* office. As she pedaled down the road, she kept an eye out for her father. She wouldn't have been surprised to meet him and Wes on the way home. She pedaled faster and prayed the chain on her bike wouldn't slip off.

It just wasn't fair. She was supposed to be there at the office when Wes went back to work. She could have done the dusting any time, or Tabitha could have surely dusted this one time. But Aunt Love never asked Tabitha to do anything. It was as if expecting a baby was a full-time, all-consuming job. Actually Tabitha had looked too miserable to dust or anything else that morning. She'd sit awhile and then get up and walk around the room.

"How much longer do you have to go?" Jocie had asked her on one of her trips through the living room to the bathroom.

"Four, five weeks. Way too long."

"A month isn't all that long," Jocie said, trying to help.

"It's forever. I feel like a bloated hippopotamus." Tabitha sent Jocie a mean look. "And don't you dare say I look like one too."

"I wasn't even thinking it." Jocie held up her hands and

waved the dust rag like a white flag. "You want me to get you some ice water?"

To Jocie's horror, Tabitha broke out in tears.

"What's the matter with you, Tabitha? Is something hurting extra bad?"

"I'm all right," Tabitha said between sobs.

"You don't sound all right," Jocie said. "Should we call the doctor?"

Aunt Love came in from the kitchen. "She's okay, child. Sometimes an expectant mother just gets a little teary." She pulled a handkerchief out of some secret pocket on her dress and handed it to Tabitha.

"Is she going to cry like this till the baby comes?"

"Probably not every day." Aunt Love put her arm around Tabitha and steered her on toward the bathroom.

By the time Jocie had finished dusting, Tabitha had mopped up the tears and was taking a nap while Aunt Love rocked on the front porch and counted stitches in her latest baby blanket. The baby wouldn't need a blanket if things didn't cool off before she was born.

The sun was relentless as it beat down on Jocie, sucking up every drop of moisture and melting the blacktop under her tires. The Sawyers' dog, Butch, just raised his head and watched her ride by from his place on the shady front porch. "Smart dog," Jocie said through lips so dry they were beginning to stick together.

Jocie was relieved to see her father's car still parked in the back of the building when she got there. "Hey, everybody, where are you?" she called as she went in the back door.

"Just the girl I wanted to see," Wes said. "Come on over here and hold this screwdriver for me."

Jocie went over to where Wes was peering down into the press. She took the screwdriver while Wes scooted his crutches up closer to the press. He looked pale, but happier than she'd seen him for a while. "You want me to tighten some screws or something?"

"Naw. I was just poking around on her some to see what she might be needing, but I think she's fine." He patted the side of the press. "I sort of missed old Betsy Lou here."

"I didn't know you'd given the press a name."

"I just thought it up right now," Wes said.

"How do you know it's a girl?" Jocie asked.

"Because she's always squeaking and complaining."

"Hey, that's not a nice thing to say." Jocie laughed and gave his arm a little poke before she looked around. "Where's Dad?"

"He went to get us a soda pop down at the A&P Store. And he said he might stop and ask Harry Saunders and some others about Sidewalk Days next weekend. Maybe take a couple of pictures." Wes leaned his shoulder against the press. "I told him I'd be fine here by myself."

"You look a little pale," Jocie said. "Maybe you should sit down awhile."

"Could be you're right. Get me that chair over there. Then after we rest a minute I might see if I can make it up the stairs."

"I'm not sure that would be a good idea," Jocie said as she helped Wes sit down in the chair. "What if you lost your balance or something?"

"When did you turn into such a worrywart?" Wes laid his crutches down on the floor beside him.

"I don't know. Maybe since a tree fell on you."

"Well, it's time you got over it and quit what-iffing everything. Look for what-if smashers instead. Say if I lost my balance, I'd just grab hold of you."

"Then we'd both fall."

"Naw. You'd have Jupiter strength and save the day. Failing that, if I thought I was going to get top heavy, I'd sit down on the steps and scoot up on my backside." Wes lifted his leg and propped his cast up on a box. He took a deep breath. "Ahh. It's good to be home."

"Don't you like being home with us?"

"No, I like visiting you."

"But you don't even have a telephone up there to call somebody if you needed something." As Wes peered over at her, she added, "I mean, I might think that might be a problem if I was a worrywart."

"Then it's a good thing you aren't one of them things 'cause I ain't getting no telephone, but no need worry-warting about that now. I promised your daddy I'd stay at Brooke Central Station till after I go to the doctor. Besides, I got more interesting news."

"News?"

"Breaking news on the romance front."

"Have you been talking to Zella?"

"No, I've been witnessing progress."

"Between Dad and Leigh?" Jocie asked.

"That's the romance I'm talking about. Your daddy has asked her to supper."

"Not some kind of church supper? He asked her out on a real date?"

"No church anything. He not only asked her out, he gave her a kiss when she said she'd go."

"How do you know all this?" Jocie frowned a little, not sure she should believe him.

"I was there. Witnessed it all firsthand." Wes raised his right hand up as if swearing himself in to tell the truth.

"That's scary," Jocie said.

"Scary? Why scary?"

"I don't know. It just is. My dad kissing a girl right out in front of somebody."

"Well, I was pretending to be snoozing, but a Jupiterian can see right through his eyelids. A handy trick sometimes."

Jocie laughed. It was so good having Wes acting like his old self. And while she couldn't quite imagine her father kissing Leigh, it didn't bother her that he had. "Don't tell Zella. She'd never get over you knowing about the first kiss before she did."

"I ain't got no way of knowing if it's the first kiss. It's just the first one I saw."

"The first what you saw?" Jocie's father asked as he came back in the pressroom with a carton of soft drinks.

"Newspaper press," Wes said and winked at Jocie. "I never had nothing to do with a newspaper press till I came to Hollyhill. Of course I'd tinkered around with lots of other machines like spaceships and motorcycles."

"A newspaper press is probably a piece of cake after spaceships," Jocie's father said as he flipped off the tops of a couple of the soft drinks with the bottle opener and handed them to Wes and Jocie. "You think you've got the thing so it'll make the run Tuesday?"

"Shh! Don't be calling Betsy Lou a thing," Wes said.

"Betsy Lou?"

"Wes named the press. Betsy Lou. It kind of fits," Jocie told her father.

"I don't care what it's called as long as it spits out papers."

"She will," Wes said. "She'll be ready to roll come Tuesday."

"Why don't you come back then too, Wes?" Jocie said.

"You can boss me and Noah around. Make us work faster."

"Be okay with me if I just stayed here till then," Wes said.

"After the doctor. I thought we agreed," Jocie's father said.

"Yeah, but I think I can get up there to my place today to give it a lookover."

It wasn't easy, but Wes made it up the stairs on his crutches. He was sweating and out of breath at the top, but still on one foot. He hadn't had to sit down and scoot up. Jocie unlocked the door and opened it up. "It feels like an oven in here," she said as they stepped inside.

"It feels like an oven outside," Wes said.

"Maybe, but it's still hotter in here. After you go to the doctor, I'll come up and air it out and clean up a little for you," Jocie said.

"I thought you hated to sweep and dust," Wes said.

"I do, but I'm still good at it. I've had lots of practice."

"And she won't mind doing it for you," Jocie's father said. "When you're able to come home. In fact, it looks like maybe she's already started." He picked up a broom sitting next to the door.

"That looks like the old broom out of the pressroom, but I didn't bring it up here," Jocie said. "All I've done is come get books and clothes. Besides, you've got a broom somewhere up here already, don't you, Wes?"

"In the closet over there," Wes said. "Don't use it much, but it's there."

Jocie's dad held the broom up. "Well, that's a mystery then. Maybe Zella came up here to clean up the place as a surprise."

"Zell? Up here?" Wes said. "That wouldn't be a surprise. That would be a catastrophe."

"And I don't think whoever brought it up here used it. Look at this cobweb," Jocie said as she took a swipe at a spiderweb hanging down from the light.

"As I said, a mystery. Whoever heard of anybody breaking into a place just to leave a broom?" Jocie's dad said.

"You think we should take a picture and run the story in the *Banner*?" Wes said. "Come on, Jo. Think up a headline."

"'Broom thief strikes again.'"

"Again? I didn't know he struck the first time, and he didn't steal a broom. He left a broom," Wes said.

"Okay. How about 'Witch from Jupiter flies in. Forgets broom,'" Jocie said.

"So how did the old hag fly out? You're gonna have to come up with something better than that," Wes said.

"Maybe she's still hiding in here waiting to jump out at you when you move back in," Jocie said.

"Now that could be," Wes said. "But is it newsworthy?"

"It might make the paper on Halloween." Jocie's dad laughed. "But I don't think news is that slow this week. We may just keep the broom mystery out of the *Banner*."

25

As she drove to Grundy, Leigh decided not to tell her mother anything about her date. At least not until later, maybe next week when she talked to her on the phone. It would just be easier that way. Leigh wouldn't have to defend her attraction to David, and her mother wouldn't have to strain her brain thinking up reasons Leigh shouldn't be attracted to him.

The first ten minutes of the visit went okay. Her mother met her at the door with a hug and a smile, in spite of the fact that Leigh was a half hour late for lunch. Her father was even still there. Leigh wasn't sure whether he had put off his golf game to see her or to get in on the food. Her mother had fixed her special chicken salad with pecans and celery and grapes on homemade bread with Leigh's favorite brand of potato chips and banana pudding for dessert. Her father tolerated Leigh's hug for a couple of seconds before he pulled free and said, "Let's dig in."

Leigh sat down at her usual spot at the table and looked at the potato chips with dismay. She'd told her mother she was trying to quit eating potato chips, but that was hard to do when the chips were staring her in the face. But she wasn't at one of the Mt. Pleasant Church women's houses. She could ignore the way her mouth could almost taste the salty chips and just eat the chicken salad.

She took a piece of bread and then looked up at her father.

"Have you been feeling better this week, Dad? Mother said you weren't feeling well last week."

She couldn't see anything different about him. His hair might be a little thinner on top since the last time she'd really looked at him. His tan scalp was peeking through his gray hair. And his nose had been sunburned one time too often this summer. But other than that, he looked the picture of health for a man in his sixties. There was obviously no problem with his appetite the way he was putting together a six-inch-thick sandwich.

Actually, it was her mother who didn't look all that well. Her face was red, and she was panting a little just from the short walk through the house to the kitchen. The summer heat had always been hard on her. Leigh took a quick look at her mother's ankles as her mother sat down and scooted her chair up to the table. They were puffed up and lapping over on the edges of her shoes. That made Leigh feel what she knew would be the first of many guilt twinges. Her mother had no doubt been on her feet all morning fixing the chicken salad and banana pudding.

Her father looked at Leigh over his sandwich. "Oh, you know your mother. She makes a mountain out of every molehill. I'm fine."

"Now, Peter, I don't do any such thing. And you are not," Leigh's mother said. She looked at Leigh. "He was practically in bed all last week."

"Just a few twinges in my back. It's not like that's anything new," Leigh's father said. "You know how my back is."

"Oh," Leigh said. "Is it better now?"

"It will be after a few rounds of golf," her father said.

"Isn't it awfully hot out on the golf course?" Leigh spread some chicken salad on her bread. "This looks delicious, Mother."

"Never too hot to play golf. I'll rent a cart. And nobody ever said your mother wasn't a great cook. She just needs to learn not to eat everything she cooks."

Leigh winced and tried to think of some way to change the subject, but she wasn't quick enough. Her mother rose right to the challenge. "There you go talking about my weight again. You could eat a horse and never gain an ounce, but not everybody can be that lucky. The way you talk, you'd think I wanted to be heavy, when heaven knows I have to pay the price for it every day. A person could hope her own husband would try to be a little more understanding."

"Oh, I understand plenty. I understand that you're the one shoveling the food in," he said through a mouthful of sandwich.

Leigh's mother stared down at her plate. Leigh held in a sigh. It was the same old dance her parents had been doing for years. Any minute now her mother might break out in tears or she might go pitch her sandwich in the trash can or who knew what new scene she'd come up with since Leigh had been there last. When Leigh was younger, she had always jumped into the middle of the act with assurances to her mother of how beautiful she was in spite of the extra pounds, or by defending her mother to her father. That usually made her father turn his attack on Leigh. Now Leigh simply wanted it to be over. She tried pretending she hadn't heard either of them. "How's your golf game, Dad? Are you beating par down at the course?"

"I've cut a stroke off my score," he said. "How about you? You playing much now?"

One summer while Leigh was in high school, her father had tried to teach her how to play golf. She had been so horrible at it he'd given up on her after a few unpleasant Saturday mornings, but ever since then they had kept up the pretense that she still played. Mostly just to have something to talk about. "No. There's no golf course over in Hollyhill."

Leigh was breathing a little easier as she took a bite of her sandwich, thinking they might have scooted around the fat scene. She should have known better. Her mother was determined to play it out.

"How can you sit there and talk to your father about golf after the horrible things he just said to me?" Her mother glared at her. "Don't you care about me at all? And why aren't you eating any potato chips?"

It seemed easiest to ignore the first two questions and just answer the last one. "I told you, Mother, I'm laying off chips right now for a while."

"But I bought them especially for you. They are still your favorite brand, aren't they?"

"I appreciate that, and they do look delicious." Leigh couldn't believe her mother was making her feel guilty for not eating potato chips.

"Leave her alone, Catherine," Leigh's father said. "Maybe she's trying to lose weight."

"I have lost weight," Leigh said. Had her father not even looked at her when she came in? Everybody in Hollyhill had noticed she'd lost weight. Surely her own parents could see the difference in her.

"Well, that's good to hear. It's certainly none too soon," her father said as he took another handful of chips. "You ready to serve that banana pudding, Catherine? I've got to get out of here. The guys will think I'm not coming and tee off without me."

"Sit still, Mother. I'll get it," Leigh said as she jumped up. She dipped her father a big helping of the still warm banana pudding and sat the dessert dish in front of him. "How about you, Mother? Are you ready for dessert?"

"Dip her out about twice this much," Leigh's father said. "I'm sure she thinks she needs the extra calories."

"I work all morning cooking something special for you, and this is the thanks I get," Leigh's mother said.

Leigh had had enough. "All right, already! Do you two do this all the time, or do you just save it all for when I'm here?"

"Do what?" her father said.

"This." Leigh threw out her hands toward them in exasperation.

"Oh, don't get your drawers in a twist, Leigh. Your mother knows I'm just picking on her a little." He spooned into the pudding. "You outdid yourself, Catherine. This is delicious."

"Why, thank you, Peter," Leigh's mother said as if she'd never been the least bit upset with him.

Leigh counted slowly to ten before she carried the other two dessert dishes to the table for her and her mother.

"You didn't get much." Her mother peered at Leigh's dish as she picked up her spoon. "If you have to starve yourself to get a man to like you, then he's not worth having to begin with." She slid a heaping spoonful of pudding into her mouth.

"I'm not starving, Mother. I'm just cutting back on how much I eat. Don't you think I look better?"

"I'm sure you're not a bit worried about what I think. It's that preacher you're worried about. I hear you haven't been at the First Baptist Church for weeks."

"I haven't been missing church." Leigh looked at the clock over the stove. She'd been there forty-five minutes. It felt more like forty-five hours. How in the world had she kept her sanity living in this house for twenty-seven years? Leigh took a slow breath and reminded herself that they were her parents and she loved them. She took a bite of her dessert.

"Is he a good preacher?" her mother asked.

"Is who a good preacher?" Leigh's father asked as he finished off the last of his banana pudding and stood up.

"Leigh's boyfriend. I told you she was chasing after this preacher over there in that town where she lives now."

"A preacher, you say. Do preachers play golf?" Leigh's father almost looked interested for a minute.

"Some of them do, I'm sure," Leigh said. "But David doesn't."

"Too bad." Her father glanced at his watch. "Well, I got to get going. Good seeing you, Leigh. Don't stay away so long next time."

"I was just here last Saturday."

"Did I see you then?"

"No, you'd already left for the golf course."

"Oh, well. You catch that preacher, you bring him around and introduce us."

"Sure," Leigh said. "If you promise to behave."

"Why? Is he the extra-preachy kind? One of those preachers who thinks you've committed a cardinal sin if you miss church even one Sunday to get a good tee time at the course?"

"I don't know. The subject has never come up, Dad," Leigh said with a smile. "But you'd like him. You both would if you gave him a chance." Leigh looked at her mother.

"Don't look at me like that," her mother said after Leigh's father went out the door. "I haven't got a thing against your preacher." She paused a minute before adding, "Except, of course, that he's too old for you. And that he already has a family. Two daughters with a grandchild on the way. Not many people even consider having more family once they have a grandchild. Having more children, I mean. You just need to think about that, Leigh. Don't you remember how much you used to talk about wanting to have babies?"

"I was younger then, Mother. And David's not too old to have children if he wanted to." Leigh couldn't believe it. Here she was considering the possibility of having children with David again. Maybe it would be better if she pushed those thoughts to the back of her mind and focused on the fact that they were having their first date. Ten dates from now, or twenty, would be time enough to find out what David thought about having more children. She knew how he loved the children he had. That was enough for her right now.

"I suppose that is the sixty-four-thousand-dollar question. Does he want to? Does he even want you chasing after him? Most men would rather do the chasing."

"You're probably right, Mother." Leigh stood up and started scraping up the dishes.

Leigh would be agreeable, let her mother be right about everything for the rest of the visit. Three or four hours wasn't too long to give her mother. Her mother had given a lot to her over the years, and Leigh knew she loved her. She had just never accepted that Leigh might grow older and into a different life than the one her mother had planned for her. Still, how could Leigh be too upset about anything today with the memory of David's hug and kiss and the promise of their date in a few hours dancing through her mind? She needed to concentrate on her blessings and not the minor irritations of life. Her mother was both of those. A blessing and an irritation, but surely Leigh could let the irritations slide off her and embrace the blessing of her mother's love.

They spent the afternoon in the living room where the window air-conditioning unit her father had bought last summer kept the air nice and cool. They drank iced tea and talked about how hot it was outside and whether the heat was going to dry up all her mother's petunias. They talked about Aunt Wilma and how she spoiled her grandchildren until surely Aunt Wilma's ears were burning. Her mother caught her up on the news about the people at her church. Leigh promised to go with her mother one night if the church had a fall revival. She sidestepped promising to come for a Sunday service.

It wasn't until four o'clock, when Leigh said she'd have to leave, that her mother got her wounded look on her face again. "But I thought you'd stay till after dinner. I baked a ham last night."

"I'm sorry, Mother, but I have to go home."

"You have to, or you want to?"

Leigh reached over and took her mother's hand. "We've had a nice visit. Let's not ruin it now."

"So you want to," her mother said. "It's something to do with that preacher, isn't it? Where are you chasing him this time? Is he preaching a revival over there somewhere?"

"No, Mother. And I'm not chasing him. He asked me out." The words were out before she thought.

"You have a date?" Her mother fell back in her chair and threw her hands up in the air.

"You don't have to look so shocked, Mother." Leigh laughed. Nothing her mother could say was going to spoil the joy bubbling up inside Leigh. In about two and a half hours David was going to show up at her door, and they were going to get in his car and go somewhere. Alone together. She had a date. A real date.

"You could have told me," her mother said.

"I did tell you. Just now." Leigh leaned over and kissed her mother on the cheek. "Be happy for me, Mother."

"But I'm worried about you, Leigh. You might get hurt."

"You know, I never once climbed on the monkey bars at school because you always said I might get hurt. All the other kids looked like they were having so much fun, but I kept my feet on the ground because I might get hurt. But if I had it to do over, I would climb right up on top of those monkey bars and sit there up high and watch the world go by."

"Monkey bars? What has monkey bars got to do with you going out with this preacher?" Her mother was frowning.

"Not a thing. And everything," Leigh said with another laugh. She squeezed her mother's hand. "Thanks for lunch, Mother. And I'm going to pray you can be happy for me."

"I pray for you every day," her mother said.

"I know. And you know, I think your prayers may be getting an answer."

"I didn't pray for you to meet this preacher."

"But surely you prayed for me to be happy."

"Of course."

"Then your prayers are being answered. He's a good man, and I think I love him." Leigh gave her mother another quick hug, picked up her purse, and was out the door before her mother could catch her breath from that revelation. By Thursday, no doubt she'd have plenty to say, but that was okay. Leigh wasn't worried about Thursday. She was just enjoying the precious present.

She rolled all her car windows down before she pulled out of her parents' driveway, and let the wind blow in on her all the way home. To her apartment. To her home. To her first date ever. To David.

I think I love him. The words echoed in her mind. Then she decided she hadn't been totally truthful with her mother. She didn't think. She knew.

26

David felt like a sixteen-year-old driving toward Leigh's apartment Saturday evening with his hands so sweaty they were slipping around on the steering wheel. His heart was doing a tango inside his chest, and he didn't have the first idea what he was going to say after he climbed the stairs and knocked on her door. He felt sort of the way he did sometimes when he stood up behind the pulpit to preach. That thought surely approached sacrilege—comparing a simple date to delivering the Lord's message.

His eyes shot heavenward with a *Sorry, Lord*, but he smiled, thinking the Lord wouldn't be that offended. Some people pictured God as solemn and ever serious, but he thought God must have a fine sense of humor. How else could anyone explain the duck-billed platypus that looked like something made out of spare parts? Or that the Lord had given catfish whiskers to taste with, monkeys tails to swing through trees, and elephants noses that doubled as shower nozzles. And he made man. Surely man was the creation that kept the Lord laughing the most.

And David was no exception. He imagined the Lord looking down on him now and shaking his head with a smile. He might even be summoning the angels over to peer down with him so they could all have a laugh or two over this middle-aged man sweating over a first date. But if he was, there was love in his laughter. God was love. Man could have joy in that truth.

David had spent much of the afternoon studying that truth in 1 John as he worked on his sermon for the next day. The beginning of the third chapter said, "Behold, what manner of love the Father hath bestowed upon us, that we should be called the sons of God."

He'd read that bit of Scripture over and over to let the meaning settle in his heart. *Sons of God*. Sons and daughters of God. People of God. He didn't want his people of God, the ones at Mt. Pleasant, to divide themselves into this kind of people or that kind of people. He wanted them to see the love the Father had bestowed on each one of them. And that love was to be received and processed in one's heart and turned around and bestowed on one's neighbors. At least David thought that was the message the Lord was trying to reveal to him out of the Scriptures.

But he'd need to study more. The afternoon had been full of interruptions. First it took awhile to get Wes settled back in the living room. The man was almost too tired to pull himself out of the car when they got home, but the trip had been more than worth it. The sight and smell of the pressroom was just what Wes had needed. He came home and ate almost every bite of the tuna salad sandwich Jocie had fixed for him.

Then once Wes was resting easy and David had just settled down in front of his desk with his back to the fan to keep the wind from flipping the pages of his Bible, Tabitha showed up in his doorway. He had to take time to talk to her. The poor girl was miserable. And lonesome. He was giving her all the love he could, but she needed more. She needed a husband to love her through this, to rub her back and massage her feet and carry her drinks.

He put his hand flat on her extended belly and felt the baby moving as he prayed for both mother and child. That always made Tabitha feel better, and she was smiling when she left in search of a cooler spot to fan away the afternoon. He'd never felt the movement of his own babies in the womb. He'd been down in a submarine during the war while Adrienne had carried Tabitha, and she had refused to let him near her while she was expecting Jocie.

He shut his eyes and mentally closed the door on his dark feelings of regret. That was past and gone. Here and now he needed to concentrate on reading the Scripture and coming up with the Lord's message.

He hadn't even gotten to the end of the chapter before Jocie knocked on his door and poked her head into his room. He looked around at her with a frown.

"Sorry, Dad." She looked worried that he might yell at her or something, but she stood her ground. "I know you don't like to be disturbed while you're getting your sermon together, but Mr. McDermott is on the phone. I told him you'd call him back, but he said he really needed to talk to you. Something about Homecoming."

David sighed and marked his place in the Bible before he stood up to go downstairs to the phone. "Then I guess I'd better go talk to him."

The Homecoming service hadn't been the reason Matt McDermott had called. He'd started out with that, wanting to have a meeting to go over their plans for Homecoming Day the third Sunday in September. A former pastor was delivering the morning message. They'd lined up special music for the afternoon service, and Harvey McMurtry would be reading the history of the church the same as always. Everything was in order, and it wouldn't even matter if that was the day Tabitha's baby decided to come. The day would go just as well whether David was there or not.

He listened to Matt and agreed to a meeting after church the next day. Then he waited for the real reason for the call. Matt had hesitated for a minute before he spit it out. "I was wondering if you'd had the chance to go by and see Bob and Charlene. Charlene's mother was telling Dorothy how unhappy Charlene was, not getting to come out to church the last few weeks."

"I've been by to see them a couple of times, Matt, but I'm afraid Bob's not very interested in talking to me right now. He thinks I insulted his integrity and his faithfulness, or at least that's my best guess at what he's thinking."

"Well, I know you didn't do that, Brother David."

"Not intentionally, at any rate." David wondered how he could make their conversation as short as possible so he could get back to his sermon notes without making his head deacon feel put off. Rehashing his and Bob Jessup's misunderstanding wasn't going to help Bob forget his hurt feelings.

David held in another sigh as he said, "But I don't think I'm going to be able to talk him back into a pew at Mt. Pleasant. At least not right now. He shuts down his ears when he sees me coming. Maybe you'd have a better chance."

"I have talked to him."

"Good, then he knows you care about him." David hoped Matt would let it drop, but he didn't. It was a kind of cleansing to unload the whole story on the preacher.

"He's thinking you'd rather see the Hearndons at church than him. I told him that the Hearndons hadn't even been back but one Sunday since he's been at church, but he said it wasn't the Hearndons he was worried about."

"Then what was he worried about?" David was sorry

he'd asked that as soon as the words were out, because of course what Bob Jessup was worried about was the preacher. All at once, David was a little afraid that Matt was worried about the preacher as well. He didn't let Matt answer his question. "Look, Matt, I'll go visit him again next week if he doesn't show up tomorrow. I'll go see him even if he does. But I don't think it will do much good. He's got his mind set against me."

"That's true enough, Brother David," Matt said. "I just hate to see the church getting split up over this."

"Split up? You think the church is getting split up over Bob not coming?"

"Not just Bob. The other thing too. The Hearndons." Matt sounded sad.

"The Hearndons are part of our church community, and I'm not going to turn anyone away from our worship services. If you want that, you'll have to turn me away first." David decided to be blunt. Sometimes you could circle around an issue until you were dizzy.

"I wasn't suggesting anything like that, Brother David," Matt said quickly. "Oh no. I wouldn't want you to even imagine I was. You've been a godsend to our church. Everybody loves you."

"Maybe we should say 'almost everybody,'" David corrected.

"Well, some of them that had reservations are coming around. I hear the Martins have got back on the list to have you for dinner on Sundays."

"They have. I'm sure we'll have a good day at their house," David said. He'd have to think through every word before he let anything come out of his mouth on that Sunday, but it was a step in the right direction. He and Ogden

Martin were on the same team for the Lord. They needed to act like they were.

"Then maybe we can hope Bob will come around."

"In time. And with prayer. You and I can covenant to pray about it, Matt."

After he had hung up the phone and checked his watch, David had prayed all the way back up the stairs to his room. He shut the door and did his best to block out every thought but what the Lord was putting in his mind as he worked on the outline for his sermon. Then he prayed all the time he was taking a shower and getting dressed.

And now he was praying as he got out of his car in front of Leigh's apartment. Wordless prayers, because he didn't know what to pray. For guidance? For a good time? For Leigh? For himself? For all of those? Maybe for inspiration on where to take her. That morning at the park he'd promised her a surprise, but then the afternoon had been so cluttered that he hadn't even thought about where they could go, much less planned anything. He might have to ask her to make some peanut butter sandwiches after all.

Mrs. Simpson, Leigh's landlady, was peeking out her back window as David crossed the yard to the stairs. When David smiled and waved, Mrs. Simpson dropped the curtain as if it had burned her fingers and stepped back from the window. *What was that about?* David wondered as he started up the outside flight of stairs to Leigh's apartment. Maybe she thought he'd caught her being nosy instead of friendly. Maybe she thought he was wrong to come calling on her young neighbor. Maybe she was right, David thought even as he started smiling before he tapped on Leigh's door.

Why was he worried about what he was going to say? He hadn't worried about what he said that morning. The words had just come out. Leaning over to hug and kiss Leigh had felt as natural as breathing. What difference did it make what Mrs. Simpson thought? What anybody thought? The Lord might be laughing at David's awkward attempts at romance, but David didn't note the least hint of disapproval in his soul. And the people he might worry about approving or disapproving were the people who had seen him off at home with smiles.

Wes had given him a thumbs-up. Aunt Love had asked him to remind her what Leigh's name was one more time before she said, "Such a sweet girl. A blessing." Tabitha had done her best to smile through a new threat of tears that had nothing at all to do with his having a date and everything to do with her condition as she waved at him from the porch, her feet in a washpan of cool water.

Jocie had trailed him out to the car before giving him that grin again that said Wes had told her all about the kiss in the park. "Have fun," she had said. "But remember you have church in the morning."

As if he could forget. He'd just have to forgo sleeping that night and get back into the Scripture when he got back home.

And then Leigh was opening the door and standing before him. A flush colored her cheeks as she smiled up at him shyly. "Oh, it's you," she said. The color darkened in her cheeks. "I mean, of course it's you. I was expecting you."

David smiled at her and put his fingers under her chin. He looked into her beautiful blue eyes. "Hello," he said.

"Oh," she said, her eyes getting wider. "Hello."

He dropped his hand but kept his smile. "Are you ready?"

"More than ready." She picked up her purse and stepped out on the landing at the top of the steps, pulling the door shut behind her. "I guess I should have just said yes, right? But truth is, I'm nervous as a cat. It's no telling what I might say. And why do you think they say that about cats being nervous? Do you think cats act all that nervous?"

"Aunt Love's cat is pretty nervous whenever Jocie's dog is around." David put his hand on her elbow as they started down the steps. "But you don't have any reason to be nervous. I'm the one who has a reason to be nervous."

"You? Why would you be nervous? You've surely had dozens of dates."

"Back in another lifetime," David said. "But what do you say we forget that four-letter word, D-A-T-E, and just think about having a good time?"

"Sounds good to me," Leigh said. "But I'm not sure everybody else will cooperate. We'll be the center of attention wherever we go. The preacher and that girl who's been chasing him."

"Have you been chasing me?"

"As fast as I can. That's why I've been doing all that walking." Leigh smiled over at him. Her blush was fading. "So I'll be in better shape and can run faster than you."

"I never could run very fast." David opened the car door for her. "And you're right about us being the center of attention. We already are." He lowered his voice a little, leaning in toward Leigh. "I think Mrs. Simpson is taking notes."

Leigh laughed. "She is the curious type, but at least she won't have to worry about my music being too loud tonight."

"No, she'll be able to hear fine while she's calling everybody in the county." David gave Leigh a quick smile as he closed her door.

"So what's the surprise?" Leigh asked when he got in behind the wheel.

"That there isn't one?" David gave her an apologetic look. "I'm sorry, but things were pretty crazy this afternoon."

"That's okay. I can run back up to my apartment and get the bread and peanut butter for a picnic at the *Banner* office if you want."

David laughed. That, he decided, was the best thing about Leigh. She made him laugh. Everywhere else he had to be so responsible. He had to take care of people. Not that he didn't laugh with them. He did. But there was something different about laughing with Leigh. Something he'd been missing for years. Maybe something he'd been missing forever. "We'll save the peanut butter for another time," he said. "We'll just go out to the Family Diner. No candles on the table, but then Zella already thinks I'm hopeless. This will just prove her right." He started the motor and pulled out on the road.

"On this date—" Leigh slapped her hand over her mouth for a second before she went on. "Oops, I wasn't supposed to say that word. Anyway, on this whatever we're having, it's what *I* think that's important. And I think candles on the table are way overrated."

David stopped at the end of the street before turning to head out to the restaurant on the other side of town. He looked over at Leigh. She was wearing a blue dress the same color as her eyes, and her hair lay in soft waves on her shoulders. "Did anybody ever tell you that you're beautiful?"

Her cheeks went rosy again, but she didn't turn her eyes away from his. "Only my mother when I was a little girl."

"You're beautiful, Leigh Jacobson," David said as he reached across the seat and took her hand.

After that, it didn't seem to matter to either one of them

that everybody at the Family Diner found a reason to come over and talk to them with a big "well, can you believe this" smile spread across his or her face. It didn't seem to matter that Jane Ellen, their waitress, hovered around their table to make sure she didn't miss anything of note. It didn't seem to matter that the baked potatoes had been cooked too long and the iced tea was a little watered down.

It didn't even seem to matter that when he took Leigh home, they had to talk in whispers as they sat on the top step of the stairs to her apartment to keep from rousing Mrs. Simpson. It didn't seem to matter that the outside air even at going on eleven p.m. was still warm as bathwater.

Nothing mattered but the way their words and laughter seemed to reach across the divide between their souls and embrace. Sometimes the Lord surprised a person with the most unexpected of blessings.

27

The first Sunday in September when Cassidy Hearndon's mama got her up and said they were going to the white people's church, Cassidy thought about sticking her finger down her throat and making herself throw up. She'd done it back in Chicago a time or two so she wouldn't have to go to school. It had worked then. It might work now, but then her mother would make her stay inside and it was way too hot to be stuck in the house all day shut up in the back bedroom to make sure she didn't share her sickness with none of the rest of the family. Not that the scaredy-cat sickness was catching or anything.

Cassidy picked up the dress her mother had laid out for her to wear. It was the white one with red tulips growing all over the skirt, her very favorite, but she didn't want to put it on. Not till she had to. It was cooler just standing there in her slip and underpants.

"What in the world is wrong with you, Cassidy Marie?" her mama asked. "Stop moping around and get dressed."

"It's too hot to get all dressed up and go to church," Cassidy complained.

"The good Lord didn't say it was too hot when he paid the price for our sins, young missy."

"Then why can't we go up to the church in town? They like us up there."

"Now listen to you. We aren't going to church to make

people like us," her mama said. "We're going to church to worship, and the good Lord has put a church right down at the end of our road for us to do that. We don't have to spend a half hour and gasoline we can't afford driving to town."

"But they look at me funny." Cassidy traced one of the tulips on the skirt of the dress with her finger. She loved tulips. They'd had tulips in their yard in Chicago. Red and yellow and purple tulips.

"Probably not a bit funnier than you look at them. And Miss Sally will be there. She thinks you're the sweetest little thing. And that preacher's daughter. What did Noah say her name was?"

"Jocie."

"That's right. Jocie. She's nice as she can be. And friendly to boot."

"She just wants to play with the twins."

"So play with the twins with her," Cassidy's mama said. "Now get your dress on so you can hold Elise while I fix her hair. That child has a positive aversion to combs."

"I could stay here and help Daddy haul rocks." Cassidy didn't know why she said it. Her mama would never let her miss church to haul rocks. Her mother didn't even think her daddy should miss church to haul rocks, but sometimes her mama didn't get her way when it came to Cassidy's daddy.

"Stop talking nonsense and get dressed. Now!"

Cassidy turned away from her to pull her dress over her head so that her mama wouldn't see the tears sneaking out the sides of her eyes. Her mama couldn't understand about the scaredy-cat sickness. She was beautiful and brave and not afraid of anything. Not even of the police down in Alabama when they'd put her in jail last summer. Cassidy had been scared. She'd thought she might never see her mama again the way they said she'd never see Uncle Darnell again. Even her daddy had been scared. He'd tried to hide it by acting mad and yelling in the phone, but Cassidy had known. When a person was scared herself, she could almost smell the same thing on somebody else.

Cassidy rubbed the front of her dress close against her face as she pulled it down to wipe the tears away, but her mama saw them anyway. She came over and buttoned up the back of Cassidy's dress. Then she turned Cassidy around to face her. She put her hand under Cassidy's chin and tipped her face up. "Now, honey, you dry up those tears, because your mama isn't going to ever let anybody hurt you. Not ever."

"Yes, Mama," Cassidy said as she wiped the last of the tears off her cheeks. She wanted to believe her. She used to believe her. Now she just pretended to believe her.

Noah said that was a sign she was growing up. He said that for sure their mama wanted to protect them, but that sometimes she got carried away making the world better for everybody, and she couldn't always keep her promises because of what he called her commitment to "the greater good." When Cassidy had asked Noah what "the greater good" was, he said it was too hard to explain, but that it had to do with how people like them got treated because of the color of their skin and how they might get treated on down the road years from now. He said if she kept her eyes and ears open, she might understand it better someday.

So she had listened when her mama was talking to her daddy or on the telephone, and she had watched what was going on around her and in the papers her mama got in the mail. That's how come she knew about those girls down south who weren't much older than her getting killed in church, and they were at their own black church, not some white church.

She sometimes thought about asking Noah about the three girls, if he knew whether they'd been scared like her, but some things were too scary to talk about. And he might not be able to tell her nothing like that would ever happen to her. He'd told her once he'd do his best to never tell her something he didn't know for absolutely sure was true. That's why he told her nobody could protect somebody else all the time no matter how much they might want to, but that he was getting big enough to protect her most of the time, and for sure he'd never let what happened to her on that march in Birmingham last year ever happen again.

For a minute the memory slipped to the front of Cassidy's mind—the thick slobber dripping off that big dog's teeth right in front of her face and the sight of Noah getting knocked clear off the street by the firemen shooting their water hoses at them. But she blocked out the thoughts. There were some things a person couldn't think about, or she'd just crawl in some dark cave somewhere and never come out. Besides, she knew Noah meant it. He wouldn't let anything like that happen again. He'd promised, and Noah didn't make promises unless he was positive certain he could keep them.

Still, she didn't think he could keep the people out there at the church at the end of the road from looking at her like she had two heads or something. Especially since they were looking at him the same way. Except for Miss Sally and Mr. Harvey and the preacher's family. And there was that little girl with pigtails who had grinned at her the last time they were there a couple of weeks ago. The little girl had pointed at her own pigtails and then at Cassidy's. And at least Cassidy's mama wasn't making them go to Sunday school. She said the white church folks needed time to get used to them being there.

Cassidy wrapped her arms around Elise and held her tight while her mama made tiny braids in her hair. Elise kicked her feet and screamed, but both Cassidy and her mama just ignored her. They could talk to Elise till they didn't have any words left, and she'd still scream and fight when they did her hair. So it was better to just hold her down and get it over with.

"I wish we were still in Chicago," Cassidy said when Elise stopped screaming for a minute to catch her breath.

"Chicago, Chicago," her mama said. "You and Noah both. Always talking about Chicago. What was so great about Chicago?"

"Saundra," Cassidy said. Saundra had lived next door, and they'd played paper dolls together every day. Now she had to play paper dolls by herself. She'd tried playing with Elise, but Elise had torn the head off her favorite girl doll, Sue Ellen. Not on purpose, but Sue Ellen lost her head anyway. Her mama taped it back on for Cassidy, but now the doll's head fell over frontwards all the time like she was praying. And a person got tired of playing her paper dolls were in church praying all the time.

"Saundra was a sweet little friend for you. Why don't you write her a letter and see how she's doing?" Cassidy's mama said. "But you'll make friends here. You've been going to school a couple of weeks. I'll bet you've already met some nice girls. Maybe we could invite one of them over sometime."

"None of them live close like Saundra did," Cassidy said. School actually hadn't been all that bad. She liked school, sitting in her own desk, filling up the lines on her notebook paper. The work had been easy. She'd done most of it already last year in Chicago, and her mama said they'd move on to some new things soon. But she hadn't really made any friends.

"That might be a problem," Cassidy's mama said as she fastened another braid on Elise's head.

"It is," Cassidy said as she loosened her hold on Elise just a smidgen. Elise had given up on screaming and was just snuffling a little now. She whispered in the little girl's ear. "Mama's almost through and you're going to look so cute."

"Don't wanna look cute." Elise stuck her lip out in a pout.

"But you can't help yourself. You just are. Cute as a bug," her mama said as she touched Elise's nose with the comb before she picked up another bit of hair. Her fingers worked fast as she braided the strands of hair even as she returned to Cassidy's problem of having somebody to play paper dolls with. "Miss Sally lives just over the hill. While she's not a little girl or anything, it's good to have friends of all ages. She told me she was coming over this afternoon with last year's Sears Roebuck catalogue so the two of you could cut out some of the models and glue them on cardboard to make you some new paper dolls."

"There aren't any black people in the Sears Roebuck catalogue," Cassidy said.

"True enough." Her mama sounded put out, but Cassidy wasn't sure whether it was at her or at the Sears Roebuck catalogue. "But if Miss Sally's nice enough to come help you make some paper dolls, you'd better be nice enough to play with them. You hear me, missy?"

"Yes, ma'am," Cassidy said. She didn't mind playing with Miss Sally. Miss Sally was extra nice. She smelled like spearmint chewing gum, and she was always smiling. Best of all, she didn't just look right past Cassidy and start talking about how cute the twins were the way most people did. Cassidy loved Elise and Eli, but them being born had made her almost disappear in front of most people's eyes, so it was good having somebody that thought she, Cassidy Marie Hearndon, was special all by herself. Even if she was a scaredy-cat.

28

Jocie was up early on Monday even though there was no school. It was Labor Day. A holiday. Jocie had never quite figured out why people got off work on Labor Day. It seemed to be the one day all year a person should have to work.

Wes told her she could labor for him since he was moving out of their living room and back into his apartment. He'd gone back to the Lexington doctor the week before and had a new lighter cast with no rods sticking out to worry about.

"You should've seen my poor old scrawny leg when they cut that old cast off it. I was almost glad when they slapped more plaster on the shriveled-up thing so I couldn't see it no more," Wes had told her Sunday afternoon as they sat on the porch and watched the clouds piling up in the west, teasing them with the idea of rain. Once or twice they even caught a whiff of the scent of rain in the air.

Zeb kept his nose on Jocie's knee. The dog didn't like storms, but the rumbling clouds only flashed a little lightning before drifting on to tease somebody over in the next county. Or perhaps the clouds watered the earth there. One of Aunt Love's oft-quoted verses was about how it rained on the just and the unjust, which Jocie's father said meant that the Lord let it rain on everybody.

"What'd the doctor say about you trimming a few inches off the cast yourself?" Jocie asked Wes as she rubbed Zeb's ears.

"Said it saved considerable wear and tear on his saw blade. Said he might start handing out pocketknives with all his casts," Wes said.

"Oh, he did not." Jocie laughed.

"And how would you know? I don't recall you being anywhere in the room when he was sawing on me."

Jocie's father had let her stay home even though Wes didn't really need a baby-sitter anymore, but it was the Martins' time to have the preacher over for Sunday dinner. Her father said she could wait till next time the Martins' turn came up to go along. He said that would give her some time to work on forgiving and then forgetting what Ronnie Martin had done, so obviously she hadn't fooled her father all that much with her pretend-like forgiving act at the big church apology scene.

She told her father she would work on the forgiving bit, but she didn't see how she could forget. Ever. Of course, her father took that opportunity to remind her of how the Lord forgave and forgot sins and to suggest she spend some time praying about what the Lord would want her to do. So Jocie supposed she'd have to start saying a forgiving heart prayer.

Still, Jocie was glad enough to stay home with Wes even if she had missed seeing Noah and his little sister and the twins who had shown up for church Sunday morning. She didn't miss sitting across a dinner table from Ronnie Martin.

It might have been hard to keep him invisible at that close range. It was bad enough at school. It seemed as if he was always hanging around every time she and Paulette were at their lockers. Paulette and Jocie had been excited when they found out their lockers were side by side so they got to meet between classes and talk about what was going on while they got their books. They didn't have but a couple of classes together, which was probably just as well. Paulette was still acting funny whenever Jocie talked to Charissa, who was in all Jocie's classes.

Jocie didn't know what Paulette's problem was. Charissa was great fun. They'd been eating lunch together, and even though they'd only been going to school a couple of weeks, already it was as if she and Charissa had known each other for years. Charissa said it was because of the preachers' kids thing, that nobody who wasn't a preacher's kid could really understand. Jocie had written that down in her journal under her section on Charissa.

It had felt funny being at the house on Sunday. The afternoon hours had seemed to linger like a visitor who got up to leave, then stretched and sat back down to stay a little longer. She and Wes went through a whole pitcher of lemonade as they whiled away the time on the porch, talking and reading. When she told Wes how her father thought she needed to work on having a forgiving heart, Wes laid his new science fiction novel facedown on the porch floor while he helped her look up some forgiveness verses in the Bible. They found more about how the Lord had forgiven them than about how they should forgive one another, but then they came across Ephesians 4:32.

Jocie leaned over to read the verse aloud out of the Bible Wes had open in his lap. "'And be ye kind one to another, tenderhearted, forgiving one another, even as God for Christ's sake hath forgiven you.' Do you think it would help if I memorized that and said it over in my head every time I saw Ronnie Martin instead of pretending he was on Neptune or somewhere?" she asked Wes.

"It might. It seems a powerful verse."

"Yeah, I think I remember Daddy preaching on it or one like it sometime or other." She looked at Wes who was tracing the verse on the page as if he was memorizing it by touch. Then she looked at his leg in the cast propped up on a stool in front of the rocking chair. "But have you forgiven him? I mean, we wouldn't have been out in that tornado if it hadn't been for Ronnie Martin and what he said."

"But they were just words, Jo. Mean words, but words." Wes looked over at her. "He didn't make you run away and not talk to your daddy about what he said."

Jocie hung her head. "I know. It was my fault. Your leg getting hurt and everything."

"The tornado wasn't your fault." Wes reached over and touched her cheek. "Look at me, Jo. Do you know who the hardest person in the world is to forgive?"

She looked up at him and asked, "Who?"

"Your very own self."

Tears jumped up into her eyes. "But I feel so guilty. You almost died, Wes. I almost caused you to die."

"That ain't true. The tree falling on me almost caused me to die."

"But—"

"No buts about it. And I didn't die. I'm right here, and even if there was some reason for you to feel bad about my leg getting banged up, I'd forgive you for it. And your daddy would forgive you for it. And the Lord would forgive you for it." Wes tapped his finger on the Bible again. "It says so right here."

"Do you really forgive me, Wes?" Jocie tried to blink back her tears, but a couple of them slid out and down her cheeks. "I mean, you can't ride your motorcycle or anything."

"I don't have no reason to forgive you, Jo, but if I did, I would." He reached over and touched her face. "In a Jupiter heartbeat." He pulled his hand back, reached into his pocket for a handkerchief, and handed it to Jocie.

"Is that fast?" Jocie asked as she wiped away her tears.

"That's so fast no mere earth doctor can even hear it," Wes said. "So get that journal of yours out and write this down on one of the pages so you won't be forgetting it. 'If Wes ever needs to forgive me, he'll do it in a Jupiter heartbeat.' You got that? You give me the pen, and I'll write it out for you if you need me to."

Jocie smiled. "No, I think I've got it." She gave Wes a hug and then did just what he said. She wrote the words down in her journal along with a lot more words since sometimes, once she got started writing in her journal, her pen didn't seem to have brakes.

While she was writing, Wes kept leafing through the Bible.

"Here's one I'll bet you've heard Lovella quote out of Psalms," he said after a while. "'For thou, Lord, art good, and ready to forgive; and plenteous in mercy unto all them that call upon thee.'"

"Yeah, Aunt Love likes that one," Jocie agreed without looking up from her journal.

"What's not to like? Even I can see that's a good one. 'Ready to forgive and plenteous in mercy.'"

"All you've got to do is ask," Jocie said, still without looking up.

"That's what your daddy tells me."

Something about his voice made Jocie stop writing and look at Wes. Suddenly it was as if her senses were heightened. She felt a whisper of breeze against her sweaty skin. She heard a bee out in the yard searching for pollen, along with the sound of Wes fingering the tissue-thin pages of the Bible. Her eyes separated out every unruly gray eyebrow sticking up above the reading glasses he wore.

As long as she could remember she'd been asking Wes to take the Lord and going to church seriously, and now it sounded like he was. She was almost afraid to say anything for fear she might scare away the moment, but at the same time, she couldn't stay quiet. "Are you thinking about asking?"

"The idea's crossed my mind," Wes said.

"Then why don't you?" Jocie held her breath as she waited for his answer.

"I don't know," Wes admitted. "I guess it's just hard for an old Jupiterian like me to believe in that plenteous mercy."

"You mean, you don't think the Lord can forgive you?"

"He'd have a lot to forgive."

Jocie frowned a little and pointed at the Bible. "But don't you think that's what 'plenteous' means? That there's a lot of mercy out there for the asking."

"That's how it sounds." Wes looked back at the words in the Bible.

"That's how it is," Jocie said.

Wes looked up at her. "And you know this yourself? You aren't just saying what you've heard your daddy say?"

"He says it, but even if he didn't, I'd know it."

"Why's that?"

Jocie hesitated a minute before she answered. "I don't know. Maybe because of what happened at Clay's Creek Church. You know, the lilacs and you and Dad showing up when I needed you and everything. And I hadn't done what I should have done that day, but the Lord helped me anyway. When I prayed, he answered."

"You do seem to be having a good return on your prayers this summer, Jo. The dog prayer. The sister prayer. The leg-healing prayer. Even the doctors are changing their tune a little and saying I might actually walk again without crutches after all."

"I knew you would. What do Earth doctors know about Jupiter bones anyway?"

"And you weren't praying about it?" Wes looked at her with lifted eyebrows.

"Well, yeah, but I always pray for you. And could be I was praying a little harder than usual since you got hurt."

"I'm not sure I'm that good at praying or walking down church aisles."

"Daddy says you don't have to be in a church to ask the Lord to save you, that you can do that anywhere."

"The book's pretty clear on that," Wes said, lifting the Bible a little out of his lap. "The Lord's all over, everywhere. But there's somewhere in here that says it ain't enough to just be private about it, that you have to step forward and do some aisle walking."

Jocie put her hand on his arm. "Aisle walking isn't all that hard. And if you decide you need to do some of it, I'll walk on one side of you and the Lord will walk on the other side."

"I might just hold you to that, Jo, if I ever do decide to do that aisle walking. But you know what happened the last time I got close to a church. It just blew clear away to Jupiter or beyond."

"Not all of it." Jocie smiled. "Folks are still bringing in pieces. Mr. Armstrong brought in one of the collection plates last Tuesday. He spotted it up in a tree somewhere. Bent a little, but it would still hold money. Daddy took a picture of him holding it. Mr. Armstrong says the people out at the church are going to make a special display case when they build their new church to hold some of the stuff people have been finding."

"Sounds like front-page news to me." Wes shut the Bible and leaned back in his rocking chair.

"There might not be room this week. We'll probably have the front page full of pictures of Sidewalk Days. We might even get some shots of the square dancing in the streets Monday night for the top fold."

"Dancing in the streets. Sounds like quite the event," Wes said. "I'll watch it from my upstairs window."

"So you really are moving out on us?"

"Ain't nothing against none of you. Could be I'll even miss you."

"Could be?" Jocie leaned over to stare into his face.

"Could be. I might even miss old Harlan or Zebedee or whatever you call him." Wes smiled at Jocie and reached over to run his hand down Zeb's back. The dog turned to grin at Wes. "He's a fine dog. But sometimes a man needs some time alone to think things through in the proper way."

"You mean, like asking for this plenteous mercy?"

"That's one of the things."

Suddenly Jocie felt like crying. "I don't want you to leave."

"I ain't going back to Jupiter or nothing, Jo. I'm just going home. And I'll be able to go down to the pressroom and keep old Betsy Lou happy and get ink under my fingernails again." Wes looked down at his hands. "It just ain't right having clean fingernails."

So Monday morning after breakfast, Jocie helped Wes pack up his books and clothes so they could ride in with her father. Even though it was a holiday, they were working on this week's issue of the *Banner* so their subscribers could get their papers on Wednesday the same as always. With every book she put in the box, she felt more like crying.

Even Aunt Love looked a little teary-eyed as she quoted a verse or two out of Psalms, and of course Tabitha had tears running down her cheeks while she watched Wes and Jocie. But that was pretty common the last couple of weeks. Tabitha claimed she wasn't all that unhappy. Miserable and hot and more than ready for the baby to get here, but that wasn't why she was crying. She said everything else about her was swollen so she supposed her tear glands were too and that maybe they had to spill over to keep her eyes from exploding. But this morning as she watched Wes packing up to move out, she had a sad look to go along with the tears.

Wes was the only one of them smiling. He was hopping around on his crutches and doing his best to tease them into smiling back at him. "You'd think somebody had died around here. Come on, girls. It's just the opposite. I'm coming back to life again." He did a little shuffle step on his crutches. "Bet you didn't think I could still dance."

"I never knew you could dance to begin with," Jocie said. "And I haven't seen anything yet to make me change my mind."

"What's the matter? Don't you recognize the Jupiterian shuffle when you see it?" Wes laughed. "Maybe I'll teach that step to you at your birthday party next week."

"I can't wait. Leigh's chocolate cake and your dance lessons. Plus new tubes for my bicycle tires. Dad promised." Jocie looked over at Wes and smiled. "What more could a girl want?"

"Strawberry ice cream and dancing in the street?" Wes said.

"I don't have to wait for my birthday for that. That's happening tonight."

"Who'd have thunk they'd have ever closed off Main Street in little holy Hollyhill so folks could dance?"

"Square dancing," Jocie said. "Church people don't mind square dancing. You just hold hands while you swing your partner and promenade. Nothing too close or wild. Leigh may even talk Daddy into trying it."

"If she does, you be sure to have a camera at ready. We wouldn't want to miss out on that top-fold picture."

29

Cassidy didn't like going to town with her mama. She'd have rather stayed home and watched Eli and Elise while her daddy was watering the apple trees. He'd watered them every day since they'd set the trees down in the holes he and Noah had dug. Cassidy and her mama had poured a bucket of water in every one of the holes while her daddy and Noah pushed the round hard dirt clods back in around the tree roots, but the ground just sucked the water up like it was nothing.

Her daddy said the ground was just too dry because of how hot it was, and so every night he asked her mama to pray for rain when she said grace at the supper table. Cassidy's daddy didn't go to church, but he believed in the Lord. He had to. Else he wouldn't be asking her mama to pray for it to rain on their trees. There wasn't any use in praying if you didn't believe the Lord was listening. And Cassidy had heard her daddy say prayer was all that was going to keep those trees they'd put in the ground from dying if they didn't get some earth-softening rain soon.

Cassidy shut her eyes and imagined the trees in rows across the field. She liked going down there and walking around the little sapling trees. She counted them over and over as she imagined them the way her daddy said they would look in a few years. All green and leafy and full of apples. He said she'd be able to just reach up and pick her off a big red apple to eat. When he talked about it, she could almost hear the pop of the apple when she bit down into it.

"We'll have us an orchard, Cassie," he'd told her. "Not just these trees but dozens more planted all over this field. We'll pick baskets and baskets of apples and take them all over to sell."

"To Chicago?" Cassidy had asked.

"Maybe even to Chicago."

Her mama had been down there in the field with them and she'd laughed as she looked from Cassidy's daddy to the little tree twigs sticking up out of the ground. "You don't be thinking on any trips to Chicago just yet, missy. All your daddy has right now is an orchard of hope."

"Your mama could be right," her daddy said as he laid his big hand on Cassidy's head and let it rest there a minute. "But hope's a mighty fine thing to have. Your mama won't argue with me on that one. As best I recall, there's even something about it in her Bible. Faith, hope, and charity."

Her mama had smiled at her daddy and reached for his hand. It made Cassidy feel all happy inside when her mama and daddy held hands like that. She didn't like it when they fussed about that freedom train her mama was always chasing after.

That's why Cassidy didn't like going to town with her mama, because she never knew when her mama was going to run after the chance to work for that "greater good" Noah had talked about. They dropped Eli and Elise off at Miss Sally's house, but her mama wouldn't let Cassidy stay. Said she needed new shoes.

"You can measure my foot and order them from Miss Sally's Sears Roebuck catalogue," Cassidy suggested. She hoped her mama would like that idea, and that way she could stay at Miss Sally's while her mama went to town.

"No, no," her mama said. "They're having a sidewalk sale in town. The shoe store had an ad in the paper with what looked like good prices, and it's always better to try a pair of shoes on to get the right fit."

Cassidy wanted to say that if it was a white person's shoe store, they probably wouldn't let her try on the shoes anyhow, even if her socks were straight off the clothesline and so white they practically sparkled. Cassidy knew. She'd been shoe shopping in the wrong stores with her mama before, but saying something like that to her mama was just like sounding the whistle of that freedom train. She'd be on it in a minute flat, pulling Cassidy right along with her. And that's why Cassidy wanted to stay at Miss Sally's, trailing after the twins to keep them from breaking her pretties, instead of going to town.

Miss Sally had a lot of pretties—glass birds and bells and angels and all sorts of trinkets, as Miss Sally called them. Eli had already broken one of the birds, but Miss Sally just swept up the pieces and threw them in the trash can and never said the first word to their mama. She told Cassidy not to worry about it, that Eli was lots more fun to have around than an old glass bird anyhow.

The street down through Hollyhill was closed off, and her mama had to go around behind where Noah worked at that newspaper office to park. Then they walked down through an alleyway to the shoe store. The stores all had tables full of stuff out on the sidewalk, and the dress stores even had racks of dresses hanging outside. At the shoe store, their sidewalk table was piled high with sneakers—just what her mama thought Cassidy needed for school.

The first pair of shoes Cassidy tried on fit, and the clerk even smiled at her when she asked Cassidy if she wanted to wear the new shoes and put her old shoes in the sack. The new ones were a pretty yellow, and Cassidy didn't want to take them off, so her mama let her wear them away from the store.

If they'd just walked straight back to the car and gone home, things would have been fine. Maybe even better than fine. But her mama decided they were thirsty. They went in the little restaurant two stores down from the shoe store. Her mother took hold of Cassidy's hand and started right for the soda counter where there were tall stools with red shiny tops fastened to the floor. Cassidy's heart was already thumping in her chest even before the waitress stepped in front of them and said, "I'm sorry. We don't serve coloreds up here. There's a table for you all in the back."

Cassidy looked at the white woman's face. She didn't look all that sorry. Everybody in the restaurant had quit talking and was looking at them. It was so quiet that Cassidy was sure her mama and the waitress would be able to hear how her heart was trying to pound a hole right through her chest. She pulled on her mama's arm. "I'm not all that thirsty, Mama."

For a minute, she didn't think her mama was going to pay any attention to her, but then her mama looked down at her and smiled. "All right, sweetie."

Her mama's smile disappeared when she looked back at the waitress. "When I come back, you can be sure I'll sit wherever I please."

"You might sit down, but we can't wait on you nowhere but that back table," the waitress said. For a minute she did look a little sorry as she added, "It's just the way things are around here."

Cassidy cringed as the memory of the dog in Birmingham crept up out of the back of her mind and snarled at her. Sirens started going off in her head. They must have been going off in her mama's head too.

"And why's that?" Cassidy's mama asked. There was fire in her eyes, but everything else about her turned stiff and cold as she stood tall and glared at the woman.

Cassidy gently tugged on her mama's arm again. She didn't tug hard, because when her mama turned to ice like that, Cassidy was always afraid her mama might just shatter into pieces.

"Let's go, Mama."

Her mama whirled without another word and went back out on the street. Cassidy had to hurry to keep up. When they passed the alleyway that led up to where they'd parked the car, Cassidy said, "Aren't we going home?"

"Not yet, sweetie. I'm taking you to where Noah works. You'll be fine there."

"I want to go back to Miss Sally's," Cassidy said as tears began to trickle out of her eyes. "I want us both to go."

Her mama slowed up, and her ice glare melted away as she smiled at Cassidy. "Now don't you be worrying about your mama, sweet child. Your mama knows exactly what needs doing, and it's going to get done."

A little of the smile stayed on her mama's face as she pulled open the screen door and stepped into the *Banner* offices. A woman with hair nearly as black as Cassidy's and covering her head in fat curls looked up from her typewriter. She peered out at them through dark-rimmed glasses and asked, "Can I help you?" She didn't smile. Cassidy looked down at her new yellow shoes and wanted to go talk to the shoe store clerk again.

Her mama didn't seem bothered by the woman's face. Her smile just got bigger as she held out her hand and stepped over to the woman's desk. "Hello, you must be Miss Curtsinger. I'm Noah's mother, Myra Hearndon, and this is my daughter, Cassidy."

Cassidy peeked up at the woman behind the desk to see if what her mama had said was going to make any difference in whether she smiled at them or not. The lady was smiling at her mouth, but there wasn't much of it leaking up to her eyes. "A pleasure to meet you," she was saying. She barely touched Cassidy's mother's hand before she jerked it away to pull a pink tissue from somewhere and blot her nose with it. She looked kind of scared.

Cassidy wasn't surprised. A lot of people got uneasy when her mama fastened her eyes straight on them. Her mama was always telling her and Noah, "Don't you ever be afraid to look somebody straight in the eyes. You be proud of who you are." She had better luck with Noah than she did Cassidy.

"The same here," her mama was saying. "I do so appreciate Rev. Brooke giving Noah a job."

"David felt we needed the help with our regular hand out with a broken leg. We have to get the *Banner* printed on time."

"And Noah is enjoying the work. He says you've been working here since even before Rev. Brooke and that the Reverend says you're the glue that holds the place together."

"Well, I do my best," Miss Curtsinger said. "I'm afraid David doesn't always have the best business sense when it comes to the financial side of things. Sometimes he trusts in the goodness of people a bit too much. And though I hate to have to say it, people will take advantage of that."

"That's so true, although I suppose trusting in the goodness of people isn't a bad failing for a preacher to have. At the same time, he's fortunate to have someone like you to keep things in business order."

The lady's smile was easier now as she warmed to the

praise. Cassidy's mama knew how to put the honey on the bread when she needed to.

"I guess you're here to see Noah," the lady said. "He's back in the pressroom with Jocelyn. Wesley and David were back there with them, but I think Wesley must have gone up to his apartment awhile ago for a rest, and David went down the street for a little bit. But he won't be gone long. I'm sure Noah and Jocelyn are fine back there by themselves." She couldn't seem to stop chattering as she stood up and led them toward a door at the back of the room.

"Don't you worry," Cassidy's mama said. "His father and I have taught Noah how to behave himself."

"Oh, I wasn't meaning to sound worried. Noah's been nice as can be. I haven't got any complaint at all about him."

The lady was sounding flustered again, and Cassidy was glad when she just pushed the door open and called out to Noah and then hustled back to her desk. Cassidy and her mama went on into the room.

Noah looked up at them from the table where he was sitting beside the preacher's daughter. "What are you doing here, Mama?"

"I came to get Cassidy some new shoes. And now I'm going to let Cassidy stay here with you while I go get something to drink."

Noah stood up and stared at their mama. She stared right back at him, and Cassidy could feel her turning back to ice. Cassidy's heart started thumping again, and the hot breath of that Birmingham dog was on her face. Still, she didn't argue. It never did one bit of good to argue with her mama, but Noah gave it a try.

"Mama, you promised Daddy you wouldn't do this here. You promised you'd let somebody else do the fighting for a while," he said.

Cassidy looked over at the preacher's daughter. Her eyes were big as she looked first at Noah, then at Cassidy's mama. Cassidy looked around for a place she could crawl under to hide. Some place the dog couldn't get to her.

"It's not your place to tell me what I promised your father." Her mama was using that voice that meant she expected her children to shut their mouths and not say another word.

Noah acted like he didn't hear the voice. "Nobody else will fight with you here. They don't mind sitting where they're told to sit and going in the back doors. Why don't you save your energy for when you go down south with the other freedom fighters?"

"I'm not doing that right now. I'm off the freedom train."

"Then don't get back on it here in Hollyhill where we have to live."

Cassidy's mama covered the distance to Noah in two steps. He was a head taller than their mama, but Cassidy knew who had the power. Her mama put her finger right in Noah's face.

"Don't you ever tell me what to do, Noah Alexander Hearndon. And you're wrong about the other people here. Everybody wants freedom. It's our inalienable right. And don't you forget it. The Jim Crow laws have been thrown out everywhere, and if they don't know that here, then it's time they found out."

Cassidy's mama whirled around and headed back to the door. She was pushing on it before Noah said, "I don't want to have to tell Daddy you're in jail, Mama." He sounded almost as ready to cry as Cassidy felt.

She let her hand fall off the door as she turned back around to look at Noah. "I'm only going to go get me something to drink. I would have already done it, but I couldn't do it with Cassidy there. You know that. If it gets to be the kind of problem you're imagining, I'll come on back down here and get a drink of water out of Rev. Brooke's sink."

"Do you promise?" Noah asked.

"I promise. You just take care of your little sister till I come back." She turned to smile a little at Cassidy. "Noah will take care of you, sweet child. Don't you be troubling your head about anything."

Cassidy's mama turned and disappeared through the door. Cassidy listened to her footsteps across the front office and heard the screen door slam behind her as she went out on the street.

It was a funny thing. The Birmingham dog poked out at Cassidy when her mama was around, but it never completely jumped out where it could get her. But once her mama was out of sight, the dog was right there, opening its big mouth to swallow Cassidy whole. She had to go hide. She had to go crawl farther back in that cave back in her mind. The dog was growling at her now.

She didn't like it back there. It was dark and lonely that far back in the cave. But it was safe—the dog couldn't get to her there. Nobody could get to her there. She heard Noah talking, but he was far away.

30

"Wow!" Jocie said softly after Mrs. Hearndon stalked out of the pressroom. Jocie's hands were shaking and Mrs. Hearndon hadn't even said the first word to her. Jocie swallowed hard and tried to think of something to say, but Noah didn't look in the mood to talk. She smiled over at Cassidy, but the girl's eyes were fixed on the wall as if she saw something horrible there. "What's wrong with her?" Jocie asked Noah.

Noah was still staring at the door his mother had just gone through. "That's just how she is. My mother thinks she has to single-handedly usher in a new age of freedom for us people of color."

"No, not your mother. Your little sister."

Jocie went over to Cassidy who was standing perfectly still as if she was playing frozen tag, only worse than that. Even her eyelids were frozen open. Jocie reached out to touch the little girl, but then stopped her hand in mid-air. Cassidy was breathing. Jocie could see her chest moving in and out, but it was as if the girl's mind had gone off and left her body behind. "Are you okay, Cassidy honey?"

Noah was beside his sister in a heartbeat. He put his face right next to hers, nose to nose, and ordered, "Cassidy, you come back out here to me right now."

For a second, his little sister didn't respond, but then her hands started trembling a little. She whispered, "The dog. It's going to eat me."

"No, it's not," Noah said firmly. "I'm here right in front of you. You're safe."

"But the water might blow you away." A tear slipped out of the corner of her right eye and slid down her cheek.

"Not this time. This time I'm right here holding on to you."

Noah wrapped his arms around her and picked her up like a baby. He pushed on her legs to make them bend enough that he could carry her over and sit down in the chair with her in his lap. She kept her head stiff up in the air away from him.

"Should I call the doctor?" Jocie asked.

"No," Noah said. "She's just scared. She'll be okay in a little bit if I can get her to listen to me. You are going to listen to me, aren't you, baby sister?"

"You want me to get a wet washcloth or something?" Jocie didn't know how that would help, but that was always what people did. When somebody acted sick, somebody else ran for a wet cloth or a glass of water. She didn't think they could get Cassidy to take a drink.

"No, just rub her hands while I talk to her."

The little girl's hands were thin, almost fragile looking, with long, graceful fingers like her mother's. Jocie gently kneaded Cassidy's palms between her thumbs and fingers as Noah whispered to his sister. "It's all right, baby. Nobody's going to hurt you. There's no dogs here. Not the first one. It's all right. We're safe and dry and the sun's shining. Daddy's got apple trees growing in the field, and nobody's going to hurt us here. It's okay. I promise. And you know I don't make promises I can't keep."

Cassidy blinked, and Jocie could feel some of the tension draining out of the little girl's hands.

"Are you feeling better, Cassidy?" she asked.

The girl's hands went stiff again as she tried to pull away from Jocie. "Is she hiding the dog?" Cassidy whispered.

"The dog?" Jocie frowned. "My dog's at home. Daddy won't let me bring him to work with me."

Noah shook his head a little at Jocie, then turned to whisper in his sister's ear. "Shh, baby. There aren't any dogs here. Jocie won't hurt you. She likes you. She might even help me sing to you." He glanced up at Jocie again. "Singing to her sometimes helps."

"How about a hymn? That's about all I know well enough to sing all the way through."

"We can try one."

He started singing "What a Friend We Have in Jesus." He sang so good Jocie sort of hated to mess up the song by adding her voice, but after he sang a verse, she joined in. Cassidy began to relax against Noah. Her head drooped and then dropped down on his shoulder. After a couple more verses, her eyes closed.

Jocie sang along with Noah as they started the first verse over. When they'd sung that verse all the way through without Cassidy opening her eyes, Jocie whispered, "Is she asleep?"

"I think so." He stroked her head gently. "Poor little girl."

"What was wrong with her?" Jocie asked. "Some kind of seizure?"

"I guess you could call it that. She just gets scared and freezes up. It started after what went on down in Birmingham last year."

"What happened in Birmingham?"

Noah looked at Jocie as if she were asking who was president or something. "I guess you probably don't know. You people here in Hollyhill just sit tight in your little town and don't worry a bit about what goes on anywhere else."

Jocie clamped down on her irritation at his attitude. "I know there were marches down there and trouble. I saw the headlines in the daily papers, but I don't know why that has Cassidy so scared that she's seeing dogs where there aren't any dogs."

Noah put his hand over Cassidy's ear as she lay against his shoulder, but she didn't show any sign of hearing them. Then he sighed. "I'm sorry, Jocie. It's just that I get so mad when I think about what happened to her. To us."

"You don't have to be mad at me. I wasn't there."

"I wish I hadn't been there either, and I especially wish Cassidy hadn't been."

"Were you down there when the church bomb killed those girls?" Jocie didn't even like to think about that. Girls her own age dying while they were at Sunday school learning about the Lord. She couldn't understand it, but her father said nobody could really understand the kind of hate that made people do things like that.

"No, that was later. This was in May last year. The Children's March in Birmingham. The city down there had just closed up everything—the parks and playgrounds and swimming pools—so they wouldn't have to let black people in after the judges said they couldn't keep us out. So the Reverend King and some others got the idea of having a thousand children marching because they thought newspapers all over the country would eat that up and print a lot of stories. Plus they didn't think the police would do anything too bad to a bunch of kids." Noah paused a second and touched Cassidy's head again before he went on. "They probably wouldn't have to a bunch of white kids."

"What happened?" Jocie asked.

"The police arrested all the children marching and took them to jail."

"Were you and Cassidy arrested?"

"No, it might've been better if that's all that happened to us. We didn't march that first day. Daddy didn't want us to march at all. He and Mama fought about it, but Mama said her family, her children needed to stand up and be counted along with all the other children. She left the twins with a neighbor and borrowed a car. We left while Daddy was at work."

"Did you want to go?"

"I could hardly wait," Noah said. "I'd caught the freedom train fever from my mother. Me and Cassidy were supposed to march that first day, but we had a flat tire on the way down south and didn't get there until after the march had already started. I don't know who was the most disappointed. Me or my mother."

"Not Cassidy?"

Noah looked down at his little sister and his voice softened a bit. "No. Cassidy didn't want to march at all. She's always been on the shy side. Never liked it when anybody had a fuss or she had to go into a new place. Mama should have let her stay back in Chicago with the twins. But she was old enough at nine years old. They wanted kids between six and eighteen, and Mama kept telling us she wanted us to be part of something bigger than ourselves. Something that would change things."

"But you got there too late."

"Too late for the first day, but the people organizing things decided not to let the police beat them. They gathered up another thousand children from somewhere. Maybe a bunch of other people had been late like us. Maybe the police turned loose the kids they'd arrested the day before. Maybe they went out and recruited Birmingham kids. I don't know. But the next day we all lined up to march again. Mama told me to keep Cassidy right beside me, and I wouldn't have been able to get away from her anyway. She practically attached herself to my leg, she was so scared. All those people yelling as we started along the street. I don't even know where we were marching. Maybe to one of the parks or to the mayor's office. Some of the older kids were leading the way in the front. Me and Cassidy were just following along."

"I remember something about that now. How what happened started riots down there last summer." Men had talked to Jocie's father about how the president should send in troops to calm things down, but it had all seemed so far away to Jocie. She listened to the talk, read about it in the papers, and even saw bits of the riots on the TV news, but it was all so alien to what was happening around her in Hollyhill that it was as if it was all going on in some foreign country a million miles away. But it hadn't been that way to the boy and girl in front of her. They'd lived it.

"The riots were later. After that day. We were home in Chicago by then. It was what happened that day that makes Cassidy try to go off somewhere to hide."

Jocie hesitated. She wasn't sure she really wanted to know. It might be easier to keep bad things off in that foreign country where she never had to think about them. But she asked anyway. "What happened?"

Noah looked down at Cassidy's face. "Are you hearing me, baby sister?" Her face stayed soft in sleep. Not even an eyelid twitched. Noah looked back up at Jocie. "I wouldn't want to send her running back into her hiding place after I've pulled her out, but I don't think she's hearing us. Mama says it would be better if we could get Cassidy to go on and talk about it anyway, but she can't even think about it, much less talk about it." He shifted in his chair as if his legs were going to sleep.

"You want to try to lay her down somewhere? The floor's out. It's filthy, but we could push two chairs together or something," Jocie said.

"No, she's fine. She's not that heavy, and she'll wake up in a minute. She sometimes goes to sleep for a while after she gets scared like that. I think her head has to reset after she sees that dog coming after her."

Jocie looked at Cassidy. She hadn't really paid that much attention to the little girl before. Cassidy had always acted so shy, almost afraid to even look at Jocie; and the twins were so cute. Jocie had the twins described in detail in her journal, but now she looked at Cassidy with new eyes. "What is it about the dog?"

"I'll get to that." Noah looked at the wall behind Jocie for a minute before he started talking again. "The police down there, they told us to go home, but we weren't going to listen to them. We were going to march through the streets and make the city of Birmingham start treating us right, the way the courts said they had to. It was exciting being in the middle of the action. I began to see why Mama liked getting on that freedom train.

"Of course, Cassidy didn't feel that. She was crying by the time we lined up to march down the street. I should have taken her back to Mama and made Mama let her stay with her, but if I'd done that, they'd have started the march without me, and I didn't want to miss being part of it. Being part of history, as Mama had said that morning. So I just held Cassidy's hand tight, and we started walking all together at once. A thousand of us. Demanding to be treated fair and equal. There were even a few cheers here and there.

"The police were in the street waiting on us." Noah frowned at the memory. "Police with dogs. And firemen with hoses. I didn't know why the firemen were there at first, but this boy next to me said he'd heard they sometimes turned water on marchers when things got out of hand. But we weren't doing nothing but walking. Peaceful as can be. We weren't even yelling. Just walking. Slower, but still walking."

"How about Cassidy?" Jocie asked.

"She was still walking too. We didn't have much choice. We were about three rows from the front, and all the kids behind us were pushing us forward toward the police and the dogs and the firehoses."

"What happened?"

"They turned on the water. You could see the firehoses on the ground filling up, turning into something live, and then the water was shooting out with so much force that it took one of the boys in front of us and threw him completely over a parked car. I tried to hold on to Cassidy and get her out of there, but then the hose turned on me. I had to turn loose of Cassidy or she would've been thrown in the air with me. The water just lifted me up and carried me with it. Then I guess the fireman turned it on some other kid, and I landed against the curb. My arm was sitting at a funny angle and my head was ringing, but I couldn't think about whether I was hurt or not. I had to find Cassidy. It took me maybe five minutes but it seemed like hours. I kept thinking about having to go back to Chicago and tell Daddy I turned loose of Cassidy's hand and lost her."

"You had to turn her loose to keep her from getting hurt."

"That's what I told myself, but I don't think Daddy would have believed it. He would have thought I should have done something." Noah tightened his arms around Cassidy a little. "I finally spotted her. She was sitting in the middle of the street with one of the police dogs right in her face. The policeman holding the dog's leash was yelling at her, I guess telling her to get up and move off the street, but she was too scared to move. I jumped right in front of that dog and put my back to its teeth. The policeman was still yelling, but I don't know what he was saying. I picked Cassidy up. My arm hurt so bad that for a minute I thought I might pass out and the dog would have us both, but then somebody came and helped me and we got to a church somewhere. That's where Mama found us. She took one look at my arm and Cassidy's face and loaded us up in the car she'd borrowed and drove us straight back to Chicago.

"Cassidy never said a word all the way home. My arm was hurting. Somebody at the church had put splints on it, but it still needed a cast. Mama said we'd take care of it when we got back to Chicago. She just wanted us out of there. She never intended on us getting hurt. She didn't say much, just drove. She prayed some now and again and tried to sing to Cassidy once, but mostly we just listened to the wheels rolling on the highway. She found a doctor to fix my arm before we even went to the house. I think she wanted the extra time before she had to face my father."

"Was he upset?"

"Oh yeah. Scary mad. You haven't met my daddy. He's big. He can grab hold of my belt and pick me up with one hand, but he hardly ever raises his voice. That day he raised his voice. Mama doesn't take to being yelled at, so she was yelling back. The babies were screaming. My arm was hurting, and it was all I could do to keep from throwing up. But then Cassidy got up off the couch and went over and stood between Mama and Daddy. She didn't say anything. She just stood there, and they quit yelling. That's when Mama promised to get off the freedom train for a while. And now she's trying to start one up here in Hollyhill."

Jocie looked over her shoulder at the door. "It won't be like that here. They'll serve her up at the Grill."

"You think? Then why was she so fired up when she was down here, and why hasn't she already come back? It doesn't take all that long to drink a soda."

"You want to go check on her?" Jocie asked.

Noah touched Cassidy's head. "I can't leave Cassidy right now. I have to be here where she can see me when she wakes up."

"Then I'll go," Jocie said. "You really think your mother's having a sit-in at the Grill?"

"It's a possibility. Your police chief may have already dragged her off to jail." Noah looked worried.

"No"—Jocie shook her head—"I can't believe that would happen."

"But you're an innocent, Jocie. You think everybody in Hollyhill reads the Bible and prays and does what the Lord wants them to do."

"That's not true. I know there are mean people everywhere. Even in Hollyhill. I've run into a few of them personally," Jocie said. "Look, I'll go check it out. If she's in jail, I'll find Dad. He'll know what to do."

On the way out to the street, Jocie picked up her camera. She wasn't sure whether or not she'd take a picture of Myra Hearndon even if she was having a sit-in at the Grill, but she hung the camera around her neck just in case.

When she passed by Zella's desk, Zella was covering up her typewriter, getting ready to leave.

"Is everything all right?" Zella asked. "I thought Noah's mother looked upset when she left."

"She was a little. Something about getting a drink at the Grill, I think."

"Oh, my heavenly days!" Zella's eyes popped open wide behind her glasses. "I knew there was going to be trouble."

"I didn't say there was trouble."

"But there will be. I've known that since the very moment that boy came through the front door with you. Those people shouldn't have expected to just move into the county and have everything change overnight."

"She just went to get a soft drink," Jocie said.

"Trouble. Mark my words." Zella wagged a finger at her. "There's going to be trouble, and you need to stay out of it, Jocelyn Brooke."

Jocie rolled her eyes at Zella and went on out the door. But all the way up to the Grill, she fingered the camera. Should she take a picture if Zella was right and trouble was there?

31

It hadn't seemed like a day that was going to end in trouble. Rain maybe, but that was far from trouble. More an answer to prayer. Storm clouds had been building up in the west all day, as if all they'd needed to do to make it rain was haul half the merchandise in the Hollyhill stores out to the sidewalk and plan a square dance in the street. David didn't think anybody would mind skipping the square dancing if some rain wanted to come their way.

But it appeared that hadn't been the only storm building up as the day slipped toward evening. Zella had hunted him down at the courthouse on her way home. Up until then, David would have said it was a good day. Hot and muggy, but the shoppers hadn't let that stop them from hunting for bargains out on the sidewalks. The merchants' cash registers had been ringing up sales all day, so maybe they'd be ready to buy more ads in the *Banner*.

Wes was settled back into his apartment with a fan in his window and a refrigerator full of sandwiches Leigh had brought him. Not peanut butter. Leigh said somebody had told her Jupiterians didn't eat much peanut butter. And so David had been leaning on the counter thanking Leigh for the sandwiches and working up the nerve to suggest another date, when Zella had blown the day apart by saying Myra Hearndon was staging a sit-in at the Grill.

Then Zella poked her finger against his chest and said,

"And Jocelyn headed up that way to get right in the middle of the trouble. As usual. I told her not to, but that girl . . ."

He didn't bother listening to the rest of Zella's complaints. He covered the two blocks from the courthouse to the Grill in record time, but a little crowd was already gathered around the Grill's door when he got there. He didn't see any anger or hostility in their faces as he edged through them toward the open door. Just curiosity as they stood around waiting to see what might happen next.

One of them, Helen Moore, put her hand on David's arm as he passed by her. She kept her voice low as she said, "You might ought to get Jocie out of there in case things go bad. I've been hearing about some things might be going to happen today. Things that might cause trouble."

David paused to look down at Helen, whose head barely came up to his shoulder. Helen worked for the sheriff, and although she was friendly enough, David could hardly ever get any kind of information out of her for a story for the *Banner*. She considered it unprofessional to talk about what she heard at the office. Now she looked seriously worried as David asked, "You heard something about this happening? You mean it was planned?"

Inside the Grill, David could see Myra Hearndon sitting straight and tall at the counter with Jocie sitting just as straight on the stool beside her.

"Not this," Helen said, her voice not much more than a whisper. "I'm guessing this was spur of the moment. That woman, she's the mother of that boy who's working for you, isn't she?" She waited for David to nod. "They tell me she just came in here to get a soft drink and didn't like being told to sit in the back booth. She's from Chicago, you know, and has done some of those marches down south, rode the freedom buses, even been arrested a time or two.

Sheriff Harpson did some checking on the Hearndons when they moved in."

"Why?"

Helen looked as if she was sorry she'd said so much. She mashed her mouth together for a moment before she said, "Just to be ahead of any trouble, I guess. And if you tell anybody I told you that, I'll say you must have heard me wrong."

David looked from Helen to Myra Hearndon. Her hand was resting on the counter with one of her long, graceful fingers touching the dollar bill that lay in front of her as she waited to be served.

Mary Jo Yeager was as far away as she could get from her and still stay behind the counter. She was staring hard at the countertop she was polishing. David could almost read her thoughts: She didn't own the place. She could just take her apron off and leave, but she'd been working there for years and her son had just gone off for his second year at the university in Lexington. She told everybody she waited on that college educations weren't cheap. Some people thought she was trying to get bigger tips, but David thought she was simply so proud her son was studying to be an engineer that she had to talk about it or burst.

She wasn't talking now as she peeked up from her counter polishing toward the door as if hoping for somebody to come rescue her. She spotted David and mouthed the words, "Do something."

He wanted to tell her to do something. He wanted to tell her to take Myra Hearndon's money and set whatever she ordered on the counter in front of her. But then David wasn't her boss. And he wouldn't want to be the cause of young Denny Yeager not getting to finish engineering school.

David was still praying about what to do when Charles

Boyer, the pastor of the West End Baptist Church, and his wife, Alice, stepped past him and went straight to the counter to sit down on the two stools next to Myra Hearndon. Mary Jo Yeager stared at them and looked close to tears.

"We'd like to get some drinks over here, Mary Jo," Rev. Boyer said. He had a deep voice that sometimes rattled the windows when he was preaching, but now he kept his voice gentle and kind.

"Now, Brother Boyer, you know I can't serve you over here. That's just the way it is."

"Then I think today is the day that needs to change," Rev. Boyer said. He turned to look at David. "Don't you agree, Brother Brooke?"

Jocie turned on her stool to look around at David. "Oh, hi, Dad," she said. Her shoulders sagged a little as she looked worried she might be in trouble. She rushed to explain, "I'm just keeping Mrs. Hearndon company."

"She is," Myra Hearndon agreed. She moved her hand off the dollar bill on the counter to touch Jocie's arm softly. "We're not here for any trouble. Just something to drink."

David stepped up behind Jocie and put his hands on her shoulders. "It is hot," he said. "Why don't you give everybody a glass of water, Mary Jo?"

"You know I can't do that, David," Mary Jo said. "You need to talk to Grover about all this. I just work here. You know that."

"Where is Grover?" David asked. Grover Flinn was the owner of the Grill.

"He's gone to get the police chief," Mary Jo said.

David's hands tightened on Jocie's shoulders. "Why don't you go on back down to the office, Jocie, and let me have your seat?"

"But, Dad, he won't arrest us, will he? We're not doing anything wrong or anything."

"Nobody's going to get arrested," David said. "But don't argue with me. Just do what I told you."

ℵ ℭ

Jocie looked at her father, stood up, and picked up her camera. "Yes, sir," she said. She didn't want to leave, but she knew when her father meant business. She looked at the woman beside her. "What should I tell Noah, Mrs. Hearndon?"

"That I'll be along to get Cassidy in a little bit and that he can ride in with me too, since it's sounding as if a storm might be coming up."

"Okay." Jocie couldn't think of any other reason to delay her leaving, and her father was giving her the look she wasn't supposed to ignore. She moved slowly toward the door to the street. None of it made any sense. What difference did it make to Mary Jo where she set down a soft drink? And what was the police chief going to do when he got there?

At the door the people scooted back to give her room to go out on the street. Behind her, her father had sat down beside Mrs. Hearndon. Jocie fingered her camera. She turned and snapped two pictures before her father pointed his finger at her and then the door. She slipped out to the street, then took a couple more pictures of the people standing around.

Her father wouldn't care if she took a few pictures. What was happening in the Grill was news. Even Wes would agree. Maybe bigger news than the tornado in July. The big daily papers might even carry this story if her father wanted to send something in to them.

Grover Flinn and Police Chief Simmons pushed past

her, not even noticing when she took a picture of them. She wanted to follow them back into the Grill, but her father had been pretty clear about wanting her out of there. He must have thought there might be trouble, and Grover Flinn's face looked like it. His nose was beet red and his eyes were bugging out as though he might be about to have a stroke any second.

Jocie glanced over her shoulder toward the Grill, but she kept moving down the street toward the office. Thunder rumbled as a sudden strong wind pushed the storm closer. The clouds piled up into a black mass overhead until it looked as if night was coming on early. On the sidewalk in front of the Fashion Shop, dresses on the racks were dancing wildly in the wind. Jocie took a picture of Miss Pauley trying to hold the dresses down while she pushed the rack toward the door. One of the dresses escaped and started flying out in the street. Jocie grabbed it and handed it to Miss Pauley before helping her maneuver the rack through the door and into the shop.

On both sides of the street, store owners were hustling to get everything off the sidewalk tables and inside before it rained. Jocie snapped a picture of Beulah Thompson, the clerk at the ten cent store, running after a basket tumbling across the street.

Beulah caught up with the basket and looked at Jocie as she went back to the front of the store. "You better quit worrying about pictures and get inside, Jocie," she said as she began raking packages of napkins off the sidewalk table into the basket. "We're in for a storm and a half from the looks of those clouds. I hope it doesn't turn out to be all wind and no rain."

"I guess we shouldn't mind getting wet if it does rain," Jocie said.

"Wet's okay," Beulah said with a worried glance up at the sky. "Struck by lightning not so good. I guess that would make some story for your paper. Clerk gets struck by lightning trying to save three dollars' worth of napkins."

"Or editor's daughter trying to get one more picture, huh?" Jocie helped her shove the stuff in the basket.

Beulah laughed. She was about Tabitha's age and had long brown hair that was whipping all around her face. She reached up to push it back out of her eyes and went stock still as she stared down the street.

"Oh my gosh! Will you look at that?"

Jocie turned to look. A group of maybe twenty men were marching up the street, the wind pushing the white robes they were wearing out around them like small sails. Some of them were holding white hoods up around their faces. Others let the wind blow the hoods off their heads. Behind them the black clouds seemed to be touching the ground, and it was almost as if the men had stepped straight out of the dark storm clouds onto Main Street.

"Who said they could come? We're not even having a parade or anything," Jocie said as she raised her camera up to take a picture.

"I don't think the Ku Klux Klan asks permission. They just do whatever they want to do," Beulah whispered as if she was afraid they might hear her.

"But what are they doing here?" Jocie had a sick feeling in the pit of her stomach as the men got closer, walking in formation up the street, not looking right or left.

"Nothing good." Beulah dropped the basket on the sidewalk. "Heck with the napkins. Let's get inside."

Jocie let Beulah drag her back toward the store while she tried to take a couple more pictures. She wasn't sure the pictures would come out. It was so dark the street lights were coming on even though it was still a couple of hours before sundown.

"Quit taking pictures," Beulah said. "No need attracting their attention."

"Why?" Jocie asked. "It's just black people they hate, isn't it?"

"Who knows with them? Just the sight of them scares me silly." Beulah stepped back inside the store. When Jocie didn't follow her in, she stuck her head back out and said, "You'd better get on in here too. They might know about that boy working for your daddy."

"You mean Noah?"

"Whatever boy your daddy gave a job to. I don't know his name."

"Noah. Why would they care about that?" Jocie asked.

"He's a colored boy, isn't he?"

"Well, yeah, but—"

"You don't have to know the reasons for everything, Jocie. You just better come on inside out of the storm and away from them."

"No, I'll be okay. I'll just wait till they go by and then go on across the street before the storm hits."

"Suit yourself, but don't say I didn't warn you." Beulah took one last look at the clouds and the men in the street before she ducked back inside and disappeared.

Jocie stepped back against the building under the awning and watched the men moving up the street. They didn't pay any attention to the wind or the thunder or even seem to be aware of the people on the sidewalks. They kept their eyes straight ahead and walked in step, moving in concert like one giant creature.

Suddenly everything was too quiet—as if the storm in the sky was holding its breath along with the people on the sidewalks while this human storm marched past. In the unnatural silence, the sound of the men's boots hitting the street jarred the air.

Jocie raised up her camera and took another picture. Her heart jumped up into her throat as, suddenly, the four men on the front row all turned their eyes toward her as if they were the head of a beast looking for prey. She hid her camera behind her back and fervently wished she had gone inside with Beulah or run on across the street to the newspaper office. She wished she were anywhere but standing pinned against the side of the ten cent store by the cold eyes staring at her. Then they turned as one to stare ahead of them up the street once more, and Jocie was able to breathe again.

She ran into the ten cent store and past Beulah, who said, "I told you to get off the street."

Jocie didn't pay any attention as she raced on out the back door to the street that ran behind the stores. Her only thought was to get to the Grill before the men out in the street did so she could warn her father that they were coming. Who knew what might happen if the white-robed men found out a sit-in was going on?

Jocie was panting by the time she opened the door into the Grill's kitchen. "For land's sake, child, what you doing coming in the back door? You trying to scare the life out of me?" Willanna, the cook, asked.

"I've got to tell Dad something."

"I think he done sent you home once. You better have a good story."

Willanna wiped her hands on her apron and followed Jocie to the swinging door out of the kitchen. She stopped there to watch as Jocie rushed out behind the counter. No glasses were sitting in front of any of the people at the counter. Myra Hearndon still had her finger holding her dollar bill forward. Grover Flinn and Chief Simmons were standing behind them with their hands on their hips as if trying to decide what to do. Mr. Flinn's nose was even redder than it had been when he passed Jocie out on the street earlier.

Jocie's father started frowning when he saw her. "I told you to go back to the newspaper office."

"I know, but this is important. The Klan's coming up the street."

32

Beside Jocie's father, Myra Hearndon pulled in a quick breath, then shut her eyes for a moment before she opened them again slowly, but she didn't move. She sat just as straight, her face forward, and didn't take the first look over her shoulder. Everyone else looked out at the street.

Grover Flinn was almost yelling at the police chief. "See what's happening? You should have gone on and run her out of here like I told you to do."

"Now, Grover, she's just sitting there. There's no law against that," Chief Simmons said.

"You could've arrested her for disturbing the peace."

"I haven't seen any peace being disturbed except maybe by you. And you surely couldn't expect me to arrest Brother Boyer or Miss Alice or David here, now could I? What would I charge them with? Being thirsty?"

"Well, somebody ought to have done something. I don't want any trouble with the Klan," Grover said.

Outside the men in the white robes had come to a halt in the street in front of the Grill. The people clustered around the Grill's door began easing away as if they were afraid of being caught in the middle of whatever trouble might come.

Suddenly Mary Jo slammed down the towel she'd been using to rub a hole in the counter. "Enough is enough!" she said, glaring at Grover. She walked around the counter past him and Chief Simmons straight to the door. She pulled it shut and turned the lock just as two of the men in white robes started walking toward the Grill.

"We're closed," she shouted through the glass door as she flipped the paper sign hanging on the door over from OPEN to CLOSED.

The two men stared at her through the door. She didn't pay them any attention as she stalked back past her boss and behind the counter again. She went straight over to Myra Hearndon, pulled out her order pad, and said, "Now what was it you wanted, ma'am?"

"What do you think you're doing, Mary Jo?" The words squeaked out of Grover Flinn as if somebody was choking him.

Mary Jo looked over at him. "I'm taking orders from these customers who got in the door before closing time. I'm hoping they won't want anything that Willanna will have to cook, but if they do, we'll stay here and cook it if the storm don't knock out the electricity."

"I haven't said you could serve them." Beads of sweat popped out on Grover's head.

"You hired me to serve customers that come in this place. Now I never gave it a whole lot of thought before where anybody sat, but I've had plenty of time to think the last couple of hours. The truth is, me and Willanna have been working here together for over ten years." Mary Jo glanced over at Willanna, who was still standing in the door to the kitchen. "We've rubbed shoulders, drank out of the same cups, sweated together over that stove back there, and she ain't never caught the white disease and I ain't never caught the black disease."

"She's telling the truth," Willanna said, lifting her eyebrows up and nodding a little.

"So I don't think it much matters where anybody sits."

Mary Jo looked back at Myra, her pen poised over her order pad. "Now that was a soft drink you wanted, wasn't it?" She totally ignored Grover Flinn, who was staring at her as if she'd sprouted horns and a tail.

"Yes, thank you," Myra said. "With plenty of ice, please."

"The same for us," Brother Boyer said. "And we appreciate it, Mary Jo."

"Just doing my job while I still have one."

"Nobody's going to fire you," David said with a look over at Grover Flinn. "Grover couldn't get by without you to wait on people, could you, Grover?"

"If he thinks he can, he'll have to get by without my cooking too," Willanna said.

"I never said anything about firing anybody," Grover said as he sank down in a chair beside one of the tables out in the middle of the restaurant.

"That's good to hear. Now you take some deep breaths, Grover, before you have a coronary," Mary Jo told him. "And Chief, you go on and make those peeping toms in sheets get away from my door. They're the ones that ought to be arrested, coming in here from who knows where trying to scare folks. And I done told them we're closed."

"We may be worse than closed before they're through," Grover said, but his nose was fading from bright red back to a more normal pink.

Jocie looked at her camera. One picture left. She thought about taking a picture of Grover slumped at the table or Chief Simmons heading toward the front door, but instead she raised the camera up and turned it toward Mary Jo putting ice in the glasses. Mary Jo looked over at her. "You take a picture of me, Jocie Brooke, and I'll take that camera away from you and stomp it flat."

Willanna laughed. "Don't you be messing with Mary

Jo today, child. She means what she says." She shook her head as she went back into the kitchen.

"We've probably got enough pictures for this week's issue, Jocie," her father said as he stood up. "We'd better get back to the office and work on getting them ready to print."

Noah's mother took a long drink of the cola Mary Jo set in front of her and then said, "I'll walk along with you, Brother Brooke." She slid gracefully off the stool. She lightly touched Brother Boyer's shoulder as she looked at him and his wife. "I do thank you both for coming to have a drink with me." She glanced out toward the street where there was no longer any sign of men in white robes. "Please pray for peace and cool heads."

"We had peace before you came in here. If it's gone now, you can take the blame," Grover said.

Myra ignored him as she turned to Mary Jo and said, "That was one of the most courageous things I've ever seen anybody do."

Mary Jo looked as if she'd just been awarded a medal. Her cheeks turned rosy as she said, "It wasn't all that much. I should have waited on you way back when, and then we wouldn't have had to worry about those yahoos out on the street."

When they left the Grill, there was no sign of the Klansmen. Jocie wondered if the ground had swallowed them up, or if they had stepped back into the storm cloud the way it had looked as if they had come. The clouds weren't quite as dark as they had been and the thunder sounded more distant. Even so, as she and her father and Noah's mother started down the street toward the newspaper office, raindrops began splattering on the sidewalk.

"It looks as if we may get wet," Noah's mother said.

"We can hope." Jocie's father held out his hand to catch a raindrop.

"And pray," Noah's mother said. "Alex's apple trees need a good rain."

"Everything could use a good rain," Jocie's father peered up at the clouds. "But it looks like the storm is moving away from us."

"Do you think the storm, this other storm that Mr. Flinn says I've started, will move away from us too? Is the . . ." She hesitated as if even saying the word was painful, but she went on, making herself say it. "Is the Klan very active in Holly County?"

"Not that I've ever known. Those men, the ones I got a good look at, I've never seen them before."

"I watched them coming up the street down in front of the ten cent store," Jocie said. "I didn't recognize any of them. Of course I couldn't get a good look at some of them with those hoods up around their faces." She looked over at her father. "Why were they here? They couldn't have known what was going on at the Grill, could they?"

"No, I don't think so," Jocie's father said. "That was just coincidence."

"It wasn't coincidence that they were here," Noah's mother said. "They may not have come because I was staging a sit-in up there, but you can be assured they were here because of us. Because we bought that land from Mr. Harvey. Poor Alex. He just wanted a farm. We didn't think we'd be challenging or breaking any barriers here just buying a piece of land. While I'm quite willing to make personal sacrifices to work toward true equality in our country, I don't want my children to be in danger."

"No good mother wants her children to be in danger," Jocie's father said.

Jocie waited for her father to say more, to assure Noah's mother that her family was safe in Holly County, that nothing bad would happen, but he was silent as they hurried on toward the newspaper office. Jocie told herself it was just because the raindrops were hitting harder. He couldn't stop and talk with the rain coming down. But even after they went inside and Cassidy was hugging her mother and Noah looked about ready to pass out with relief, Jocie's father didn't say anything to reassure Noah's mother that things were going to be all right. Jocie waved at Noah and Cassidy as they followed their mother out the back door and dashed across the street through the rain to their car. Jocie's father watched too, but he still didn't say what she was wanting to hear.

Finally Jocie asked him straight out. "They'll be okay? Nobody will bother them out on their farm, will they?"

Her father put both his hands on her shoulders, turned her toward him, and looked straight into her eyes. "I wish I could promise you that, Jocie, but I can't. All I can promise you is that we will pray that nothing bad will happen and that Mr. Hearndon's apple trees will grow tall and bear much fruit. It would be good to have an apple orchard in Holly County."

"But bad things do sometimes happen even when we pray that they won't."

"They do," her father admitted.

"Even when people aren't doing anything wrong?"

"Even then." Her father's fingers tightened on Jocie's shoulders. "But remember, the Lord never leaves us even when those bad things happen. He's there right beside us to help us make it through whatever life throws at us. You know that firsthand after the Lord took care of you in the tornado."

"But I caused that. Well, not the tornado, but being in its path. If I'd done the right thing and not run away, me and Wes wouldn't have been there."

"You're going to have to forgive yourself for that, Jocie. Nobody else has ever blamed you for what happened to Wes."

"That doesn't change it being my fault," Jocie said matter-of-factly. "But Noah and his family aren't doing anything wrong. They ought to be able to live anywhere they want."

"Yes, they should."

"Then it doesn't seem fair that they have to worry about bad things happening if they haven't done anything to deserve it."

"No, it doesn't."

Jocie didn't want her father to agree with her. She didn't know what she wanted him to say, but something to take away the echo of the sound of boots hitting on Hollyhill's Main Street. She concentrated on the rain hitting the front windows, an answer to prayer.

"Maybe we should thank God for the rain," she said after a minute.

"We should," he said. "And we can pray for the Hearndons, that the Lord will protect them and keep them safe."

"Can we do it right now?"

Jocie wanted to pray for the Hearndons now. Not wait till Sunday or bedtime. The bad things might not wait that long.

"We certainly can." Jocie's father kept his hands on her shoulders as he looked up at the ceiling and shut his eyes.

"Dear Lord, thank you for the blessings of the rain. You are a great and mighty God, and we look to you for all our needs. Help us to know your will and to follow your leadership. Watch over Noah and Myra and Cassidy and Alex and Elise and Eli this day and every day. Keep them safe in your mighty hands." Jocie's father's hands tightened again on her shoulders. "And thank you for this child you have given me to love and call my own. Amen."

33

Tuesday morning Zella left her house even earlier than usual to walk the five blocks to the *Banner* offices. She'd always been an early riser. The best time to work on her roses was in the morning as the sun was coming up. Not that there'd been much she could do with them lately except watch them dry up. In spite of all the thunder and lightning, the rain the night before had come and gone too quickly. Her rain gauge only showed two-tenths of an inch. Not enough to give a dandelion a good drink.

Of course, Zella's father used to say that once any kind of rain broke the drought, it was easier for the next rain to come. And thunderclouds had been building in the west nearly every evening for the last couple of weeks. Last night's was the first shower from any of the thunder, but maybe the next thunder would bring some real rain.

That was what the preachers needed to pray for. Not just a rain that wet the sidewalk and was nothing but a misty memory as soon as the sun came back out. A real rain. The kind that set in and stayed awhile. Though now the preachers might better spend their time praying away the other storm that was trying to settle over their town. That storm had nothing to do with the weather, but it was lying there on the horizon, dark and threatening.

Zella didn't understand why David was being so blind about it all. It was one thing to be in the middle of the storm just because that's where you happened to be when the storm hit. It was a whole different matter walking right out into the dark cloud and standing there daring the lightning to strike you.

She'd told him hiring that boy was a mistake. Not that she saw anything all that wrong with the boy other than being a bit disrespectful at times, but that probably had more to do with him being around Jocelyn than what color his skin was. And that other girl who had been coming in to see Jocelyn after school every once in while, that Rev. Boyer's daughter. She was nice as can be. Zella could only hope some of that girl's good manners would rub off on Jocelyn. She'd told Jocelyn as much just last week.

But not everybody in Holly County was as forward thinking as Zella was. A lot of people were just out-and-out prejudiced against colored people. That was simply the way they'd been brought up, and they hadn't ever seen any reason to change. Not Zella. She thought it was fine that the schools had been desegregated. It was high time. The state was going to make them do it anyhow. And she had no idea why three people had canceled their subscriptions because David put the story about Francine Rowlett on the front page. It wasn't like he put the colored teacher's picture on the top fold.

David said that surely wasn't the real reason they canceled, even after he read their letters saying it was. He said they must have already had some kind of problem with the paper or him. Sometimes David just closed his eyes and wouldn't look to keep from seeing the bad in people. That's why he'd never known what was going on with Adrienne. The day she drove out of town was everybody's lucky day.

But praise the Lord, David had opened his eyes and seen Leigh Jacobson at last. Zella had been pushing the girl in front of him for months. And now he was not only seeing

Leigh, he was calling her, finding reasons to walk down to the courthouse to talk to her, taking her to dinner—even if it was just to the Family Diner here in town. The man surely lacked any romantic instincts. And after Zella had told him he needed a restaurant with candles on the tables.

Still, things were progressing. Zella could tell that by the way Leigh's face colored up when she asked her straight out if David had given her a good-night kiss after they went out to eat. And if they'd kissed, David was definitely serious. He wasn't the type of man who would casually throw his kisses around without caring who he might hurt.

Of course the two of them still had plenty of obstacles in their road to romance. Jocelyn for one. Jocelyn always wanted to be right in the middle of everything. She'd been right in the middle of what went on the day before up at the Grill.

Leigh had called last night and filled her in on what had happened, since Zella walked on home after she'd found David at the courthouse. She wasn't about to stick around town and watch everybody make fools of themselves, swinging their partner and doing some sort of do-si-do dancing out in the middle of Main Street. Besides, the storm was coming up.

She hadn't realized the other storm was coming. She heard rumors about the Klan, but she never thought they'd just put on their sheets and march right down the middle of Main Street. Where in the world was the sheriff? She knew where the chief of police was. He was up at the Grill trying to get that Myra Hearndon to quit sitting where Grover Flinn didn't want her to sit while she tried to order a soft drink. And Zella could still hardly believe what Mary Jo had done. People could surprise you sometimes.

But somebody, and not just Mary Jo, should have been out there telling that bunch of hoodlums to take their sheets elsewhere. From what Leigh had told her, the men weren't even from Hollyhill. Not that there weren't men in Hollyhill who might be in the Klan. Zella knew a few who liked to get in your face and spit all over you while they told you giving coloreds the same rights as whites would be the downfall of the country. Some men could be such idiots. Thank the heavens above she didn't have to look at one of them over the breakfast table every morning.

As she passed by the Christian Church, the bells began ringing out the hour. The hymn wouldn't play until eight o'clock. Tuesday. That was "The Lily of the Valley." Or maybe that was on Wednesday and today was "What a Friend We Have in Jesus." She heard them every livelong day, whether she was at the newspaper or at home. Even down at the Baptist church where she went, those songs started playing, she heard them. She ought to know them all by heart, but the songs didn't sound right being bonged out the top of a church. It would have been plenty good enough to just let the clock chime out the hours.

Zella picked up her pace. She was a block away. She didn't really think Wesley would beat her into the office. It would take him awhile to get up and going with that big cast on his leg, but he'd always been an early riser too. She didn't want to take the chance he might clump down the steps and be in the office before she was.

Of course even if he did beat her into the office, he probably wouldn't mess around her desk, but then you never knew. And there were things she didn't want him to see. She'd stuck the letter under her typewriter pad. It wasn't in plain sight or anything. Still, that would be the first place Zella would look if she was searching for something at somebody else's desk.

Not that she would poke around somebody else's desk.

Except for David's. If she didn't check his piles of stuff every little bit, some bill would go missing and then they might not get their newsprint on time or the electric company would turn off their lights. And she always put back anything of a personal nature in the exact same spot she found it. The first time she'd found Leigh's name and telephone number on a scrap of paper slid halfway under David's phone, Zella had wanted to shout. It just made her feel so good when things turned out the way they should, and if a person had to prod a little here and there to get things to go the way they should, then there surely wasn't anything so wrong with that.

That's all she was doing with Wesley. Making things turn out the way they should. A man needed family, and Jocelyn saying she was family didn't count. Blood family was what was important. Relatives had to see to you when you needed help. Just like Vera Louise, Zella's niece, might have to someday see to Zella's needs whether she wanted to or not. It would be her obligation since Zella didn't have any children of her own to take care of her when she got old.

She unlocked the front door of the *Banner* and went inside. No sign of Wesley or David. She went straight to her desk, stuffed her purse in the bottom drawer, and took a pink tissue out of the box on top of the desk to dab the sweat off her forehead. If another shower hadn't come before evening to cool things off, that pressroom was going to be hot as blue blazes when they had to start folding the papers. She sat down and lifted the cover off her typewriter. Then she lifted up the pad and pulled the letter out.

It had come in the mail last week. She'd made sure she was the first to go through the mail ever since she'd written to the address she got from the friendly clerk up in

Pelphrey, Ohio. Zella hadn't told the woman the whole truth, but she hadn't exactly lied. She just said there might be an inheritance, and that was true enough. Wesley had been at the point of death for a while, and Zella supposed a motorcycle and a bunch of books might constitute an estate. Besides, for all she knew Wesley could have a sock full of money hidden away somewhere. Just because she herself hadn't found it when she was up there in his apartment didn't mean it wasn't there. She hadn't looked everywhere.

She slipped the letter out of the envelope, then sat still and listened to make sure she was still alone in the offices. No sound from the back. In fact, she could hear Wesley clomping around on his crutches over her head. She supposed she'd have to tell Wesley about the letter sooner or later. But she was waiting for the right time. There wasn't any hurry. The boy who'd written wouldn't show up on anybody's doorstep until she wrote back to him, and she hadn't done that yet.

Zella unfolded the letter and looked at the neat handwriting there. Wesley had neat handwriting too. A person wouldn't think it from looking at him, with his hair that sprangled out in a dozen directions and printing ink stains or grease spots on his shirts all the time. But he wrote notes in small precise letters. Not exactly like this boy's, but a person could see a likeness if she looked for it.

Dear Mrs. Curtsinger, . . .

Everybody always assumed a woman was married, as if being unmarried was some kind of unnatural state. Zella shook away her irritation and went on reading.

I was very excited to receive your letter regarding Wesley Green. I think he may be my grandfather. He left here over twenty years ago and my father has always told me that he must be dead. So your letter was a surprise. My father is still not sure that this Wesley Green is his father and would like to have more information. The name, Wesley Green, is not that unusual, and before any of us make a trip to your area, we would like to be sure this man is really our father and grandfather. If he has recovered enough from his injuries, please show him this letter and ask him to write us.

As far as your question about my grandfather perhaps having some sort of legal problems, my father is unaware of anything of that sort. We couldn't be completely sure since he has been gone so long, but no one has ever contacted us looking for him until we received your letter. My father feels my grandfather's grief over the tragic loss of his wife and daughter in an automobile accident may have led to my grandfather leaving home.

I will look forward to hearing from you or from my grandfather if he is indeed the right Wesley Green. I am a college student majoring in science education, but if this man is my grandfather I would like to come see him at my first opportunity and perhaps write to him prior to that.

Thank you so much for contacting us.

Sincerely yours,
Robert Wesley Green, Jr.

So much for being from Jupiter, Zella thought. She folded the letter and carefully stuck it all the way in the back behind a pile of envelopes in her top desk drawer as she heard Wesley stepping out of his door up above her head. She would tell Wesley in time. Just as soon as she figured out how.

34

By the time Jocie's father dropped her off in front of the high school on Tuesday morning, the sun had already burned off every trace of the rain from the night before and the heat had returned in force. The weatherman was saying it might be the hottest day of the year with the chance of more thunderstorms in the evening.

Jocie didn't usually pay much attention to what the weatherman said was going to happen other than to try to figure out whether to wear long sleeves or short sleeves. No sleeves suited best now with the heat. And shorts, but of course the school didn't allow shorts even if the school building was like an oven by lunchtime. But now with everybody praying for rain, Jocie listened to the weather forecasts and tried to remember to say her rain prayer at least three times a day.

Without rain, the farmers' crops would dry up in the fields, and the cows wouldn't have any grass to eat and would stop giving milk. Then the farmers wouldn't have any money to come to Hollyhill and buy things. They wouldn't have money to put in the collection plates at church. They might even quit buying the *Banner* to find out the news.

Zella kept saying they might do that anyway because of Noah. Sometimes Zella could come up with the craziest things to worry about. Noah was working out great at the paper. He didn't mind Jocie telling him how to do things, and he was learning fast. Best of all, he and Wes had hit it off fine. Since Wes had been sort of down in the dumps a lot lately, Jocie had been a little worried he might think Noah was trying to take his place at the paper, but he'd not been a bit bothered. He just watched Noah tossing the bundles of newsprint around like they were cotton balls and said it was about time her father hired some young muscle. Said he'd had muscles like that back when he lived on Jupiter.

It was great having Wes back to keep the press clicking along smoothly as they ran the inside pages of the *Banner*. And he'd been almost like his old self, talking about Jupiter and cajoling the press as if it was a reluctant girlfriend. He even had Noah laughing when he called the press Betsy Lou.

Of course, that was before Noah's mother sat down at the counter at the Grill and the men in their white robes came stomping up Main Street. Wes had missed all that excitement. He'd already made his way up the stairs to his rooms to prop his leg up and sit in front of his fan. Unless he'd been looking out his window, he probably wouldn't know anything about what had gone on until her father told him this morning. Jocie wished she could be there to hear them talk about it. Maybe they'd say something to take away the bad feelings she had about the men staring at them through the door of the Grill.

Jocie had even dreamed about them staring at her. Only it wasn't just the two men, but all the men surrounding her and linking their arms together so she couldn't get away. Then when she'd taken pictures of them, they just laughed. Horrid loud laughs that made her drop her camera and hold her hands over her ears. That's when she had jerked awake.

She had lain there in the dark and wished Wes was still in the living room so she could creep in there by his cot and let him put his hand on her head and tell her it was just some kind of Neptunian nightmare. Her father would have told her the same thing without the Neptunian part, but she didn't want to wake him up. Wes would have already been awake.

But Wes was gone, so she had just stared at the stars in the sky outside the windows and let her hand fall down to touch Zeb's head beside her bed. Aunt Love was always saying it was better to pray and count your blessings instead of sheep when a person couldn't sleep, so Jocie whispered a prayer into the night.

"Dear Lord, thank you for the night. And the stars in the sky. Thank you for letting Daddy love me. Thank you for sending me Zeb. Thank you that Wes is better. Thank you that it's almost time for Tabitha's baby to be born. Thank you that Aunt Love hasn't forgotten her Bible verses, because she wouldn't be able to stand it if that happened. But of course, you already know that. Thank you for being here in the dark with me. Watch over Noah and his family. Please send us rain. And help me to go back to sleep so I can stay awake in civics class tomorrow. Amen."

Then Jocie had repeated Psalm 23 over in her head. *The Lord is my shepherd; I shall not want.* She could remember saying it all the way through two times, but then she must have fallen asleep before she got to the *surely goodness and mercy* part the third time.

Jocie thought maybe she should repeat it over again this morning as she went in the school and down the hall to her locker. There was just a funny feeling in the air as if what had happened on Main Street the day before had somehow carried over to the school. Nobody looked happy. Instead, everybody looked worried, like they were going to have a test in every class and they'd all forgotten to study.

When Jocie got to her locker, Paulette was already there. And so was Ronnie Martin, leaning against the wall opposite the lockers. Jocie looked right past him as if he wasn't there, but that was getting harder and harder to do. It seemed as if he was always around somewhere. At church, here at school. It was wearing on Jocie, like water dripping on rock, to keep making him invisible.

Jocie looked over at Paulette as she twisted the combination on her locker. "How come he's always hanging around here?"

Paulette looked a little uncomfortable as she said, "Who?"

"Who do you think?" Jocie jerked her head in the direction of Ronnie Martin. "Him."

Paulette looked even more uncomfortable. "Oh, you mean Ronnie. I've been meaning to talk to you about that, Jocie. You know, Ronnie's actually pretty cute. And he's going to be sixteen next month."

Jocie's hand froze on the English book she was reaching for in her locker. She looked over at Paulette. "So?"

Paulette started talking faster. "So, I think you need to give Ronnie a break. I mean, I know he shouldn't have said what he said to you. That was bad, but he told you he was sorry."

"He didn't mean it."

"And you obviously didn't mean it when you said you forgave him." Paulette's eyes narrowed and her mouth tightened as she stared at Jocie. "I mean, isn't your father always preaching that we should forgive each other?"

"I think that's only if the other person's really sorry."

Jocie couldn't believe this. Her best friend, Paulette, taking up for Ronnie Martin. Her best friend, Paulette, thinking Ronnie Martin was cute. All at once Jocie remembered how

Paulette had disappeared for a while after church let out the Sunday before last and then had come around from the cemetery behind the building with cheeks a little too red. She'd told Jocie she'd been running after some of the little kids, but now it appeared she'd been running after Ronnie Martin.

"But he is now," Paulette said, losing her mad look and using her best pleading voice. "Honest. He's really sorry any of that ever happened."

"I guess he told you that so you'd kiss him or something," Jocie said.

"Don't be mean, Jocie."

"Sorry. You're right. That was mean, but so was Ronnie Martin. He was being mean to poor old Sallie that day and talking about Tabitha even before he started in on me."

"I know," Paulette said. "But people can change. That's why we go to church to learn how we ought to act, isn't it? And he's trying. So I think you should try too."

Jocie pulled in her breath and held it a minute before she let it out. She didn't want to try to forgive Ronnie Martin. She wanted Ronnie Martin to disappear off the face of the earth. *Forgive us our debts, as we forgive our debtors.* Forgive and be forgiven. Paulette was right. Her father was always preaching on that. It was all over the place in the Bible. She and Wes had found a lot of those verses on Sunday afternoon. And it wasn't as if Jocie thought she was perfect. She had plenty to be forgiven for.

"Okay," Jocie said finally. "What do you want me to do?"

"Just give Ronnie a chance. Talk to him."

"Now?" Jocie wanted to slam her locker shut and run the other way. Any way that got her away from Ronnie Martin. But Paulette was her friend, and she'd told her she'd try.

"Yeah, why not? We've got to head to class. The bell's

going to be ringing any minute, but Ronnie's class is down the same hall as ours." Paulette smiled over at Ronnie, who pushed away from the wall and came over to them. "Come on, Ronnie. Walk us to class."

Jocie made herself look at him. He'd been nothing but mean to her ever since she'd started going to Mt. Pleasant Church. He'd made fun of her. He'd said those horrible things to her. He'd tried to destroy her very world.

"Hello, Jocie," he said. He looked the same, and yet he didn't. He was still big with broad shoulders. The sleeves of his T-shirt were tight on his upper arms where he'd been lifting weights to get ready for football season. His face was red and not all from being out in the sun. And his smirk was more of a smile. Not exactly a smile, but closer to one.

Jocie didn't feel close to a smile at all. "Hi, Ronnie," she made her mouth say.

And then the first bell was ringing and they didn't have time to do anything except run for class so they wouldn't all end up in the principal's office with tardy slips. Jocie had never been so thankful to hear a bell ringing.

The reprieve didn't last long. When Jocie came out of her second-period algebra class, Ronnie was there by the door waiting for her. She kept her eyes away from him, but he still fell into step beside her.

"Hi, Jocie. You got a minute?"

"I've got to go to class." Jocie hugged her books up against her chest and still didn't look at him. "Where's Paulette?"

"Her next class is upstairs."

"Oh, yeah." Jocie didn't know what else to say. As she walked down the hall with Ronnie beside her, she couldn't remember the last time she'd felt so awkward. Heaven forbid that anybody would think they were a couple. She eased a couple of inches away from him.

"Besides, I thought it might be easier if we talked without Paulette being around. That way we could say whatever we wanted to say without worrying about what Paulette wanted us to say."

"And what does Paulette want us to say?" Jocie kept her head down but peeked out of the side of her eyes at him.

"Oh, you know Paulette. She wants everybody to get along, be buddies."

"I'm not sure we can be buddies." Actually she was pretty sure they couldn't, but she'd promised Paulette she'd try.

"Yeah, well, maybe not, but how about a truce?"

"I thought that was what we had already. A truce. No active hostilities," Jocie said.

"I don't know about that. Your hostility still feels pretty active. If hostility means hate."

"Hate?" Jocie flinched a little at the word. "I don't hate you."

"You don't like me either."

"No."

"And I guess I can't blame you. I did pick on you when you first came to church and my daddy didn't like your daddy, but he likes him better now. Says you might not be able to agree with everything Brother David says, but the man practices what he preaches."

Jocie was gripping her books so tight that her arms were going to be bruised. She debated which would be easier to do—sock him in the nose or stomp on his foot. She didn't even like hearing him say her father's name.

"Mt. Pleasant is lucky to have my father as their preacher," she said.

"Yeah, most everybody out there thinks so. And I've been paying more attention in church lately and trying to remember to love my neighbor and that kind of stuff. You know, the stuff he's always preaching about."

Jocie couldn't believe she was hearing right. Ronnie Martin worried about loving his neighbor? She stopped in the middle of the hall and turned to look squarely at him while the other kids gave them funny looks as they went around them.

"Are you sure you aren't just wanting to love your neighbor Paulette?"

"That too," Ronnie admitted. "But that's not the only reason for all this."

"Oh? What is the reason then?" Jocie wished the bell would ring so she could make a run for her class.

"All right, I'll just be out with it. I know you didn't believe me when I said I was sorry out at church that day, and maybe you were right. Maybe I wasn't sorry enough. But I am now."

"Wes almost got killed," Jocie said.

"I know that, but you don't have to act so all holier than thou." Ronnie was frowning. "You don't act like you think I can feel sorry or want to change. But maybe it's you that can't change. Maybe it's you that doesn't want to forgive your neighbor."

Jocie looked at him, but she couldn't say that she forgave him. Not without lying. So instead she said, "I've got to get to class." The first bell rang right on cue.

"Yeah, me too."

"I'll work on it," she said. "The forgiving thing."

"Okay." He started to turn back down the hall but then he stopped. "Oh, by the way, maybe you should tell your friend Noah to be careful. I've been hearing talk."

"What kind of talk?"

"Oh, just the regular stuff. You know, what went on last night. I hear you were there."

"Are you talking about those men? The Klan?" Jocie

shivered a little as she said the word. "You don't have anything to do with them, do you?"

"No, no. Never." Ronnie looked totally shocked that she'd even think such a thing. "But I know some guys that know some other guys. Anyway, maybe you ought to warn Noah to be watching out. Him and his family. The talk isn't good."

"If you know something bad's happening, you should go tell the sheriff."

"I don't really know anything for sure. I'm just hearing stuff. Why don't you tell Brother David and maybe he can find out more about it, okay?"

"Okay," Jocie said as the second bell sounded. She was right beside the door to her class so she might be able to slip in without getting a tardy, but Ronnie wasn't going to be so lucky.

She watched him head back down the hall. It was going to take some getting used to not making him invisible when she saw him. And he'd actually sounded almost nice. As if he really cared if she forgave him or not—and about Noah and his family. That was going to take even more getting used to. Ronnie Martin being nice. In fact, the question now was whether she could feel nice enough to wipe the slate clean and start over with him. She'd just have to pray about it.

She seemed to keep piling up prayers. The rain prayer. Tabitha's baby prayer. Wes getting better prayer. A forgiving spirit prayer. But maybe the Lord wouldn't mind. Her father was always saying the Lord wanted to hear from his people. That was good. For sure she couldn't do this forgiving thing on her own.

35

David spread out the pictures that he and Jocie had taken the day before at Sidewalk Days on the table in the press-room. Wes had come down early and had the pictures ready before David even got to the office.

"It sure is good having you back in the saddle," David told Wes, who was sitting over by the press with his leg propped up on another chair, waiting for David to pick the pictures for this week's issue.

"Well, I don't know about being in no saddle, but I've got my head full of the smell of ink again, and coffee just tastes better out of this old pot out here." He held up his cup.

"I'm not sure better's the right word."

"Oh yeah," Wes said and took a sip. "Strong and mean."

David shook his head a little. "I don't know how you can keep drinking coffee as hot as it is in here."

"I figure my insides might as well be as hot as my outsides," Wes said. "Besides, the heat never bothered me. I ain't so sure about old Zell. Something wrong with her?"

"What do you mean, wrong with her?"

"She's been sort of jumpy ever since I come back. Like a frog leg in a skillet of hot grease. It's like she thinks I'm gonna look cross-eyed at her and say boo or something."

"I guess now that you mention it, Zella has been a little short with everybody lately. Could be the heat. Maybe

I should see about getting a fan to put out there by her desk."

"No, that would never work. Might blow one of her curls out of place and then she'd really get curious on us. Besides, when you think about it, she's always been a little short with everybody. Excepting maybe Leigh, and who in their right mind could be short with that girl? She's got the sweetness market cornered."

"You won't get any argument about that out of me," David said. He made a mental note to plan something special with Leigh for Friday night. Of course, the high school was playing a home football game that night, so David would have to take pictures. Saturday night might be better if he could get his sermon prepared early enough. Maybe they could drive over to Dove Lake and rent a rowboat. A rowboat and moonlight. Even Zella would think that was romantic.

"Well, see, that should make old Zell happy, what with her matchmaking going so well. But then maybe it's just me. Or maybe it's Noah. She don't seem too happy about him being on board even though he seems to be a right smart help."

"He is. And you're right about Zella." David looked over his shoulder at the door out of the pressroom. "She didn't want me to hire Noah. Thought it might cause problems with some of our subscribers. I still can't imagine why."

"From the looks of those pictures there, the problems have already shown up. Whatever the cause might be. Jo got some interesting shots." Wes pointed over at the table. "Looks like I missed all the excitement when I went up the stairs to contemplate my window fan."

"Were you okay by yourself last night?" David glanced at Wes and then back at the pictures.

"It was a heap quieter, but some lonesome. And tuna fish sandwiches ain't near so good for breakfast as they are supper. Besides, I done got used to the girls around. Jo waiting on me, Lovella talking Bible to me, and Tabby creeping down to the john in the wee hours of the morning. Poor child looks about ready to pop."

"She's ready, but the doctor says it may still be a couple of weeks or longer." David picked up a couple of the pictures and laid them aside.

"She's taking it well. Being in the family way, I mean. But she does seem awful set on having a girl. Done come up with a name for her and everything."

"I know, but once the baby is here, she'll be happy whether it's a boy or a girl." David kept telling himself that, hoping it was true.

"Maybe so, but you'd better be ready with some words of wisdom just in case." Wes took another drink of his coffee.

"My wisdom reservoir has been pretty empty the last few weeks."

"Now that ain't the case. Unless you used them all up on me."

David turned to look at Wes. "I don't know if my words to you were wise enough."

"You mean, because I haven't come out and walked the aisle?" Wes kept his eyes on the press.

"Walking the aisle's not what's most important. What's in your heart is the most important thing, and that's what the Lord pays attention to."

"I'm still thinking. You got to give me some time, David."

"But none of us know how much time we have."

"I've been shown that's true enough." Wes mashed his mouth together and stared a hole in the press.

David wished he'd picked his words a little more wisely at this moment. "I'm sorry, Wes. I didn't aim to bring back bad memories for you."

"Them kind of memories don't have to be brought back, David. They just lay there ready to spring up and bite you all the time."

"The Lord is ready all the time too. He can help you with that. With everything. He'll walk side by side with you and help you through hard times and rejoice with you in good times." David stopped himself before he started really preaching.

"Is that the way it is for you?" Wes looked around at him.

"It is. Proverbs says he's 'a friend that sticketh closer than a brother.' And it can be that way for you too. All you have to do is trust him." He kept his eyes locked on Wes as he offered up a silent prayer.

For a few seconds, there was a stillness in the air between them, and David thought Wes might take that step into trust, but then Wes was saying, "You've been a friend better than a brother to me, David. I thank you for it." He turned his eyes back toward the press. "And I ain't ignoring your wise words. I'll keep thinking on them."

David gave it one more try. "Sometimes it's more important what you feel in your heart than what you think in your head." He never understood why some people fought so hard against the pull of the Lord on their hearts. Why couldn't they just accept the love the Lord so freely offered? All they had to do was believe. If only David could believe for them, but each person had to make his own choice.

"I'll try to remember that," Wes said before he looked around and pointed toward the pictures on the table again. "But we'd better get back to work if we're going to get the *Banner* run on time. What do you think about those pictures? I'm betting there's some you won't be putting in our good paper."

David looked down at the pictures laid out in rows, starting with the ones he'd taken of the shoppers and merchants while the sun was beating down and the sky was a merciless blue. People looked hot, but happy enough as they shopped. Then Jocie had taken the pictures of him and Myra Hearndon and Rev. and Mrs. Boyer at the counter with Mary Jo hovering in the background looking worried. The picture of Grover Flinn and the sheriff rushing up the street toward the Grill was black and white, but even without Grover's red nose, it was easy to see the man's agitation. David couldn't put that one in the paper. Not if he ever wanted to eat at the Grill again.

He could definitely use the one of the dancing dress in the wind as Miss Pauley tried to push the dress rack inside her store ahead of the storm. Jocie had an eye for capturing the moment. She had captured the moment with the KKK too. The men in their white against the black storm cloud was chilling. He picked the picture up and moved over closer to the light.

Wes got up and hobbled over to look at the picture. "You know any of them?"

"Not that I can make out. Some of their faces aren't that plain," David pulled the photo up for a closer look. "But I heard they were all from out of town."

"It's a great shot."

"It is."

"You gonna run it?"

"No. No need giving them free ink."

"But they were here. Marching right down our Main Street. You could say that was news," Wes said.

"You could. And it is." David put the picture back down on the table. "But if I put that in the paper it would be like printing an obscenity in big black letters. I wish Jocie hadn't taken the picture."

"You give that girl a camera, she turns into a regular Lois Lane."

"But with no Superman to rescue her if she gets in trouble."

"She's got you."

"And you," David said.

"I can't do much flying right now. Leg's too heavy." Wes shook his head a little. "What about the other one? The one of the sit-in at the Grill. Who'd have ever thought we'd have a sit-in here in Hollyhill? By the way, how'd it turn out? Seems like we're missing the end photo."

"Mary Jo took things in hand. Locked out the Klan. Told Grover to sit down and shut up. Made the chief do his job and get rid of the men out on the street. Then poured us all soft drinks."

"Mary Jo?" Wes sounded surprised.

"Mary Jo."

"Jo should have taken a picture of her."

"She started to, but Mary Jo threatened to smash her camera."

"And Jo listened?" Wes sounded even more surprised.

"It wasn't a good time to cross Mary Jo."

"You don't say? Sounds like a good story."

"I don't know. I'll have to think about that." David frowned down at the photo. "I wouldn't want to cause trouble for Mrs. Hearndon or the Boyers. Or Mary Jo."

Wes tapped his finger on the picture of the Klan. "I think the trouble is already here."

In the end they put the sit-in story on the back page. It was front-page news, but David put it on the back. Maybe being a preacher and a newspaperman wasn't a good combination when real news happened. He didn't want his town torn apart, but at the same time he knew Myra Hearndon had every right to sit wherever she wanted to sit. It was time things changed in Hollyhill, but he wanted the change to be peaceful. He didn't want front-page news like the big papers had. Marches and riots. Policemen making arrests. National Guard troops in the streets to keep the peace. That kind of thing happened in Birmingham or Atlanta maybe, but not here in little Hollyhill. At least David was praying not.

By the time Jocie and Noah showed up at the office after school, David and Wes had the papers nearly ready to run. Leigh showed up right on schedule as they began putting the papers together. "I think we're going to get another storm," she said when she came in. "Let's hope this one has some rain and not just thunder and lightning."

"It rained last night," Jocie said.

"Just enough to make the grass sizzle," Leigh said as she sat a plate of sandwiches and a pan of brownies down on one of the chairs.

"You're a girl after my own heart, Miss Leigh." Wes smiled at Leigh and then shot a look at David. "Course I know it ain't my heart you're after, but that's okay. I can still eat a brownie."

Leigh's cheeks flashed red as she laughed. "Now, Wes, I believe you're trying to embarrass me." She went over and gave him a hug. "But it's good to see you back in the thick of things. It's been pretty dull around here without you."

"You know, I used to think Hollyhill and Dullville were one and the same, but things has been changing some here lately. Churches getting blown away. Sit-ins up at the Grill. Preachers going courting," Wes said.

"You just never know what might happen around here," David said with a smile at Leigh. "Thanks for coming and bringing food."

"I'll second that," Noah said as he grabbed a sandwich. "We can just dig in, can't we? I missed lunch."

"We're supposed to fold papers and then eat," Jocie told Noah.

"How about if I eat one sandwich now to keep from fainting away and then another one later?" Noah took a bite of the sandwich.

Leigh laughed. "Don't worry about it, Jocie. There's plenty and Noah's a growing boy. He has to keep his strength up."

David watched Leigh and silently thanked the Lord that she hadn't given up on getting him to notice her. For sure he was noticing her now. Noticing her gift of lighting up a place. Noticing how she had a way of making all of them smile. Even Noah, who had come in after school looking as if he'd been in a fight. He had refused to talk about it to David or Jocie other than to say a boy like him with a mother like his had to expect a few black eyes now and again.

And David was smiling too. Inside and out as he watched Leigh work her magic with Noah. He'd find a minute before the night was over to suggest the rowboat and moonlight. And maybe he could give Jocie the camera at the football game Friday night while he sat up in the stands with Leigh and cheered the Hollyhill Bulldogs on to victory or, if that was too much to hope for, then to a few first downs. In between plays they could decide on a time for Jocie's birthday party the next weekend.

"Where's Zella?" Leigh asked as she looked around.

"She was out here awhile ago, but I think she was afraid I was going to put my crutch down on her toe or something," Wes said.

"Oh, she probably just had a curl out of place or needed a fresh coating of lipstick before she could start folding papers," Jocie said. "You know Zella. Everything has to be just so. Or then again, she might be hiding in the restroom. She doesn't like storms." Thunder rumbled outside and the lights flickered.

"I hope the electricity doesn't go off before we get done," David said.

Leigh eased over closer to David and lowered her voice. "But then Zella's been after us to do something by candlelight."

"I don't think it was folding papers." David kept his voice low too.

"But we have sandwiches and brownies. That could equal a candlelight supper just like we talked about last week. It's not peanut butter, but chicken salad's okay." Leigh smiled.

"With the whole crew? About as romantic as you can get, right?" David grimaced.

"Well, fun anyway." Lightning flashed outside and the following clap of thunder rattled the windows. Leigh looked toward the small window in the back. "That was a close one. Maybe I'd better go check on Zella. See if she *is* hiding out in the restroom or under her desk."

Leigh was almost to the door out of the pressroom when there was a crash that had nothing to do with the thunder and lightning. When Zella screamed, David ran past Leigh into the front offices. Wind carrying the moist feel of rain hit David in the face as he went through the door. The front window, the one with *Hollyhill Banner* painted across it, lay shattered on the floor. Zella was staring down at the blood bubbling up out of a cut on her arm.

"What in the world happened?" he asked her.

Zella looked up at him with eyes almost popping out of her head as she held up her arm for him to see. "They could have killed me! A piece of that glass could have killed me!"

"What happened?" David repeated. "Did the storm blow something into the window?"

"It wasn't the wind." Zella pointed toward a rock in the middle of the shattered glass.

David stared at the rock. A rubber band held a folded piece of white paper to it. He didn't want to pick it up. He didn't want to read what was sure to be written on the paper. He wanted to be back in the pressroom laughing with Leigh. Not standing here with storms breaking out all around him.

36

Jocie stared at the rock surrounded by the broken glass, but she didn't try to step past her father to pick it up. It was as if the rock was a snake coiled, ready to strike and sink its poisonous fangs into whoever reached for it. Perhaps the poison was already in the air, sinking in through their pores, and that was why they were all just standing there not moving.

The wind pushed in through the shattered window, making the pieces of glass still stuck in the window frame screech as their broken sides rubbed together. Jocie jumped as one of the shards of glass was jarred loose and crashed to the floor.

Wes eased up beside her father on his crutches. "It's just a rock," he said.

"But somebody threw it," Noah said, standing beside Jocie.

"They did for a fact," Wes said. "But the damage is done now. It's over."

"I'm not so sure about that," Jocie's father said as he took a step toward the rock. Glass crunched under his shoes.

"Wait, David," Wes said. "Jo, go get a camera. This is news."

"Maybe I won't want to print this in the paper," Jocie's father said.

"No, it ain't that you're not wanting. What you don't want is for the rock to be laying there in the first place,"

Wes said. "But it is, and folks will be expecting to read about what happened. We'll need pictures."

As Jocie ran to get a camera, Zella said, "Doesn't anybody care that I'm bleeding?"

"Of course we do, Zella," Jocie's father said as he moved over to look at her arm. "How bad is it? Do you want me to call Dr. Markum?"

"No, I don't think it needs stitches, but it could have been cut deeper." Zella rolled her arm over to get a better look. "I could have been hurt bad."

Jocie reappeared and held up the camera. "Want me to take a picture of you, Zella?"

"Don't be silly, Jocelyn. Heaven knows, you waste enough film. Nobody wants to see a picture of me bleeding on the front page of the *Banner*." She dabbed at the cut with the handful of pink tissues Leigh handed her.

Once the blood was wiped off, the cut wasn't much more than a scratch, but there were bits of glass scattered all over Zella's desk. So Jocie took a picture of that instead of Zella's arm. Then she focused in on the rock lying in its glass nest. She popped in a new flashbulb and took a picture of a large piece of glass with the letters *BA* on it. She looked through the viewfinder at the pieces of glass still stuck in the window frame with their sharp, jagged ends, like fingers pointing toward the gaping hole in the window. Some of the letters of the word *Hollyhill* were still there, some were gone, and others were broken in half. She needed the picture from the outside, not the inside.

She was pushing open the door when her father stopped her. "Don't go out there, Jocie."

"But, Dad, I need to take the picture from out there. So the letters will be right. I mean, look. See how *Hollyhill* is all broken up."

"I'm afraid I do," he said as he leaned down to pick up the rock.

She turned away from the door to watch him pull the rubber band off the rock and unfold the paper. Maybe the rain would hold off a few more minutes so she could still get the outside picture, but she couldn't miss her father reading the message on the rock.

He stared down at the paper in his hand. Nobody in the room said anything as they waited for him to speak, but he didn't. Instead, his mouth tightened into a thin line as he dropped the rock back on the floor and tore the paper through the middle. Then he put the pieces together and tore them twice more.

He kept the pieces clutched in the fist of one hand as he grabbed Zella's trash can with his other hand and dumped it out. Zella gasped as pink tissues flew everywhere along with torn envelopes and crumpled papers. Jocie's father didn't seem to notice as he dropped the ripped-up paper down into the trash can. He kept his eyes on the bits of paper as though expecting them to try to make an escape.

He finally spoke. "Get me a match."

Jocie, along with everybody else in the room, just stood there and stared at her father. She couldn't imagine what might have been on the paper that had her father looking so grim. Then Zella pulled open a drawer on her desk and handed Leigh a book of matches. Without a word, Leigh handed the matches on to Jocie's father.

Jocie crept closer so she could see down in the trash can, but she didn't lift her camera up to take a picture as her father struck the match and dropped it into the papers. The flame flared up for a couple of seconds before vanishing into wisps of smoke. Jocie's father reached down and mashed the black remains of the paper into nothing but ash.

Outside, the thunder and lightning were easing away from Hollyhill taking with it the promise of rain, but nobody in the room paid much attention even with the window wide open to the weather. They were still staring at the trash can as if it might reveal answers to questions none of them dared ask.

Then Wes was saying, "All right, that's done. Now we better get going on all this or we'll be folding papers all night. Jo, you finish your picture taking. Noah, go hunt around back behind the press and see if you can dig up some boards or something we can cover up the window with."

Jocie's father interrupted him. "There's plastic back there. Some I got when we were thinking about painting the place last spring. It'll do to cover the window temporarily."

"Well, that might be easier," Wes admitted and went back to assigning duties. "David, you go call the police, and Leigh, you hunt up the broom out by the back door."

"Broom?" Zella gasped and turned pale.

"Are you feeling faint, Zella?" Leigh asked. "Maybe you should sit down." Leigh scooted Zella's chair out and leaned it over to dump any bits of glass out of it.

"I'm fine," Zella said, even as she sank down into the chair. "I'm just not sure we have a broom. It may have gotten thrown away or something."

"Don't worry about it. We'll find a broom somewhere," Leigh said. "Here, let me help you put a bandage over your cut before it starts bleeding again."

Jocie started toward the door to get the picture she wanted of the window from out on the street. But then she stopped and looked at her father, who was stooped down, picking up the bigger pieces of glass. "What did it say, Dad?"

He looked up at her after picking up another piece of glass. "No words you will ever hear passing out of my lips." He dropped the glass into the trash can. It crashed into more pieces. "Just let your curiosity rest this time, Jocie, with the knowledge that it was nothing but words of hate. Nothing any of our eyes or ears need to see or hear."

"Does somebody hate us?" Jocie didn't like saying the word. Not when she was talking about real hate. She didn't mind saying she hated dusting or washing windows. She hated mosquitoes whining in her ears. She hated boiled cabbage. But this was a different kind of hate.

Her father looked straight into her eyes. "I don't know, Jocie. I want to say no, but I don't know." Then he reached up and touched her cheek. "But maybe not. Maybe it was just a stupid prank."

She knew he didn't really believe that. He was just handing her a way to think of it without having to have the word "hate" bouncing around in her head. The problem was, she couldn't believe it either. She turned her mind back to the business at hand.

"I've got to take a picture from outside. It's okay if I go out there now, isn't it? The storm's moving off."

Her father stood up. "I'll go with you."

"You don't think whoever threw the rock is still hanging around out here, do you?" Jocie said as she stepped through the door out onto the sidewalk and looked around. Dark shadows lurked at the edges of the pools of light from the streetlamps. People could be standing there ready to throw more rocks.

"No, probably not. People who do things like this are cowards who don't want to take the chance of being seen."

"Do you think they broke other windows or just ours?"

"I don't know. I hadn't thought about that possibility,

but I'll ask the chief when I call him in a minute. If so, I might have to go take more pictures."

"Everything looks okay from here." Jocie looked up the street. She couldn't see anything but more shadows. The street looked deserted. That wasn't unusual for the nights they folded the *Banner*. All the other businesses were closed and locked up. Maybe whoever threw the rock knew that. They would have seen the lights and probably Zella at her desk. At night it was easy to see into the office when the lights were on. Jocie looked in now. She could see Leigh in there plain as day, opening another Band-Aid for Zella's arm, and Noah and Wes unfolding the plastic sheeting Noah had found.

"Take your picture," her father said. "We've got a lot to do."

Jocie looked through her camera at the broken window framed in the viewfinder. She brushed aside all the questions swirling around in her head. She didn't have to think about the reasons why in order to take the picture. She just had to think about how best to capture the shot so that other people might look at it and ask why.

She snapped one picture before she moved down the sidewalk for a different angle. Her father stayed by the door, and the shadows behind Jocie began reaching long fingers toward her. She took a deep breath, willed her hands to stop trembling, and braced the camera against her face. She concentrated on the square of the world in front of her eye as she squeezed the shutter and the flashbulb exploded in a burst of bright light.

For the rest of the night she was just going to concentrate on doing one thing at a time. The window was broken. Jocie couldn't fit the pieces back together. She couldn't do anything about rocks with hate words tied to them. Or about what might be in the shadows behind her other than to try to stay in the light out of reach. She couldn't do anything about yet another thunderstorm moving away without gifting them with rain. Nothing but pray. Yet wasn't that the best thing to do? Pray first. Do something second.

She hurried away from the shadows breathing down her neck to where her father waited. "It isn't going to rain, is it?" she said as she looked toward the east where thunder was still rumbling as the storm rolled away from them.

"Not out of that one," her father said. "But it will rain."

"But when?"

"I don't know, Jocie. We just have to keep praying."

"But we have so much to pray about. And now this too," Jocie said. Maybe she should just forget about all her other prayers and concentrate on a no-hate prayer.

"Yes, this too, but the Lord knows what we need, and he will take care of us."

"If he already knows what we need, why do we need to pray?"

"Because he wants to hear from his people and because it helps us when we pray." He put his arm around her shoulders and moved her toward the door. "But now we've got to get this mess cleaned up and back to work to get the *Banner* ready to go out."

"Nothing stops the *Hollyhill Banner*."

"I don't know about that, but this isn't going to." Her father waved his hand toward the broken glass on the floor as they went through the door.

For the last couple of months, folding papers hadn't been so bad with Leigh showing up with food to give it sort of a party atmosphere. And with Wes back, Jocie had been expecting a really fun night, but now nobody was smiling or saying much as they did what had to be done.

After Leigh had helped Zella put a row of Band-Aids up and down her arm, she helped Jocie sweep the glass up off the floor while Noah and Jocie's father carefully worked the remaining shards of glass out of the window frame. Wes tried to stay out of the way, and Zella disappeared into the restroom to try to dab a couple of spots of blood off her white blouse before the stain set up.

By the time Chief Simmons showed up to give the broken window an official once-over, Noah and Jocie's father were already tacking the plastic over the opening. "Looks like you got on somebody's bad side," the chief said.

"So it seems," Jocie's father said as he and the chief stepped inside.

"You know who?"

"Not who, but what."

"So there must have been a note," Chief Simmons said.

"There was." Jocie's father looked straight at the chief. "I got rid of it."

Chief Simmons frowned at him. "We might have got some leads off it."

"I doubt it. The letters were all cut out of the newspaper and pasted on."

"So where'd you throw it away? That trash can?" Chief Simmons stepped toward the trash can full of glass shards. "We can fish it out, I guess."

"Nothing to fish out. Nothing but ashes. I told you I got rid of it." Jocie's dad mashed his mouth together in a thin hard line as he waited for whatever the chief might say next.

"Well, I guess it's too late to do anything about that now. So you think it was the Klan?"

"I know it was the Klan, and so do you."

Chief Simmons sighed. "Yeah. I've been hearing things."

"Did you know they were going to be marching here yesterday?" Her father narrowed his eyes as he waited for the chief's answer.

"Come on, David. You don't think I would have let them be here if I could have done anything about it, but it's a free country. A person can walk down whatever street they decide to walk down."

Jocie was glad Noah was outside hammering the plastic in place instead of inside hearing Chief Simmons. Things were weird enough without Noah having to set the police chief straight on how it didn't always work that way, that sometimes the police brought out dogs and firehoses to keep certain people from walking down certain streets.

Her father said, "And sit wherever he or she wants to?"

"Well, it looks like they can now. At least at the Grill. And I'm not saying it shouldn't have always been that way, but people being people, it isn't always that easy."

"No, not easy at all. Are the windows up there okay?" Jocie's father asked. "And Brother Boyer's church? You haven't gotten any other calls?"

"I came by the Grill. As far as I could tell, everything looked okay. And I'll go by the church when I leave here. But surely they wouldn't bother a church."

"Tell that to those people down there in Birmingham. The families of those little girls."

"But we aren't Birmingham, David. We've never had that kind of trouble in our town, " the chief said. "We need to keep a level head here. It's just a broken window."

"This time." Jocie's father looked from Chief Simmons toward the plastic over the window flapping in the wind.

Jocie didn't like the way her father said those words. Did he think whoever threw the rock would be back with more rocks? More hate? She suddenly remembered what Ronnie

Martin had told her earlier that day. She moved closer to her father's side and touched his arm to get his attention.

"Not now, Jocie," her father said.

"But it's probably something Chief Simmons will want to know too." Jocie rushed on, not waiting for her father's permission. "Somebody at school told me I should warn Noah and his family to be on the lookout. That something bad might be going to happen."

"Did they give you any details?" Chief Simmons asked. "What or when or anything?"

"No, he just said he'd been hearing things."

"Well, that's not much help," the chief said. "I've been hearing things. Of course, where the Hearndons live out in the county is out of my jurisdiction anyway. But I'll pass it along to the sheriff so he can keep an eye out about that."

"This is in your jurisdiction," Jocie's father said. "The West End Church is in your jurisdiction."

"And I'm going to investigate and drive up there through the West End to be sure everything is peaceful. You don't have to tell me how to do my job, David."

"Sorry, Randy." Jocie's father shook his head a little. "I wasn't meaning to do that."

"That's all right. I understand." Chief Simmons put his hand on Jocie's father's shoulder. "It's been a long day. But the truth of the matter is we aren't ever going to find whoever threw that rock. You know that and I know that. The best we can hope to do is make them think we might so that they won't throw another one."

"You're probably right," Jocie's father said.

"Of course I am," Chief Simmons said. "You let me know if you have any more trouble."

Jocie and her father watched Chief Simmons go out the

door. Wes hobbled up behind them. "You get past writing out parking tickets, the chief's done in over his head," Wes said.

"Maybe we shouldn't be too hard on him. He's probably right. We'll never know who threw that rock," Jocie's father said.

"We might not want to know," Wes said.

37

The *Banner* got folded that night, but Leigh wasn't quite sure how. Things were all turned upside down after the rock came through the window. Wes was pale and drawn from being up on his leg too long. Zella jumped at the slightest noise. Noah hardly said two words except to ask David to drive him home after they were through. He couldn't very well ride his bike all those miles home with that evil lurking out there somewhere in the dark.

Even Jocie was silent as they folded the papers. Leigh wasn't sure she'd ever seen Jocie without something to say for so long. But then again maybe that was because David was so grim. He hardly managed a smile even when he told Leigh good night, but she knew it didn't have anything to do with her. It was whatever had been written on that paper.

He wouldn't talk about it. Not even several days later when they went to the high school football game on Friday night. He said he didn't want to talk about any of it. He said that was all anybody in town had wanted to talk about all week, and that was true enough. Leigh heard it every day at the courthouse. Who did what? Why whoever did what? And the most asked question, what were they going to do next? Everybody had their opinion, but nobody had any answers.

But David said he wanted to give his mind a rest, and

then he smiled at her. Leigh was ready to talk about anything he wanted to—or not talk about anything he didn't want to—as long as he kept smiling at her like that. He gave his camera to Jocie and let her run along the sidelines to get the pictures they needed for the *Banner*.

"She's better at taking pictures than I am anyway," he said.

"I don't know about better, but she does seem to be having fun," Leigh said after they found a seat up in the bleachers.

As Jocie made her way out to the field with the camera, kids kept yelling at her and striking poses. Jocie turned the camera toward them and focused in.

"She'll run out of film before the second quarter," Leigh said.

"She's not really taking all those pictures. She's just pretending so they'll leave her alone."

"Gee, I should have carried around a camera when I was in high school. It looks like an instant ticket to popularity."

"I'm glad you didn't," David said.

"Why?"

"Because then you might have taken a picture of some guy and one thing would have led to another and you'd be married now with three kids."

"Three kids?" Leigh's cheeks warmed and her heart started beating faster.

"Well, two at least."

"So what would be so bad about that?"

David reached over and took her hand. "Then I'd still be a lonesome old man who might have completely forgotten how good a regular old peanut butter sandwich could be."

Leigh leaned closer to David and didn't even think about

all the people around them who would be seeing them holding hands. It was as if they were the only two people on the bleachers. "You know, we've never really had that peanut butter sandwich picnic. We just keep talking about it."

"How about tomorrow night? If it doesn't rain. And from the looks of the weather maps, we're not even going to get any thunder or lightning for a while. I'd thought about us maybe going to the lake, but the way Tabitha's been feeling, I'd better stay closer to home."

So they went on their picnic. She made the peanut butter sandwiches. David brought grapes and lemonade. They didn't go anywhere special, just carried a blanket out into the old apple orchard behind his house since he had to stay close in case Tabitha's baby decided to come early.

The sun was going down by the time they got the picnic spread out, but it was still hot. Leigh's face was moist with perspiration and her hair was going frizzy. She should have borrowed some of Zella's armor hair spray. The fruit flies and bees that had been buzzing around the faulty apples on the ground came over to check out the new feast in the area. Then before they'd taken two bites of their peanut butter sandwiches, mosquitoes started humming in their ears. To add to the country ambiance, now and again a whiff of the neighbor's cow pasture drifted over to them.

"Maybe a picnic wasn't such a good idea," David said as he swatted at a mosquito on his arm.

"Or the peanut butter sandwiches," Leigh said. "I think my mouth is going to stick together. I should have put some jelly on them."

"Maybe lemonade will help," David said as he poured her some out of the thermos.

She took a drink and tried to wiggle around to find a more comfortable spot on the hard ground under the blanket.

David looked as uncomfortable as she was, sitting on the ground. Leigh put down her peanut butter sandwich and laughed. "You think maybe we're too old for picnics?"

"Maybe not too old, just too sensible." David waved his hand around his face. "Every mosquito in the county must be swarming us."

"Zella's going to be really disappointed."

"Just tell her we went and let her imagine the rest. You can leave out the mosquitoes and fruit flies and the pungent country odor." David stood up and reached down a hand to help Leigh up. "Come on. Let's walk a little. At least then we'll be a moving target for the mosquitoes."

"Okay. We'll take the food back to the house and share it with everybody later. Maybe Aunt Love can hunt us up some blackberry jam for the sandwiches."

So maybe it wasn't the picnic Leigh had imagined or that Zella read about in her romance novels, but it was still perfect. Absolutely, completely perfect. Even after they gathered up their things and went back inside to sit around the kitchen table and peel off the tops of the sandwiches to add Aunt Love's blackberry jam, it was still perfect. She felt at home in David's kitchen with David's family. She felt at home with David.

ꝏ ꝏ

By the time they folded papers again on Tuesday, the window in the newspaper office had been fixed. David hadn't found anybody to paint the *Hollyhill Banner* name back on it, but just having the window in was a relief after a week of listening to the plastic flop in and out with every breath of air. That noise had worn on all their nerves, especially Zella's. She was constantly rearranging the papers on her desk and patting down her hair.

Finally on Monday, David had asked her if anything was bothering her.

"No, of course not," she'd said as she grabbed a tissue to dab the end of her nose. "Well then, of course, this with the window. And my arm." She held up her arm where the long scratch was still an angry red. "And then Ralph and his son putting the window in this morning. They must both be deaf the way they kept yelling at one another. I mean, that would surely bother anybody. Keep them from being able to concentrate on their work. Not that I haven't been doing my work. Of course I've been doing my work. I always do my work. I sold three ads this morning."

"I know, Zella. I wouldn't be able to get by without you. I just thought maybe there was something you wanted to talk about. Something in particular that was bothering you. Jocie and Noah haven't been giving you a hard time, have they? Or Wes?"

Zella looked down quickly at her desk and straightened her piles of papers. "No, of course not. Not at all. I'm so relieved that Wesley is able to be back to help you. To help us all. And I'm not a bit worried about anything he says. Not a bit."

"Good," David said. "But just remember I'm ready to listen if you do have a complaint or a problem."

"Problem? What kind of problem could I have? I mean, other than my roses drying up and that's a problem everybody in Holly County is having right now. But if I did have a problem I couldn't handle myself, why, of course, you'd be the first person I'd tell. Especially about anything here at the office."

So she hadn't told him what was bothering her, but something was. Still, the whole town was jumpy. Nobody wanted to talk about the storm hanging over their heads that had nothing to do with the rain they needed, but it was there. They talked about how hot it was and how ponds were drying up all over the county. They talked about how the football team had actually won a game on Friday night. They skirted around it when they talked about the coach starting three of the black boys who'd played at the black high school over in Grundy the year before. They came closer to admitting that storm clouds hung over Hollyhill when they talked about the *Banner*'s window getting fixed or about Mary Jo going toe to toe with Grover Flinn and serving Myra Hearndon and the Reverend and Mrs. Boyer a soft drink at the counter in the Grill.

They hadn't wanted to look the problem in the face at Mt. Pleasant on Sunday either, although it was harder to ignore with Myra's beautiful voice ringing out from the pews as they sang the morning hymns. Jocie and Miss Sally had sat in the pew behind Myra and kept Eli and Elise entertained. Cassidy sat with them too, the first time she'd gotten away from her mother's side at church. Miss Sally kept putting her arm around Cassidy or touching her hand, even as she held on to Eli in her lap, to be sure Cassidy knew she wasn't forgotten. David doubted if Miss Sally heard a word of his sermon, but he didn't care about that. He'd never seen Miss Sally looking so happy.

She told David after church that it was as if the Lord had answered a prayer she'd never even thought to offer up for some years now, and given her a family of children to love. "You know, I've loved a pile of children who have grown up here in this church, but I've never had children reaching for my heart like these three little ones. They're a gift straight from the Lord. I know they are. And their mother too. I know she's not my daughter, could never be my daughter, but sometimes it feels like she is."

"The Lord blesses us in ways we don't always expect," David said.

"That's true." Miss Sally's smile faded away as she looked out the door toward the members who had already filed out of the church and were talking out in the yard. "But I'm afraid some of the people here at Mt. Pleasant aren't seeing Myra and the children as the blessings they are."

"They'll come around. They just need a little time."

"Attendance is down. The offering is down," Miss Sally said as she held up the envelope of money she'd gathered up out of the offering plates.

"It's been a hard summer with the dry weather. And the people will be back." David pushed as much confidence as he could into his voice. "They'll be here for Homecoming Day in a couple of weeks."

Miss Sally was able to believe that, and she looked relieved. "You're probably right. People won't want to miss Homecoming even if Myra is here. Harvey has been working on the history of the church to read. Of course he reads it every year, but he likes to go over it and make a few changes here and there, put in some new things so it won't be the same old thing every year. You know, he's been doing this since our father died back in 1940. And Father did it for thirty some years before that."

"You and Harvey are the backbone of our church." David put his hand on her arm.

She smiled and waved off the compliment. "I don't know about that, but we do love the church. And we're praying that we haven't brought it harm by selling the land to Alex." Her smile faded. "He's a good man, Brother David. He really is. Even if he doesn't come to church."

"Perhaps we can pray him into wanting fellowship with us here at the church." He squeezed her arm a little.

"And pray for the others too. And pray that those others, those that want to make trouble, will have a change of heart." Miss Sally reached over to give David a hug. "You're a fine pastor, Brother David. Thank you for helping me see that I don't have to solve all the problems, that I can turn them over to the Lord."

"That's something I need to remind myself from time to time as well, Miss Sally."

"Me and Harvey pray for you every day. And for the church," Miss Sally said. "You're at the Sandersons' house today, aren't you?"

"We are."

"Did they invite Leigh?"

"I think it's expected now that Leigh will be along."

"Is it now?" Miss Sally's eyes twinkled as she smiled at David. "Well, that's good news."

"It is," David agreed. "And Leigh tells me you and Mr. Harvey are coming to Jocie's birthday party Saturday afternoon."

"That's right. We're looking forward to it." Miss Sally looked around to be sure Jocie wasn't in earshot. "The you-know-what is still a surprise, isn't it?"

"She thinks she's getting inner tubes for her bike tires."

"Well, that isn't a falsehood," Miss Sally said with a laugh.

And so each day they managed to push the storm into the background of their lives. It was there rumbling its warnings, but nobody wanted to listen. They had other things to worry about. Rain. Birthday parties. Getting the *Banner* out on time. Figuring out what was wrong with Zella. Trying not to melt in the heat.

David picked up one of the *Banner*s and looked at it as Noah and Jocie bundled the papers up to be delivered to the post office and the stores. Leigh had already left with Zella. David had whispered in her ear to find out what was wrong with Zella if she could. And Zella had smiled, really smiled for the first time since the window was knocked out, but that was just because David was whispering in Leigh's ear.

Noah came up beside David to look at the picture of the rock on the top fold of the paper. "Do you think that will cause new trouble?" he asked.

"I don't know. But Wes was right. We did have to print it."

"Even if it causes more trouble."

"The trouble is already here," David said.

"That's the truth," Noah said.

David looked around at Noah. "Are things all right out at the farm?"

"As right as they can be. The pond's still got water. Dad says there must be some kind of deep spring feeding it, so our trees are still living. And we've done all we can about getting ready for whatever might happen. It's hard to know what to do when you don't know what face is going to be on the trouble coming. But we're keeping our eyes open and not taking chances. Mama's promised she'll stay away from town for a while."

"That might be best."

"She didn't aim to make trouble. She just can't help herself when somebody tells her she can't do something. But she doesn't want to have any dealings with those kind of men." He touched the picture of the rock in the paper. "She's been talking about packing up Cassidy and the twins and going to stay with Dad's sister up in Chicago till winter. She says most of the time this kind of thing settles down a little once it starts snowing."

"Why's that?"

"I don't know. Too cold to run around in sheets, maybe." Noah attempted a joke.

David didn't smile. "I'm sorry, Noah. I never thought anything like this would happen in Hollyhill."

"People are just people everywhere."

"And some of them are good people."

"Some of them are. But some of them aren't."

"If anybody bothers you, you call the sheriff."

"Are you sure he won't be under one of the hoods himself? A lot of sheriffs down here in the South are, you know."

"Not ours. Not Sheriff Harpson. He hates what's going on."

"I'll tell Dad," Noah said. "But you and me both know that Hoopole Road is a long way from town and the sheriff's office." Noah turned his eyes back to the picture on the paper. "And they couldn't even protect you here right in the middle of town."

38

Tabitha woke up early Saturday morning. It was too hot to sleep late even if she hadn't been too miserable to sleep. She was beginning to wonder just how big her stomach was going to get. The doctor said everything was just fine, that she wasn't too big, but Tabitha felt huge. She waddled instead of walked. It took a major effort to get up out of a chair. Sometimes Aunt Love had to help her. She couldn't even reach her toenails to paint them. She wasn't sure she still had toes, it had been so long since she'd seen them.

Aunt Love promised her it wouldn't be long now. That she looked ready, whatever that meant. But the doctor said it could be two more weeks. That was what he said every time she went. He put his cold stethoscope on her belly until he found Stephanie Grace's heartbeat, then he smiled and said to come back next week. He hadn't even told her to pack her suitcase for the hospital yet, but of course she had. She had an overnight case with a robe and two nighties and a bed jacket Leigh had given her and the pink terry cloth sleeper for Stephanie Grace to wear home.

It was the only pink one she had, and she'd had to buy it herself. The people at church had given her a shower in the church basement one Sunday afternoon a month ago, but they'd given her yellow and green sleepers and gowns and such. To be safe, they said, in case she had a boy instead of a girl. The mothers all had stories about expecting girls and having boys, or expecting boys and having girls. They told her there was no way to be sure until somebody invented a way to look through your belly into the womb, and there wasn't much chance of that happening.

Tabitha had felt okay on Friday, and a good thing, with having to help Aunt Love get ready for Jocie's big birthday party. Of course it wasn't a surprise like Tabitha's party had been back in July. Jocie knew they were having cake and ice cream for her that afternoon. She'd even helped with the cleaning and getting ready. Wes was coming, and Zella. Miss Sally and Mr. Harvey had promised to come too.

Miss Sally was such a sweetheart. She'd probably bring Tabitha something new for the baby even though she'd already given her the sweetest cradle. Mr. Harvey had pulled it out of their attic, and Miss Sally had painted it white and made a little mattress for it and bumper pads with rainbows on them. The cradle was up in Tabitha's room just waiting for Stephanie Grace with all the sleepers and diapers and soft receiving blankets folded up in it.

And of course Leigh was coming. Leigh was a fixture now. Tabitha didn't mind. She was glad her father had decided to fall in love. Even if Leigh wasn't all that much older than Tabitha herself. She was old enough. And Tabitha's father needed somebody who loved him that way, that man-and-wife way. For sure, DeeDee had never loved him properly, if at all.

Tabitha tried to push DeeDee out of her mind. She hadn't expected it to bother her when DeeDee didn't write her or call. But it had. Her father said that was natural enough. A girl needed a mother when she was getting ready to be a mother herself. Not that DeeDee would have been much help that way. She'd never wanted to be a mother. Had never really been much of a mother even though she'd seen to Tabitha's physical needs over the years.

Tabitha caught her long hair up in a ponytail and then tucked the hair under and pinned it up. It was too hot for long hair. She thought about just taking some scissors and whacking it all off, but it was probably cooler tucked up off her neck. She dropped her hands back down and rubbed her lower back.

Her back was giving her fits. If it hadn't been Jocie's birthday, she'd have fixed her bed up with lots of pillows, turned the fan so it would blow right on her, and gone back to bed for a while. She'd never had a backache quite this bad. It seemed to come in spasms. But for Jocie, she'd have to try to ignore it. She didn't want to spoil her party.

The party was at two, the hottest part of the day, but nobody had parties in the morning, and once the day had heated up, it stayed hot until midnight anyway. The forecast had been the same all week. Hot and dry. Too hot for September. Tabitha remembered crisp fall days in September from when she was a child in Hollyhill. Mornings when she had to wear a sweater. Evenings when her grandmother, Mama Mae, talked about lighting a fire in the fireplace. But nobody needed to light a fire to keep warm so far this September.

By the time Leigh showed up with the cake and Zella and Wes, Tabitha had given up trying to help Aunt Love. She was just sitting in front of the fan and holding her ice-water glass against first one cheek then the other one to cool down. Her back was hurting even worse than when she got up, but she thought she could make it two more hours. By then the party would be over. Jocie would have her new bike, and Tabitha could just go to bed and try to go to sleep and block out the pain. Something was always hurting when you got this far along carrying a baby, or that was what the other mothers at church were always telling her.

ꙮ ꙮ

It was exciting being fourteen. Jocie had awakened sometime in the middle of the night, looked up at the stars out the window, and thought, now she was fourteen. That sounded lots better than thirteen. She was into her teens. She was on her way to being an adult. She knew worlds more than she had last year when she was just turning thirteen.

So much had happened since her last birthday. Everything had changed. Everybody had changed. When she'd told her father that at breakfast, he had smiled and said that happened every year. But Jocie thought this year had to be different, special in the changing department.

All she had to do was look around at the people at her party to prove that. Aunt Love was smiling. She'd been smiling a lot lately. She still quoted just as many Bible verses, but more of them sounded joyful now. Her father was laughing with Leigh as she put the candles on Jocie's specially ordered chocolate cake. He'd met Leigh at the door and hugged her right in front of everybody. The two of them had even held hands like a couple of teenagers in front of the whole county at the football game. That had to be more than a normal change.

Tabitha was sitting there right in the middle of them holding her hands over her belly instead of being off in California. She was going to be a mother just any time, and that would make Jocie an aunt. That certainly didn't happen every year. Miss Sally and Mr. Harvey were sitting on the couch, drinking lemonade and waiting for her to blow out her birthday candles. Jocie hadn't even known them last year, and now they were like a favorite aunt and uncle, and her father was the pastor of their church. That was a change. A big change. Her father actually having a church again.

Wes had been there to help her celebrate turning thirteen last year, and Jocie was thankful he was still there to celebrate with her this year. In another month or two he might even get rid of the cast and be able to ride his motorcycle again. She would give all the little packages people had brought to be able to climb up behind him on his motorcycle again and go for a ride through the country.

Maybe that was a change. In her. She didn't really care about what she was getting. Of course, she did want the inner tubes for her bike tires her father had promised. She had to carry the air pump with her everywhere now if she wanted to ride her bike.

Jocie looked around. Everybody was talking, but Jocie sort of kept herself outside the talk so she could watch them. She'd have to write all this down in her notebook later. How everybody had changed.

Her eyes fell on Zella sitting beside Miss Sally. Zella never changed. Jocie almost felt relieved. She could count on Zella to be the same every day, every week, every month, every year. Even her success matchmaking Leigh and Jocie's father hadn't seemed to cheer her up much lately. Not that she'd ever admit she was cranky, but she was. Lately more than usual. Wes said it had to be the hot weather. Maybe Jocie could make Zella her next year's project—to see if she could change Zella into a kinder, sweeter model. Jocie shut her eyes and tried to imagine it and almost giggled. Some things surely weren't supposed to change.

"What's so funny, Jo?" Wes hobbled over to stand beside her.

"Everything," Jocie said. "Not funny. Just great. Having everybody here. And Leigh making me a cake. Do you remember your fourteenth birthday, Wes?"

"Well, now that's a long time ago in Jupiter years. Could be I took my first spaceship ride that day."

"I wonder what everybody else did."

"Probably not what you're fixing to do. Blow out candles. Miss Leigh's about ready to light them. You'd better be gathering your breath and thinking up a good wish." Wes leaned on his crutches and fished a handkerchief out of his pocket to wipe the sweat off his face. "We don't need no extra heat in here."

"But I have so many wishes that I don't know which one to pick." Jocie watched Leigh arranging the fourteen candles just so.

"Then wish them all, Jo. Don't short yourself on nothing."

"You're one of my wishes, Wes. That your leg gets better and we can go riding on your motorcycle again." She looked back at Wes.

"Well, wish that one for certain. I'm ready to do some riding."

"And I want to wish Tabitha's baby here and okay. And Aunt Love to be able to remember what she wants to remember. And Daddy to be happy and for Leigh to stay the way she is." Jocie's eyes touched on each person as she said their names.

"And make us a few more cakes." Wes eased down into a chair, then looked up at Jocie to say, "But are you sure you're doing wishes? All that sounds sort of like the prayer list you was giving me last week. Your healthy-baby prayer. Your Aunt Love's memory prayer. Your rain prayer. Your leg-healing prayer."

"Can't wishes be prayers or prayers wishes?"

"Don't ask me. I'm no prayer expert. I expect you know a heap more about that than I do. But you should wish something for yourself, Jo. That's what birthday wishes are for. For yourself."

"But all that would be for me," Jocie said.

Wes smiled at her and reached up to touch her hand. "Well, tell you what. You wish all them prayers and blow out all your candles and while you're doing that, I'll sit over here and wish something especially for you."

"What?"

"Now you know the rules. You can't tell your wishes before the candles are out."

"But I just told you all mine."

"My ears don't count. That's like talking to yourself," Wes said. "Look, I think they're ready for you. Better hurry before all that fire melts your icing."

Leigh started singing "Happy Birthday to You," and then everybody was joining in. Jocie gathered up all her wish prayers and tried to run them through her mind while she was blowing out the candles. It took every bit of her breath, but she got them all out. Then everybody was laughing and clapping and making her feel loved and special.

Jocie looked at Wes and wondered if that was what he'd wished for her, because when she thought about it, she was probably the one who had changed the most of anybody in the room. She imagined what she might write in her journal later after everyone was gone.

Today I turned fourteen. In the year since I was thirteen, I have been given back my sister who was gone for so many years. I have a dog named Zeb. I found out that Aunt Love was young once. I had my father taken away from me and given back. I may have a stepmother before long. I learned for sure without any doubt that the Lord answers prayers.

She'd be able to write for hours about that. Maybe she should have asked for a flashlight for her birthday so she could write in her journal all night.

She opened her presents. A book about taking pictures from Wes. Some peppermints from Zella. A pen with red ink from Leigh. A pair of socks from Aunt Love. A notebook from Tabitha. A crystal bell that had belonged to their mother from Miss Sally and Mr. Harvey. But no inner tubes for her bike from her father. She couldn't be disappointed with all these other things, but she couldn't believe he'd forgotten. Then her father was calling her out on the porch and there was the most beautiful blue bicycle Jocie had ever seen.

"And you thought I'd forgotten your inner tubes, didn't you? Here they are in a little bit different package than you were expecting," her father said. "From all of us. Leigh, Aunt Love, Zella, Wes, Tabitha, Miss Sally, Mr. Harvey, and me."

Jocie looked at the bike and then at everybody watching her and burst into tears.

Her father laughed. "I think that means she likes it."

39

David should have noticed, but he hadn't. Aunt Love had to tell him. Jocie's birthday party had broken up soon after Jocie took a ride down the drive to the road and back on her new bicycle. Leigh left to take Wes and Zella home. David didn't try to get her to stay longer because he still had to get his sermon together. There'd been no time that morning with all the preparations for the party. He needed to study the Scripture and spend time in prayer to be sure he found the message the Lord wanted him to preach.

Prayer was why Miss Sally and Mr. Harvey hadn't left when the others did. Mr. Harvey wanted to pray with David. Mr. Harvey said he'd been especially burdened the last few days. "I don't know what it is, Brother David, but I can feel something's wrong. Like I'm missing something the Lord wants me to do. I was hoping you could help me pray through it."

"Well, certainly, Mr. Harvey. Let's step out on the porch while the women put the cake away," David said.

They had hardly bowed their heads when Aunt Love came after him. "I hate to interrupt you, David, but I think Tabitha is in labor. It's likely she has been all day."

"All day?" David said. He had noticed that Tabitha had been extra quiet and had only picked at her cake. "But why didn't she tell us?"

"She says she didn't want to ruin Jocie's birthday party,

but she got up with a backache. You know some women labor in their backs first. And there seems to be some rhythm to her pains. I've no doubt she's having contractions."

David's heart started pumping harder and his hands felt shaky. He wanted to run somewhere, do something, but he wasn't sure what. "There's still time to get her to the hospital, isn't there?"

"It might have been better if she'd told us sooner," Aunt Love said. "It is a good drive to Grundy. I've got Jocelyn trying to reach the doctor."

David looked at Mr. Harvey who smiled and patted him on the back. "Now don't you worry about me, Brother David. You go take care of the girl. Looks like you might just be a granddaddy before the night's out."

"I'll pray for you on the way to Grundy," David promised. He started down the porch steps toward the car.

"Hold on there, Brother David. Don't you think you'd better take the girl with you?" Mr. Harvey said and laughed.

David stopped. "I guess that would be best, wouldn't it?"

He didn't know who looked the most scared when he went back into the living room—Jocie or Tabitha. Or maybe himself if he'd had a mirror, he thought. Jocie looked at him and said, "The doctor said to bring her on in. Right away."

"All right." David made an effort to keep his voice calm. "Why don't you go get Tabitha's suitcase, Jocie?"

Then Tabitha stiffened. Her eyes got big and she held her breath.

Aunt Love leaned over her. "Keep breathing, child. In and out. And keep thinking on the Lord who is able to help you." She pulled out a verse of Scripture. "'Preserve me, O God: for in thee do I put my trust.' Now breathe. Slowly, in and out." Aunt Love looked around at David. "Maybe you'd better take a few deep breaths too, David."

Tabitha grabbed hold of Aunt Love's hands. "You've got to go with me, Aunt Love. Please."

"It's going to be all right, Tabitha. You're going to be fine."

"But you have to go with me." Tabitha sounded ready to cry. "You and Daddy both."

"Your sister can't stay here by herself," Aunt Love said kindly. "Not all night. And first babies sometimes take awhile."

David was hoping so. If not all night, then at least until they reached the hospital in Grundy. "Maybe we should just call Dr. Markum or maybe get the ambulance," he said.

"No, she needs to be at a hospital and the ambulance would take longer than you driving," Aunt Love said. "Jocelyn will just have to go with us, but I don't think they allow children on the maternity floor at the hospital."

"I'm fourteen now," Jocie said as she came back with Tabitha's suitcase.

"That might be old enough," Aunt Love said.

"I'm sure it is. I think it's thirteen," Miss Sally spoke up. "But your Aunt Love is right about first babies, Jocie. It promises to be a long night. Why don't you just come home with us instead? You can spend the night and go to church with us in the morning."

"Church," David said. "Maybe I should try to find someone to fill in for me in case I can't make it on time."

"Now don't you be worrying a bit about us out at Mt. Pleasant," Mr. Harvey said. "You make it if you can, and if you can't, me or one of the other deacons can carry on. We'll make out at the church just fine. You just take care of your girl."

ꙮ ꙮ

So it was settled even though her father never really asked to see if that was what Jocie actually wanted to do. And the truth was, Jocie wasn't sure which she'd rather do. She thought it might be exciting to be there when Stephanie Grace made her entrance into the world, but at the same time, when Tabitha got all stiff and started groaning, it was scary. It might be better to skip over being part of the laboring process and just wait and see the baby once she was here.

Jocie carried Tabitha's suitcase out and put it in the trunk while her father got Tabitha settled in the backseat. Jocie tried to think of something encouraging to say to her sister. Something like good luck or hope everything comes out okay, but neither of them sounded right. Jocie was leaning into the car to just say good-bye when Tabitha dug her fingers into Jocie's arm and said, "Start saying your baby prayer." Then she was going stiff again with her eyes wide open almost as if surprised by what was happening.

Her father pushed Jocie back and shut the door. He gave Jocie some last-minute instructions about being good at Miss Sally's house and praying and putting up the cake, but the words got all jumbled up and didn't make much sense. Jocie smiled at him and promised to do it all. Then she stood on the porch and watched the car until it disappeared down the road.

Miss Sally came over to stand beside her. "She'll be fine, and the next time you see her she'll have a sweet little baby."

"I'm a little more worried about Dad. I don't think I've ever seen him so jumpy."

Miss Sally laughed. "That's the way it is with men. The

women have to do the laboring to get the babies here while the fathers fall apart at the seams."

"But Daddy's not even the father," Jocie said.

"He's the father of the mother. That might be even harder. But he'll be okay. He'll settle down and say a prayer and the Lord will get him through it." Miss Sally put her arm around her. "Come on. Let's get that cake put away and the dishes washed up so we can go on home. We have to go by the church for a minute, and Harvey has a cow he needs to check on before dark. More babies on the way."

"Do you think he'll let me go with him? I love baby calves."

"I'm sure he'd be tickled to have some company. And we've got several little babies right now. Cute little things. I saw them frisking around together this morning out in the field back behind the house," Miss Sally said. She gave Jocie a little push toward the door. "Now go gather up your church clothes and a nightie, and I'll start on the dishes."

The sun was on the way down by the time they got to Miss Sally and Mr. Harvey's house. Mr. Harvey got out of the car and picked up his walking stick. "We'd better not waste any time, Jocie girl. It'll be too dark to see whether the little bugger has come or not if we don't get a move on it."

"How do you know which direction to go in the field to find the cow?" Jocie asked as she fell in step beside him. She liked Mr. Harvey. He was easy to talk to and always had some story to tell that could make her smile. She had a special section in her journal for his stories of the old days. Her favorite was the one about how he'd gotten lost in the woods once when he was just a little boy, and his old coon dog, Jake, had tracked him down and led him home.

"That's easy enough," Mr. Harvey said now. "They always just go straight to the hospital field."

"You don't have a hospital field," Jocie said, disbelief in her voice.

"Nearest thing to it. A cow gets ready to calve, she just moves right over to that hill yonder and goes to it." Mr. Harvey pointed across the way. "See, I think I can make out the old girl over there already."

Sure enough, the cow was picking at the dry grass with her new calf curled up beside her. She raised her head to moo softly, and the little calf clambered to its feet.

"No need bothering her," Mr. Harvey said, stopping a respectable distance from the cow. "We can see they're both fine from here."

The calf took a couple of staggering steps and then moved with more assurance straight to the cow's udder to suck. The cow reached around and touched the calf's back with her nose.

"I wish I had my camera," Jocie said.

"It is a peaceful picture. The way of nature. Birth and life and death, a continuing cycle."

Jocie looked from the calf to Mr. Harvey. "But we don't like to talk about the death part."

"No, we don't, but it's part of God's plan. Man is born and has his time on earth, but the day comes to us all when we must move on to our eternal reward."

"Aunt Love's always quoting stuff out of Ecclesiastes about that. A time to be born. A time to die. You know, that chapter with all the opposites. She's on me all the time with that one about a time to keep silence, and a time to speak. I'm not too good at the keeping silence part."

Mr. Harvey laughed. "Well, some of us have a harder time with the time for silence than others, I suppose. Come on, let's head back to the house and see what Sally's found us for supper."

"We should have brought some of my birthday cake."

"Oh, I'm sure Sally has something sweet in the cupboard for us. She generally does. We'll have you a good birthday supper."

"It is still my birthday, isn't it?"

"Birthdays generally last all day. And could be your little niece or nephew will be sharing your birthday next year."

"That might be fun." As they started back across the field, Jocie looked up at the sky and silently said a prayer for Tabitha and the baby. After all, she'd promised her she'd say the baby prayer. One star had popped out in the blue over their heads. Jocie couldn't decide whether she should use her first-star wish for rain the way she'd been doing for days now or whether tonight she should make some kind of wish for the baby, so she asked Mr. Harvey, "Do you think it might rain soon?"

"Doesn't look too promising for tonight," Mr. Harvey said as he looked up at the clear sky. "But it will rain. It always has. The Lord takes care of us."

When Mr. Harvey said it, Jocie could almost smell the rain in the air even though there wasn't a sign of a cloud in the sky. So tonight she'd let Mr. Harvey handle the rain getting there as she stared up at the star over her head and wished Tabitha's baby would be healthy.

"Do you think it's wrong to wish on stars?" she said.

Mr. Harvey smiled at her. "No, I don't. I've been wishing on stars all my life, and the Lord's been turning those wishes into blessings."

"Thanks for letting me come out here with you."

"Glad to have the company, Jocie girl."

Dusk was falling and more stars began making their appearance in the sky. As they came over the hill, they could see the lights of cars and trucks passing out on the road beyond the house.

"Looks like an awful lot of traffic out on the road tonight," Mr. Harvey said. "Hope nothing's wrong somewhere in the neighborhood."

40

Cassidy woke up with a start and sat up in bed. Her heart was pounding so hard she thought it might jump out of her chest. At first she didn't know what had made her wake up. All she could hear was the fan whirring in her window. Cassidy drew in a deep breath and looked across the room at Eli and Elise in their cribs to see if one of them had been what had wakened her. In the dim light drifting in the top of the window she could see the twins both sprawled on their backs, breathing slow and easy in their sleep. They hardly ever woke her up anyway. Cassidy was used to the rattle of their cribs when they turned over or the noises they made when they had a bad dream or something.

Maybe that was what it was. What had made her wake up. The bad dream. She'd been having it a lot ever since her mama had to buy a soft drink last week in town. But if the dog growling at her had jerked her out of sleep, she couldn't remember it, and most of the time its big pointed teeth were there in the dark in front of her nose even after she opened her eyes. She didn't yell much anymore when it happened, because her mama and daddy got upset if she said anything about the dog.

Besides, nobody got much sleep if she hollered and woke up the babies. And then everybody was upset. Her mama told her just to count to a hundred when she had the bad dream and it would go away. Most of the time it did. Other times she had to yank the cover up over her head even if it was so hot under there she could barely breathe. But she stayed there, sweating and taking quiet little breaths, until the dog would finally give up on her coming out and run away to growl at somebody else.

She started to count in a whisper that not even Eli or Elise would be able to hear over the sound of the fan. "One, two, three, four, five . . ." But it wasn't the dog dream. It was something else. Something outside. She stopped counting and got out of bed. She pushed a chair over to the window and stood on it to peer out the window over top of the fan.

A truck was coming up their lane, and then another one. But it was funny. It was dark, but they didn't have their lights on. The wheels on the rocks her daddy had put on the lane to their house last month sounded like the dog growling in her ears. And then more dogs were growling.

Cassidy got down off the chair. She looked at her bed and thought about getting under the covers, but instead she went out to the living room. It was quiet in the house. All the growling was outside. Cassidy peeked out the front window. Now there were five trucks. All trucks, no cars. Two of the trucks drove on past the house toward the field where their apple trees were growing into an orchard. Her daddy's orchard of hope.

One of the trucks stopped in front of their yard gate. The next truck didn't stop, just drove right over their fence and the lilac bushes her mama had gotten from Miss Sally. That wasn't right. Cassidy wanted to go back into the cave in her mind and just curl up there for a while, but somebody had to tell her daddy. Somebody had to come out and do something about her mama's lilac bushes. They'd been carrying out the rinse water from their laundry to water them, and her mama talked about the pretty purple blooms that would be on them next year and how good they'd smell. They hadn't had any lilac bushes in Chicago.

Somebody got out of one of the trucks. Somebody—or something. It didn't have a face. Only something like a pointy white pillowcase with holes for eyes. White floated around the rest of the thing the way it did around ghosts on the cartoon shows. But under the white, down on the ground, were boots. Cassidy stared at the boots and knew it was one of those men her mama and daddy had talked about after she and her mama had gone to town shoe shopping. Her daddy had called them cowards hiding under sheets, and her mama had frowned and said it was like the men thought the Lord couldn't see under their hoods. That they could do whatever they wanted as long as nobody saw their faces. But of course the Lord could see through anything.

Other ghost men came up behind the first one, and Cassidy raced toward her parents' bedroom.

"Daddy," she whispered as loud as she could. Fans were running in their room too, so she was almost to the bed before her daddy heard her. "Daddy!"

He sat up but didn't reach for the light. "What's the matter, Cassidy?"

"The ghost men are here. The ones you've been talking about," Cassidy said. "The ones that think the Lord can't see them when they do bad things."

She could tell her daddy and mama were looking at each other. They were afraid. The same as she was. The opening to the cave was still there in her mind. She could crawl inside and nobody could reach her. But what if they came after her? What if they reached their white arms in and pulled her out and fed her to their dogs? She hadn't seen any dogs, but that didn't mean they weren't there.

"Shh, baby, it'll be okay," her daddy said. "You stay here with your mama. I'll take care of everything." He was on his feet with his pants on already.

Her mama reached over and pulled Cassidy tight against her a few seconds before she got out of the bed and began getting dressed. "How many?" she asked.

"I don't know," Cassidy said. Tears were rolling down her cheeks. She was going to have to go into the cave. It was the only safe place. But she didn't want to leave her mama behind. And she knew her mama wouldn't go in the cave with her. "I saw five trucks. Some went down in the field. One ran over your lilac bushes, Mama."

Her mama stopped in the middle of putting on her shoes. "Over the fence?" She didn't wait for Cassidy to answer her. She looked at Cassidy's daddy and said, "Maybe we should call the sheriff."

"As if that would do any good," her daddy muttered.

"Brother David said it would. He said the sheriff wouldn't be part of any of this."

"About the only thing we can be sure of, Myra, is that your Brother David isn't out there under any of those sheets."

Then Noah was at the bedroom door. "We can't call anybody. The phone's dead."

Again Cassidy felt the fear in the room like a live thing trying to eat them. She inched into the entrance to her cave. She could still hear her mama and daddy and Noah, but it was like she sometimes heard her mama and daddy's voices at night through the walls. Muffled and soft. A private sound.

"I love you, Myra, more than life itself," her daddy was saying.

"Don't go out there, Alex. Just stay in here and they'll go away."

"You know they won't."

Her mama was almost crying. "You can't fight them, Alex."

Cassidy inched farther into her cave. Even Noah didn't come after her.

"I'm not fighting anybody. I'm just going out there to see what they want."

"You know what they want."

"This is our land. They have no right to be here." For a second her daddy's voice was louder. Then it was softer again. "It'll be all right, Myra. You take care of Cassidy and the twins and talk to the Lord for us. Isn't your Lord supposed to take care of us?"

"I am praying, Alex. Oh, dear Lord, sweet Jesus, I am praying," Cassidy's mama said.

Noah went with her daddy. Cassidy could see him from where she'd inched inside the cave. He didn't tell her to come out the way he usually did. So maybe it was okay for her to be there. But then her mama was peering back at her, reaching for her.

Her mama didn't yell like Noah always did. Her voice was soft, the way it was when she sang to Eli and Elise when she put them to bed, but it was very close. Cassidy could feel her mama's breath on her ear. "Cassidy, darling, you have to stay here with me now. I might need you to help me with Eli and Elise. You'll have to go play with your dragons another time. Not now."

Cassidy didn't know why her mama said that about the dragons. There weren't any dragons in her cave. But it might be nice if there were. Then Cassidy could get on one of the dragons and ride it out and let it breathe fire on the ghost men outside.

"Cassidy." Her mama's voice got a little louder as she lifted up Cassidy's chin with her hand. "Do what I say. Right now! I need you paying attention."

Cassidy always minded her mama. She reached a hand

out of her cave and touched her mama's hand. Her mama gripped her hand so tightly that it hurt.

"I'm afraid, Mama," she said.

"I know, sugar. You just think on how much the Lord surely loves us and keep helping your mama pray that he will watch over us." Her mama held her hand even tighter for a moment before she said, "Now we're going back to your room to see about our babies."

Cassidy's mama opened the bedroom door. The trucks outside must have turned on their headlights, and now bright beams of light snaked in through the windows and bounced off the mirror on the wall behind the couch. Men were yelling outside, but Cassidy couldn't hear her daddy or Noah saying anything.

Her mama didn't go through the door. Instead she pushed it back shut against the light and got down on her knees beside Cassidy. "We're going to play a game. We're going to play hide-and-seek with those lights out in the living room and crawl under them to your room. Okay?"

"Okay," Cassidy said. "But are those lights trying to find us?"

"I don't know. Maybe not, but we can play anyway," her mama said as she got down on her hands and knees and opened the bedroom door again. "Follow me."

It was funny crawling after her mama. Cassidy sometimes played crawling games with Eli and Elise, but her mama never did. Her mama was always tall and in control. But of course, Cassidy knew her mama wasn't playing a game now. She just didn't want the ghost men to see them.

They were almost to Cassidy's bedroom door when there was a loud bang outside. Her mama stopped crawling and said, "Oh dear God, have mercy on these your children. Please, not guns."

Eli began whimpering in their bedroom. Elise would be crying too in a minute. She always woke up and cried when Eli did. But Cassidy's mama acted as if she didn't hear Eli. She stayed down on her hands and knees and crept over to the window off the porch where the least light was coming in. Cassidy didn't hesitate. She crawled after her. When her mama peeked out the window, so did Cassidy.

Back in the bedroom, Eli was crying a little louder and now Elise was joining in. In a few more minutes both of them would be standing up, shaking the sides of their cribs and screaming. But Cassidy's mama didn't even look over her shoulder and call out a soft word of promise to the twins.

Her mama was so stiff beside her that for a moment Cassidy thought she must have gone off into her own cave. But then Cassidy's daddy was talking out on the porch, and her mama let out her breath.

"This is my property. You have no right to be here," Cassidy's daddy was saying. His voice was strong and steady. And he looked strong, standing there on the porch staring out at the ghost men. Noah stood behind him, in his shadow.

The men out in the yard made a half circle around the porch. Cassidy started counting, but when she got to seven and thought that was all of them, more stepped out of darkness beside the trucks up into the light. They carried big flashlights that they pointed at her daddy. He had to hold his arm up above his eyes to keep the lights from blinding him.

The man standing in the middle, right on the rock path that led up to the steps of their porch, answered her daddy. "We've come to tell you that *you* are the one who has no right to be here."

"This is my land," Cassidy's daddy repeated, his voice still strong and a little louder than it had been.

The man on the rock path paid no attention to what her daddy said. "Sell your land back to the one you bought it from. That way no one will have to get hurt."

"He wouldn't buy it," Cassidy's daddy said.

"We'll convince him. We have many convincing ways." The rest of the men took a step closer to the porch as the man in the middle spoke. "Many ways. Ways you won't want to know about."

"You're trespassing. Now get off my land," Cassidy's daddy said.

"We'll leave. This time. But remember we can come back and next time we might not be so polite." The man paused a moment before he went on. "We hear you have a beautiful wife."

Beside Cassidy, her mama went stiff again.

"You leave my family alone." Cassidy's daddy sounded mad now. He stepped toward the edge of the porch. Noah grabbed his arm.

Cassidy's mama began whispering, "Dear God, put your hand between him and the evil out there. Oh, dear Lord, I beg you."

The white ghost hoods shook as the men in the yard began making a horrible sound like the way the rocks screeched when the shovel scraped against them in the holes Cassidy's daddy and Noah dug for the trees. Back in the bedroom, Eli and Elise were crying louder and yelling for their mama in between sobs.

"A man should take care of his family," the white ghost man said. "Take them back to where you came from. We don't want your kind here. You've been warned. Next time there won't be any talking."

The men flicked off their flashlights and began melting back into the darkness beside their trucks. Truck doors opened and shut. When they were all gone except the man on the path, that man said, "One last thing. You should have listened when the people around here told you trees wouldn't grow in this ground. At least not nigger trees." Then he too disappeared into the darkness.

Cassidy's mama waited until the trucks backed up over her flower beds again and went through the fence back to the road before she went to get the twins. She picked Elise up and hugged her before she handed her to Cassidy and went to get Eli. Cassidy stayed right beside her mama, moving when she did, stopping when she did. She smelled her mama's perfume and felt the moisture of perspiration on the skin of her arm. Cassidy held Elise and told her to stop crying, but she kept hold of her mama too. If she didn't do that, she might just fall into a deep black hole and never come out. She glanced around in her mind for the opening to her safe cave, but she couldn't find it. It didn't matter. Her mama would never let her take Elise in the cave with her.

When her daddy and Noah came in off the porch after even the sound of the trucks had disappeared into the night, Cassidy's mama hugged her daddy so tight that Eli, who was mashed between them, started crying again. Then they all huddled together, and her mama said they should say a thanksgiving prayer.

"And why's that?" Cassidy's daddy said as he pulled away from Cassidy's mama. "What's there to be thankful about in all this?"

"We're all here together. The Lord took care of us. He kept us safe in his hands."

"If we're in his hands, he must be clenching his fists, mashing the very juice of life out of us."

"Alex! Stop that kind of talk."

"You know they tore up our trees." His voice sounded funny, not like her daddy at all.

Cassidy's mama was quiet for a minute, and then she said, "Maybe we should go look."

And so they went together down to the orchard field. All of them. Her daddy led the way, walking a few steps in front of Noah, who put Eli up on his shoulders. Eli didn't pay the first bit of attention to how quiet the rest of them were and whooped with delight to be walking outside in the moonlight. Cassidy's mama carried Elise, who laid her head down on her mama's shoulder and fell back to sleep. Cassidy matched her steps to her mama's and kept her hand where it brushed her mama's arm.

She'd slipped on her shoes, but she was still in her nightgown that used to be blue but now was faded out to almost white. She wondered if she would look like a cartoon ghost to anybody watching. Her arms and face would disappear in the dark of the night, and it would look like just a white dress walking along. A ghost girl like the ghost men.

She turned her mind away from that thought. She didn't want to think about the ghost men. But when they got down to the orchard field, it was hard to keep from it. The trees were no longer standing up with their little leaves reaching for the sky. They were mashed and broken.

Her daddy stood at the gate into the field for a long moment, as if he could keep it from being true by not walking into the orchard. His orchard of hope. Their orchard of hope.

Finally he said, "They drove the trucks over them. Didn't even have enough honor about them to pull them up. Just let their trucks do their dirty work for them."

He went into the field and knelt down by one of the broken trees. Cassidy remembered that one. It had been the biggest tree, the one her daddy always gave two dips of water because it was going to be the tree leader to show the other trees how to grow and make apples. Tears rolled down Cassidy's cheeks. She'd helped her daddy water these trees and wrap their trunks to keep the rabbits from eating them. She'd walked through them, imagining them tall over her head loaded with apples. And now they would never grow.

Her mama walked over and put her free hand on Cassidy's daddy's shoulder. "We'll get more trees."

"And they'll come and destroy those too. What then, Myra?"

Her voice got stronger, sounded surer. "Then we'll plant more trees."

Cassidy's daddy shook his head. "Is that what your Lord tells you? Is that how he answers your prayers? Just keep starting over?"

"The Bible says, 'Tribulation worketh patience; and patience, experience; and experience, hope.'"

"I can't feel much of that right now." He stood up, still holding a bit of the broken tree.

"That's because you aren't leaning on the understanding of the Lord," Cassidy's mama said.

"Don't you be preaching at me tonight, woman." Cassidy's daddy threw the branch he held as far as he could into the field. But then his anger seemed to leak away, and he sounded almost sad as he said, "Not tonight."

They turned and began making their sad procession back to the house when Noah pointed at the sky beyond the barn. "Something's on fire over that way," he said.

They stopped walking to look. Off across the fields, the sky was glowing red.

"Oh dear Lord," Cassidy's mama said. "Miss Sally's house is over there."

"I hope your Lord can help you understand that," Cassidy's daddy said.

41

By the time Jocie helped Miss Sally put fresh sheets on the bed in the parlor, she was beginning to wish she'd gone on to the hospital with her father and Aunt Love. It wasn't that she didn't like Miss Sally and Mr. Harvey. She did. A lot. But she just felt out of place here in this room of memories that was fine when the sun was shining through the windows, but sort of spooky when night shadows lurked behind the doors.

Plus once she went to bed, she wouldn't know till morning about Tabitha's baby. Her father had called earlier to say they made it to the hospital and that the doctor said Tabitha was definitely getting ready to give birth, but the baby wasn't expected to make an appearance for several more hours, maybe not till morning. Jocie's father said Tabitha was doing fine or at least as well as could be expected for somebody about to have a baby. Or so the nurses told him. They wouldn't let him stay with Tabitha.

"It's just as well you're not here, Jocie. You wouldn't believe how hard these chairs are out here in the waiting room. Aunt Love's wishing she had a cushion. And the only magazines are about fishing."

"You like fishing," Jocie said.

"I like to go fishing. Not read about somebody else going fishing."

"No Bible?"

"I haven't seen one," her father said.

"Aunt Love can quote some verses for you."

"That might work," he said. "Everything okay there with Miss Sally and Mr. Harvey?"

"It's fine."

"Good. I'll call you early tomorrow morning. By then we should have a new baby and I can come on to church. I don't know what kind of sermon it will be. The Lord keeps telling me not to put off my sermon preparation until the last minute. Maybe I'll start paying attention now."

"It'll be okay, Dad. You can just preach the same one you did last week."

Her father laughed. "Are you trying to say they will all have forgotten it by now anyway?"

"No, not that. You can just say you thought they needed to hear it again. I mean, all sermons are some the same. Believe and be saved. Treat others the way you want to be treated. Love one another. That kind of thing."

"The people expect me to preach a little longer than that."

"But why do sermons have to be so many minutes long? Is there a rule book for sermon giving?"

"No rule book. Just the Bible," Jocie's father said. "Now behave yourself and don't drive Miss Sally and Mr. Harvey crazy asking questions like that." And then he laughed again before he said good-bye.

Now in Miss Sally's parlor, Jocie shut her eyes and tried to go to sleep. Mr. Harvey had offered to bring his fan down for her from his bedroom upstairs, but she'd told him she didn't need it. And with the windows open to the night air it was hot, but not too hot to sleep. That wasn't the problem. It was the feeling that Miss Sally's mother's ghost might be hovering over Jocie trying to see who was sleeping in her bed.

Jocie told herself firmly there were no such things as ghosts, and even if there were, Miss Sally's mother was probably just as sweet as Miss Sally and wouldn't mind Jocie sleeping there. The spooky ghost feelings faded away, but then other worries came to poke at her. Wes on his crutches. Figuring out how to forgive Ronnie Martin—and Paulette for wanting her to. Tabitha having a baby. Not just expecting one, but actually having one. The Klan. Thinking about the men in sheets and boots was scarier than thinking about ghosts watching her.

Jocie started repeating Psalm 23 the way she did when she couldn't sleep at home. She was on the part about the shadow of death when she heard wheels crunching the gravel of Mr. Harvey's driveway. At first she thought it might be her father coming to tell her about the baby, but it didn't sound like just one car but several. Why would people be coming to see Mr. Harvey and Miss Sally in the middle of the night?

Jocie got up and went over to the window. Up above her head she could hear the vibration of the fan on the floor of Mr. Harvey's bedroom. Outside, it wasn't cars but pickup trucks. They stopped before they got to the house, and men started getting out. For a minute Jocie thought she must have actually fallen asleep and was in her dream when she saw their white robes. They were moving without any noise. Surely that could only happen in a dream.

One of the men carried a torch high above his head. Behind him, several men carried a wooden cross. Jocie wanted to yell, but her mouth wouldn't work. That's the way it sometimes was with dreams. A person was frozen, unable to run or do anything.

The men laid the cross down in the yard in front of the porch. Then other men were splashing something on it. That was when Jocie knew for sure she wasn't dreaming.

She could smell kerosene. One of the men laughed softly as he told the other man to be careful not to get his robe soaked or he might get lit up too. The sound of the man's voice was muffled by the hood over his head.

And then the man threw his torch on the wooden cross and jumped back as the flames swooshed up and licked the porch roof. One of the other men ran over to them and said, "You idiots! You put it too close to the house. We didn't want to burn them alive. Just put a scare into them."

The flames licked out at the dry grass, and the whole yard was suddenly on fire. Jocie ran for the steps. Smoke was already sweeping through the house, and the flames crackled as they bit into the porch roof.

"Miss Sally! Mr. Harvey!" she screamed. "Wake up!"

Outside there were some loud bangs and lots of shouting. Jocie couldn't make out the words, but she could hear the panic. The same feeling was blasting through her. Then even the shouts faded away as the roar of the fire grew louder. It was hot in the stairway and hard to breathe. Jocie pulled her gown up over her nose and mouth, and kept going.

Miss Sally met her at the door to her bedroom. She had on her robe and slippers with a hair net over her gray hair. "What's happening?"

"The house is on fire!"

"Oh, my word! We've got to get Harvey."

Jocie started banging on Mr. Harvey's bedroom door. The smoke was getting thicker. She pushed the door open. Mr. Harvey was sitting on the side of his bed holding his chest. Aunt Love did that a lot, but most of the time it didn't mean anything. Jocie wasn't so sure about Mr. Harvey.

Miss Sally moved past her and put her hands on Mr. Harvey's shoulders. "Get up, Harvey! We've got to get out of here."

He just looked at her as if he hadn't quite heard what she said. Then he took a couple of deep breaths and said, "Do I smell smoke?"

"The house is on fire," Jocie said. "Please, Mr. Harvey, we've got to hurry."

He stood up and reached for his pants. Miss Sally yanked them away from him. "You don't have time to get dressed, Harvey. I'll carry them for you. Jocie, get his shoes. Once we get outside, then you can put them on."

Jocie grabbed the shoes sitting on the floor by the bed and led the way out toward the stairs. She was almost afraid to look back to see if they were following her. What would she do if they weren't? She whispered a prayer. "Dear Lord, help us."

The smoke was getting thicker, swirling around them, making her cough. She stopped at the top of the stairs. It was too late. Maybe she hadn't prayed soon enough. Flames had raced from the porch and across the hall to the stairs. The bottom step was burning. Jocie tried to take little breaths to keep from breathing in the smoke, but the flames were sucking up all the air. It was so hot that she couldn't breathe.

Behind her, Mr. Harvey and Miss Sally were coughing. Jocie's lungs were hurting and black spots were forming in front of her eyes. She couldn't pass out. She'd die if she passed out and so would Mr. Harvey and Miss Sally.

Then Mr. Harvey was pulling her back from the top of the stairs and talking in her ear. "We'll have to go out the window in Sally's room."

Out the window. Jocie might do that, but dear Lord, could Mr. Harvey and Miss Sally? Still, it was that or trying to run through the flames to one of the downstairs doors. And none of them could do that.

Mr. Harvey opened Miss Sally's bedroom door. The flames

swooshed up the staircase like a live thing, ready to devour the fresh air from the bedroom. Jocie pushed Mr. Harvey and Miss Sally inside and slammed shut the bedroom door. She took a couple of breaths, but that just seemed to make her cough harder. Outside there was an unnatural glow.

Mr. Harvey was holding his chest again as he leaned on Miss Sally. "Do we need to tie sheets together to make a rope to the ground?" Jocie asked.

"No, child," Miss Sally said. "The back porch roof slants away from the window. We can crawl out and over to the cellar mound and down. Me and Harvey used to do it all the time when we were kids just for the fun of it."

Jocie looked at them. "You're not kids now."

Miss Sally actually smiled. "You go first and help us remember how."

"No. I'm okay. You go, then Mr. Harvey, and I'll come last so I can help you if you need me to."

"No time to argue," Mr. Harvey said. He was panting a little. "Just push the screen out and go, girl. We'll need you out there on the roof to keep us from rolling off when we come out."

Jocie knocked the screen out of the window, dropped Mr. Harvey's shoes outside, and then slid out after them. The roof was right under her feet, not even a full step down. Maybe they were going to get out after all. She picked up Mr. Harvey's shoes and moved them out of the way. She wished she'd put on her own shoes when she'd gotten out of bed to go look out the window. The roof shingles were scratchy under her feet.

Miss Sally hiked up her nightgown, grabbed her leg below the knee, and pulled it up until she could push her foot out the window. Jocie helped her balance as she pulled her other foot out and stood up on the porch.

"It's more slanted than I remember, Harvey. Be careful," Miss Sally said back in the window.

"Hurry, Mr. Harvey!" Jocie could smell the fire coming after them.

Mr. Harvey stuck one foot out and then sat straddling the window frame in his nightshirt. Sweat was running down his face.

"You two go on ahead," he said after a couple of seconds. "I'll catch up."

"I'm not going without you, Harvey. So you just take a couple of deep breaths and come on out of there," Miss Sally said.

"Go, Sally. For the girl's sake."

Jocie's heart was pounding, and she imagined she could feel the shingles heating up under her feet. Still, she couldn't run away and leave them stranded on the roof. Jocie moved over and put her arm around Mr. Harvey. "You can lean on me," she said. "Please, Mr. Harvey. You have to get out. We can't leave you here. We just can't."

"No, I suppose not." He sounded very tired, but he leaned toward Jocie and held on to the window frame as he worked his other leg out through the window. He was panting again. He looked up when he stood down on the roof and said, "Dear Lord, just a few more minutes."

Jocie wasn't sure if he was talking to her and Miss Sally, or the Lord. Then they were making their way over the shingles to where the roof dropped down to almost touch the dirt mounded up over the root cellar. The fire was licking up the sides of the front of the house and coming through the roof to light up the sky, but the back of the house was still okay.

They were off the cellar and moving away from the house when the men in white were suddenly around them. Eyes stared out through the hoods at Jocie. Just like in her dream, except Mr. Harvey and Miss Sally weren't with her in the dream.

Mr. Harvey straightened up. His anger seemed to give him strength. "You men did this!"

"We didn't aim to burn the house. We just wanted to give you a message," one of the men said through his hood.

"Bob, is that you?" Mr. Harvey peered over at the man.

"No, you don't know any of us," one of the other men said.

"It doesn't matter what I know. The Lord knows all of you. You can't hide your evil under hoods and expect the Lord not to see you."

"You brought this down on yourself," the man in front said. "You should have never sold your land to that—"

"Go! Leave! You've done enough harm for one night," Mr. Harvey said, not letting him finish. His voice was cold. "And I'll pray the good Lord can forgive you."

"We don't need your prayers, old man," one of the men said, stepping toward Mr. Harvey. But a couple of the other men grabbed the man's arms and pulled him back. They fell back out of the light of the fire and melted away into the night.

From the front of the house, Jocie heard truck doors slamming and motors starting up. And then there was only the noise of the fire crackling and devouring all Mr. Harvey and Miss Sally's things. Jocie wished she could run back inside and grab the old clock off the mantel that Miss Sally said had belonged to her father. It had never quit ticking through all those years, and now it was burning. All their precious keepsakes were burning.

They moved a few more feet away from the house and turned to look back at the flames leaping through the roof toward the sky now. "So fast," Miss Sally whispered.

And then Mr. Harvey leaned forward and clutched his chest again. "I'm really sorry to do this to you right now, Sally—" he gasped for breath before he was able to go on—"but I think I'm having a heart attack."

"Oh no, Harvey. No!" Miss Sally cried.

But Mr. Harvey wasn't listening. He was staring straight ahead. "Look, Sally. Have you ever seen anything so beautiful? They must be angels." And then he was slumping.

Jocie tried to hold Mr. Harvey up, but he was too heavy. He slid away from her arms down to the ground. Miss Sally dropped to her knees beside him. She put her ear down on his chest. After a couple of seconds she said, "He's still breathing. We've got to get him to the hospital."

"But how?" Jocie said. Miss Sally couldn't drive, but Jocie could if she had to, at least to a neighbor's house. But she and Miss Sally would never be able to get Mr. Harvey in the car by themselves. They wouldn't be able to lift him off the ground.

"I don't know," Miss Sally said. It sounded as if she was crying.

Pray. The word echoed in Jocie's head. The Lord would help her. Hadn't he always helped her before? And hadn't he helped Mr. Harvey and Miss Sally by putting Jocie in their house so she could wake them up when the house caught on fire? Another five minutes and they wouldn't have gotten out. "Dear Lord, please help us. Show me what to do next."

She'd no sooner finished whispering the prayer than she saw headlights out on the road. "There's a car coming."

"Praise the Lord," Miss Sally said. "Go get them, and bring them here."

Jocie started around the house, but then hesitated. "What if it's some of those men coming back?"

"If it is, they're surely coming back to help. Use what the Lord sends."

It wasn't any of the men. It was Noah and his whole family, even the twins and Cassidy. Cassidy's eyes were big as they stared out of the car window at Jocie and then at the flames behind her.

Noah and his father carried Mr. Harvey to the car. Mr. Hearndon touched Mrs. Hearndon's arm. "You take them. Noah and me will stay here and try to keep the fire from spreading to the other buildings."

Jocie and Miss Sally climbed in the backseat with Cassidy and the twins. Cassidy scooted as close to Miss Sally as she could get, and Elise climbed over into Jocie's lap and said, "Hot."

Jocie pulled her tight to her with one arm and put her other arm around Eli. He snuggled against her without a word as his mother pulled out on the road to head toward the nearest hospital in Grundy. Too far away. Other cars, neighbors Miss Sally said, passed them headed toward the fire.

"Sweet Jesus," Mrs. Hearndon said in a voice not much over a whisper. "Watch over our menfolk this night. Bring them into the sunlight of another day."

Miss Sally reached up and put her hand on Mrs. Hearndon's shoulder. "The neighbors are good people. They weren't part of any of this."

"I pray you're right," Mrs. Hearndon said before she mashed on the gas and sent the car flying through the night.

Jocie tightened her arms around the twins, and Cassidy scooted even closer to Miss Sally. In the front seat they could hear Mr. Harvey's labored breathing. Jocie kept her eyes wide open, but she never stopped praying all the way to the hospital.

42

Tabitha lay in the hospital bed and stared at the tiny holes in the ceiling tiles over her head. She squinted her eyes and started counting them row by row to distract herself from the pain. She was on the third row when a new contraction grabbed her. The holes in the tiles blurred and ran together as she grabbed the sides of the bed and braced herself. She was breathing the way Aunt Love had said she should, but it still hurt. Way worse than anything she had expected.

She needed Aunt Love in the room with her to tell her it was okay. That she was going to make it. That thousands of women had babies every day and it hurt, but they lived through it. Even Aunt Love had lived through it. And she hadn't even been in a hospital with doctors and nurses the way Tabitha was.

Tabitha needed somebody beside her. She needed to be able to reach out and touch a real person instead of the cold metal rails on the bed. The nurses had swarmed in on her at first, getting her in a hospital gown, checking her blood pressure and the baby's heartbeat, shaving her down there. Tabitha hadn't been expecting them to do that, but the nurse said it had to be done to keep down the chance of infections or something like that. Faces came and went—looming over her, telling her this or that—but she could hardly remember anything they had said.

She did remember what the doctor had said after he examined her. She was doing fine. Just fine. If she was doing fine, she was glad she wasn't doing bad. She'd never be able to stand "bad" if this was "fine." Then he said it would be awhile. That she might not deliver till morning. He acted as if he might go on home and go back to bed.

How was she going to stand this pain until morning? And all by herself. As the pain began to ease back, a couple of tears slid out of the corners of her eyes and down her cheeks. She hadn't expected to be all alone.

No nurse had even been in to see about her since one of them had put up the side rails on the bed, as if she was some little kid who might fall out. If they were going to lock her in the bed, the least they could have done was let somebody, Aunt Love or her father or anybody, stay with her. Maybe they made her be alone because she didn't have a husband. Maybe this was part of her punishment.

She tried to say a prayer, but she wasn't very good at praying. Her father said she didn't have to be good at praying. That the Lord didn't care if her prayers were fancy or not, as long as they came from the heart. But Tabitha felt funny praying. She'd gotten too out of the habit all those years she'd been gone from Hollyhill with her mother, who thought praying was nothing but a big waste of time. Better to be out doing, DeeDee had always said, instead of hiding somewhere in a corner, praying to a God that never listened anyway.

Tabitha hadn't believed that. She knew God listened, at least to some people. She'd just never been sure he would listen to her. At least not then, while she was with her mother. Why would he? They never went to church, and the truth was, she hardly ever even thought about praying except when she was thinking about her father. And then it wasn't her praying, but him praying.

Of course, she was going to church now. Had gone most every Sunday since July except when she stayed home with Wes. And Aunt Love was always talking church stuff to her at home too. Tabitha didn't mind. She liked it when Aunt Love assured her that the Lord loved her and her unborn baby and would take care of them no matter what.

But now Aunt Love was out there somewhere in the hospital where they wouldn't let her come and talk to Tabitha. And the pain was rolling back toward her. She could feel it coming. Then it didn't seem to hardly pause until it was rolling back at her again. This couldn't be the way it was supposed to be. Not with her in here all by herself. Maybe if she screamed as loud as she could, her father would hear her and come help her.

The door to her room opened, and one of the nurses came in. She didn't come to the bed to look at Tabitha's belly or anything, but just walked over and looked out the window as if checking the weather or to see if her ride was in the parking lot down below. She didn't even look around at Tabitha as she said, "How are you doing?"

"The pains aren't stopping. Please, I need my father or my aunt to help me. The pain isn't stopping." Tabitha hated the way her voice sounded. Weak and teary, but it hurt. She wanted to be strong for Stephanie Grace, but nobody had told her it was going to hurt so bad. Or maybe they had, and she just hadn't understood until she was feeling it herself.

The nurse left. Didn't even pat her arm or check her pulse. Just left. Tabitha had to scream. She wanted to be a good girl and do what they told her, but for Stephanie Grace, she had to scream. There wasn't anything left to do. But the sound was swallowed up by all the holes in the ceiling tiles. And the pain rolled on, crushing her.

Then the door was pushing open and nurses were swarming all around her. One shoved a gas mask over her nose while another one put her hands on Tabitha's stomach. Suddenly Tabitha had to push. Stephanie Grace wanted out and Tabitha's whole body was pushing.

The nurse with the gas mask held it tighter over Tabitha's nose and mouth and said, "Breathe in. Don't push. Breathe. Don't push."

But she couldn't keep from pushing. She had to push. And breathe. And then she began sinking away from the noise and the pain.

ꟹ ꟹ

David heard Tabitha scream all the way out in the waiting room on the other side of the double doors. The sound pierced his heart. He shouldn't have let them push him away from her side. He'd known she needed him, needed someone to cling to, but they said he and Aunt Love would have to wait out where the fathers had to wait. They said they'd take care of Tabitha. They told him not to worry. As if that was even possible. His daughter was having a baby. A woman could die having a baby.

"That was Tabitha," Aunt Love said. "They should've let one of us stay with her."

David was out of his seat and across the room. He went right through the doors to the nurses' station. He wouldn't have stopped there if he'd known which room held Tabitha.

The nurse at the desk looked up at him and said, "You're not supposed to be back here."

"I want to see my daughter."

"I'm sure you've already been told, sir. No one is allowed in the labor rooms with the patients. Not even the fathers-to-be." She stood up and came around the desk to usher David back through the doors to the waiting area. She didn't appear to be much older than Tabitha, but she looked very determined to make sure he obeyed the rules.

"Well, that needs to change. Right now. I heard my daughter scream, and I intend to see with my own eyes that she's all right."

The nurse changed tack and brought out a sympathetic tone. "I know it must be difficult for you to wait, but I assure you your daughter is being cared for by our very best nurses. She'll be fine." The nurse put her hand under David's elbow and tried to steer him back toward the waiting room.

David didn't budge. "I want to see my daughter. Now."

The nurse looked at him, and David stared back. He was expecting her to call in reinforcements to manually move him back where it had been decreed that he must stay, but then she was saying, "All right, sir, I can certainly understand your concern. You wait there a minute, and I'll call back and check on her for you." The nurse went back around the desk and picked up a phone.

David stood still and listened. Not to the nurse talking softly into her phone but for Tabitha. One more sound from her and he'd be able to pick out the door she was behind. He couldn't very well just go barging through the doors willy-nilly, invading the privacy of the other mothers-to-be. Of course, there weren't but two other families out in the waiting room. He'd already prayed with both of the fathers. They'd been sharing nervous conversation, but that was before Tabitha screamed.

So even if he guessed wrong the first few times, the rooms would either be empty or have one of the women he'd already prayed for in them. The nurse was still on the phone behind the desk when he started down the hall. She called after him, but he didn't stop.

Then another nurse came out of one of the rooms. David recognized her from other visits he'd made to the hospital as a pastor. She was older, surer of herself than the nurse at the nurses' station, as she came over to block his path. She was smiling. "Now, Brother Brooke, what do you think you're doing? You know you can't be back here with the mommies."

"Linda," David said. "When did you get moved to the maternity floor?"

"A couple of months ago. The job came open, so I thought I'd try babies awhile." Linda gave him a stern look. "But I didn't think I'd have to be reminding you of hospital rules."

"Tabitha—that's my daughter—she screamed."

"I know," Linda said and put her arm around his waist to turn him back toward the waiting area. "But she's okay. Really. Things are just going a little faster for her than we were expecting. In fact, they're getting ready to wheel her into the delivery room, darling. So you can't see her now. Not till after the baby comes." She walked with him to the double doors. "I can't believe you're old enough to be a granddaddy."

"Me either," David said. He felt ready to jump out of his skin. "This is harder than my own kids. Of course, I was half a world away when Tabitha was born. Didn't even know she had arrived until she was almost a month old. I was in a submarine, and it took that long to get the news."

"During the war, right?"

"Right."

And then there was Jocie. He'd been right there on the other side of the bedroom door at their house when Jocie was born. Adrienne had refused to go to the hospital, as if even up to the end she could deny the fact that she was pregnant. Then all David had wanted was for the baby to come, in hopes that afterward he and Adrienne could start over and perhaps find a way to make their marriage work. That had been a vain hope, but the baby, Jocie, had been healthy. And a blessing. The Lord often did that. Sent a special blessing even in the worst of times. Tabitha's baby would be a blessing too.

Linda was patting his arm as she said, "Don't you worry one bit. Your baby's going to be just fine, honey. Both of your babies. Tabitha let out a little yelp, but that's not uncommon with the mommies. It's not easy work getting a baby here." Linda looked over her shoulder back down the hallway. "Poor little thing. She doesn't have a hubby waiting out there with you, does she?"

"No."

"Well, she's lucky to have a daddy like you to take care of her. Just as soon as that baby's here, I'll come tell you, Brother Brooke. You can depend on it. I enjoy carrying out good news."

ꟸ ꟹ

Tabitha heard the baby crying even before she was able to push her eyelids open. She was in a different place on a hard table with bright lights beaming down on her. Her feet were up in stirrups and her legs were wrapped in sheets. Everything was stainless steel or white. No color.

One of the nurses standing by her head said something, and Dr. Roland stood up at the end of the table and smiled at Tabitha. "All over. You did great. I'm just finishing up a few stitches down here."

"Stitches?" Tabitha's mouth was so dry her lips were sticking together.

"Yes, you remember. I told you about the little cut we'd make so you'd have an easier time delivering. You did fine."

"My baby? Is Stephanie Grace all right?" Tabitha turned her head toward the sound of crying. She could see a nurse doing something to a baby on a table over at the wall. Her baby. Tabitha felt all soft inside.

The doctor laughed and the nurses joined in. "Your baby's fine. Healthy and strong. Curly black hair. Nurse Haskins is just checking everything out, but I think you'll have to come up with a new name. You've got a fine baby boy. Six pounds seven ounces."

At first Tabitha wasn't sure she was hearing them right. She thought she might still be under the effects of whatever they had made her breathe. Drifting off to some strange place where doctors laughed and told jokes.

"No," she said. "I had a girl. Stephanie Grace. Where is she?"

Again they laughed. The nurse over by the wall picked up the baby and wrapped him in a blanket and brought him over to Tabitha. She laid the baby in Tabitha's arms and opened up the blanket so she could see his fingers and toes and that he was very definitely a boy. The nurse said, "He's a beautiful boy."

Tabitha looked at the baby and said, "But I was supposed to have a girl. Not a boy." What would she do with a boy? She didn't know anything about boys.

The nurse smiled. "The Lord blesses us with whatever he chooses. A boy this time. A girl the next. Put your hand up here and touch his cheek."

Tabitha touched the baby's soft cheek. He stopped crying and turned his head toward her.

"See, he knows his mama's touch already," the nurse said.

ꕥ ꕥ

David thought his heart would explode when he looked at the baby boy lying in Tabitha's arms. True to her promise, the nurse, Linda, had come and gotten him and Aunt Love and led them back to see Tabitha and the baby for a few minutes before they whisked the baby back behind the glass in the nursery.

He was crying, his mouth a wide circle of protest at being thrust out of his safe haven into the world. But even so, he was beautiful. He had an abundance of black hair, and his skin was tan as if the hours Tabitha had spent in the sun while she was carrying him had burned straight through to her womb. David stroked the baby's tiny hand and remembered how Tabitha had never wanted to talk about the baby's father, but that didn't matter now. As soon as his eyes touched on the baby, David's heart enveloped him. Secure and loved. This baby, this child, his grandchild, was beautiful. The wonder of it brought tears to his eyes.

David looked from the baby to Tabitha. Her eyes held tears as well, but not of joy. She looked confused, almost sad.

"Sweetheart, are you okay?" David asked.

"He's a boy," Tabitha said.

"And a beautiful one," David said, with Aunt Love agreeing as she stood beside him.

"But where's Stephanie Grace?" Tabitha said. "I was supposed to have Stephanie Grace."

"It's all right, sweetheart. Stephanie Grace is still right here in your head waiting for another time to be born." He leaned over and kissed her forehead. "But now the Lord has blessed you, blessed us, with this beautiful baby boy. And he will be a joy to you and to me."

"And me," Aunt Love echoed. "'Joy cometh in the morning.'"

Tabitha smiled through her tears and looked down at the baby. She ran her fingers across the baby's cheek, and he stopped crying. "I don't have a name for him."

"You will," David said. "Just give yourself some time. And rest. Right now you need to rest."

"He is pretty, isn't he?" Tabitha said.

"The most beautiful baby boy I've ever seen," David said.

A nurse carried the baby away, and David and Aunt Love kissed Tabitha and left with promises to bring Jocie back that afternoon to see the baby. David waited by the elevators while Aunt Love made a visit to the ladies room before they headed down to the car.

It was a few minutes past four o'clock in the morning. No time for sleeping, but plenty of time for him to get home and make a few sermon notes before time for Sunday school. David smiled. Instead of his congregation dozing off on his sermon this morning, he might be the one dozing off himself. But the Lord was good. He'd lift David up and carry him through it. And the people at Mt. Pleasant would be so excited to hear about the baby that they wouldn't be too critical about whatever he managed to preach. This baby would be a bridge for them all to step closer and see what was important about life.

As he leaned against the wall and waited for Aunt Love, he idly watched the elevator lights climbing to the floor he was on. Perhaps it was bringing another doctor ready to deliver another baby into the world or maybe one of the waiting fathers with a cup of coffee.

The doors slid open and there was Jocie. For a second, David couldn't believe his eyes. But no, she was standing there in the middle of the elevator in front of him, barefoot with a blanket draped around her shoulders over her nightgown. She reeked of smoke as she stared at him out of black-rimmed eyes. Tears had made streaks down through the gray smudges on her cheeks, but she wasn't crying now. The despair etched on her face went past tears.

"Jocie," David said, reaching for the open-door button before the elevator doors could slide together and take her away from him. "What on earth has happened?"

"It's Mr. Harvey. I think he's dead. They haven't told me that, but I think he is."

43

David reached out and pulled Jocie to him. The smoke smell in her hair was so strong it burned his nose. What was it about this summer that made Jocie keep landing in the middle of disasters? "Are you okay, baby?" he asked.

"I think so. They say they need to check my lungs, but they were trying to get hold of you first." Her voice was raspy sounding, and she had to push back from him so she could cough before she could go on. "I told them you were here at the hospital, but they didn't pay any attention to me. So I just got on the elevator when nobody was looking and came on up here. Miss Sally told me which floor, and I was praying you'd be somewhere I could see you right off. I'm glad the Lord answered that prayer, Daddy." She looked up at him.

"He put me out here right by the elevators," David said as he gently touched her cheek. She looked so bruised and fragile that it made his heart hurt. "Can you tell me what happened?"

"There was a fire. We barely got out of the house, but we did get out. Then Mr. Harvey—he just . . . fell down." Her bottom lip started trembling, but then she mashed her mouth together and looked around. "Where's Aunt Love?"

"In the ladies room. We were heading home." He could barely keep from bombarding her with questions, but he'd sat with enough people in the aftermath of a tragic event to know it would be easier for her if he didn't demand to know everything at once. He had to wait for her to be ready to tell him more. He put his arm around her shoulders.

"Oh," Jocie said. "Does that mean Tabitha had her baby?"

"She did. A beautiful little boy."

For a second Jocie's eyes had a flicker of life back in them. "A boy. Oops, guess Tabitha will have to come up with a new name." She almost smiled as she looked up at him out of her smoke-rimmed eyes, but then she was coughing again. Hard coughs that shook her whole body.

"That she will," David said as he tightened his hold on her shoulders. He wanted to take the cough from her, put it inside his own body. More than that, he wanted to take the sadness, the bad things that had happened to take the joy out of her eyes, and make them disappear. He wanted them to be able to laugh and talk about Tabitha's baby and not have to worry about death. Surely she was wrong. Surely Mr. Harvey wasn't dead.

Jocie took a couple of breaths when she finally stopped coughing and then wiped her eyes on a corner of the blanket. "I feel like I'm trying to cough up my whole insides. Mrs. Hearndon says I must have breathed too much smoke."

"Mrs. Hearndon? Is she here too?"

"She's in the emergency room with Miss Sally." She coughed again.

"I think that's where you need to be too. We can talk on the way down there."

"But what about Aunt Love? We can't just leave her up here by herself. She'd be lost." Jocie's eyes turned sad again. "I don't want to lose anybody else tonight."

David looked over Jocie's head down the hall toward the ladies room. "She's coming," he said.

Aunt Love clapped her hands over her heart and looked faint when she saw Jocie. "My stars, child. What has happened to you?"

"I'm all right, Aunt Love. Honest. Just coughing a little. From the smoke. And the air, it was so hot. I think it scorched my nose." Jocie pushed on the side of her nose and took a breath.

"Was there a fire?" Aunt Love frowned and looked even more worried. "At our house?"

"No, I wasn't at our house, remember," Jocie said quietly. Her eyes turned inward as if she was seeing it play out again in her head. "It was Miss Sally's house. The whole thing just went up in a big swoosh. Everything was burning up. Even their clock. You know, the one on Miss Sally's mantel that had never stopped ticking. I wanted to go get it, but I couldn't go back inside. Nobody could. Miss Sally said none of that mattered anyway. She just didn't want to lose Mr. Harvey."

David pushed the elevator down button, and when the door slid open, he ushered them inside. "What happened to Mr. Harvey?" he asked as the doors shut and the elevator started down.

"He didn't burn up." Jocie trembled a little and pulled her blanket closer around her, but she kept talking. "We got out, but the house went fast. We had to climb through a window in Miss Sally's bedroom out on the roof. I didn't think Mr. Harvey was going to make it. He kept stopping and talking to the Lord. Not like me praying, but talking to him as if he was standing right there beside us. And then once we got down to the ground and the men were gone, he said he saw angels."

"The men? What men?" David asked.

"The Klan. They had on hoods, so I don't know who

they were, but Mr. Harvey knew one of them. He called him Bob."

"The Klan burned down Mr. Harvey's house?" David couldn't believe what he was hearing. Surely not Mr. Harvey and Miss Sally's house. Everybody loved them.

"I don't think they aimed to. It just happened. They had this big wooden cross they put in the front yard. Then they threw kerosene all over it and lit it, but one of the men started yelling that it was too close to the house."

"Didn't they know you were inside?" Aunt Love asked.

"I guess so. Well, not me, but Miss Sally and Mr. Harvey. They didn't know I was there watching them." Jocie stared at the elevator doors for a minute before she started talking again. "But I saw them. I was in that room downstairs that used to be Miss Sally's mother's, but I was having trouble going to sleep. I was thinking about Tabitha and everything. Anyway, I heard them when they came. I should have run and got Mr. Harvey and Miss Sally then, but I thought maybe I had actually fallen asleep and was dreaming."

Jocie looked over at David and went on. "You see, I'd been having this dream about them. About the men in hoods, ever since they were in town, so I thought I might be dreaming. But I wasn't. I knew that as soon as I smelled the kerosene. I shouldn't have waited so long to go get Mr. Harvey and Miss Sally."

"It's okay, baby. You couldn't know the house was going to catch fire," David said softly.

Jocie got too still and shut her eyes for a moment. The elevator came to a stop on the bottom floor, but David pressed in the close-door button. She needed to finish telling them so they could take some of the pain from her into their own hearts.

Jocie licked her lips and started talking again. "I've never seen fire like that. One of the men had a torch, and when he threw it down to the kerosene, there was this awful explosion of flames. The whole yard caught fire and then the porch. It was like the fire turned into some kind of monster and it was hungry. Very hungry."

Aunt Love whispered a bit of Scripture. "'What time I am afraid, I will trust in thee.'"

"I was afraid, Aunt Love. I thought we were going to burn up. Smoke was everywhere and I couldn't breathe. I got Miss Sally and Mr. Harvey awake. Miss Sally wouldn't let Mr. Harvey put on his pants and shoes. We carried them for him. We went to the stairs, but the fire had gotten inside. It wasn't just smoke anymore. The bottom steps were on fire. And the walls down there. It was so hot. I couldn't breathe. Things started going black in front of my eyes."

"What were the men outside doing?" David asked.

"They were yelling, shooting guns, I think. But then I couldn't hear them anymore. The fire was too loud. Mr. Harvey said we'd have to go out the window. I didn't think they could, but they did. It wasn't too hard. But Mr. Harvey kept holding his chest, and then when we got down on the ground, the men in the sheets came up around us. Just like in my dream. They said the house burning down was all Mr. Harvey's fault. For selling his land to Noah's father. Then they left and the fire was burning behind us and Mr. Harvey told Miss Sally he thought he was having a heart attack and then he saw angels."

"How did you get to the hospital?"

"Noah's mother. They saw the fire and came. Mrs. Hearndon is with Miss Sally. And Cassidy and Eli and Elise. They're all down there. Eli and Elise went to sleep, but Cassidy's too scared to go to sleep. I wish she didn't have to be so scared." Jocie leaned against David.

"So do I, sweetie," David said as he rubbed her hair.

She didn't seem to hear him. "But I guess she has reason. The men went to their house first. Didn't burn anything there, just tore up all their apple trees. All of them. Ran over them with their trucks and broke them up." Jocie looked up at David. "Why did the Lord let them do that, Daddy? Why didn't he stop them?"

"I don't know, Jocie."

"Why did those men want to hurt Miss Sally and Mr. Harvey?"

Jocie was still looking at David, waiting for him to say something to help her make sense of what had happened, but he had no answers. "I don't know the answer to that either, baby. Some things are just beyond understanding," he said.

Aunt Love spoke up. "'For their feet run to evil.'"

Evil. That surely was the only explanation. Men allowing hatred to rule their actions. David took his finger off the close-door button. The elevator doors slid open, and they were back in the antiseptic confines of the hospital.

A nurse led them back to the curtained alcove where Miss Sally sat on an examining table. Myra Hearndon sat in a chair beside the table with Eli asleep in her lap. Elise was stretched out asleep on a hospital blanket on the floor. Cassidy was leaning against her mother with her eyes closed, but when they came through the curtains, the little girl opened her eyes and looked at them. Jocie was right. The child was scared. Deep down scared.

Some of that same fear, along with sorrow, was in Myra Hearndon's eyes as she looked at David and then back to Miss Sally. "Oh, Rev. Brooke, I'm so glad Jocie found you. The doctors want to check her lungs. Just to be sure she's okay."

Miss Sally looked small and forlorn, sitting on the examining table with the hospital gown draped around her and a blanket over her knees. Somebody had washed some of the smoke and soot off her face, but there were still traces of black around her eyes and nose. And yet she looked at David and smiled. "The child, has she had her baby?"

David thought he might cry, but he swallowed the tears and managed a smile for Miss Sally. "She did. A boy, six pounds seven ounces."

"Oh, that's wonderful," Miss Sally said as, for just a moment, the tiny alcove was filled with the miracle of birth instead of the sadness of death. "Harvey would have been so happy. He would have been promising him a ride on his tractor." Then her face clouded a bit as she looked at Myra. "Did the tractor burn too?"

"I'm sure Alex and Noah and the neighbors were able to save the tractor," Myra said.

"Oh, I hope so. Harvey loved that old tractor," Miss Sally said. "I remember when he got it. He was just like a little boy with a new toy."

A nurse came in and said too many people were with Miss Sally and that the doctors were ready for Jocie. Jocie said Aunt Love could go with her, that they were just going to make her do some breathing stuff the way they had with Miss Sally and maybe take an x-ray. Myra stood up to take Cassidy to the restroom.

"Lay Eli down there with Elise, Myra," Miss Sally said. "If they fuss about it, I'll just tell them to hush, and Brother David can help with them if they happen to wake up before you get back." Miss Sally smiled at Cassidy. "And get your mommy to get you a soft drink out of the machine down there, sweetheart. I know you have to be thirsty. You've got some change, don't you, Brother David?"

David handed Myra all the change he had in his pocket after she laid Eli down on the floor. The little boy's eyelids didn't even flicker as he settled beside his sister on the blanket.

"You can't argue with her," Myra said with a smile toward Miss Sally as she took the coins. Then she turned toward David and lowered her voice a little. "She's just so kind. You know, she's not even mad. I want to tear apart something, maybe everything, but she says the Lord will make something good come of this." Her eyes filled with tears. "And I know that's true, but what they did was still wicked."

And then David was alone with Miss Sally and the two sleeping toddlers. He stood close beside her and held her hands for a moment. All around them outside the curtains there was noise as the hospital personnel took care of emergencies, but he and Miss Sally seemed to be in a pocket of deep silence. Finally David asked, "What about Mr. Harvey?"

"He's gone," Miss Sally said sadly. "They told us for sure a little while ago, but I knew it back at the house."

"I'm sorry . . . Did they think it was a heart attack?"

"Heart attack, broken heart, sorrow. Whatever name you want to give it. I think he could have stood it if it had been lightning striking the house and burning it down, but for men he knew to be doing it was just more than he could bear."

"Jocie said he knew one of the men. That he called him by name. Bob."

"Well, there's no knowing for sure, and Bob is a common name."

"Did you recognize any of them, Miss Sally?"

"It's hard to say. They had on hoods, you know." Miss Sally dropped her eyes away from David's. "The sheriff was in here a little bit ago asking me the same thing, but I wouldn't want to accuse a man when I couldn't be sure."

"But they need to be punished for what they've done."

Miss Sally looked up at him again. "I'm going to leave that up to the Lord, Brother David. He can take care of all that for me. And for Harvey." Her face softened a bit. "You know, we wouldn't either of us have made it out of the fire if your little girl hadn't been there with us. We'd have burned up in our beds for sure. I'm sorry she had to be part of it, though. To see the hate. It's pierced her heart, Brother David. That and Harvey going on."

"I know. I'll talk to her later." After he prayed for answers himself.

"Tell her Harvey's okay. That he's in a better place."

"I'm still sorry he's gone. I'm going to miss him."

"I know, Brother David." She patted his hand. "But you can't be wishing a person back no matter how much you love him once he's seen the angels. He went right on with them, you know. Ran right out of his body and left that fiery hell behind us. Took off across the fields with them straight up to heaven. If the fire hadn't been crackling and popping so loud, we could have probably heard him laughing."

Miss Sally blinked away her tears and laughed a little herself at the thought. "I know he kept breathing till after we got him to the hospital, but it was just because his spirit took off so fast his body got caught by surprise. As soon as he saw those angels coming after him, he was gone. I know he was."

"Do you wish you could have gone along with him?"

"Oh, no, Brother David." She looked surprised he could even think such a thing. "The Lord's still got some things for me to do down here. I think that's why he put your sweet little girl there with us tonight." She looked over at the two children curled asleep on the floor. "The Lord knows what he's doing. He's just given me a family, you know. Myra says I can come live with them for as long as I want. The Lord's hand is in that. I know it is."

"But will you be safe? Jocie said the Klan had been at their house too."

"Now don't you be worrying. I told you the sheriff was in here a bit ago. And Jimmy, he promises me that wherever I go to stay, he'll be sure to see that I'm safe. See, the Lord is going to use this. If Jimmy keeps me safe, he'll have to keep Myra and Alex safe. Don't you think?"

"I pray so," David said. "Maybe we should pray so together."

He held her hands and felt strength coming through to him as he prayed. Here she was the one who'd lost her brother and all her possessions and yet she was pushing strength toward him.

When he said amen, she told him, "Now you go on and see about Jocie. Make sure she's okay. She took an awful chance running up the stairs after us with the smoke so bad." She squeezed his hands before she turned them loose. "I'll be just fine. Myra and little Cassidy will be back in a few minutes. Myra will take care of me.

"And you tell all the folk at Mt. Pleasant what I told you about Harvey and the angels. That way maybe they won't be so sad. Tell them that we'll be having Homecoming next week same as always. Harvey would have wanted us to."

ᘓ ᘕ

The next morning the Mt. Pleasant Baptist Church members came and sat in the pews the same as always, but they didn't have church the same as always. David didn't preach a sermon. They didn't even sing any songs. Jessica Sanderson tried playing "What a Friend We Have in Jesus," but she didn't get through the first verse before she just stood up and went back and sat in the second pew with her family.

There wasn't a dry eye in the church when David told them what Miss Sally had told him to say. And everybody prayed. Really prayed. There had probably never been a better message straight from the Lord in all the many years the Mt. Pleasant Church had been meeting. It was a message that didn't have to come out of a preacher's mouth. It was a message that just went heart to heart.

44

Mr. Harvey's funeral was on Wednesday afternoon at two o'clock. Hollyhill shut down. Jocie didn't go to school. She didn't go Monday or Tuesday either. She was still coughing, still had that nasty smoke smell in her nose. She could have gone to school, but she just didn't want to, and her father said she didn't have to. At least, until after the funeral.

Besides, Wes had needed her to help get the *Banner* out. Her father was busy helping Miss Sally. He took Miss Sally to Hazelton's Funeral Home on Monday morning to get everything arranged for Mr. Harvey's funeral service. And then he and Mrs. Hearndon took her out to see what was left of her house. He looked grim when he brought his film back to the office for Wes to develop for the paper. That was all he'd done for this week's issue.

He'd said he didn't care whether they printed a paper this week or not, but Zella said they had to. She said they were just like the post office that never let anything stop the mail. Blizzards, floods, gloom of night, whatever. She said it had to be the same with the *Banner*. They couldn't just decide to skip a week.

"Why, if we don't put out some kind of paper, there will be people lined up here Thursday morning with their hands out for a refund for this week's cost of their subscriptions," she'd told Jocie's father. "Can you imagine what kind of headache that would be? Refunding a week's worth of their subscription."

"They wouldn't do that," Jocie's father said, but he didn't sound too sure of it.

"You know some of them would. Besides, we need the money from the counter sales to stay out of the red, and the people that have bought ads have a right to see them in the paper when they thought they would be in there." She looked hard at Jocie's father. "I'm as tore up as anybody about Harvey. He was a fine man, a godly man, but he wouldn't have wanted us to just sit down and hold our heads in our hands and say 'oh, me.'"

"I'm not doing that."

"Well, no, you're helping Sally, which you ought to be doing, but Harvey would be the first to tell us to go on about our lives, and part of that is putting out a paper. Besides, don't you think this is a story that ought to be told? As a testimony to him. To Harvey."

"You're preaching at me, Zella," David said.

"Turnabout's fair play," Zella snapped. "We can't just hide our heads in the sand on this one. Let Jocelyn write a story about it. She was there."

Jocie's father said she didn't have to if it was too hard for her to think about what had happened, but it had helped to write some of it down. And then she'd been so busy helping Wes and Noah get the pages ready to run and running them that she hadn't had time to think about the flames racing up the stairs to trap her and Miss Sally and Mr. Harvey.

Her father had been there on Tuesday when they folded the papers. So had Leigh with her brownies, but the folding session was solemn and somber as they folded the papers with Mr. Harvey's picture on the front page, top fold.

Wednesday, Leigh took off work. That morning after they

took the papers to the post office, she drove Jocie over to the hospital to see Tabitha and her baby. He was the cutest thing Jocie had ever seen as he lay there in his little bed on wheels behind the viewing window. He kept waving his fists and fussing at the nurses.

Jocie told Tabitha how cute he was and that she needed to hurry up and come up with a name or they'd just have to call him Boy Brooke the way she'd heard some people name their dogs Pup or Dog. And then she suggested Stephen Lee. Stephen for Aunt Love's baby and Lee for Mr. Harvey. That had been his middle name. It was in the obituary they'd printed in the *Banner*.

"Stephen Lee. That does have a nice sound, and I liked Mr. Harvey. He was sweet to me," Tabitha said and then looked worried. "But do you think, you know, if I ever do have another baby that I could still name her Stephanie Grace? Would that be too confusing having a Stephen and a Stephanie?"

"Not for anybody with half a brain," Jocie said. "The names don't sound a thing alike. And who cares what anybody thinks, anyway? He's so cute. He needs a good name."

"He looks like his father," Tabitha said.

"Well, you did tell me once that his father had beautiful brown eyes," Jocie reminded her.

"But I forgot to add the part about the beautiful brown skin," Tabitha said.

"It won't matter," Jocie and Leigh both said at once.

But Tabitha just looked at them without smiling. "How can you say that after what just happened to Mr. Harvey? It will matter."

Leigh stepped closer to give Tabitha a hug before she said, "All right, you're right. It might matter to some people, but it won't matter to the people who are most important to you and now to him. Your father and Jocie. Aunt Love and me. Wes. We'll be there to help you and him through whatever happens."

"So name him already," Jocie said.

"Okay, okay, I will." Tabitha had made a face at Jocie, then looked sad as she'd asked them to be sure to tell Miss Sally how sorry she was about Mr. Harvey.

And now her father had preached the funeral, and they were at the cemetery getting ready to put Mr. Harvey beneath the ground. It was still hot, even though some clouds had drifted in to cover the sun. People had looked up at the sky as they'd walked from their cars across the graveyard to crowd around the tent set up over the grave. In hushed voices they talked about how much they needed rain.

Miss Sally was sitting under the tent with Myra and Alex Hearndon on either side of her. Cassidy sat close to Myra, and Noah had the twins at the back of the tent. Dorothy McDermott had moved up beside him to help with the children if she was needed. A few nieces and nephews filled up the rest of the chairs under the tent.

Miss Sally dabbed her eyes with her handkerchief as Jocie's father read the graveside Scriptures. Jocie had attended a lot of funerals with her father. She knew how they went. Most of the crying happened in the funeral home before Mr. Hazelton shut the casket. The graveside was just one final good-bye, but today everybody was crying. Everybody but her.

Jocie didn't have any tears. It was as if the fire had been so hot that it had seared every tear out of her heart. Beside her, tears ran down Leigh's cheeks. Even her father had to wipe away tears as he read from his Bible. But Jocie just listened with her eyes so dry they almost hurt as she looked around at the people gathered there and wondered if any of them had been under the hoods.

None of it seemed real when she thought about it. The white-hooded men around Miss Sally's house. The fire. Crawling out the window and across the roof with Mr. Harvey talking to the Lord. But it *was* real. Her father was reading from his Bible. The people around her were weeping. Mr. Harvey was dead.

What was it Mr. Harvey had told her when they went out to see the new calf? That birth and death were all part of God's plan for his people. But the fire had nothing to do with God's plans. That was hatred with feet and torches.

Her father was through praying, and Mr. Hazelton was picking a rose out of the spray on top of the casket to give to Miss Sally. When he handed the rose to Miss Sally, she whispered something to him. He looked a little surprised before he went back to the casket for two more roses to hand to Mrs. Hearndon and Cassidy. Cassidy wouldn't take hers, so Mrs. Hearndon had to take them both.

The first raindrop hit Jocie's head as Miss Sally stood up on the green fake-grass rug under the tent. And then more drops splattered against the tent. There was no sign of a storm, no thunder or lightning, no wind. The clouds overhead just broke open and rain began falling, almost as if the very sky was weeping for Mr. Harvey. It was a gentle rain, and nobody ran for their cars. They just stood there and held out their hands to catch the drops.

Miss Sally came out from under the tent and looked up toward the sky, letting the rain wash the tears off her face. And then she laughed. Right out loud. "Isn't that just like Harvey?" She looked at the people around her. "He just went right to the source of all rain and talked the Lord into sending it on down to us."

It rained the rest of the day and all night long and into the next morning. The same gentle steady rain that let the ground drink in every drop. And all the time it was raining, everybody in Holly County kept thinking about Mr. Harvey and how much he had loved his land and his neighbors and how the rain was saving the crops. Of course, Noah and his family didn't have any apple trees left to be saved by the rain.

Jocie went back to school on Thursday. Everybody was extra nice to her. Paulette even left Janice and Linda to sit with Jocie and Charissa at lunchtime. Of course, that might not have had as much to do with the fire as Paulette still hoping Jocie would say it was okay for her to like Ronnie Martin. Jocie didn't know why Paulette needed her okay, but for some reason, she did.

But Jocie had too much other stuff on her mind to worry about whether she'd ever be able to forgive Ronnie Martin. She didn't even have time to pray about that right now. She had to pray for Miss Sally and Noah's family. And she had to pray that somehow she would be able to close her eyes and go to sleep again without seeing flames and men in hoods. She thought about asking her father to help her pray on that one, but he'd been so busy helping everybody that they barely had the chance to talk about anything except what needed to be done at the *Banner*.

Thursday, her dad took Wes back to the doctor. Wes came home wearing what he called a walking cast. He still had to use his crutches, but he got to put weight on his leg, and he started eyeing his motorcycle. When Jocie went by the newspaper office after school, he told her, "You know, I think if somebody helped me climb on the thing, I could take a ride now."

"Don't even think about it," Jocie told him. "Enough bad things have happened this year already."

"Wouldn't be nothing bad about me taking a ride."

"It would be bad when you had a wreck because your leg was in a cast."

"I didn't say I'd do the driving. Noah could. Or maybe you," Wes said with a grin.

"Don't either one of us have a license," Jocie reminded him.

Wes sighed. "Well, I guess that is a problem. Maybe I can talk your daddy into being a preacher on a hog. Might make Miss Leigh think he was dashing and handsome."

"She already does," Jocie said.

"Yeah, I guess you're right. Then how about old Zell? You think she'd take me for a spin?"

The thought of Zella on Wes's motorcycle was so crazy that Jocie had to laugh. For the first time all week.

"There, that's more like it," he said. "You can't stop laughing, Jo."

"You weren't doing all that much laughing a few weeks ago yourself." Jocie peered over at him. "Then it was me trying to get you to laugh."

"That's what friends and family are for." Wes reached over and touched her hand. "What is that verse Lovella sometimes says? That one about the merry heart."

"'A merry heart doeth good like a medicine.'"

"It's medicine all of us need." Wes sat back in his chair.

"But how can your heart be merry when bad things are happening?" Sadness welled up inside Jocie as she thought about Mr. Harvey.

"That's too hard a question for an old Jupiterian like me," Wes said. "But could be it has something to do with that peace that passeth understanding your daddy talks about sometimes. And with how even when bad things are happening, good things are still happening too."

"Like Tabitha's baby?"

"That's one of the good things for sure. Did she ever decide on a name for the little feller?"

"Finally. Stephen Lee. She's supposed to bring him home tomorrow. She had to stay an extra day or two because she had a fever or something, but she's okay now."

"Yeah, that's what your daddy told me. He said me and Zell would have to hold down the fort here while he goes after her. Of course, the way old Zell's been acting like she's afraid to look sideways at me, she may take the day off too."

"Oh, you know Zella. She's always strange." Jocie made a face as she looked out toward the front office where Zella was banging on her typewriter.

"You got that right, but then so am I." Wes ran his fingers through his hair until it was spiking out in all directions. "You think I'll scare little Stevie when I come see him? Miss Leigh says she'll drive me out there. In her car. She won't talk about getting on my motorcycle. Turns right pale at the thought of it."

Jocie giggled again before she said, "No. He'll like you." She hesitated a couple of seconds. "You haven't seen him yet, have you?"

"Not yet."

"His father was black."

"So your daddy told me."

Again Jocie hesitated before she said, "Do you think the Klan will hear about that and try to burn a cross in our yard?"

Wes leaned closer and put his hand on Jocie's cheek. "It's going to be all right, Jo. You and your daddy have a higher power watching over you."

"I want him to watch over you too."

"Well, maybe he already is, Jo." He patted her cheek and

sat back again. "Just think about that tree falling on me back when the tornado tried to blow us to kingdom come. He helped us live through that. Not just you but me too, when by rights I shouldn't have."

"But why didn't he watch over Mr. Harvey?" She kept her eyes intently on Wes as she waited for him to answer. She needed an answer.

But he shook his head. "More questions too hard for an old Jupiterian. But then again, how do you know he wasn't? Didn't you say Harvey saw angels?"

"That's what he said, but do you think there were really angels there? That the Lord could have opened my eyes and let me see them the way he did for Elisha's servant in that Old Testament story where the Lord's army of horses and chariots were on the mountain around them protecting Elisha?"

"I don't know, Jo, but the one thing I think we can be sure of is that Harvey saw them. They were real for him."

Friday, Tabitha and the baby came home, and the minute Jocie got home from school, Tabitha made her sit down on the couch to hold the baby. He was so tiny, so soft, so new. Jocie touched his hand. He opened his eyes and smiled.

"Oh look," Aunt Love said. "He must be dreaming of angels."

Angels. Jocie wondered if they were the same angels Mr. Harvey had seen. Then she was remembering walking out to the field with Mr. Harvey to find the new calf. A time to be born. A time to die. Tears filled Jocie's eyes and overflowed onto her cheeks. Stephen Lee didn't seem to mind even when the tears began dripping off her chin onto his blanket. He just kept smiling his seeing-angels smile.

"'I have heard thy prayer, I have seen thy tears,'" Aunt Love whispered the verse.

45

On Sunday, a former pastor, Brother Perry, delivered the Homecoming sermon. David was glad he didn't have to preach. It was hard enough just standing in front of the church making the announcements and leading the prayers and watching the deacons come forward to take up the collection without Mr. Harvey.

Miss Sally was there, smiling the same as always, with a kind word for everybody who came over to talk to her before the services started. Now, as the deacons moved back up the aisle with the offering plates, she had Elise on her lap and Cassidy sandwiched between her and Myra Hearndon, who held Eli. Noah sat straight and tall beside his mother, but he kept looking over his shoulder as if afraid something or somebody might be trying to sneak up on him.

Alex Hearndon wasn't there. He'd told David that he had been giving some thought to coming to church with Myra, but after what had happened to Mr. Harvey, he didn't see how he'd ever be able to go inside a church house again. He didn't see how anybody could.

"The Lord's not to blame for what happened to Mr. Harvey," David had told him. "Or to your apple trees."

"You credit the Lord for the good things that happen. Why not the bad?"

"Because the Lord has given man the freedom to choose good or evil. 'A good man out of the good treasure of the heart bringeth forth good things; and an evil man out of the evil treasure bringeth forth evil things.'"

"Scripture, I'm thinking," Alex said.

"The words of Jesus in the Gospel of Matthew. It's up to us to choose the treasure we're going to store up in our hearts."

"A bunch of people around here have been choosing the evil treasure."

"But that shouldn't turn us away from the love of the Lord. I believe the Lord can make good come out of anything," David said.

"That's what Miss Sally says too, but I can't think of the first thing good that could come out of their house burning down or Mr. Harvey dying or my trees being beat down and ruined. Not one good thing." The man stared at David, daring him to say any of that was good.

"Nor can I," David agreed with him. "But the workings of the Lord are wondrous and mysterious."

"I'll let you and Myra talk about that. Me, I'm wondering if your Lord is working at all."

David wished Alex was there beside him now, watching his congregation and seeing the workings of the Lord that morning. Tabitha had insisted on bringing her baby even though Aunt Love thought it too soon for her to get out. But Tabitha said she felt fine and she wanted to be there for Miss Sally and for David. And the church people, Tabitha's Christian brothers and sisters, had looked at her baby and smiled with joy for her. If there were whispers of disapproval, David hadn't heard them. Perhaps the Lord was blocking David's ears, and if that was so, he was thankful.

Leigh was sitting beside Tabitha, ready to help with the baby if Tabitha needed her to. She didn't know anything about babies, but she had a loving heart. David's eyes touched on Leigh, and his own heart lightened—almost sang—even with all the problems pressing down on him. Surely without a doubt Leigh coming into his life was the working of the Lord. And again he was thankful.

The church was full. They'd had to bring out extra chairs from the Sunday school rooms. Bob Jessup and his family were there for the first time since he'd thought David had doubted his spiritual commitment. Another working of the Lord. Bob had come to see David after Mr. Harvey's funeral. What they had said would forever remain just between the two men and God. But Bob was changed. He'd driven to Atlanta, Georgia, and bought apple trees. They were out in his truck, pulled over in the shade in the church parking area. He'd asked David to go with him to take them to the Hearndons after the services were over that afternoon. David was praying that Alex Hearndon would see the working of the Lord in that and accept the trees.

But maybe the most joyous sign of the working of the Lord was Wes sitting in a chair at the end of the pew beside Jocie. She kept reaching over to touch his arm as if to make sure he was really there. David himself had blinked a couple of times when Wes had come in that morning with Leigh. When he went back to greet them, Wes narrowed his eyes and said, "Now don't go expecting me to do no aisle walking. I just thought I'd come along with Miss Leigh to cheer up Jo a little this morning."

"She'll be excited to see you," David said. And a bit of Scripture had echoed in his heart. *O Lord, how great are thy works!*

ꘐ ꘐ

Cassidy hadn't wanted to come to church. Not even for the morning services, much less all day long. Not because she didn't love the Lord. She told her mama she loved the Lord, but she didn't like all those eyes looking at her. White eyes. Eyes maybe hating her enough to tear up her daddy's beautiful trees. Now they'd never have that orchard of hope he'd talked about.

Cassidy had heard them talking last night. Her mama and daddy. Her daddy said he didn't have the heart to plant any more trees that would just get tore up too. He said they might have to go back to Chicago so he could get a job, which was okay with Cassidy. Except for Miss Sally.

That's what her mama told her daddy. That they couldn't leave yet. That they'd have to wait a little while because of Miss Sally. Cassidy didn't think her mama wanted to leave Miss Sally at all. But her daddy said they couldn't expect Miss Sally to take care of them after all the trouble she'd just had. He said if the white people were mad before, when they'd just been living there minding their own business planting trees, then they'd be crazy mad if they thought they were taking advantage of Miss Sally's kind heart. He said it was no telling what they might do.

Cassidy had heard them. It was in the middle of the night, but Cassidy had been awake. She was awake a lot anymore. She got up out of her bed and went out into the living room to look out the window to make sure the men in the trucks weren't coming back. She moved real quiet to keep from waking up Miss Sally, who'd been sleeping on the couch ever since the men burned down her house and made Mr. Harvey die, but Miss Sally was already awake. She was sitting up on the couch in the moonlight coming through the front windows.

Cassidy looked close at her face to see if what her mama and daddy had been saying made her cry, but she didn't look worried. She smiled at Cassidy and held out her arms to her. Cassidy forgot about checking out the window as Miss Sally held her close.

"It's all right, Cassidy sweetheart," Miss Sally whispered in her ear. "Don't you worry a minute. The Lord is going to take care of us. He's going to keep us safe and bring your daddy some new trees. That will make your daddy feel better."

"How do you know?" Cassidy asked.

"The Lord told me," Miss Sally said. "And I believe him. You can always believe the Lord. He knows."

Now the morning service was over. They'd eaten all the food people had brought and were back in the church house with the preacher talking. Cassidy hoped it wouldn't be much longer before they could go home. She wanted to be at home instead of here with all these eyes on her, seeing her black skin and wanting to hurt her because of it. She could just crawl back in her safe cave, but that was sort of scary too, since back in there she couldn't touch her mama. She felt better when she could touch her mama. And now, sitting between her mama and Miss Sally while the preacher talked, Cassidy felt almost safe enough to shut her eyes and take a nap.

Then Miss Sally was standing up, going down the aisle toward the front, and that side of Cassidy's body felt too cold. Cassidy had known Miss Sally was going to go up front to talk. Miss Sally explained it all to her that morning on the way to church, how she had to give the history of the church since Mr. Harvey wasn't there to do it. A few minutes before she stood up, she'd whispered to Cassidy to not worry if she cried a little while she was talking. That the right kind of tears were good.

Miss Sally stood up behind the pulpit. It was extra quiet in the church as Miss Sally looked down at the sheets of paper she had in her hands. And then she looked out at the church people and said, "This is the annual reading of the history of Mt. Pleasant Baptist Church founded by thirteen men and women in the year 1821."

Miss Sally touched her eyes with her handkerchief and then said, "Now all of you know that Harvey has been doing this ever since 1940 and that, before that, our father read the history for many years. Harvey knew it all by heart. When this building was built. When the sidewalk was laid. Who the preachers were and when they were here. I never heard him say one bad word about any of the preachers we've had here. Not one. Even when the rest of us weren't being quite as nice. Of course, we weren't talking about you, Brother Perry. We all liked you."

Miss Sally smiled over at the man who'd done the preaching that morning and then looked back at the people. "Most of you out there know the history by heart too, but you liked hearing Harvey tell it, and he liked telling it to anybody who'd stand still to listen. And on Homecoming Day he had a captive audience."

Cassidy jumped when a few people chuckled. Then everything went quiet again as Miss Sally stopped and swallowed. She kept her mouth mashed together for a long time before she folded up her papers and moved them off to the side of the pulpit. Now there was absolutely no noise at all in the church. Even Eli and Elise were sitting still, watching Miss Sally. Cassidy scooted over closer to her mama and wished she was on the other side of her mama between her and Noah.

Miss Sally started talking again. "So since you already know the history, I'm not going to read it today. Next year you can find a new deacon to give the report. Today I'm going to stand here and use the history-reading time to tell you what Harvey would tell you if somehow he could come across the great divide between us and talk to us. Not that I think he wants to come back across that divide. He ran off to heaven with the angels, and now he's up there with the Lord. So the first thing I think he would tell you is that he's happy. Happy the way none of us can even imagine, but the way all of us, if our hearts are right, won't have to imagine someday. We'll be there. We'll know about the kind of happy Harvey's feeling.

"Now all of you know neither me nor Harvey ever got married. Harvey had a girl once, but she married somebody else. Broke his heart and he never went out courting again. Me, nobody ever came calling. I prayed about it when I was young. And even harder when I was not so young. I wanted to marry. I saw you here at church with your children and grandchildren, and I wanted a family so much it tore a hole inside me, but the Lord didn't answer that prayer. I used to think it might be because maybe I was just too ugly, but I look out there at you and some of you aren't a bit prettier than I am, and you're sitting there surrounded by your children."

There was a little more laughter as Miss Sally smiled out at the people. Then tears were in her eyes again. "You know Harvey. You know what a tender heart he had, how he cared for the helpless things. He knew how I felt and he prayed with me, but when the years passed and the Lord didn't send a husband my way, he told me that the Lord must have something else planned for my life. Something special.

"That's another thing Harvey would tell you if he was here today. That the Lord has a plan for everybody, and everybody has a place in the kingdom of God. He said there were always children to love, and so I took the children here at the church into my heart. I look around and see so many of you back today, and it makes my heart glad that you are remembering to honor the Lord and your families. I've got a list at home of every child who was ever in my Sunday school class."

A frown flickered across Miss Sally's face. "Well, at least I did have a list. Now I guess the list is just here in my heart." She put her hand up over her heart for a second. "And I thought that was what the Lord intended for me. That you were the family he aimed me to have. Until Harvey decided to sell the farm over on Hoopole Road.

"Our cousin Ben—you remember Ben, our aunt Clara's youngest boy. He moved on up to Chicago some years ago. Claims he likes it up there in the north. Snow and all. Anyway, he said he knew a man who'd been wanting to buy some land to grow an orchard. Well, as soon as Ben said that, Harvey could already see his fields full of apple and peach trees. He was so excited. He felt like the Lord had ordained that farm for something special. An orchard of hope."

Miss Sally looked straight at Cassidy when she said that. Cassidy blinked away tears at the thought of her daddy's orchard of hope being just broken sticks now, but she kept looking at Miss Sally as she went on talking.

"So we sold it to them. We'd never seen them, but Ben said they were good people and that was good enough for us. He didn't mention anything about color, and it never occurred to us to ask. I'm glad we didn't." Miss Sally looked at Cassidy's mama and smiled. "Because you know what? After all these years, when I thought I was way too old to even think about having a daughter, the Lord sent me one. She wasn't born to me, but the minute I saw her she was in my heart, and I knew the Lord had done it. That's the only way it could have happened."

Cassidy's mama had tears rolling out of her eyes and down her cheeks. One of the tears fell on Cassidy's arm.

"The Lord does love us. 'Delight thyself also in the Lord: and he shall give thee the desires of thine heart.' He wants to do that. And he has done that many times for many of you and for me. I wanted a daughter and now I have one. I wanted to be a granny and now I am. Maybe not by the natural order of things, but like Paul, who was an apostle as one born out of due time. I'm a granny by the Lord's special dispensation." Miss Sally looked at Noah and Eli and Elise, and last of all, she settled her eyes on Cassidy.

Then she was looking at the other people, the white people. "And I think that's the most important thing Harvey would tell you if he was here. He'd tell you that the color of our skin doesn't matter one little bit, that the Lord loves what's inside that skin. And that's what we should love too. That's what Harvey would say—and that he's waiting for the day when we all join him at that homecoming of all homecomings. The one he just had early last Sunday morning when the angels came down to escort him to paradise. May you all have the hope of that homecoming in your hearts.

"Last of all, Harvey would tell you bad things happened because some people let evil take control of them, but the Lord is making good come out of it. I can see that good in your faces and feel it in the love of your hearts. I know you will embrace my new family."

Cassidy stood up. Her heart was beating hard inside her chest, but she knew what she had to do. Her mama reached out a hand to stop her, but Cassidy stepped away from her touch. It was scary, standing there not touching her mama, but then she moved out to the aisle and, with her eyes on Miss Sally, she went straight to the front of the church and climbed up on the podium to stand beside Miss Sally. To stand by her granny.

46

Jocie had been in a lot of church services, attended a lot of revival meetings, heard a lot of preachers urging people to come down the aisle and turn their lives over to the Lord, and sometimes they did. She had once herself. But whatever happened at Mt. Pleasant Church after Miss Sally quit talking and Cassidy walked up the aisle to climb up on the podium to stand beside her was different. It was as if the Lord had heard them singing "Showers of Blessings" that morning and now was raining them down on everybody in the church building.

Maybe it was all Mr. Harvey's doing, the same as the rain they had after his funeral to end the drought. Maybe now Mr. Harvey was up there telling the Lord what needed to happen at Mt. Pleasant Church to make folks there better and happier.

Jocie was already feeling tingles up and down her spine and getting what Aunt Love called holy goose bumps before Wes looked over at her.

"You know, if that little bitty girl can make it down that aisle as scared as she's been, then I guess I can. Maybe I'll just go on down there and ask your daddy to say that prayer with me."

Jocie wasn't sure she could trust her ears, but Wes was reaching for his crutches. Her heart bounced around like crazy inside her as she put her hand on his arm and asked, "You want me to go with you?"

"No, I'm a big boy. And this is between me and the Lord." Wes stood up and swung down the aisle on his crutches.

By now everybody in the church was standing up. Jocie wasn't sure why except that it didn't seem possible to stay sitting down. Nobody was singing "Just As I Am" or any of the other invitation hymns, but it didn't matter. The invitation was floating around in the air, touching all of them.

Jocie's dad met Wes at the front of the church, and she thought he might break out in a dance he looked so happy. Then Bob Jessup and his wife were walking down the aisle to rededicate their lives. When Miss Sally came down off the podium to give him a hug, Mr. Jessup started crying. Not little tears that just slipped out of the corner of the eyes like Jocie had seen some men cry, but big boo-hoo tears. He tried to say something to the church, but he couldn't talk. His wife led him over to the front pew and helped him find his handkerchief. More people came forward to promise to live better for Christ. Even people who weren't members at Mt. Pleasant and were just visiting for the Homecoming service.

What with the way everybody in the church seemed to be making some kind of decision, Jocie wasn't surprised when Tabitha stepped out of the pew, carrying her baby. But it must've surprised the other people in the church. It got quiet again for a minute as Tabitha stood in front of the church and said, "My baby's father didn't want him. He wanted me to do something to see that he was never born, but I couldn't do that. I want to thank all of you for loving him even before he was born and for loving him still now that you see him." She looked down at her baby a minute and then held him up as if presenting him to the church. "I named him Stephen Lee. Stephen for a baby a mother lost a long time ago and Lee for Mr. Harvey. He would have liked that, I think."

More tears started flowing. Things hadn't calmed down

much from that when Leigh went down the aisle to move her membership to Mt. Pleasant since, as she told them, she was there all the time anyway. And Jocie's father looked like that was exactly where he wanted Leigh to be.

Jocie was beginning to think the church was going to explode with all the blessings hitting everybody. She wanted to run down the aisle to be there beside Wes and her father, but for some reason her feet stayed nailed to the floor where she was. It was like the Lord was telling her not yet. That more had to happen.

And more did happen. Noah and his mother moved out of their pew and carried Eli and Elise down the aisle. At first Jocie thought it was just so they could be there with Cassidy and Miss Sally, but then Noah's mother was talking one on one with Jocie's dad before she turned to look out at people still in the pews. Suddenly everybody was silent again.

"I'm presenting myself and Noah is presenting himself to the church for membership. I believe in the Lord and made a profession of faith when I was ten years old. Noah has also made a profession of faith and been baptized into the church. We're not doing this as any kind of protest or challenge. If you refuse me and Noah membership, we will understand and not harbor any resentment. But the Lord stirred up my spirit and Noah's this day."

Mrs. Hearndon looked around at Miss Sally and then back at the people. She swiped the tears off her face with the palms of her hands and drew in a deep breath before she was able to go on. "And if you'll have me, I want to be a member of the same church my mother belongs to."

A stillness settled over the church as Jocie's father stepped forward. He looked a little worried as he said, "And what is the pleasure of the church? Of course, the rededication decisions require no action, but do you accept these other decisions that have been brought before the church? Wesley Green as a candidate for baptism into the full fellowship of our church, Leigh Jacobson as a member on promise of her letter from the Hollyhill First Baptist Church, and Myra Hearndon and Noah Hearndon on statements of faith?"

Noah's mother put a hand on Jocie's father's arm. Her voice was calm, sure. "No, Rev. Brooke. You can't do it that way. Each vote needs to be taken individually. Wesley. Leigh. Me. Noah. Separately."

Where a few minutes ago there had been movement and joy throughout the church, now it was as if everybody was afraid to breathe. Jocie looked around at the deacons, who were always the ones to make a motion to accept a new member candidate. Matt McDermott was holding up his hand to speak, but Ogden Martin jumped in front of him. Jocie wanted to hide under the pew and not hear what he was going to say. He was always against everything her father proposed.

But then he was saying, "I move that we accept each of these people, individually and one by one. First Wesley Green. I'm sure Deacon McDermott will second each of my motions." Mr. Martin looked over at Mr. McDermott, who nodded. "If that is your pleasure, say amen."

The amens were loud, unanimous.

"Leigh Jacobson? Amens again, please."

Again the amens rang out all over the church.

"Myra Hearndon? On her statement of faith. Amens?"

Without hesitation the amens sounded loud again and then the same for Noah. No sooner had the amens died out than Jim Sanderson was saying, "You wouldn't want to lead the singing, would you, Mrs. Hearndon?"

Everybody laughed, and again Jocie wanted to go to the front. Again her feet couldn't seem to move off their space on the floor. Again the Lord was saying not yet. Saying that maybe there was something she needed to do before she could go share the joy. She looked behind her where Paulette had been sitting on the back pew with Ronnie Martin. They weren't sitting now. They were standing the way everybody else was, but they were there. And the Lord was prodding Jocie.

She picked up her feet and moved not toward the front of the church but toward the back. She stopped in front of Ronnie Martin.

"I forgive you," she said. "I don't just pretend to forgive you. I really forgive you."

Ronnie didn't seem to know what to say as he looked at her without smiling. After an uncomfortable minute, he said, "Okay. Good."

Then as she started to turn away, he went on. "Wait a minute, Jocie. I want you to know that I really am sorry for what I did and not just because of Paulette. Honest."

"I believe you," Jocie said. And she did. She felt lighter, as though a weight had been lifted off her shoulders, or maybe it was that when she forgave—really forgave—Ronnie, only then did she feel the forgiveness she had needed. She actually thought about reaching out and hugging Ronnie, but then it seemed better to just smile before she rushed down the aisle to hug Wes.

Jessica Sanderson had to play through "Trust and Obey" twenty times while everybody shook hands with everybody else who had made decisions. And then Bob Jessup was asking for anybody who wanted to help, to follow him to the Hearndon farm to help plant the apple trees that were out in his truck.

Leigh took Tabitha and little Stephen and Aunt Love home. But Wes stayed and rode down to the Hearndon place with Jocie and her father. Every deacon came and their wives. In all, over twenty people descended on Alex

Hearndon, who didn't look as if he could believe his eyes when Bob Jessup showed him the trees. He stared hard at Mr. Jessup for a long minute, but then Miss Sally was stepping up beside him to say something into his ear, and Noah's father stuck his hand out and shook Mr. Jessup's hand.

They all went down into the field. Even Wes, who sat on the tailgate of one of the trucks and told Jocie and Cassidy how trees were planted on Jupiter while they watched the men dig out the broken trees.

Jocie smiled at him. "I'll bet they don't even have apple trees on Jupiter."

"Well, not exactly apples, but something close. They're called jupples, and if you eat one of them you can jump twice as high as you could. So you don't have to worry about a ladder or anything when you're picking them. You just grab one, take a big bite, and then you can jump right up and pick off the rest of them."

Cassidy giggled, and Wes smiled at her. "Fresh ears. The Lord is blessing me for sure."

Jocie laughed too, more with relief than because the story was funny. "I'm glad you're still from Jupiter," she said.

"What's the matter, Jo? You think the good Lord can't love somebody from Jupiter?" Wes raised his eyebrows as he peered over at Jocie.

"No. Today I think anything is possible," Jocie said.

"Just 'think'?" Wes asked.

"Okay. Today I *know* anything is possible." She looked at Cassidy. "What do you know, Cassidy?"

Cassidy looked at Jocie and Wes with sparkling brown eyes as she said, "That my Granny Sally says Mr. Harvey's angels are going to be watching over me and my daddy's apple trees. And she knows."

Ann H. Gabhart and her husband live on a farm just over the hill from where she was born, in central Kentucky. Ann is the author of over a dozen novels for adults and young adults. She's active in her country church, and her husband sings bass in a southern gospel quartet.